Dear bookseller,

I'm delighted to be introducing you to t.....
early proof of A. Rae Dunlap's outstanding debut, *The Resurrection-ist*. This is a decadently macabre piece of gothic historical fiction, intertwined with elements of dark academia, true crime and queer romance, which we are proud to have acquired in a pre-empt. Set in the murky underworld of Georgian Edinburgh's anatomy schools, it follows James Willoughby, a young medical student who descends into the illicit business of body snatching... and unexpectedly falls in love. This copy of the manuscript – which is currently undergoing final edits – is one of the very first to be shared with the world.

Love stories don't often play out in cemeteries and dissection theatres. But I'm certain that James and Nye, the tenacious, unconventionally loveable protagonists in *The Resurrectionist*, will stay with me until the grave – as will their obsessive pursuit of scientific progress, and the deliciously grim methods they use to obtain it. So if, like me, your intrigue is piqued by a story that's as ghoulishly thrilling as it is darkly sweet, please grab a shovel, and dig in!

I hope you fall in love with *The Resurrectionist*, and would be very happy to hear from you if so.

With all my best wishes,

Daisy Watt
Commissioning Editor
HarperNorth
daisy.watt@harpercollins.co.uk

THE
RESURRECTIONIST

A. RAE DUNLAP

Harper
North

HarperNorth
Windmill Green
24 Mount Street
Manchester M2 3NX

A division of
HarperCollins*Publishers*
1 London Bridge Street
London SE1 9GF

www.harpercollins.co.uk

HarperCollins*Publishers*
Macken House, 39/40 Mayor Street Upper
Dublin 1, D01 C9W8, Ireland

First published by HarperNorth in 2024

1 3 5 7 9 10 8 6 4 2

A catalogue record for this book
is available from the British Library

HB ISBN: 978-0-00-871153-5

Printed and bound in the UK using 100%
renewable electricity at CPI Group (UK) Ltd, Croydon

This novel is a work of fiction.
Some of the names, characters and incidents portrayed
in it are the work
of the author's imagination.

MIX
Paper | Supporting
responsible forestry
FSC™ C007454

This book contains FSC™ certified paper and other controlled
sources to ensure responsible forest management.

For more information visit: www.harpercollins.co.uk/green

For Karen & Georgia

An Introduction

To hear my mother tell the story, my decision to abandon my studies at Oxford was enough to disgrace my father into an early grave. Regardless of his habits—his drinking, his gambling, his debts—in her mind, it was my own act of reckless rebellion that finally put him under for good.

To that end, it's perhaps for the best that he wasn't alive six months later, when I was nearly arrested for smuggling a naked corpse in a wheelbarrow down Chambers Street at half past midnight, but I fear that's getting rather ahead of myself. The point is, my father's shame in me apparently drove him to his untimely death, making the events which transpired in the wake of his passing the fault of no one but myself and myself alone.

In all fairness, my father never had particularly high aspirations for me, so the fact that I was able to underwhelm him so completely was quite the accomplishment indeed. As the third son of a modestly landed family, it was impressed upon me from an early age that I would require a livelihood—and not just any livelihood, but one becoming of a man of my station. In my early childhood, my father assumed that I would follow my uncle's path into the military, but it quickly became apparent that neither steadfast leadership nor brazen feats of daring were amongst my stronger suits, as I exclusively pursued activities of a much gentler persuasion. I would notoriously steal away from my brothers' reckless exploits and wild marauding about the grounds of the family estate to hide inside the library with a book, more content in the company of words than my siblings. What's more, my diminutive stature made athletic competition too humiliating to endure, so I therefore declared it outside my natural inclination and avoided it whenever possible, much to my father's dismay.

So it was to be a clerical vocation for me—the Church being the next best chance for an unlanded gentleman to excel in society—and preparations were made for my attendance at Oxford, where I could procure a degree while maneuvering my way to a prominent parish position. This edict of intent was dictated to me by my father in his unmistakable blithe monotone across the mahogany expanse of his desk three days before my departure for University in the summer of 1828, along with a comprehensive summary of my weekly allowance and the names and titles of class-appropriate peers with whom I was explicitly instructed to rub shoulders.

However, it quickly became clear to me that life in the Church could never suffice. As ill-suited as I was to be a leader, it was evident that I was a considerably worse follower. I was uniquely repelled by both mundanity and tradition. Classics bored me, rhetoric confounded me, and the few Theology lectures I attended failed to ignite wonder. I abruptly began to realise that I could no more devote my life to antiquity and myth than I could take up arms and command a battalion. To me, military maneuvers and ecclesiastical quandaries paled in comparison to the passion that I felt when reading about the biological facts of life. The insuppressible notion began to dawn on me that I was, in my core, a man of Science.

And not just any science: human science, the study of the body, of man himself, of sinew and bone and humour and blood. The essence of life, the very organs that granted our being, that was the wonder of it all! To unlock the mysteries of the human form was to behold God's masterpiece firsthand, and that is what sparked the fire within me for the very first time. Turning each riveting page of every volume in the University's well-curated collection of anatomy texts, I knew then and there that my calling was to be a physician.

And to a modern man, a call to be a physician was a call to Edinburgh, shining beacon of medical discovery, home of Hume and the New Enlightenment, a city unparalleled even on the Continent in its quest for progress on the scientific front. To be a truly contemporary physician of the era, one could aim no higher than a diploma from the University there.

And so as the withering chill of autumn descended, I repacked my trunks, settled my debts, and returned to the family stead brimming with fervor and bursting with pride to announce my new career with all the careless haste of a young man possessed. Much to my chagrin, my intentions were met with staunch opposition from all parties involved, yet I persisted. From teatime to dinner, my resolution was brought under fiercest scrutiny, but I refused to allow my temper to get the better of me, civilly commanding that the relentless interrogation cease. The remainder of the evening was spent in a predictably grim and heavy silence as I held firm in my resolve.

On that very night, my father died in his sleep. So it could be said that my mother's less-than-equitable placement of blame was not entirely far-fetched, though I maintain it was a small mercy he did not survive to see the deepest depths of my eventual moral compromisings—the aforementioned corpse in the wheelbarrow being the least of it. Little did I know that that brush with death would be my first of many, and at the time, it both consumed and compelled me in a way that only one's first encounter with mortality can.

Yet I must insist that, in the end, this is not a story about Death. It is perhaps a Life story—or even, yes, a Love story. It is the story of how I clawed my way from the decay of a crumbling legacy into the modern era of Reason and Science. It is the story of how I escaped the prison of archaic superstition to the freedom of enlightenment. It is the story of how a rose can blossom from even the bloodiest soil, of how light can grow from shadow, how love can grow from despair.

This, dear reader, is the story of my Resurrection.

1.

An Invitation

My arrival in Edinburgh was heralded, quite fittingly, by a deluge of rain, the volume and frigidity of which took me embarrassingly by surprise. I'd ventured that far north only twice before in my life, both times in the basking embrace of summer. Unfortunately, this experience had filled my head with romantic notions of Scotland based upon hazy recollections of carefree days spent upon sun-kissed moors, with the temperate winds of the rugged highlands ruffling my hair, heather and thistle beneath my feet.

The reality of Edinburgh, however, was a harsh contrast to my fond memories not just of the untamed countryside, but to my sparse experience of metropolitan life thus far. Juxtaposed against Oxford's dreaming spires, the jumbles of soot-singed bricks slicing jagged black angles into the sky appeared primitive to my discerning eyes, to say nothing of the coal-black sludge lining the cobblestone streets. I'd arrived in the first week in November, just in time for the start of Winter Session, and quickly grasped that the expressions of amusement exchanged amongst my acquaintances at home upon hearing of my intention to disembark for the north in such a season may not have been without merit. It was staggeringly obvious to me that my tweed overcoat was utterly insufficient before I'd even set foot outside my carriage.

I'd resolved to take a room based upon an advertisement posted in the hall of the Royal Medical Society, which was the first stop upon my arrival. This would have undoubtedly horrified my mother, who was already offended enough that, unlike Oxford, the University here provided neither porters nor bedders, so I would be responsible for maintaining my own accommodations. But it would seem luck was on my side, as there were plenty of vacancies listed that boasted proximity to the lecture halls and a set-rate fare for breakfast and I'd simply pointed my coachman towards the first lodging house on the list.

In any other circumstance, my initial impression of the Hope & Anchor Inn would have been one of profound revulsion: the windows were caked in several layers of grime; the door handle was disconcertingly slippery to the touch, the interior dim and smokey. But following the interminable journey from Bath, coupled with the disorientation of a stranger in a foreign city and the demoralisingly inclement weather, it seemed to my weary eyes to be the coziest, quaintest lodging house imaginable. The barman was endearingly gruff (just as I'd imagined every native Scotsman to be), and I was charmed by the prospect of living amongst the local populace. I secured a room, then promptly returned to my coach to await a porter.

It soon became obvious, however, that porters were not part of the standard service at the Hope & Anchor Inn. What's more, my coachman declined to provide any further assistance besides depositing my trunk and valise unceremoniously upon the rain-soaked street and stealing off into the descending night with barely a tip of his hat in my direction. Thus, it was with the strength of my own two hands and the gritty determination of a man in the throes of newfound independence that I made my first official entrance as a resident of the Hope & Anchor Inn.

It was not, truth be told, a particularly graceful entrance. I was unable to completely lift the trunk due to its cumbersome shape, so I was relegated to dragging it behind me as the brass tacks securing the underframe screeched in protest against the wooden floor. The handle of my valise had grown slick with rain, and I fumbled it no fewer than three times as I wove my way between the densely packed tables, filled with wary-eyed patrons hunched over pints of dark ale. A disconcerting silence seemed to follow me, but I resolutely ignored it and made my way to the interior staircase and proceeded to ascend.

Well, I *attempted* to ascend. As it turned out, scaling steep stairs beneath the weight of my luggage was considerably more challenging than the porters of my past had led me to believe, and I had barely struggled past the halfway point when I lost my grip on the trunk entirely and whirled to watch as it thundered down the stairs in a deafening cacophony—and to my compounded horror, directly into the outstretched arms of a young, curly-haired stranger who'd had the misfortune of rounding the corner into the stairwell at the least opportune moment possible.

With a startled shout, he braced himself just in time to bring the trunk to an abrupt halt, still perched at a precarious angle and threatening to continue its descent as he strained against its unwieldy bulk. To his credit, the stranger recomposed himself in the blink of an eye, his expression turning from surprise to amusement as he cast a glance up the stairs in my direction.

"Drop something?" His lip was quirked in the hint of a smile, but his blasé attitude towards nearly meeting an untimely end beneath a piece of rampaging luggage did little to fade the blush of humiliation I could feel scalding my cheeks.

"Sorry, so sorry, a thousand apologies—" I somehow dropped my valise again in my haste to retreat down the stairs to free the young man from his current quagmire, and to my relief (and perhaps mild indignation), he laughed.

"Keep your head on, I've got it. Why not pop your bag up on the landing, then come back here and we'll hoist this beast up together, shall we?"

"Oh! Um, yes, of course, quite right you are . . ." I hastily followed his directive, and we were soon working in tandem to shepherd the offending beast up the stairs, which proved to be considerably easier than maneuvering it solo. The stranger showed no hesitation in providing me instructions as I struggled awkwardly backwards up the stairs, and I in return duly hid my chagrin at his continued sniggering at my clumsiness.

An unspoken gentlemen's agreement reached, we summited the staircase with a collective shout of triumph and gave The Beast a final heave in the general direction of the bed chambers before collapsing on either side of it in mutually undignified surrender.

The stranger was still grinning, his amusement apparently unimpeded by exertion. I found the sentiment to be contagious and grinned back.

He recovered his breath first. "So. I take it you're new in town, and not just carting this about for the entertainment of local bystanders?" He gave the trunk a good-natured pat.

I took a gulp of air and mopped the sweat from my brow with the back of my hand, only to discover it had mixed with the rainwater to form a rather unsavoury salty sheen. "Just arrived from Bath. I'm starting at the Medical School this week."

His smile grew even brighter. "You, too? Brilliant! There's a whole group of lads here from the new class; we were just enjoying some pints downstairs. You ought to join us."

Transferring the sweat from my hand onto the twill of my breeches, I shook my head forlornly. "Look at me. I'm clearly in no state for socialising. I haven't even dressed for dinner, let alone—"

To my surprise, the stranger let out a bark of laughter. "Listen, mate. Not sure what pubs were like in Bath, but around here, we tend to be a bit more informal."

I eyed him appraisingly, attempting to determine his backstory in the few details illuminated by the sparse lamplight of the hall. His accent sounded civilised enough— London, or thereabouts at least—his boots well-cobbled, and his shirt finely tailored. But he wore no jacket or waistcoat, his cravat was loose at his throat, and his sleeves were rolled above his wrists. After months of the rigorous cap-and-gown standards at Oxford, to me he appeared nearly charlatan in his approach to propriety, and a part of me wanted to doubt his seemingly earnest intent.

This being said, there was no malice in his eyes, no judgement in his tone, and no hesitation in his speech. What reason would he have, I puzzled, to cause me more indignity than what I'd already suffered as a result of my own poor coordination and physical ineptitude at something as simple as wrangling my own valise? After all, I was a stranger in this city—no family name to honour, no tradition to uphold. I was, at last, free from the rigid mores of my past! It seemed that the very least I could do was indulge in a well-earned pint with my new peers.

With a curt nod of assent, I extended my hand. "In that case, it would be a pleasure to join you. My name's James, by the way." This didn't seem to be the proper place for titles.

He took my hand and, much to my surprise, rose to his feet and pulled me up bodily with him, our sudden proximity exuding an air of familiarity that was my first cherished hint of welcome in so foreign a place. "I'm Charlie. Now, let's get The Beast to your room and head back downstairs before we miss all the fun."

We made quick work of depositing my trunk into the darkened chamber whose number coincided with that of my newly acquired key. I admittedly made no effort to assess my new abode, as Charlie seemed keen to rejoin the revelries at the pub and I had no wish to detain him further. Mere moments later, he was leading me back into the smokey din, a flush of excitement on his cheeks—a condition I found mirrored in my own. For this, right here, was to be my new life! A life of independence, of personal discovery, of raucous barrooms and newfound mates, of loosened cravats and rolled-up sleeves, of dark ale and smudged glasses and sticky floors, high-minded ideas and low-minded gossip and everything in between. For while it was the sanctified surgical theatre that had called me north, it struck me then and there that it was only the base of the bargain. For the first time ever, my life was mine, and I was determined to live it to the fullest.

We approached a booth into which were crowded three young gentlemen of a similar age as myself, all huddled over an unidentifiable object resting upon the surface of the dark oak table. The tallest of the men, capped with a shock of red hair offset by a brilliant green overcoat, was poking at the object in question with a fork, while the other two hissed on encouragement.

"Oy! Lads!"

At once, three heads snapped our way in perfect unison with uniformly guilt-stricken expressions upon their faces, but seeing it was only Charlie on the approach, they quickly shifted back to conspiratorial excitement.

"Charlie, where've you been?" The red-haired gentleman beckoned him frantically. "Hamish is here, and he's brought an ear!"

"Hush. Christ, you'll get us thrown out again!" spat the beak-nosed boy to his left, who looked considerably younger than the other two upon second glance, though the glower on his face conveyed an anachronistic maturity about him.

The red-haired gentleman (or, perhaps boy would be a better descriptor, considering his distinctly ungentlemanly conduct) rolled his eyes before proceeding in an exaggerated whisper. "It's still got the cochlea on it!"

Repulsed, I turned towards Charlie, who, to my surprise, looked beyond delighted at the prospect. "Really? Attached?"

"Indeed."

"Excellent!" He pressed forward and snatched the fork from Red-Hair's hand before leaning over the table to inspect the specimen himself, leaving me standing in an awkward hover.

My presence wasn't lost on Beak-Nose, who eyed me up and down incredulously. "Who're you?" His Scottish accent was so thick I could barely understand him.

"Oh, that there's James," quipped Charlie, without raising his gaze from where he was poking a disturbing tangle of pale, stringy threads protruding from the apparent ear. "He's just come up from Bath, starting Winter Session with us this week."

Red-Hair raised his eyebrows. "Ah, another aspiring medical man, eh?"

I gave a hapless shrug. "Hopefully."

"Better be more graceful with a scalpel than you are with luggage," Beak-Nose interjected, and Red-Hair elbowed him good-naturedly as I felt yet another blush rise in my cheeks; apparently my less-than-distinguished entrance hadn't gone unnoticed by these particular patrons.

"Ignore him; he's just being vazey," Red-Hair continued with a grin. "I'm Phillip, by the way, and this here's

Hamish, our man on the inside, who brings us all sorts of delightful toys to play with."

I swallowed uncertainly. "Toys?"

Hamish gave a coy shrug and leaned back in his seat. "Just bits and bobs from the school where I work. Fancy a go at the ear? We've got a spare fork." He held it up and waggled it suggestively in my direction.

"Erm, not right now, thank you . . ." I cast about for a valid excuse, but was luckily interrupted by the stocky, sandy-haired fellow seated to Hamish's right.

"I'm Luke," he said cheerfully. "And seeing as how you're already standing, I think it's only fair you buy us all a drink."

"Gladly." Relieved to have a chance to collect myself, I turned and made my way towards the bar to procure our pints, my mind reeling a mile a minute.

So these were the students of the medical persuasion, destined to be my companions on our quest for the highest level of knowledge that humble Man had yet attained? Gathered around a gritty pub table, poking a human ear with a fork? My stomach churned as I contemplated the prospect.

Of course, I was well aware that I would encounter cadavers during my medical training, but in my mind it had always been in a very civilised manner: within the hallowed walls of the Operating Theatre, beneath the watchful eye of a master physician demonstrating proper technique in a hushed tone of reverence and respect. The thought of confronting a disembodied appendage over a few pints at the local watering hole without so much as a by your leave was abhorrent to me in the utmost.

And yet . . .

These men were, for better or worse, to be my colleagues. I'd known all along that the University at Edinburgh was unlike Oxford or Cambridge, not just in the vastly more varied breeding of the pupils but in the pragmatic philosophy of their education. They had come here for the same purpose as I, to further their knowledge of the human form, to attain comprehension where before there had been nothing but prejudice and superstition, to learn to heal and cure and prosper. That was to be our unified mission, each and every one of us, and far be it from me—a newcomer to this flourishing academic scene—to define what constituted propriety in the fast-changing world of medical scholarship.

Resolve revived, I gathered the pints on a tray and wound my way back to the booth, where I was met with a round of raucous cheers. This simple gesture of camaraderie fortified me, and it was with a sigh of relief that I slid into the spare seat beside Charlie, and we raised our pints to my arrival. Glancing around the table at their eager faces, I found it all too easy to ignore the disembodied ear which served as the macabre centrepiece to the jolly tableau.

"So," Charlie ventured, slapping his half-drained glass down and turning in my direction, "what brought you here, James?"

I took a sip of my own ale (it was bitter and almost alarmingly thick, but I willed it down) and attempted to apply a casual air. "I want to be a physician. I was at Oxford before"—I deliberately ignored the rather rude murmur from Hamish at this admission—"but I knew that if I wanted to pursue the medical profession the proper way—in the manner of the New Enlightenment, that is—Edinburgh was the only place for me. So . . . I left Oxford, and here I am."

"Well, that explains a lot," muttered Hamish into his pint, and despite my good nature, I found myself narrowing on his continued obstinance.

"What exactly do you mean by that?"

Hamish drained another swallow of ale and wiped his mouth with the back of his hand. "Nothing at all, mate. Just that you seem a bit of a toff to be around these parts. Not the type to . . . get your hands dirty, as it were." He leaned forward and gave the lobe of the ear a rather menacing flick in my direction.

"Ay, Hamish, lay off, he's just—"

"No, Charlie," I interjected, "it's quite alright." Despite my family background and my profound respect for etiquette, I'd never been one to bow out of a verbal altercation, and I most certainly wasn't going to start tonight, the first night of my new life. "As a matter of fact, I left Oxford for that very reason. It was all thought and hypothesis, no action and conclusion. All play and no work. All brain and no hands. Here, I aspire to use both."

"Ah, so you'll be joining the Surgery lectures, too, then?" Luke inquired eagerly.

Surgery lectures? There was a difference between that and the Physicians' training? It slowly began to dawn on me that I should perhaps have put in a bit more research about my exact course of study prior to my arrival.

But now was no time to back down; the lads were all staring intently in my direction, and the correct answer was more than obvious. "Of course! The Surgery lectures. Absolutely."

"Brilliant!" Charlie chimed in. "And Hamish has got our inside track into one of the best private schools in town."

"Private . . . schools?" I was utterly confounded; wasn't the University to be our place of training?

But my consternation was summarily drowned out by Hamish, who was waving his hands and clicking his tongue. "Ah, sorry to disappoint you all, but Knox is full up this term already. Yer on yer own."

There was a chorus of groans, which luckily gave me the opportunity to interject my private inquiry with Charlie. "What's Knox?" I was growing more disquieted by my ignorance with each passing moment.

Charlie clearly didn't pick up on the sensitive nature of my question and responded loudly enough for all to hear. "Dr. Knox owns one of the private surgical schools here in town. Hamish over there works as an assistant in his labs, which is where he gets his hands on all of this delightful stuff." He gestured vaguely towards the ear.

"But . . . pardon my asking, aren't you all attending the University? Why do you need a private surgical school if you're already enrolled in all the lectures required for a degree?"

A round of laughter ensued, but to my relief, it was neither mean-spirited nor dismissive; instead, it smacked of honest amusement.

Phillip was the first to respond. "Have you ever been to an anatomy lecture before? Here at the University, I mean."

I shook my head. "No."

"Well, it's a bit . . . useless," he continued diplomatically. "A hundred and twenty students in the theatre, craning their necks around the crowd to get so much as a glimpse of the demonstration. I'm in my third year now, and I've never been closer than thirty feet from a body on University grounds."

I furrowed my brow; this information was quite contrary to what I'd come to understand about medical training in Edinburgh; the city was meant to be the heart of practical surgical training. How was it possible a third-year student had such limited access to the necessary syllabus?

"And so . . . the private schools are different?" I ventured.

Hamish snorted into his ale. "That's one way of putting it," he muttered.

I resolutely ignored him and turned my attention back to Phillip. "How so?"

Phillip steepled his fingers in front of himself, a mischievous look on his face. "Have you ever heard of the Parisian Manner of dissection?" Once again, I shook my head. "It's a method of learning in which each anatomy student is provided with a corpse of their own for dissection."

The thought was utterly confounding. "Their own . . . corpse? For every student?"

Next to me, Charlie nodded, his eyes alight with enthusiasm. "Exactly. You get practical experience in anatomy, dissection, diagnosis—before you even meet your first patient! It's how they do it on the Continent, you see, and Edinburgh's the only city here that's caught on. That's what makes it so special. That's why this is the City of Science. That's why we're all here." He gestured towards the nodding faces around the table, and I marveled at the possibilities.

"So . . . how do we gain admission to a private school?"

Hamish interjected once again, this time with considerably less derision, much to my relief. "Knox is already full up this term, but plenty of other schools will be hosting their open houses for prospective new students this week. Malstrom's gallery will be accepting twenty, I've heard—you ought to try there first. There's a demonstration Thursday next."

"Fantastic." Charlie raised his eyebrows in my direction. "So, James. Ready to get those toff hands dirty?"

2.

An Observation

The first fortnight of my new education passed without much cause for notation. I found my lectures enlightening, my new peers welcoming, the locals enchantingly warm (if a bit rough around the edges), and my lodgings tolerable enough. For all the talk of its incomparable convenience, the Hope & Anchor proved to be convenient in its proximity to the University alone; the rest of its features left much to be desired. Despite my satisfaction with the location, my chamber itself was sorely lacking. There was no hot water, the bedclothes were weathered beyond reasonable repair, the floor ice-cold save for a small threadbare rug, and the breakfast consisted of no more than unbuttered bread, an overboiled egg, and a tepid pot of tea. Yet I held my tongue rather than observe all of this aloud, as it seemed that the accommodations were deemed sufficient not only by Charlie but by the myriad of other students who took their lodgings there. And as I had quickly learned upon my arrival, it was not my place to comment upon the quality of my surroundings, lest I catch wind of a less-than-courteous hiss of "Toff-Boy" uttered in my direction beneath Hamish's breath whenever he was within earshot.

The only observation I had dared make public was my reaction to the rather surprising view from my chamber window. I had awoken the morning after that first night at the pub to blink out beyond the pearled glass to see, to my horror, a kirkyard cemetery positioned directly beneath my windowsill.

"Grim, isn't it?" Charlie had beamed back at me over the gelatinous ash-grey yolk of his egg as we took our breakfast together. "Dates back to 1560. A place that old, you know it must be haunted." He gave me a devious wink.

I found myself distinctly perturbed by the prospect. "Have . . . I mean, have you ever seen a ghost there?" My heart pounded at the thought. As a man of Science, I of course eschewed all belief in the supernatural and occult, but something about the jagged tombstones rising like ravenous teeth from beneath the frosted earth evoked an inevitable sense of foreboding.

"Naw, not me," Charlie replied around a mouthful of bread. "But you ought to ask Lawrence from room 11. His chamber looks out over the MacKenzie mausoleum, and he swears he's seen figures coming and going at all hours of the night."

I pointedly did not ask Lawrence about any such thing.

After all, the hours of the day were limited, and there was so much to learn, so much to take in, so much to read and ponder and know. Never before had I been more certain that I had made the right decision when I'd left Oxford; it was ever clearer to me by the day that this was my intended vocation, my irrevocable calling, my inescapable destiny. While it was true that the classes were cramped and impersonal (sometimes consisting of over 140 pupils, by my own calculations), we had unfettered access to the most brilliant medical minds and the most up-to-date journals available to modern man. It was a privilege in the truest sense of the word. But—

"It's all bollocks, really, until you see a dissection at a proper school," Hamish gloated over his pint the night before the open lecture at Malstrom's. The other lads were listening to him with the kind of rapt attention I'd come to resent; it had been plain from the beginning that Hamish hadn't taken much of a shine to me, and I found myself returning the sentiment twofold. He was precocious, self-righteous, and relentlessly smug about his position within Knox's school, and the way he lorded it over the other boys struck me as nothing short of infuriating. "Best drink light tonight, mates, because tomorrow you're about to see the real thing—the kind of nightmare that makes your stomach turn."

Anticipatory titters erupted from amongst his enraptured audience, and it took all of the willpower I had within me not to roll my eyes. After all, we had been exposed to a dissection our very first week in the lecture hall. Granted, it had been from a considerable distance and consisted of no more than the removal of a gangrenous limb, but surely that ought to count for something in the summation of our journey to medical manhood.

"So, Toff-Boy," Hamish swiveled his gaze in my direction. From over his beaked nose, he reminded me

markedly of a large, gawky bird of prey. "You ever seen
a dead body before?"

I cleared my throat and adjusted my cravat, diplomatically electing to omit the obvious example of the
cadaver I'd observed in the lecture hall a mere six days
prior. I had seen one other corpse in my lifetime, but the
memory of my father laid out in his coffin a mere three
months prior was a mental picture I'd sooner forget than
divulge with any new acquaintance. "Not exactly, no.
But I did have the privilege of accompanying our family
physician on some local rounds in my childhood."

"See anything good?" Hamish pressed, a malignant
gleam in his eye.

I took a swill of ale. "Define good." I knew exactly
what Hamish was insinuating, of course, and the truth
was that this apprenticeship had consisted of no more
than a carriage ride to the neighbouring estate, where
the Lady of the house had been experiencing debilitat-
ing headaches. But it had quickly become apparent to
me that coded language and slight exaggeration were
all part of the jostling for prestige amongst my scholastic
comrades.

From beside me, Phillip gave me a playful jab of his
elbow. "You know! Did you see anything . . . disturbing?"

All of the faces at the table were turned in my direction and plastered with identically rapt expressions, and
for the near-dozenth time that week, I found myself
mildly affronted by their uniquely yet universally macabre dispositions. There was a pregnant pause before I
demurely replied: "A gentleman physician never reveals
the details of his patients."

There was an explosion of disappointed exclamations, a call for more ale, and a rapid dissolution into more mundane chatter. But I couldn't shake the feeling of Hamish's gaze upon me as all around us, the others speculated about what wondrous horrors awaited us in the sanctum of the private surgical theatre.

The next morning, we breakfasted early so as to arrive at Number 14 Surgeon's Square a fair half hour before the presentation was scheduled to begin, yet found that a queue had already begun to form. It was with resigned sighs that we took our places at the end of it, sharing nervous glances at the heavy grey sky that was threatening to unleash yet another torrential downpour.

"Do you think we'll get in?" Phillip posited nervously, hugging his overcoat more snugly around himself. The air was unforgivingly brisk, and I could already feel my toes numbing.

Charlie used his height to his advantage and craned his neck to take stock of our lot. "I think we'll be fine. There's only twenty or so ahead of us."

We huddled together against the cold, breathing puffs into our gloves and listening intently to the murmurs of anticipation exchanged by our fellow pupils.

"I heard yesterday Knox did a full decapitation—"

"Malstrom's been known to have a volunteer hold the intestines—"

"Three students passed out during the bloodletting alone—"

"A billfold made of skin—"

"A candle made of fat—"

I willed my ears to close against these exclamations, lest I allow my softer nature to get the best of me. For I had not come all the way to Edinburgh to be simply another mild-mannered physician, lost in theories and textbooks and vague pharmaceutical remedies. I had come here for the science, for the awe of it all, and I was determined to witness the miracle of the human form firsthand.

An excited murmur rippled through the crowd as the line began to move. We shuffled determinedly forward and were soon poised before the heavy oaken door. Beside it, a young man with a gaunt, pale face and a wild shock of jet-black hair stood with a wooden box in his hands, which he extended in our direction.

"One crown each, lads," he muttered in a heavy brogue, shaking the contents of the box with a demanding jangle. We forked over the coin—nearly half my weekly allowance, I noted with chagrin—and my friends and I at long last stepped across the threshold into the fabled fold.

We proceeded through the entryway into a large, surprisingly bright room, with high ceilings and tall windows that rose in graceful arches up to the elaborate crown molding. The walls were painted a pale greyish-white, and dozens of lamps illuminated the space. It seemed jarringly, shockingly . . . cheerful? Surprisingly absent was the clinical chemical smell I'd warily anticipated.

A small scrum had formed near the door-frame, as the excitement of anticipation quickly evaporated in confluence with reality, rendering my fellow observers with a bout of shyness supremely at odds with the brags and boasts I'd overheard in the queue mere minutes before.

"Come in, yes, please come in, don't be shy!" My gaze fixed upon a tall, broad-shouldered man with a wild white beard, wearing a navy houndstooth jacket of a most admirable stock, gesticulating broadly in our direction. He spoke with a thick French accent, but his familiar manner and contagious enthusiasm were not akin to any of my previous impressions of a Continental Frenchman. With tenacious resolve, I stepped forward with a confidence I in no way possessed, yet that was all that was required for the man's satisfaction.

"Yes, good sir, come along, right along, that's the way. Right up to the front with you; now's not the time to be coy," he continued with a wink.

As if of their own volition, my feet spirited me on to stand before this most peculiar man, who was beaming down at me with the affection of a long-lost uncle.

"That is it, that is it, my boy. I see from your face you are most prepared for the wonders that await you here, in this most sacred of studios." And with that, he draped an arm around my shoulder, theatrically twirled me clear around, and whisked away a thin white sheet which until that moment, my addled mind had neglected to register.

And there, but a foot in front of me, was a true corpse, supine upon a great marble slab.

All the world seemed to stop. But to my credit, I did not recoil or faint. Instead, it was as if every fibre of my being had seized into a stunned paralysis, and I could feel my eyes grow wide at the sight before me.

"Ah, good lad! I knew from the look of you that you'd be one of the sturdiest ones. It is the kindness in your face, no? Some see this as weakness but no, non, it is the sign of a healer, oui, a true spirit of science." I resisted the urge to balk at the compliment; I'd grown up hearing my mother describe my blond hair and fair features as cherubic to anyone within earshot, an accusation which my elder brothers delighted in using as something akin to an expletive outside her presence. Yet I refused to let such history deter me, pulled myself to my full height, and gave a curt nod of affirmation. He grinned even wider in return. "Come closer, good sir—and the rest of you, aussi! Allez, allez, now is not the time to be shy!"

From behind me, there was a pressing crush of bodies as the remaining prospective pupils jostled and bickered, each trying to maneuver his way closer to the perceived action. I hazarded a quick glance over my shoulder only to find that I'd lost Luke, Phillip, and Charlie entirely. I was utterly on my own.

"Bien, bien!" With two quick claps of his hands, the broad-shouldered man elicited silence amongst the gathered crowd. "Welcome, gentlemen, to the Malstrom Surgical School. I am your instructor and the proprietor of this establishment, Doctor Louis Malstrom—à votre service. Today, I shall provide for you a demonstration of what you might expect were you to enroll in my course. As I am sure you are aware, I teach in the venerable Méthode Parisienne, and should you choose to attend, I can assure each and every one of you that you shall have a true human subject upon which to hone your developing skills." A palpable thrill resonated through the assembled crowd.

"Now! We begin." With another clap of his hands, Malstrom gestured towards the back of the room, from which the pale young man who'd collected our fee at the door suddenly reemerged and strode through the parting crowd to produce a tray of instruments, which he positioned beside the body with a reverent bow before receding into the background once more.

"Merci, MacKinnon," Malstrom exclaimed with a clap. "Now, let's see. You, dear sir. What is your name?" The doctor was staring straight at me, and I could feel the blood rush to my face in a hot flush at being the centre of attention once more.

I cleared my throat and gathered my courage. "Willoughby, sir. James Willoughby."

"Excellent, excellent. Mr. Willoughby, perhaps you'd do me the honour of assisting me with today's demonstration?"

I mentally uttered a prayer to God and all that was Holy that the rumour about holding the intestines was a falsehood, but externally willed myself to exude a calm purposefulness, a demeanour befitting a man of medicine. "Gladly, sir."

"Wonderful! Now step close here, lad, stand by my right side, perfect, perfect, there you are."

I resolutely did not look down at the body splayed out in front of me, but the unfortunate side effect of this decision was that I found myself staring straight into the crowd of spellbound faces, which did little to assuage my anxiety.

"Mr. Willoughby, I have assessed by your disposition that you are not simply one of the bawdy gawkers who attends my demonstrations for morally dubious reasons. Can you affirm I am correct?"

"Y-y-yes, sir." To my horror, my voice shook slightly.

"Then I take you to be a man of your word, sir." With a flourish, he plucked a scalpel off the tray of instruments and extended it in my direction. "I should like you to make an incision from the bottom of the brachial artery, between the radial and posterior interosseous arteries, culminating at the carpus. Understood?"

For a moment, my mind was as blank as the slate-grey Edinburgh sky, and a wave of nauseating panic rose up inside me. The faces of the crowd seemed suddenly to be leering at me, daring me to admit my own ignorance.

But . . . but I was not ignorant! Not of this! I'd studied the vascular systems of the forearm in one of the scant medical texts I'd found in my father's library, rendered in hauntingly pale reds and blues. As a child, it had mesmerised me, and as a man, it had astounded me. I knew the Latin. I knew the map. I knew it . . . well, like the back of my hand.

I took a deep breath, and with a solemn nod, took the corpse by the wrist to turn his forearm up. Then slowly, delicately, I placed the blade to the crook of his elbow and pressed down as gently as I could.

The sensation was . . . stunning. There was no other way to describe it. I had expected surgery, with its low-class connotations, to be rough and gritty and blunt. But the blade sliced through the epidermis like paper, gliding in an elegant line as I guided it between the two parallel arteries in a slow, methodical pull. I allowed my gaze to flick to the wrist, my terminus, and steered my hand steadfastly towards it. To my own considerable shock, my fingers did not quake.

I completed the incision and lifted the blade, releasing a breath I didn't know I'd been holding as I turned to seek Malstrom's approval.

He looked distinctly pleased, and I could feel the hint of a smug smile tug at the corners of my lips, but I forced them down—after all, I had just opened the flesh of a man; surely the primary sensation for such a sombre moment should not be smug satisfaction.

"Bien, très bien, most impressive, Mr. Willoughby. And now, please, two more incisions, perpendicular to your first. At the very top and bottom."

Carefully, I lowered the scalpel back to the flesh and rendered the requested cuts.

"Parfait! Most impressive! I must ask, was your father a surgeon?"

"No, Doctor."

"Perhaps a veterinarian?"

"No—"

"A butcher?"

A smattering of laughter erupted from the onlookers.

"No, sir."

"I must say, you have the technique of a natural. Now for the next part: we open the forearm for observation by pinning back the epidermis." He proceeded to do this part himself, for which I was quite grateful; the heady high of my first true incision was quickly fading, and the stark reality that I was looking inside a human body was compounding by the second as the flesh was pulled back and secured to a board placed beneath it. The gore within gleamed grotesquely in the lamplight, and for a moment, I was tempted to sway.

Yet once again, Malstrom pulled me back from the brink with a deafening clap far too close to my ear. "Mr. MacKinnon! The wax, tout de suite, if you please!"

As if out of nowhere, his young assistant materialized once more, this time carefully balancing a bowl of what was apparently melted black wax swaying in a stand over a flaming candle. He bent to place it on the instrument tray, his elegant fingers delicate as a musician's in the flickering light. For just a moment, the illumination of the flame upon his pronounced cheekbones cast him in an otherworldly glow, and my attention was momentarily riveted by his ethereal appearance. But no sooner had the bowl been set than he disappeared again, leaving nothing in his wake but a faint whiff of wool and wood smoke, and I was hastily jarred from my diversion back to the task at hand.

"And now for your true test, Mr. Willoughby." Malstrom's eyes glistened with anticipation, and I heard myself audibly swallow. "You shall take this syringe and inject the wax into the brachial artery. We shall then watch its path through the arteries of the forearm, and then, with a second injection to the cephalic vein, we shall observe its journey in the opposite direction. Oui?" With that, he dipped an extraordinarily large syringe (which to my frantic mind more closely resembled our cook's kitchen baster than a medical instrument) into the melted wax, drew it full, and extended it in my direction.

I took it willingly, feeling the heat of the wax even through the sturdy glass of the cylinder. I looked down at the exposed arm before me and took a deep breath to steady myself.

"Hurry, hurry, Mr. Willoughby. If the wax cools before it is injected, our results will be most severely compromised."

Allowing myself not a moment's more hesitation, I reached down and pierced the artery in question and plunged the wax inside.

And felt my breath catch in my lungs in wonder.

For with the deep black colour of the dyed wax, I could indeed observe the true path of the liquid through the elaborate series of tunnels buried between the bone and sinew! Down the forearm, past the wrist, into each individual finger I watched it slide, the illustrations of my father's textbook suddenly rendered into life in dazzling, dizzying detail! It was a marvel beyond my greatest imagination, to watch something so sacred as the journey of blood through the human body, the very pathway of this vessel of life revealed before me.

I repeated the process as directed to the vein and was doubly enraptured to observe the liquid's return journey from the wrist to the upper arm. All around me, murmurs of awe rippled through the crowd, some of the onlookers in the back hopping up and down for so much as a glance. How fortunate was I to be here, the one holding the syringe!

"Thank you, Mr. Willoughby! A most impressive demonstration, my boy. You will be a true asset to this school, should you decide to join." With another beaming wink, he took the syringe back from me and clapped me fondly on the shoulder.

"But, gentlemen! We are not through yet! For now, before the wax grows brittle, is the true prestige of today's experiment!" With that, he reached down, hooked his fingers beneath the blackened veins, and slowly, gently pulled.

And as if summoned from the depths of the unknowable deep by the spell of a great sorcerer, the veins separated from their fleshy surroundings and allowed themselves to be pulled, whole and joined, from the corpse. With an odd pop the extraction was complete, and Malstrom placed the hand-shaped web on the slab for all to see.

"And with this, gentlemen, the wax will set. And we will have before us a full, functioning vascular rendition of the forearm for our continued study and the good of all mankind."

There was a breathless pause which was quickly broken by a raucous round of applause. Malstrom bowed theatrically, grinning and flipping his wrists like a magician having just performed his final act. And that is what it had seemed to me—an act of real magic.

"Malheureusement, that is all we have time for today. If you would like to sign up for this term, Mr. MacKinnon will see you in my offices to schedule your enrollment and take your tuition fee—a mere twenty-four pounds for the full session!" He gestured towards an open door at the back of the room. "The best rate in town, gentlemen; you shall find none better. Merci for your time today—it is my sincerest hope that you've found it worthwhile." And with a final bob of his head, he turned on his heel and retreated in the direction of the entryway, leaving the flabbergasted crowd in his wake.

To my shock, more than half the gentlemen in attendance followed his lead out into the street, the mass exodus allowing me to locate Phillip, Luke, and Charlie, all of whom were making their way towards the office door to secure their enrollment. I took a few brisk steps to catch up.

Charlie turned and beamed at me, slinging an arm around my shoulder. "James, mate, that was brilliant! Incredible! Was that your first time making a cut?"

"Euh, yes, it was, but . . . where are all the prospective pupils going?" I was entirely fixated on the fact that half the bystanders seemingly showed no interest in obtaining a position at the school, despite the marvelous demonstration we had just witnessed.

"Oh, they're just gawkers. Not even medical students," Charlie replied matter-of-factly.

"What?!" I couldn't believe there had been so many interlopers in our very midst.

"Yup," Luke concurred. "Hamish says they get them all the time at Knox's open demonstrations, too. They pay the fee for the entertainment, just a good story to tell at the pub."

I swallowed down my disgust. "But that's . . . that's awful. This isn't entertainment, it's science!"

"Oh, come on, James," Charlie gave my shoulder a good-hearted shake. "No use getting yourself in a twist about it. Besides, that means there should be plenty of places for us! Shall we go pay our tuition, gents?"

A pit of a completely different origin formed in my stomach at his words. For the moment I'd heard the full cost of tuition—and that it was due immediately—I'd realised that my cavalier declaration that I'd join my friends in attending may have been premature. For despite my monied upbringing, since my father's death, I certainly didn't have a spare twenty-four pounds to my name, despite Hamish's constant insinuations to the contrary.

Over the past two weeks of our acquaintanceship, I'd become increasingly familiar with the financial backgrounds of my new friends. Before my arrival, I'd known for a fact that the University of Edinburgh allowed men of middle-class backgrounds to enroll; they didn't even have a Latin requirement for admission. So my assumption that Phillip, Luke, and Charlie weren't members of landed families was entirely reasonable.

But as it turns out, though they were all indeed middle-class, they were still gentlemen of means. Charlie's father owned a shipping company based in London, Phillip had inherited a large sum from a distant uncle whose existence he hadn't even been aware of until after his death, and Luke's father occupied a none-too-minor role in the Church. Landed they were not, but they certainly weren't poor, either.

By contrast, the weeks following my father's death had been marked by a series of dire financial discoveries on my eldest brother Richard's part. My father's gambling debts proved to be far greater than he had ever acknowledged to any of us, and our presumed fortune was severely compromised. My brother announced that we were henceforth compelled to live in a state of frugality until he'd had a chance to get matters sorted (by which I assumed he meant my sister Edith would work out the figures, since she'd always been the secret brains of the family). But until further notice, my allowance was a modest fixed sum, and there was to be no further investment under any circumstances, meaning that a downpayment of twenty-four pounds on top of my University tuition was well and truly out of the question.

But how could I decline the opportunity? And it wasn't merely a matter of saving face in front of my friends. It was more abundantly clear to me than ever that enrollment at a private surgical school was the only way to become properly trained, and Malstrom had insisted that his were the best rates in town; there simply was no other choice.

These thoughts swirled in my head as we took our place in the short queue. A thousand impractical fantasies sprung to life in my mind: selling all my earthly belongings! Giving up my lodging and living in the poorhouse! Quitting University altogether and forsaking a proper degree in lieu of a private school! My fingers wrapped reflexively around the pocket watch nestled safely in the fold of my waistcoat. It was my sole material inheritance from my father: a piece of finery befitting a proper gentleman, solid gold and etched with our family crest. It was the last visceral connection I had to the man, and I was scandalised to discover my brain performing an unseemly calculation of its worth. Would it pay for one term's tuition? Perhaps more?

I suppressed the thought as quickly as it arose. Not a single of my hare-brained solutions were practical, and all would likely result in me being disowned by my family and losing what little income I had left. If only Hamish knew my true predicament; perhaps then he'd keep his smart mouth shut about my Toff-Boy origins.

But just then, a marvelous idea occurred to me: Hamish had secured work at Knox's school in lieu of his tuition, had he not? Perhaps such an opportunity would be available here at Malstrom's establishment as well! After all, the doctor had taken a noticeable shine to me, and I was confident that if I could pose the question to him, he would acquiesce.

Of course, Malstrom himself was no longer present. There was merely his assistant, MacKinnon, and I had no gauge of whether he could be easily swayed. Alas, I would simply have to try my luck. I intentionally sidled to the back of the line, behind my three friends. As the last of them (Charlie) emerged from Malstrom's office, admission papers in hand, I plastered an expression of faux-nonchalance upon my face.

"Why don't you and the lads go on ahead? There are a few matters I need to discuss with Mr. MacKinnon privately."

Charlie shot me a quizzical glance. "How about we just wait for you outside?"

"Suit yourself," I replied with a shrug, before proceeding into the office and doing my best not to make a scene of closing the door behind me.

MacKinnon was seated behind a grandiose desk, the top of which was cluttered with an array of intriguing brass instruments. Before him sat a ledger upon which he was diligently recording something with his quill, and beside him was his trusty wooden box, presumably containing the tuition fees of my classmates. He looked up when he heard the clack of the closing door, and his eyes narrowed hawkishly in the lamplight.

For a moment, I was frozen in place. For while I had previously noted the midnight hue of his hair, the ghostly porcelain tone of his skin, and the unique angles of his features, I had failed to notice his eyes, which proved to be the palest grey, unlike any others I had ever seen—hauntingly intense, and of bottomless depth. They were silhouetted by a delicate web of obsidian lashes from beneath which he glared at me with an expression of deep discontent. His petal-pale lips pursed into an unamused moue. I felt utterly dumbstruck by his ethereal appearance, and the power of vocalisation left me completely bereft.

"May I help you?" His voice was surprisingly soft now, despite the severity of his countenance. I was certain that, a mere few weeks ago, his brogue would have been too thick for my southerner's ears to comprehend, but I'd spent enough time in Hamish's presence that I mercifully didn't have to request he repeat himself.

"May—um, may I speak with you in private, sir?" I stumbled.

His eyes flicked again towards the closed door. "Seems I have little choice in the matter," he replied with a sigh, tipping his quill back into its holder. He steepled his slender fingers beneath his chin and tilted his face downwards at such an angle that the lamplight cast a ghastly shadow across his razor-sharp cheekbones. He suddenly appeared more spectre than man, and I shuddered beneath the intensity of his gaze.

"I. Um, I wanted to inquire . . . about . . . about the potential to serve as an assistant to Doctor Malstrom. In exchange . . . in exchange for . . . for perhaps, a decrease in tuition."

MacKinnon snorted rudely and leaned back in his chair, shaking his head firmly. "No discounts. No scholarships. No exceptions."

I steadied myself against his dismissal. After all, my very future was at stake here. And hadn't he witnessed how Malstrom had praised my skills during the demonstration?

"If I could just speak to Doctor Malstrom myself—"

"What's your name?"

The interruption took me by surprise, but I felt abnormally pleased to be posited a question to which I knew the answer. "James."

"Well, Mr. James, Doctor Malstrom is incredibly busy and unavailable for appointments at this time." With that, he leaned forward, plucked his quill from its stand, and resumed scribbling upon his ledger.

I doubled my resolve. "Mr. MacKinnon, if you please. I believe today I demonstrated my knack for surgical skills, and I feel I could be quite an asset to Doctor Malstrom's practice—"

With that, he slapped his quill down on the desktop with such force that I started. "Sir, with all due respect, I am Doctor Malstrom's personal secretary, dissectionist, and assemblist. We've no use for you here."

"Assemblist?" Once more, my curiosity got the better of me. "What's . . . what's an assemblist?"

MacKinnon's eyebrows rose in a clear indication of acute exasperation. "I articulate the skeletons of the dissected cadavers so that we may sell them to the other medical colleges in the region. It produces a tidy profit."

"Oh." I hadn't known such a skill existed. "You see, sir, there is clearly so much more I have to learn—"

"And learn it you can. For twenty-four pounds. Sir."

"But if you'd just—"

My plea was interrupted by three quick raps at the door. I whirled around as it opened and was startled to see Charlie's head pop into the room. I wanted to bury my face in my hands; had I not requested privacy?

"James, mate, hurry it along! There are a few new lads we met at the lecture, and they want to buy us some pints at the H&A."

"I'll just be a moment," I replied in my most even tone, despite staring daggers in his direction.

Charlie looked perfectly confused by my sour disposition. "As you were." He retreated at last, and I slowly turned back towards MacKinnon, freshly kindled shame burning in my cheeks.

But to my astonishment, MacKinnon's demeanour was wholly changed. He was staring at me appraisingly, all traces of malice evaporated from his face. "Did your friend just say the H&A?"

I was completely disorientated. What did that have to do with anything? But if local watering holes were what piqued MacKinnon's curiosity, who was I to deny him? Perhaps he was the type whose judgement could be altered after a few pints . . .

"Um, yes. The . . . the Hope & Anchor? On Candlemaker Row? Perhaps you've heard of it? A few of us take our lodgings there, myself included."

MacKinnon's eyes widened with interest. "Is that so? In the rooms right above?"

"Yes?"

"Interesting, most interesting indeed!"

"Is it?"

"In these most special of circumstances, absolutely. Listen, Mr. James, I'll need to discuss a few details privately with Doctor Malstrom first, but would you be willing to come back here tomorrow evening? I think we may just be able to strike a deal regarding your tuition."

His sudden change in tune had taken me so off guard that I found myself stumbling over my words yet again. "Oh! Y-y-yes, absolutely, please, thank you, that's ever so kind . . ."

MacKinnon gave me a calculated smile that didn't quite reach his eyes. "But of course, Mr. James. Always happy to help out a fellow man of science. I'll see you back here tomorrow at, say, five o'clock?"

"Yes, yes, absolutely, I'll be here, thank you, a thousand times over!" I strode forward and extended my hand. To my great relief, MacKinnon rose and took it, his grip stronger than his delicate fingers would suggest, his palm rough and calloused.

I turned to take my leave, but my hand paused on the door handle. I turned back over my shoulder towards where MacKinnon was already back at work. "One . . . one more thing?" He glanced up to hold my gaze. "James—that's . . . that's my given name. Not my family name. Just . . . if we're to be colleagues, I thought perhaps you should know. To avoid . . . future confusion."

Another smile flickered across his lips, this time catching his sea-grey eyes alight with amusement at my tenacity. "Begging your pardon, James. And I suppose, in that case, you may call me Aneurin."

I hesitated. "Ah . . . ni . . . sorry?"

He actually laughed a bit at that, to my relief. "Don't worry; you're not the first Englishman to trip over it. Ah-NYE-run. Aneurin."

I repeated the sounds, the rolling, lilting syllables foreign on my tongue, but it must have been an improvement because he gave me a curt nod. "Much better. Until tomorrow, James."

"Tomorrow, Aneurin."

And with that, I took my leave, feeling lighter than I had in weeks.

3.

A Proposition

I was nearly late to our meeting the following evening as a result of nothing more than my own self-doubt. I wanted to make a good impression—no, an excellent impression. I wanted to appear competent yet eager to learn. I wanted to appear fashionable yet not overly vain. I wanted to convey that I was well-mannered yet more than willing to get my hands dirty. It was indeed a delicate line to tread, and I changed my waistcoat and cravat no fewer than three times apiece before finally realising that unless I departed that very instant, I would be late, which would surely undermine any additional efforts at a good impression entirely.

I wound my way towards Surgeon's Square at nearly twice my normal pace, thankful I was now familiar with this meandering route upon the uneven cobblestone streets, even daring to take a few of the narrow Closes that served as short cuts (to which I'd recently been introduced by some my University colleagues).

I was feeling more at home in Edinburgh day by day, and it was with a smirk of satisfaction that I arrived upon the stoop of Malstrom's school at precisely one minute to five.

I rang the bell, expecting to be greeted by a house hand, and was startled when Aneurin himself flung open the door in haphazard haste. His hair was somehow even more disheveled than it had been the day before, and he was wearing a thick canvas apron with tanned leather trim over a plain muslin shirt wide open at the neck. I immediately felt egregiously overdressed.

He didn't seem to notice one whit. "James! My apologies, I'm barely decent. I got carried away with my work and entirely lost track of the time. Please, come in." He ushered me through the entryway (not even offering to relieve me of my overcoat or hat, I noted with mild annoyance), through the dissection room, and into Malstrom's office. He stripped off his apron and flung it over the back of the stately leather chair behind the desk, strode over to the bar-cart, plucked up a bottle, and procured two glasses. I took the liberty of divesting myself of my overclothes and stowed them neatly on the hat rack in the corner; it was quickly becoming evident that this was yet another space in which the social niceties to which I had grown accustomed in my youth were flouted with casual disregard. Taking advantage of Aneurin's turned back, I used what little stealth I possessed to loosen my cravat and unfasten the top two buttons of my waistcoat. The last thing I wanted was to appear unfashionably formal in such a new and enlightened profession.

"Gin alright?" he asked as he turned to place the two glasses on the desk with a resounding clink. "I find it's best never to strike a deal without a proper drink first."

Once again, I found myself disarmed by the complete reversal of his initial disposition the previous day. Gone was the standoffish air of an aloof businessman, replaced by the aura of a familiar, charming companion. It was endlessly perplexing.

"Yes, gin is fine, thank you."

He poured the liquid and handed me a glass. "To the finer points of a deal," he offered with an affable smile. We toasted, and I waited for the customary *by your leave* to take a seat, but he simply flung himself down in his chair behind the desk with rakish abandon. Suppressing my manners, I pulled out the chair opposite and seated myself.

"So. A bit of backstory." He deposited his glass on the desk, and his eyes met mine. They were even more hypnotizing than I'd remembered, the sheer colour of them so alluringly surreal that I had to force myself to remember to blink, lest I allow myself to fixate completely. "I've discussed it with Dr. Malstrom, and he finds himself in complete agreement with me about the prospect of your employment here. However, I must explain that the opportunity we have for you, it's not . . . well, it's not for the school, not exactly. It's more of a personal favour to Dr. Malstrom, in exchange for which he's happy to waive fifty percent of the tuition fee."

I did the mathematics quickly in my head. If I further minimized my few personal expenses, my allowance would be just enough to cover half-price tuition. "That's excellent news," I responded enthusiastically. "A fair bargain to be sure. I'll take the job, whatever it is."

Aneurin grinned, accentuating the sharp angle of his jaw and the soft curve of his lips. His appearance was so fascinatingly changeable, oscillating each moment between staunchly masculine and almost *feminine*. I found my mind conjuring up tales from my youth about the changeling faerie-people of the wild North who were known to possess such fluid physical qualities.

The levity of his tone quickly snapped me out of my reverie, however. "You're not even going to ask what the job is? No offense, James, but you're a rubbish negotiator. Probably a good thing you're not studying business."

I scowled at the jab and couldn't resist injecting a bit of sarcasm into my retort. "Well, forgive my enthusiasm: what you're offering me is merely the chance to fulfil my lifelong ambition."

He held up his hands in mock surrender. "Far be it from me to interfere with your agreeable nature, then! So you'll be willing to slop out the pigsty out back every morning at four o'clock on the dot?"

I could feel the colour drain from my face. "Slop out the . . . what now?"

Aneurin burst out laughing at my abject mortification. "Christ, you might be the most gullible man I've ever met. I'll have to use all my better instincts not to take advantage of you."

For the briefest of moments, I could swear I saw a shadow of something deep and hungry flicker across his eyes. But I quickly broke the silence by taking a resounding swill of my gin, then clapped the glass down on the desk.

"Alright, enough pulling my leg. What's the job, really?"

Aneurin took another measured sip of his drink before leaning back in his chair. "Dr. Malstrom's dear brother is the minister at Greyfriars Kirk—the one which, as I believe you mentioned, your current lodging overlooks."

I nodded in mute affirmation, intrigued by where this was headed.

"Well, recently the cemetery has been the victim of a series of grave robbings."

I cocked my head. "Grave robbings?" The concept seemed strangely antiquated for a kirkyard in the centre of a bustling city.

Aneurin nodded solemnly. "Indeed. A ghastly business, really, the robbers making off with the jewellery and valuables of the sacred souls interred there."

I shook my head in disbelief. "That's awful!"

"Indeed. Now, the sexton has been employed at the kirk for nearly twenty years, but Dr. Malstrom's brother has reason to believe he may have been paid off to turn a blind eye to the intruders. After all, he's supposed to make rounds about the grounds twice per night; the odds of him missing a robbery entirely seem slim to none, you see."

"I do."

"So, you'll understand why Dr. Malstrom and his brother are anxious to discover exactly how the robberies have been allowed to continue."

I shook my head at the disgrace of it. "What can I do to help?"

"It's very simple," Aneurin continued amicably, leaning (seemingly impossibly) further back in his chair. "A few times per week on prearranged nights, you'll be our eyes on the kirkyard—all from the convenience of your own bedchamber. Any time you see the sexton emerge from his cottage, you'll place a single lit lamp in your window. When he returns, you'll extinguish the lamp. His rounds are at nine o'clock and midnight, but you'll need to be on guard in case he does another round in between."

I blinked at him, puzzled. "What . . . beg your pardon if I've missed something here, but what, precisely, will this exercise accomplish?"

"Well, on the nights you're keeping watch from above, I'll be keeping watch from outside the gates. I'll see if the sexton is unlocking them for interlopers, and if he's timing his rounds to avoid encountering them during their subsequent escape. Simple!"

I furrowed my brow. "Why not just . . . stop the robbers? Or alert the authorities?"

Aneurin leaned forward, his expression alight with kindled passion. "Because then we'd simply catch the robbers, not the man enabling them! He'd just go on to do it again. It's best we catch him red-handed with a bit of police work of our own."

I paused to consider this. While this was not what I'd been expecting when I agreed to be on Dr. Malstrom's payroll, I was in no position to question his motives. After all, in exchange for the simple task of keeping watch a few nights a week and lighting a lamp in my chamber window, I could have access to one of the finest surgical educations in the kingdom! To my calculations, there was little downside at all (the minor exception being I'd have to skip pints with the lads the nights I was called upon, though further reflection led me to the conclusion that that should help me keep my purse strings tight—merely an added benefit, I reasoned).

I showed restraint in my eagerness to accept this proposal, however, and gave a slow, pensive nod as if carefully considering the benefits of such an endeavour. Knocking back the last of my gin, I finally spoke.

"It's a good plan. And a fair offer, one which I'm prepared to formally accept."

"Excellent!" He hoisted his glass in delight. "I look forward to our collaborative success, James." He tipped it in my direction and drained the dregs.

"Much obliged, Aneurin." The name still felt foreign and stilted on my tongue, in spite of my best efforts. I paused, then tossed my pride to the wind. "Am I pronouncing it correctly, now? Ah-nye-wren?"

He rolled his eyes good-naturedly and plucked the bottle of gin off the bar-cart. "Oy, if we're going to plumb the depths of Welsh pronunciation, we'll need a bit more of this to help us along." He gave the bottle a brisk shake, then refilled both our glasses.

I cocked my head, baffled. "I'm sorry, you're Welsh?" I was no expert in accents, but he certainly didn't sound like a Welshman—at least, no Welshman I'd ever met.

He laughed and took a strong pull from his glass. "No, I'm not Welsh, but my name certainly is. That's what happens when your drunkard of a father loses a bet to a Welsh sailor over the naming rights of their respective firstborns."

I could feel my eyes widen in disbelief. "Seriously? He lost your name in a bet?"

"Indeed. Evidently what he lacked in restraint he made up for in honour, so alas, here I am—a full-blooded Scotsman with an entirely unpronounceable Welsh name."

I took a measured sip of my own drink. Something about Aneurin's easy manner (or perhaps the rate at which we were consuming the gin) made me feel as though he could be entrusted with my deepest confidence.

"For what it's worth, my father was a gambling man, too," I ventured.

He raised an eyebrow. "Is that so?"

"Mmm. We didn't know how bad it was at the time, but he nearly bankrupted the family estate. Only discovered the depths of it after he died. Hence . . . well, hence my presence here, begging for a cut rate on tuition when, a year ago, I'd've scoffed you off at the mere prospect." I took another drink. "But then he went ahead and shook off his mortal coil, and his moral façade along with it."

Aneurin's face had gone sombre, his grey eyes laced with sympathy. "For what it's worth, I'm sorry to hear of his passing."

I shrugged. "It is what it is."

Aneurin quirked his lip. "At least he didn't saddle you with the unpronounceable name of a complete stranger before kicking the bucket."

I barked out a laugh. "To be fair, he wasn't all bad He did keep a rather spectacular library."

"I'm afraid mine was rather lacking scholastically, but he did teach me everything I know. At least, enough to get me the position here."

"Really?" I was doubly fascinated at this prospect. "Was he a surgeon, too?"

He snorted into the glass from which he'd presently been procuring another sip and paused a moment to compose himself. "No, not a surgeon. I'm from the island of Iona, in the Outer Hebrides. I don't suppose you've heard of it?"

I shook my head.

"No surprise there—it's an isolated place, home to no more than five hundred souls. The closest we had to a surgeon was the town's self-proclaimed physician, who'd pour half a bottle of Scotch on your wound and the other half down your throat and declare you cured."

I couldn't help but snicker at that image. "So your father wasn't a medical man. What was he, then?"

"A butcher."

"Really? I thought Malstrom was joking when he suggested that qualified as experience in the field! But that's honestly where you got your start?"

He shrugged impishly. "A cut of meat's a cut of meat, no matter how you slice it."

I wrinkled my nose, and he laughed in response.

"It was the family business for generations. My father's father. His father before him. And so on and so forth, to the dawn of time, to hear them tell the tale."

I furrowed my brow. "So . . . why did you leave?"

Our gazes met, and for a mere millisecond, I felt a crackle of pure energy between us—the sort of sensation one experiences just before the world turns resoundingly upon its head.

"For opportunity."

I raised my glass before me. "Well then, Aneurin MacKinnon. To opportunity."

He clinked his glass to mine. "To opportunity."

We drank.

* * *

To be truthful, dear reader, the next three weeks were amongst the most inspiring and exhilarating of my life. The cause was certainly not my new employment (the kirkyard night watch proved to be uneventful at best and dauntingly dull at its worst), nor was it my new employer (Aneurin was politely austere each time our paths crossed during the course of my classes at Malstrom's school, offering barely so much as a tip of his head or the vague hint of a smile in my direction to formalise our acquaintance—a detachment, I reasoned, ultimately necessary to preserve the professional boundaries required by my status as a student; after all, if word got out that Malstrom was offering cut-rate tuition, Aneurin would surely be swamped with more demands for accommodation! Our only form of communication was the tiny folds of parchment I'd discover at my dissection table when my services were to be required: Tonight).

No, the cause for my joy was in my studies. For there, within the walls of Malstrom's dissection rooms, I was, as promised, granted access to a cadaver of my very own. And side by side with my class of twelve esteemed peers, we embarked upon that most noble of quests: the quest for true scientific enlightenment. And with each hour I passed within those hallowed halls, beneath the discerning gaze and firm hand of Malstrom's tutelage, the wonders of the human body unfolded before me, uncensored and visceral beneath my own two hands. Dissection was no glamorous business—I should never wish to imply otherwise—and while it required a fair bit of conditioning before I became accustomed to the morbid sights, smells, and sounds that rose up around us in a macabre assault on our senses, I found that the deep devotion to purpose that our mission entailed was justification enough to keep any of my more delicate inclinations at bay.

Edinburgh began to feel, more or less, like a home to me. My deepening intimacy with Charlie, Phillip, and Luke proved them to be companions of the highest regard, with whom I could exchange our strictest confidences and deepest doubts about our vocational training without fear of judgement or mockery. Even Hamish seemed to have lost interest in making constant jabs at me after I shared a particularly gory story about my first encounter with a gallbladder; he'd simply raised his eyebrows, tipped his glass, and smirked as if to say, not bad, Toff-Boy, not bad. And thus from our nook at the Hope & Anchor pub, warm and dry and full of ale and spirits, my friends and I forged a bond that I shall never forget despite the darkness that would soon overshadow the jolly tableau.

The maze of Edinburgh's city streets slowly revealed its hidden logic to me, like invisible ink on lemon-streaked parchment. I began to move as a local, down the narrow alleys and shadowed closes, cutting through kirkyards and up winding, cobbled stairs. I scarcely noticed the grey sludge that caked my boots or the torrential rain that soaked my hat —for this city breathed new knowledge into me, invigorated me in ways I'd never dreamed of before setting foot in this wild patch of North. Each and every day, as I stared down into the face of Death himself, I felt achingly, blazingly alive.

But as I've forewarned, this is not the tale of my life as it was. This is the tale of how that life ended and my new life began.

My old life was buried one idle Monday in the fifth week of my night watch. And like all avalanches of the most ominous designs, this one began with the near-imperceptible ping of a single pebble against my windowpane.

4.

A Confession

Over the brief course of my employment as the unofficial Night Watchman of the Greyfriars Kirkyard, I'd developed a rigorous routine of self-imposed tasks infused with the dual purpose of furthering my intellectual pursuits and fending off the temptation of sleep.

Firstly (and most importantly), I avoided any opportunity to imbibe in alcohol on the nights I was to be on duty. I'd march resolutely past our crowded booth at the H&A with a tip of my hat in the lads' direction, expressing my regrets at my inability to join them, and notify Angus (the barkeep and proprietor, who, even after more than a month of my residency there, showed no sign of fondness or familiarity towards me) that I was to take my dinner in my room. I'd spend the next hour fastidiously transcribing my notes from Malstrom's classes that week from the scribbled margins of my anatomy textbook into proper leather bound journals. My evenings on duty were my chance to process, absorb, and organize these haphazard notations without the enticing, if often insalubrious, distractions of the dissection theatre.

Then I would allow myself a short respite for dinner, and by the time my meal was complete, it was time for me to take my perch at the window, eyes fixed upon the sexton's cottage with steadfast resolve. The sexton, corrupt as he perhaps was, also had the courtesy of being invariably prompt. As the silhouette of his figure dissolved into darkness, I would lift my lamp from the table and place it upon my window ledge. Then I would situate myself at my desk, positioned so I had a clear view of the returning pathway, and resume my studies.

For as much as I may have wished it were so, Malstrom's classes were not my only academic duty. At the University, I had lectures in physics, chemistry, Latin, and botany, as well as additional responsibilities I'd taken on as a volunteer secretary at the Friday meetings of the Royal Medical Society, whose rotating cast of guest lecturers kept both my quill and my mind engaged. I could scarcely believe my luck that I was, more or less, being compensated merely for staying awake and filling my mind to the brim with all the knowledge my academic life had to offer.

But like all arrangements that appeared too good to be true, this one was doomed to crumble at the first minor deviation from routine. It was a little after ten o'clock at night, the only sound from the kirkyard the brittle shudders of the tree branches against the relentless winter wind. I was hunched over my chemistry textbook, deep in contemplation, when suddenly, a flash of light from the grounds below caught my eye.

My head jerked up, and I rose to my feet at once to peer out the window. Much to my surprise, the sexton had emerged from his cottage, wholly unscheduled, and was scuttling off in the direction of the front gates at a pace I'd prior thought him incapable of. Heart racing I raised my lantern and placed it on the window ledge. Was he on his way to let the robbers in? Was Aneurin watching my window at this very moment, his grey eyes alight with the flame of my lantern, poised to catch the perpetrators in the act? Would there be confrontation? An altercation? I braced my hands against the frame and cursed my own breath for fogging the glass, and I squinted haplessly down into the impenetrable darkness.

Minutes ticked by as the silence enveloped me, and the kirkyard below remained dim and vacant. Slowly, I could feel my muscles relax, my instincts settling back into a subdued, distant curiosity. Even if there were to be an altercation, the gates were well beyond my line of sight, and there was little I could do from here within my chamber. And perhaps I'd allowed myself to be caught up in the melodrama of it all; there was surely little chance Aneurin would confront the sexton and his merry band of thieves alone.

I settled back into my chair with a defeated sigh, a slight tug of disappointment in my chest. Was it so wrong that I wished to be part of the excitement myself, joining Aneurin and Malstrom and whoever else in vigilante fisticuffs, instead of being cloistered away in my ivory tower with nothing but a beam of lamplight to offer in allegiance?

Of course, I mentally chastised myself. Aneurin, Malstrom, their inner circle of acquaintances—I knew in my core they existed in an underworld operating beneath the surface of Edinburgh's rule of noble civility; they were locals here, established members of the community, with their own ethics and alliances and enemies. I was still an outsider upon these streets in comparison with them; their quest for justice was hardly my own. Was it strange that the thought made me oddly melancholy? It was a full turnabout from my pronounced aversion to confrontation I'd experienced in my youth—yet another notable change in my disposition since I'd ventured north as an independent man.

I was snatched from my revery by a sharp tap against my windowpane. I blinked twice, attempting to discern the source; my window was far enough from the nearest tree branch that there was no chance the wind was the culprit. Perhaps precipitation, then—the first sign of hail?

Another ping, more distinct this time; there could be no mistaking it for ice. Something was assailing my window, and it was certainly not of natural origin. I rose to my feet and approached, cupping my hands around my face to block out the ambient light as I peered down into the infernal darkness. No sooner had my gaze settled than another ping against the very pane through which I was peering nearly made me jump out of my skin. There was a figure out there—obscure but unmistakable—poorly hidden by the vegetation beside the kirkyard path below.

Curiosity, trepidation, and excitement rose in equal tides, and I found my fingers shaking as I clumsily fumbled with the ancient iron latch holding my window shut. In the few weeks since my arrival, there had been no cause to open it, and I found the process considerably more complex than I'd anticipated.

A thoroughly humiliating amount of time later, I finally managed to unwedge the latch from its locked position and fling open the window with a gasp of relief. The frigid night air struck me full force, and gooseflesh rose on my skin as my eyes adjusted to the moonlight. And there, hunched in the bushes below my window, was a wild-eyed shadow with a shock of jet-black hair I'd recognize anywhere.

"Aneurin?"

"Shhh! Keep your voice down!" He responded in a frantic whisper, his features still obscured by the blanket of darkness surrounding him. "You have to let me up!"

I leaned further forward and shivered in the cold, replying in an exaggerated hiss of my own. "With what?" It wasn't as if I kept a ladder handy in the event that a late-night visitor should need to be rescued from the kirkyard; the situation was wholly unprecedented.

"I have a rope. Catch!" With an undignified yelp, I jumped backwards as a coil of rope nearly stuck me in the face before falling straight back down into the brush whence it had emerged. "The hell was that, Willoughby? I said, Catch!"

"A little warning would be nice," I snapped back, irritation getting the better of me. Something about the action had rather reminded me of when my elder brothers used to throw objects in my direction at random under the guise of testing my reflexes.

There was a lingering silence followed by a haughty, faux-English accent: "Well, then, by your leave, dear sir! At your convenience, henceforth!"

I rolled my eyes. "There's no need to be terse, I simply requested—"

"You won't have time to simply request anything of me if the sexton catches me down here! For the love of God, take the damn rope!"

"Fine! Just—" The coil of rope was hurled in my direction once more, but this time I was ready for it and caught it with steady hands, the tail end still dangling down to brush the earth below.

"Alright, you hold that end and I'll hoist myself up."

"You'll—Wait, you'll what?" I scanned my chamber frantically, looking for something to tie the spare end to that could support Aneurin's body weight. "I can't—I haven't got anything solid enough to secure the rope to!"

"Didn't they teach you physics at school, or were you too busy doing something more pressing, like reciting the Bible in Latin?" Aneurin's tone was dripping with sarcasm. I opened my mouth to issue a retort which hastily died on my tongue. "Crouch down. Brace your legs against the wall. Counterbalance. I'm coming up."

My body obeyed as if of its own accord, and before my brain could catch up and take stock of the situation, the rope pulled taut and my fingers wrapped sturdily around the coil as I braced my feet firmly against the wall, using my whole body as a counterweight.

There was an interminable pause, punctuated by the sporadic sounds of heavy breathing, boot soles scuffing against stone, and a few choice words I'd never before heard uttered in polite company. I steadied my resolve and strained against the rope, providing the required resistance. Then another pause, a break, a sweet moment of levity, and Aneurin tumbled over the window ledge and into my room, landing directly on top of me in the process.

Extracting himself quickly from our jumbled heap of limbs, he leapt to his feet, slammed the window shut, fastened the latch, and extinguished the lamp in a series of deft, unhesitating movements before collapsing to a crouch beside me, back against the wall, huddled below the windowsill, his breath erratic.

I blinked up at him from where I was still sprawled on the splintered floor boards, propped up on my elbows with the tangled coil of rope splayed across me, chest heaving and legs trembling from the exertion of aiding his escape. He was staring down at me, pale eyes owlishly wide in the singular moonbeam illuminating the room, a flush of what may well have been exhilaration dotting his pronounced cheekbones. To my utter astonishment, he was smiling.

"Thanks."

I gawped up at him. "Thanks? That's all you have to say for yourself?"

He gave a good-natured shrug, raking his fingers through his hair to push it back from his perspiration-slicked forehead. "I mean, you did just help me evade arrest and several months' subsequent hard labour, so yes, Thanks seemed rather in order."

"Hard labour?" My mind was spinning; I had no idea what he was talking about.

He cocked his head, his smile turning more lopsided, more relaxed. He seemed almost infuriatingly amused with the situation. "Fair point. Perhaps to return the favour, I ought to buy you a drink as well?"

Shoving myself up off my elbows and into a seated position, I found myself blushing crimson and quaking with self-righteous fury. The realisation was beginning to dawn on me that it seemed I'd been played the fool in more ways than one—and while I still had no idea what Aneurin had been up to in the kirkyard below, it most certainly was not enacting vengeance on behalf of Malstrom's clergyman brother.

"You lied to me." I tried to keep the quiver out of my voice as the puzzle pieces slowly fell into place. "You weren't trying to catch the grave robbers. It was you robbing the graves all along!" The betrayal sliced like a scalpel through my fortified self-resolve. Though I could objectively acknowledge that Aneurin and I were hardly dearest bosom friends, it felt bitter indeed to realise that our budding familiarity that day in Malstrom's office had been a feint. He didn't see me as a promising pupil or a fellow disciple of the Enlightenment; he saw me as financially desperate and woefully gullible. I thought of the moment I'd divulged my father's past transgressions to him, lured into a false sense of security by his own confidence in me, and shame welled up hot as bile in my throat.

But in a fraction of an instant, all traces of mirth seemed to slip from his face. His hands rose up before him and reached out to me as if in placation, and it was with a sense of surreal horror that I saw they were covered in soil. "No, James, please. You have to let me explain."

"You're a grave robber," I said again, recoiling both from him and from the damning ramifications of my own words. "I should turn you in."

He shook his head desperately, his expression turning earnest. "No, you've got it all wrong. I'm many unsavoury things, yes, but a grave robber is not one of them. I swear it upon my life; I've never lifted so much as a shroud of cloth from those interred below. I have never. I would never."

I narrowed my eyes, attempting to assess his degree of sincerity. Again, I saw in him that strange changeling semblance I'd noticed in Malstrom's office, all shifting angles and blurred edges, defying quantification. I couldn't read him now. And I certainly hadn't before.

I shook my head. "I want to believe you. I want to believe you wouldn't use me so unscrupulously. But all the evidence is to the contrary."

For a moment, he paused. Then, in a sudden flurry of movement, he was back upon his feet, hastily divesting his palm of the incriminating spoil upon his trousers before extending his hand towards me. "Please. Let me buy you a drink."

I cast a look of disdain towards his outstretched palm. "Pardon me for thinking I'd best stay sober when dealing with the likes of you from now on."

This rejection seemed to momentarily disarm him, and I could have sworn I saw something like hurt flicker across his face. But it was gone as quickly as it had appeared, replaced with a careful casualness I was beginning to identify as his mask. "Fine. You don't have to drink. Just . . . let me take you somewhere that's not here."

"So you can murder me in an alley for my cufflinks?" I was being incorrigible, that much I knew, but I was quickly learning better than to give strangers the benefit of the doubt in this city.

Aneurin just heaved a withering sigh and took another step towards me, still not withdrawing his hand. "James. Please."

Our eyes locked. I tried to run a tabulation of the risk involved; I tried to mentally triage my bloodied dignity. But his grey eyes were fixed on mine, his dark lashes an otherworldly halo around those mesmerising orbs. I was charmed by him, despite myself, and could offer no hope of resistance when such a plea was uttered in his soft brogue.

Cursing under my breath, I clasped my hand to his and allowed myself to be hauled to my feet. His face broke into a grin—one that certainly seemed sincere—which I found myself returning, against my better judgement. "Excellent. Fetch your coat, it's freezing." And with a flourish, he strode across my chamber and flung open the door, proceeding to turn right into the hallway and march off in the completely wrong direction.

I scampered after him, shrugging on my overcoat, and frantically trying to silence my inner voice inquiring whether I was really going out in public without my cravat.

"Oy!" I half-whispered as I jogged to catch up with him. Though it was not yet an absurdly late hour, I didn't want to risk disturbing my fellow lodgers, who would surely have some rather prying questions about what an unidentified man was doing upstairs in the

living quarters. "Stairs down to the pub are that way." I
gestured vaguely in the opposite direction.

"We're not going to *this* pub," he countered over his
shoulder.

"And why not?" I followed him to the end of the hall
where, to my surprise, he jimmied open a door to his
left to reveal a rickety, unlit staircase apparently leading
to the alley beside the inn.

"Because I've been banned from this one for life."
With that, he tossed me an impish wink over his shoulder and then descended the stairs two at a time.

For a moment, I hesitated. While I didn't honestly
think he was about to murder me, I didn't actually know
much about him at all, and what I did know painted a
rather tawdry picture indeed: he was up to some sort of
illegal business in a kirkyard multiple times a week, and
he'd been banned for life from one of the least whole-
some pubs I'd ever set foot in. Following him down an
unlit stairwell into an empty alleyway and then on to
an unidentified ale house seemed . . . well, reckless, to
say the least.

But a part of me wanted to be reckless. For while
I'd come to appreciate my life in Edinburgh—my
classes, my peers, the whole steady, certain predictability of a meaningful routine outside the confines
of my elite pedigree, I had still been itching with a
niggling, nagging desire for more. I felt like I was
standing upon the tip of an iceberg, marveling at its
beauty but knowing that further below, there was so
much more to attain, to experience, to know. And
here was Aneurin, this enigmatic stranger, cunning
and manipulative and yet so charismatic that to not

follow him down those darkened stairs into the dismal recesses of whatever world he wanted to show me—well, that seemed to me to be the true madness, indeed.

With a (slightly troubling) spring in my step, I followed him.

We wound through the empty streets in lockstep and in silence, our breath a foggy halo in the brisk December air. He unexpectedly turned left off the main road down a close that was unfamiliar to me, winding around the piles of the South Bridge and then twisting through a strange cobbled alley, at the base of which, I was shocked to see, were the gaily glowing windows of a tiny structure burrowed back against the narrow brick wall of the subterranean Vaults.

I'd never been to the Vaults myself, but I'd heard plenty of stories of the debauchery that took place therein: gambling taverns, unlicensed distilleries, dens of ill repute . . . Yet the pub whose door Aneurin was currently pushing open wasn't technically inside the Vaults, I reasoned. It was merely adjacent to them, which surely meant it couldn't be entirely unreputable. After two steps across the threshold, however, I was forced to seriously reconsider. If I had thought the Hope & Anchor was unsavoury, this establishment put it entirely to shame.

The tables were an unmatched jumble of what appeared to be ancient cast-offs from God only knows where; the tops were nearly black with grime, and I could almost feel the tacky grit caked upon them without laying down a finger. There were no proper lamps, the only source of light being fragrant, fat-wax candles poured into cracked pint glasses, acrid smoke rising from them and clouding the air with a foul stench. The patrons were no more refined than their surroundings; while I'd grown accustomed to the rough edges of the customers at the H&A, I rarely spotted anyone there I'd suspect of being a criminal. In the shadowy light of this pub, however, I was fairly certain every patron in attendance probably had a warrant out for his arrest. Such was the dazzling array of ragged overcoats and eye patches, wild hair and grizzled scars, gold teeth and fingerless gloves, I half-expected the two of us to be eyed over, like two dinners upon a silver tray, the moment the bell above the door announced our entrance.

But to my considerable shock, not a single patron looked up from his conversation. Aneurin maneuvered his way towards the bar as confidently as a fish in water, and I chased closely at his heels. Without even taking the courtesy to ask my preference in refreshment, he signaled the barkeep for two whiskeys, then whirled around to face me squarely for the first time since we'd left my chamber. His eyes gleamed maniacally in the dim light as he gave a theatrical wave of his hands at our dismal surroundings. "So. Welcome to the Pig & Swindle."

I glared at him. This was distinctly not what I'd been expecting when he'd offered to buy me a drink—I didn't think he'd drag me to some squalid den halfway to Hell when his purported intent was to win back my trust. I was at least assured that my cravat would not be missed in present company.

"What is this place?" I murmured half under my breath (lest my repulsion offend one of the nearby patrons).

"My watering hole of choice. Best bootleg whiskey in the city." The barkeep returned and thrust in our direction two grease-smudged glasses, brimming with cloudy amber liquid. Aneurin beamed at him and tossed a single coin onto the bar; I quickly deduced that while this was probably not the best whiskey in the city, it was certainly some of the cheapest. I wondered if Aneurin was less well-off than his manner of dress and station at Malstrom's would suggest.

I didn't have much time to contemplate the matter. No sooner had the thought crossed my mind than Aneurin was pressing one of the glasses into my hand and shepherding me between the series of rotting wood beams that seemed to barely be staving off the sagging ceiling from imminent collapse, guiding me to a vacant table in the far corner. He settled breezily into one of the two rickety chairs, and I pulled out the one opposite, forcing myself not to inspect the seat for grime before lowering myself reluctantly into it.

He raised his glass in my direction. "To new beginnings."

I glowered at him once more, depositing my full glass resolutely upon the table. "I told you I wasn't drinking with you anymore."

He shrugged. "Suit yourself." He knocked back half his glass in a single swill, grimaced, and sputtered. "On second thought, that might not be a bad idea. The brew's a bit off tonight." The disgust was clearly evident on my face, and he gave me a winning smile in return. "Alright, so I must confess, I don't come here for the whiskey. I come here because this is the type of place where people mind their own business. No one will ask what we're doing here; all they ask is that we return their ignorance in kind. There's no eavesdropping here at the Pig. No tattlers."

I narrowed my eyes. "Honour amongst thieves."

"Something of that nature." He rapped his fingertips briskly against the tabletop and leaned back in his chair, eyeing me appraisingly in the dim light. "So I imagine you have questions."

"A few."

"By all means. I'm an open book." He spread his hands placatingly before himself, in what seemed to me a gesture of practiced sincerity.

I bit my lip, hardly sure where to start. I turned over a few options in my mind, then finally settled upon what I deemed to be an acceptable course of inquiry.

"Fine. What were you doing in the kirkyard tonight?"

"I was working for Malstrom." His reply was diplomatic. Even. Infuriatingly vague.

"You were working for Malstrom doing what, exactly?"

He propped his fingertips beneath his chin, apparently weighing the nature of his response. He blinked twice, then replied, "I was procuring specimens."

My stomach gave an uneven lurch. "Specimens?"

"Yes, specimens. For the school."

I could feel my brow furrow in consternation. "And precisely what types of specimens were you procuring in the Greyfriars Kirkyard in the dead of night?"

His lip turned up into a half grin, and he took another steady swig of his drink. "I think you know the answer to that."

My pulse was hammering at my temples, a peculiar tightening manifesting in my lungs. The story was slowly shifting into focus, but I found the sharper it got, the less I wanted to see. "You were robbing graves."

"Ah-ah. That, I demonstrably was not." He wagged a finger in my direction. "Grave robbing is a felony. To purloin the possessions of the dead is punishable by hanging." He seemed insufferably smug about it.

I gritted my teeth. "I wasn't talking about the possessions of the dead."

A steady smile spread across his ethereal features. "Ah. Now there's the rub."

For lack of a better distraction, I peered intently at my whiskey. It smelled ghastly—smokey and bitter but somehow soothing in a way I couldn't quite define. "I need to know why."

Aneurin's eyes raked across my face, and I had the uncomfortable sensation of being dissected without so much as a single incision. At long last, he responded. "I can't tell whether you're stupider than you seem, more naïve than I'd come to believe, or so intentionally obtuse as to be a rare and volatile combination of the two."

Anger flared red-hot in my chest, and I found myself gripping my glass with wholly more fortitude than I'd intended. "What, precisely, are you implying?"

He placed his own glass softly on the table, tracing the rim with the pad of his index finger, his gaze still pointed and sharp. "James, how many medical students are there at the University proper?"

I drew a quick mental tabulation. "One hundred fifty or so in my class. I'd imagine the same in the levels above me."

"Mmm. And how many independent anatomy schools are there in Edinburgh?"

I shrugged. "A dozen? Give or take?"

"Twelve. Twelve exactly." His answer was curt, precise. "And how many pupils attend Malstrom's school with you?"

I could feel the grisly summation gathering inside my head, an abacus of grotesque accounting. "Twelve others."

"Indeed. Now, I presume you consider yourself well-versed in mathematics, being a civilised gentleman of a certain upbringing."

I could barely breathe under the weight of the insinuation. "Yes."

"And so. If there are twelve anatomy schools in Edinburgh, each with thirteen pupils and each guaranteed their own cadaver, how many cadavers are required to educate the pupils of Edinburgh's private anatomy halls each term?"

I cleared my throat. "One hundred and fifty-six."

"Quite so. And if the University itself exercises its exclusive claim to all bodies obtained by legal means—which, as I'm sure you know, is restricted to the corpses of convicted murderers sentenced to death by hanging, amounting to an average total of four per term—how, do you suppose, we make up for the deficit?"

I could feel my eyes darting frantically about the room; it all seemed so suddenly obvious, I had no greater wish than to disguise my gross negligence. "Through . . . through theft."

Aneurin pursed his lips in a guise of contemplation. "Through theft. Not just petty, reckless theft, for grave robbing is a felony. But did you know that procurement of a body alone through unlawful means is merely a misdemeanor, punishable solely by fine so long as you are . . . a man of certain standing within the medical community?"

My gaze snapped to his. "No. No, I didn't know that."

His fingers returned to the rim of his glass, resuming the same lazy circles around its circumference. "It's true. And as a fellow man of Science, you must now understand the stakes in all of this. The ends, as it's said, surely justify the means."

"You rob graves—"

"I snatch bodies. There is a difference. I do not desecrate or dishonour the dead. I do not deprive them of their worldly possessions. Everything that they carry with them beneath the ground into their hallowed tomb remains there, save for their corpse. I simply give their death meaning."

"By placing them on my slab."

"Instead of what, allowing them to rot beneath the earth as God and the worms intended? You've seen Malstrom's mind at work, James—for Heaven's sake, I've seen your mind at work! Without a subject beneath your hands, your talents, your intellect—they would all be wasted." He all but spat the last word as if it were poison in his mouth.

"This is unholy, Aneurin, it's—it's an aberration."

"Those are the words of the Church speaking." He tilted his head, analyzing me. "Were you once a man of Faith?"

I was taken wholly aback by his astute observation. "I . . . I initially endeavored to join the Church when I attended Oxford, yes, but—"

"But now you are here." He pounded the table so suddenly as to startle me from my thoughts. He was staring at me so intently, with such passion and vigour, I felt certain now that his words were genuine. "We are sons of the Enlightenment. All of us. To allow all that potential to moulder beneath the soil, like the specimens we require but are legally denied—tell me, what would be the holy cause in that?"

"So you believe what you do is moral."

"Morality is hardly the half of it. We take the greatest of care to remove all the personal effects of a corpse, from the funeral shroud to the smallest jewels and trinkets. Therefore, the taking of the body itself is not a felony, merely a distasteful taboo in the eyes of the law."

"And in the eyes of the Church?"

"Mercifully for us, the Church does not operate the gallows any longer."

I glared down at my still-full whiskey glass, willing my heart to steady its galloping against my sternum.

At long last, I endeavoured to speak. "So that's what you were doing in the kirkyard tonight. You were . . . body snatching."

He gave a vague nod of affirmation. "As I said. I was procuring specimens for the school."

"Alone?"

"Hardly. In fact . . ." Aneurin turned to peer over his shoulder. "Now where is she, I'd just seen her—ah!" He raised his arm in an enthusiastic salute, and much to my surprise, his gesture was returned by a young woman weaving her way through the crowd, drink in hand, before arriving breathless and flushed by his side. He took her hand in his and pressed his lips against it, staring up at her with delight. "James, may I introduce the incomparable Mary Paterson. Mary, this is James." He didn't even take his eyes off her as he gestured in my direction.

And I couldn't blame him. For while I had seen any number of fair faces in my day, I could say with utter certainty that none compared to the perfection of Mary Paterson.

Her skin was milk-pale and even, glowing with a feminine blush offsetting the tempting tone of her lips. Her cheekbones were high, her nose sharply angled, and her jaw defined, yet the sum was still elegantly feminine. Her hair was a rich, shimmering auburn, flowing from manicured waves into an elaborate chignon gracing the nape of her neck, from which had escaped a few unruly curls that only accentuated the perfection of her visage. Her eyes, when they met mine, were a warm, inviting brown, and there was a kindness in them that made me feel instantly at home. To look upon her face was to witness a pristine example of feminine beauty, and I found myself stumbling and tongue-tied as I rose to my feet to greet her.

I performed a curt bow, and her expression transformed into one of delight (with perhaps an undertone of amusement). With a nod of her head, she spoke at last, her voice lovely and low. "It's a true pleasure to meet you, James. Aneurin has told me so much about you—and I can see you're as much a gentleman as he described!"

I smiled, flattered that Aneurin had thought to mention me in conversation—perhaps my role in his operation was more consequential than I'd initially assessed. "I'm relieved to hear my manners have not disappointed in the first five seconds of our acquaintance; my mother would be most assured."

She tipped her head back and laughed more openly than I'd seen any lady of my social status do; it was delightfully refreshing to see a young woman so at ease and not endlessly concerned with matters of poise.

"I think that may be the first time a gentleman has sought to mention me to his mother," she continued with a wink. Then she turned back to Aneurin, who was gazing up at her affectionately. "What brings you here tonight, my love? I thought you were working."

Something strange and red-hot flared in my chest at their flagrant display of affection. Aneurin gave a casual shrug. "We got ourselves in a bit of a hobble, but James here sorted us out. I owed him a debt for his invaluable assistance."

Mary raised her eyebrows, apparently impressed by my antics. "I'm relieved to hear you've found such a worthy cohort." My cheeks flushed as she once more turned her gaze to me.

"It was nothing really," I protested feebly, but she waved me off.

"Nonsense, James. I have a strong feeling you'll be a most welcome member of our little crew." With that, she bent to press a kiss to the top of Aneurin's head. "Anyways, I must be off. Anderson's demanding an audience, and I'm afraid I can't dodge him forever."

Nye narrowed his eyes. "Let me know if he gives you any more trouble. I've carried a scalpel up my sleeve ever since the last time he attempted liberties with you."

She laughed again and rolled her eyes. "You know I can look after myself, love." And with a twirl of her skirts, she disappeared back into the crowd.

I took my seat beside Aneurin once more and, taking another (reluctant) sip of my drink, turned to meet his eye.

"So, Mary . . . is your betrothed?"

Aneurin, who had been mid-sip of his own drink, promptly choked and sputtered in a most undignified fashion before barking out a laugh. "My betrothed? What on earth would give you that impression?"

I blinked uncomprehendingly at him. "Well, the two of you seem quite familiar."

"Christ, I forget that men of your status interact only with ladies of high rank. Did you not frequent local watering holes in Oxford with women of a . . . different station?"

I shot him a dirty look. "Well, there were indeed certain pubs known for harbouring women of loose standards, but I myself didn't frequent them."

He raised an eyebrow. "No, of course you wouldn't."

"And what's that supposed to mean?"

He shrugged. "Nothing at all, simply that your commitment to maintaining your good standing makes your presence here with the likes of me all the more unlikely."

I managed to choke down another sip of my drink. "Well, needs must." I glanced across the room, attempting to catch another glimpse of Mary; she was currently seated at a table occupied by a portly, well-dressed gentleman, nursing her drink. "So Mary is not your betrothed, then. But do you intend her to be?" I was slightly unclear on what the courtship practices of the lower classes entailed.

Aneurin gave me a quizzical glance. "I would have thought it was fairly obvious that I am not the kind to take a wife, James."

My brain seemed to hit a stumbling block, and for a moment, I was rendered mute by this admission. There was the obvious explanation, of course: that as a man of meagre means from a rural town and with no family money, Aneurin simply could not afford the responsibility of taking a wife. Though it was clear from his dress and manner that his position at Malstrom's afforded him a semblance of proper living, I was well aware that the need to provide for a wife and subsequent offspring could often be the thin line between relative comfort and dire poverty.

But something snagged at the back of my mind as I conjured this excuse. Something about his tone, his manner, the way he held my gaze as he said it—left me struck speechless, dumbly staring back at him.

I eagerly sought to change the subject. "So . . . Mary works the kirkyard with you?" I was incredulous at the thought of such a stunning creature skulking about cemeteries under the cover of the darkness.

Aneurin barked out a laugh. "Mary is undoubtedly the most valuable member of our crew, but she's never been on a dig. She attends funerals throughout the city under the guise of a fellow mourner and reports back to us any pitfalls or traps we may encounter during our extraction."

"Pitfalls or . . . traps?"

Aneurin put down his drink and took his standard posture with his fingers steepled beneath his chin; the gesture was growing reassuringly familiar to me. "The families of the deceased are not ignorant to what's been happening in the graveyards of this city, and they have developed increasingly elaborate ways to ensure that their loved one's remains are not desecrated by those of our ilk. Most commonly used are tokens, tiny trifles placed upon a fresh grave that are seemingly unnoticeable to anyone not looking for them. But if the token is moved—suggesting the grave has been disturbed—the family members will alert the authorities and pound down the doors of the anatomy schools until their loved one is recovered."

I was aghast at the prospect. "Has anyone ever been reclaimed from Malstrom's?"

"Nah, Mary's far too good for that. Nothing gets past her; she lets us know just where the tokens are so we can replace them unnoticed. She also warns us of any more dangerous ploys, such as hidden lookouts or trip guns."

"Trip guns?"

"An elaborate scheme devised to deter snatchers: the guardians of the deceased rig a series of wires low to the ground around the fresh grave and connect them to a loaded pistol hidden behind the headstone."

"My God." It hadn't occurred to me before just how dangerous this work would be.

Aneurin waved his hand dismissively. "Not to worry; the device is rarely rigged properly to begin with, so it seldom triggers the pistol. And even if it does, it would take an unlucky man indeed to be standing directly in the bullet's narrow path. More than anything, the noise is intended to alert the sexton to intruders."

I wasn't entirely reassured.

"And then there are the mortsafes, which pose no danger but have become an irritation beyond compare: wrought-iron cages rented from the kirk and placed over the fresh grave for a week or two, until the body is in such a state of decomposition as to render it useless for study. They're expensive—a luxury afforded only by the wealthy—but still discouragingly prevalent these days." He sounded so distinctly mournful at the thought that I could not suppress an indulgent smile. It was clear from his demeanour that he was exceptionally well-versed in his distinctly unorthodox profession, a deep well of knowledge from which I myself was increasingly eager to draw.

"So Mary gathers the intelligence required, and then you orchestrate the snatch based on her reports in order to avoid injury or capture?"

Aneurin grinned. "Precisely."

"And where is the rest of your party?"

"They made it past the gates before the sexton was able to lock them again. I found myself trapped inside the kirkyard, quite without a point of egress, with a rather displeased groundskeeper on my tail."

My brow furrowed. "Until I rescued you."

He blinked up at me from beneath lowered lashes, looking nearly demure at the prospect. "Until you rescued me."

I broke eye contact first, pretending to be suddenly utterly absorbed in a fascinating stain on the tabletop. "And so . . . what now?"

"How do you mean?"

I scraped at the stain half-heartedly with my fingernail. Unsurprisingly, it didn't budge. "Well, you've bought me my drink. What's your next move? Do you aim to convince me to remain employed as your lookout?" I could hardly keep the accusatory tone from my voice.

He raised an eyebrow incredulously. "Have you come up with the full price of your tuition?"

My smugness turned quickly to civility. "No. Not as such, no."

"Then it seems you have little choice."

"Mmm." I allowed my eyeline to wander to the flames dancing low in the fireplace. "So then why am I here?"

"I'm afraid I don't understand."

"I mean, if it's my tuition at stake, you hardly needed to bribe me with bootleg whiskey to keep my silence."

Aneurin cleared his throat. "Well . . . I must admit, it's not . . . it's not just about your position at the school. Or your tuition. I'm afraid my sights were set a bit shorter than that."

I eyed him skeptically. "How do you mean?"

"I mean, the more pressing issue is that of . . . the body."

"What body?"

"The . . . well, the body currently hidden in the shrubberies beneath your chamber window."

It was probably for the best that I'd not been tempted to consume my drink, as I found myself sputtering upon my own saliva as it was. "My—the what?!"

Aneurin looked sincerely placating from his position across from me. "Well, I didn't want the night's labour to be for naught, and I managed to stow it before the sexton caught up with me. To have abandoned it would have been a terrible waste, would it not?"

I was certain my eyes were bulging out of my head at the insinuation. "You are telling me that there is a body stowed in the bushes outside my window?"

"Yes."

"Well then, for God's sake, put it back!" The words were barely a hiss, and despite the fact Aneurin had assured me we were in sympathetic company, I couldn't help but cast frantically about for anyone who might be overhearing this.

"It's not as simple as all that, you see—we'd already refilled the grave by the time the sexton came around; it would take ages to dig it back up again."

"So—so then just put it in the path where the sexton will find it! Surely the Church will simply cover the reburial!"

Aneurin shot me a pointed look across the table. "You know, sometimes when bodies are found in such a state, the families believe they must have been buried alive. Can you imagine, having to live with such a weight upon your soul?"

He was playing me, I could tell this time, and I glared at him accordingly. "Fine. What's your brilliant solution?"

"We use my rope to haul it up into your chamber and then cart it away tomorrow morning."

I was fairly certain my eyebrows had raised straight off of my forehead. "Are you out of your mind?"

"Tell me why that's a bad idea."

"Tell you why—why—why hoisting a stolen corpse into my bedchamber is a bad idea? For God's sake, I don't even know where to begin—"

"And I'll tell you why it's a good idea: because it's worth two guineas and a crown, and I'll give you half."

I was utterly gobsmacked. "It's . . . it's worth what?!" The fact that a near-mouldering corpse could be worth a small fortune had caught me completely off guard.

"Two guineas and a crown is the going price for the corpse of a grown man."

"For a grown man? As opposed to—"

"Six shillings per foot and nine-pence per inch thereafter for a child."

I was struck dumb. "That's . . . that's obscene. You're insane."

"Well, that makes me and the entire medical community of Edinburgh insane. I don't set the prices, and I didn't start the trade. This is what it is. You came here for knowledge, and this is the price of it. Now that you know, you can't look away. No more pleading innocence for you."

"You dragged me into this," I snarled. There was something raw and feral clawing at the inside of my chest; I felt caged and near-frantic.

Aneurin simply narrowed his gaze steadily. "You came to Edinburgh because you were looking for the face of God and couldn't find it in your Bible. Don't cast blame on me if His true appearance is not the one of beatific serenity you'd been deceived into believing. This is the face of Progress, James. Don't you dare look away."

For a beat, there was nothing but the sound of our syncopated breathing, the crackling of the fire, and the dim chatter of the other patrons. I felt dizzy, wholly unmoored, my head swimming, and for once, I could be certain it wasn't the effect of the drink.

At long last, I folded my hands carefully on the table. "Alright."

His eyes met mine. "Alright?"

"Alright. Let's go rescue a corpse from some shrubbery."

5.

An Endeavour

The walk back to my lodgings was similarly silent to the one preceding it, but the air between the two of us was thick with a much different kind of apprehension than had been there a mere hour ago. Whereas before I had been brimming with righteous indignation coupled with astute curiosity, I now found myself filled with an excitement of considerably darker origins.

Was I, the noble son of a landed family, about to tow a freshly stolen corpse into my chamber window and exchange it for money?

No, not money, but Progress, I reminded myself firmly. It was simply a matter of supply and demand. The need was great and immediate, and the law refused to acknowledge it—of that much, Aneurin had left no uncertainty in my mind. The fault was not with us and our business, but with the antiquated thinking of the backwards-facing politicians crowding the halls of Parliament. They knew nothing of the New Enlightenment;

they profited from its gains, but turned a blind eye to its costs. They benefited from the sudden prominence of Edinburgh on the scientific world stage, but preferred to keep their archaic edicts in the dark ages. Aneurin had made this all abundantly clear as he polished off his whiskey, eyes bright and conspiratorial in the dim light of the dying fire.

And thus I found myself once again trailing helplessly in his footsteps as he expertly maneuvered open the door to the alley entrance of the H&A, ascended the stairs (two at a time, of course), and practically waltzed down the hallway before throwing open the door to my chamber and depositing his overcoat on the bed as if he owned the place. I scowled at his presumed familiarity; though we were now arguably accomplices in this current undertaking, he had yet to fully regain my trust, and I inwardly stewed over his growing list of impolite transgressions.

"Now. Let's see what we're working with." He flicked the latch on the window and gave it a shove.

"It's a bit sticky—"

Of course, the window flew open with nary a hitch. He threw me a withering look over his shoulder, and I blushed at my own perceived ineptitude. Could I not even advise on opening a window without making myself seem hopelessly helpless in front of him? It was infuriating.

He scarcely seemed to notice. He was too busy leaning out the window, then popping back inside, staring up at the ceiling, and muttering to himself, his hair wild in the frigid night air that swirled in past his lanky form. I shivered and pulled my overcoat more tightly around myself, and silently hoped he'd be done with whatever this odd ritual was with due haste.

At last, he whirled back around and snapped the window shut. "Alright, James, I have excellent news."

I eyed him skeptically; I was quickly beginning to learn that Aneurin's definition of excellent was often at odds with my own. "And that would be?"

"The window of your lodging is approximately fourteen feet off the ground. And that beam holding up your ceiling is approximately eight feet off the ground."

"And that's excellent news because . . ."

He gestured towards the coil of rope still splayed in the middle of the floor from where we'd previously abandoned it. "That there is a forty-foot cut of rope. So we've just enough to run it from shrubbery outside, up over that beam, and back down to the floor, where we can position ourselves to hoist the corpse up with it. A pulley system, see?"

I traced the pattern he described, running the figures in my head. "I . . . yes, I suppose that might work."

He broke into a wide grin. "Of course it will work, o ye of little faith! For a man of science, you're awfully skeptical of basic physics." With that, he briskly retrieved the rope from the floor and tossed one end effortlessly over the beam. This time, I caught it upon its descent. He rewarded my improved dexterity with a pleased nod. "Alright, then. Have you got a good grip?" Before I could summon an answer, he strode back over to the window, flung it open, and hopped up onto the ledge as if poised to jump.

My hands gripped the rope instinctively, but a hot rush of panic overcame me. "Stop! What in God's name are you doing?"

"Why, I'm going to go down and secure the rope to the corpse, of course. Then I'll climb back up just as I did before, and then we'll haul it up together."

I rolled my eyes. "That's a fine plan, but you need to tell me these things. You can't just go launching yourself out windows and expect I'll catch you."

His expression transformed into one of brazen confidence. "Why, won't you?" And with that, he toppled out the window and rappelled into the darkness below.

It was fair fortune indeed that I'd been holding tight to the rope already, because the weight of his descent nearly rocked me from my foundation outright. But as luck (or, as Aneurin would surely insist, physics) would have it, I was able to plant my feet and square my shoulders to instantaneously impart the counterbalance required to keep him from crashing into the foliage fourteen feet below. After mere moments of tension, the rope went slack, and there was a prolonged, disquieting silence. I stood frozen and mute, still quite stunned by the speed at which this escapade was progressing. My breath came in short, aborted heaves, and I could feel sweat beading at my temples.

Two tugs on the rope snapped me from my stupor. I knew what it meant without requiring translation; the corpse had been secured, and Aneurin was prepared to ascend. Unthinkingly, I returned the two tugs, and was summarily rewarded by the return of steady pressure upon the coils threaded within my hands. A curse, a grunt, a squeak, and Aneurin tumbled back through the window frame and somehow managed to land upon his feet this time, beaming as though he'd personally hung the moon.

"Success! Now we only need to haul it up, and we're in the clear!" He dusted some errant soil from his hands; I shuddered to consider its origins.

I gave the rope another exploratory tug. "It seems . . . heavy?"

Aneurin's smile grew unmistakably wider. "Oh, it's a grand one indeed. Quite large. We'll sell off the surplus as candle fat." I must have visibly blanched, because he rolled his eyes and gave my shoulder a playful punch. "Do lighten up; it's just standard practice in the business. You needn't be alarmed." With that, he snatched up the end of the rope from the floor and maneuvered himself behind me, a look of deviant determination on his face that was clearly not mirrored in my own. "Come on, James. You've come this far—no turning back now. You just need to hold, and heave. On three. One, two—"

"Wait!"

"What?" I rounded to find Aneurin's face painted with what was quickly becoming a trademark withering glance.

"So we're just going to . . . to haul him up here, and then what?"

Aneurin shrugged. "I fear that's a problem for our future selves."

"Our future—"

"One, two, three!"

And despite every instinct in my body telling me to abort, to run, to hide, to report this transgression to the local authorities and retreat back to Bath and a life of sanctified solitude, instead I turned, and pulled.

"Again—two, three!"

I pulled, harder.

"Again—two, three!"

Another heave, a frantic shuffling of feet, the sensation of Aneurin struggling in unison behind me, the taut chafe of the rope against my palms, the creak of the boards beneath us, the escalating crescendo of our unified efforts—

"Two, three . . . Nearly there, one more, two, three—"

And with a final victorious yank, an imposing mass shrouded in a sheet of coarse white linen ascended up over the window frame and swung freely into my bedchamber, nearly bowling over both Aneurin and myself, whose shouts of surprise echoed deafeningly against the clapboard walls as we collapsed to the floor in tandem to avoid the macabre pendulum. For one infinite, horrifying second, the corpse swayed gaily above our heads like some obscene chandelier before collapsing mere inches from where we'd landed with an unholy thud.

The silence was deafening. And then out of nowhere came the unmistakable sound of snickering.

I whirled around to see Aneurin convulsing with suppressed laughter, shoulders shaking, cheeks flushed, hands clasped over his mouth to contain his amusement.

"Are you seriously laughing right now?" I hissed.

Aneurin wiped an errant tear from the corner of his eye, drawing an unsteady breath. "Begging your pardon, but it was a bit funny. The look on your face when it nearly struck you—"

"Oh, shut up. I'm sure you were no portrait of dignity and grace yourself; you're down here on your arse just like me, after all."

"I mean, better on my arse than—" He gestured vaguely towards the rotund heap in the middle of the floor, which, I quickly deduced, had landed sprawled out face-down in a most unseemly fashion.

And that was the last straw.

I burst out laughing. Aneurin looked momentarily startled and then promptly lost his barely regained composure as well, and soon both of us were giggling and gasping like a pair of naughty children raiding the sweets cabinet.

I knew it was wrong to laugh, of course; we were in the presence of the deceased, who, while no longer occupying his mortal form, still deserved to be treated with far more respect than the current situation could command. But in the sheer absurdity of the moment, the adrenaline rush had gone straight to my head, and I found myself laughing more out of relief than any sense of cold-hearted heresy.

"James?" A familiar voice accompanied a rap against my chamber door, and Aneurin and I fell instantly into a sharp and sheepish silence.

"Um . . . yes?" My heart felt lodged in my throat as I struggled to produce a tone of casual indifference.

"Everything alright in there?" Charlie sounded sincerely concerned, and I wracked my brain in earnest for an excuse for such nocturnal commotion.

"Fine! Everything is fine, thanks. I just . . . awoke in need of relief and was too lazy to light my lamp. Tripped over the desk is all."

There was an eternal hesitation. "You're sure you're unharmed? It all sounded quite . . . violent."

Before me, Aneurin snorted helplessly and buried his face in the crook of his elbow, attempting to muffle his laughter. I shot him a look full of daggers.

"Yes, of course, just a slight abrasion to my shin is all."

To my horror, the doorknob twisted ominously, and it was an interminable second before I remembered I'd securely locked it.

"Open up; let me take a look and be sure you're sorted."

"Don't be ridiculous, Charlie, I'm fine."

"Please, I'm—"

"If you say, 'a doctor,' I'm never speaking to you again."

At this, Charlie chuckled, and I could feel the tension ease from my shoulders ever so slightly.

"I was going to say concerned, but now that you mention it—"

I raised my voice ever so slightly in agitation. "Honestly, Charlie, I still haven't made it to my pot, and I'm in desperate need of relief—which I cannot attain in present company. Please, I beg of you, stop acting like a mother hen and just let me piss in peace."

That conjured an outright laugh from him. Next to me, Aneurin had all but collapsed in suppressed tittering. I was half-concerned he'd suffocate himself if I didn't dispose of the intruder imminently.

"Right you are, carry on. Library tomorrow?"

"Of course."

"Night, James."

"Night, Charlie." With that, his footsteps receded down the hall.

No sooner had they disappeared than Aneurin, apparently unable to contain himself any longer, let out a most inappropriate hoot of laughter before doubling over completely. One look at his decidedly undignified state broke my stoic composure once more, and I found myself dissolving into helpless giggles as well. The welcome levity was contagious, and it was a fair few minutes before either of us were able to speak with any degree of coherence.

"So . . . what now?" As my bout of hysteria subsided, I was growing acutely aware that our precarious situation was far from resolved.

"Well," Aneurin mused, clamoring to his feet and dusting off his knees before traversing the room to pull the window shut. "Now we devise a plan to get him to Malstrom's."

I pulled myself to my feet as well, cringing as I extended and flexed my fingers; the rope had taken a toll on my palms, and my joints ached from the effort. "Oughtn't we have done that before hauling a dead body into my chamber?"

"Nonsense, a snatcher's work happens on the fly. A problem arises, you find the simplest viable solution and take it. Just do the next cleverest thing. The best-laid schemes o' mice and men, James." He shot me a wicked grin, but I simply pursed my lips in return; I was beginning to recognise Aneurin had quite the flair for melodrama, of which I myself rarely partook.

"Don't quote Burns and expect me to swoon at you; I'm not some blushing damsel. You've convinced me to haul a purloined human cadaver into my lodgings; I'd now be much obliged if you'd devise a scheme to get it out."

He cast his eyes warily about my chamber, no doubt analysing the most intimate details of my daily life and habits, and I felt suddenly rather exposed. His gaze traced over my desk, my bed, my tiny table still strewn with the discarded dishes from my lackluster dinner, the remnants of my soup congealing in an unappetizing puddle from a meal consumed what now felt like several lifetimes ago. The world shifted surreally, and I felt once more the strange unsteadiness come over me that seemed to be so often instilled by Aneurin's presence. I found myself holding my breath.

Aneurin blinked, and the corner of his lip twitched. I followed his eyeline.

"No. Absolutely not."

"James, be reasonable—"

"We are absolutely NOT putting a dead body in my travelling trunk!"

"And why not?"

"Because it's my travelling trunk, for God's sake! I . . . I use it! For—"

"Travelling?"

"Shut up. But yes. For travelling. You can't put a body in there; it will smell!"

Aneurin sighed in apparent exasperation. "Do you smell anything right now?"

I paused to assess. "No."

"Of course you don't. We have chemicals we use for preservation during transport. This isn't an amateur science, you know."

I glared at him. "I don't care if you're a self-proclaimed professional scientist—"

"Don't be daft, I'm a dissectionist and assemblist—"

"You will not defile The Beast like that."

Aneurin snorted in amusement. "I'm sorry, you named your travelling trunk? And not only did you name your travelling trunk, but you named it The Beast? You're a fair bit less sane than I had you pegged for."

I felt my cheeks flush with mortification. "For the record, I didn't name it. Charlie did."

Aneurin's expression soured. "The same Charlie knocking on your chamber door just now?"

"Of course! From my class at Malstrom's? Do you not pay any attention during the lectures? You know what, never mind; that's hardly the point. The point is, I will not allow you to defile my travelling trunk. End of story. No further negotiation."Ten minutes later, Aneurin snapped the top of the trunk shut and fastened the clasps with a satisfied snick that seemed to match the smirk on his face. Across from him, I mopped the sweat from my brow, still panting from the exertion of hoisting the body inside and manipulating it into a form that would allow for the lid of the trunk to fasten properly.

"I still can't believe I let you talk me into this," I muttered mutinously under my breath.

Aneurin just shrugged. "It wasn't like there were loads of other options, James. We can't be careless about this."

"Speak for yourself. It's in my chamber, in a trunk with my initials monogrammed onto it!"

"Well, then it's certainly in your best interest that it not be discovered!"

I collapsed into my desk chair with an unamused harrumph. "So what now? We wait until daybreak and then walk it to Malstrom's?"

Aneurin barked out a laugh. "Are you mad? We'd never make it without drawing unwanted attention to ourselves."

"Why would it matter? It just looks like a standard travelling trunk."

Aneurin sighed. "Though you may have been oblivious to the body trade in Surgeon's Square, I assure you the local authorities are not. You can't just stroll down Infirmary Street with a travelling trunk and enter an anatomy school. You'll be arrested on the spot."

I resisted the urge to bang my head onto my own desk and settled instead for pinching the bridge of my nose. "Then please tell me you've at least thought this part through."

"As luck would have it, indeed I have. You just need to stay here while I pop out to make some arrangements. I'll be back at first daylight."

I glared at him. "You're going to leave me alone with this?" I waved pointedly in the direction of the trunk.

He cocked his head. "What? Corpses aren't unpleasant company. Rubbish conversationalists, but I can attest that they are excellent listeners."

I buried my face in my hands. "I hate you."

"Liar; you find me endlessly intriguing compared to your society friends. Now get some sleep. Be ready at sunup." And with that, he plucked his overcoat off my bed and swung it about his shoulders, then strode out of the room with an air of effortless ease, as though venturing out for a nighttime stroll. The door shut resolutely behind him.

I glanced over at The Beast. "Well, old friend," I murmured. "Guess it's just you and me."

Sleep did not come easily, as I knew that mere feet away was a neatly stowed corpse fresh from the sacred earth right outside my window. As I tossed and turned beneath the covers, the chill of the night air settling into the hollows of my bones, I couldn't resist glancing over every few seconds at the trunk positioned innocuously beside the doorway, awaiting Aneurin's return.

This is wrong.

Then why doesn't it feel wrong?

You should go back on your word, refuse to carry on.

Then why don't I want to?

I chased the tail of my thoughts round and round into a dozy stupor. Whether I truly slept I couldn't be sure, but the next thing I knew, the pale grey light of dawn was blotting the sky behind the silhouette of the kirk, and I jolted upright, suddenly more awake than I had felt in ages.

For a moment, I wondered if it had perhaps all been a mad dream, but one glance at my trunk affirmed that it was indeed quite real—and quite pressing. I sniffed the air cautiously. Aneurin had been right—still no smell. Fascinating.

I roused myself and dressed, then, in a fit of self-conscious fretting, spent the next few minutes arranging my chamber to a less distressed state: placing my dinner dishes outside the door for Angus to collect, organizing my desk, and pulling my bedclothes into as orderly an arrangement as I could muster. I felt somehow compelled to demonstrate to Aneurin that, while my lodgings were perhaps not the most impressive, I was still, in fact, a gentleman capable of maintaining a lifestyle of practiced civility.

I was just recoiling the pile of rope that had been left strewn in the corner of the room after Aneurin's hasty departure when my chamber door swung open and Aneurin entered without so much as announcing himself.

"Do you ever knock?"

He seemed to consider this. "Do you . . . want me to? Thought I shouldn't risk waking your neighbours at such an hour."

I sighed, internally capitulating to his lack of manners once more. "Never mind. What news?"

"Everything's been arranged, but I'm afraid we're pressed for time. We need to have your trunk outside by nine o'clock or we're in for a world of trouble."

I glanced at my pocket watch and found it to be a mere four minutes to the hour. I resisted the urge to mutter something along the lines of "typical." Aneurin appeared to take high-pressure situations with an air of infuriating nonchalance, which was quite contrary to my natural inclination towards fastidious timeliness. But rather than waste my breath on yet another pointless argument, I simply threw on my overcoat, pulled on my gloves, and crouched to grasp one handle of The Beast.

"So? Are you helping, or what?"

Aneurin grinned. "Let's get to it."

As I'd learned the evening of my arrival in Edinburgh, maneuvering The Beast was considerably easier with two sets of hands than one. We were able to spirit the trunk through the dim, silent hallway and down the back staircase with nary a hitch, save for a few false steps and curses exchanged as we maneuvered the steep incline. To my best approximation, we presented upon the street corner at precisely one minute to eight, and I let out a sigh of relief.

"So what now? Are we—"

My inquiry was interrupted by the rattling of the milk cart upon its daily round. It pulled to a halt directly in front of us, and the driver disembarked and procured two stout pails from his stock, briskly tipping his head in our direction before turning to deliver them to the kitchen door at the H&A.

"Come on; this is our ride." Aneurin bent and grasped the handle of the trunk, and I was too surprised to reply as I followed suit. With a quick glance in each direction (the streets were still and vacant, the dim winter sun making little progress against the persistent cloud cover and dreary December darkness), we briskly raised the trunk and loaded it onto the back of the cart. Aneurin hopped up beside it and extended his hand. "You joining me?"

I hesitated. "Do you need me to?"

"Much easier to get this into Malstrom's with you there. Plus I can pay you out for your services once we arrive and he confirms the delivery."

With a curt nod, I accepted his hand and allowed myself to be pulled up beside him, whereupon he casually took a seat upon the trunk; I followed his lead. Moments later, the driver reappeared and didn't even cast us a second look as he ascended to his perch and took up the reins, spurring the horse into motion.

We were silent for a few moments, but my curiosity got the better of me. "So . . . the driver is a friend of yours?"

Aneurin shot a vague half-smile in my direction. "Something of the sort. You see, James, this business I'm in—there's a whole organisation here in the city set up to keep it running. Porters, watchers, drivers, sextons—all can be bought for a price, and all are gainfully employed by the anatomy schools for the purpose of keeping our supply uninterrupted. And fortunately for us, for the most part, the law turns a blind eye. So long as we're not so obvious about what we're doing, they're not about to pound down our doors just for the sake of stirring the pot."

I shook my head in disbelief, still attempting to square this new reality with my prior perception of it. To think that, a mere twenty-four hours ago, I'd had no idea the trade even existed . . .

"So, the milk-cart driver . . ."

"Is willing to transport trunks for a fee, no questions asked."

"And you said there are sextons on the payroll?"

He shrugged. "Sextons, groundskeepers, undertakers, the occasional priest. At the start of the season, we pay them Opening money, guaranteeing us admission to the grounds undeterred for the duration of the term. And once the term concludes, we deliver them a supplemental Closing sum, based on our haul for the year."

I swallowed. "What . . . dare I ask, what determines the season?"

"The weather. We do our work between October and May, and it's no coincidence those months coincide with the terms at the Anatomy schools."

I furrowed my brow. "What happens from June to September?"

Aneurin cast me a sideways glance. "It gets hot." I must have still looked confused because he rolled his eyes and continued. "It smells. The bodies don't keep well underground, and they certainly wouldn't last long in the dissection halls."

"But don't the chemical compounds you mentioned take care of that?"

"No amount of chemicals can beat heat."

I resisted the urge to gag. The swaying of the cart, coupled with the reminder that we were currently sitting upon one such specimen, did little to alleviate my queasiness.

I swallowed hard and steeled myself. "So . . . is the sexton at Greyfriars in on the scheme?"

Aneurin shook his head woefully. "Sadly not, hence our need to employ you as lookout. Our crew's made headway at plenty of other kirkyards around the city, but Greyfriars remains a tough nut to crack. Its location makes it the holy grail of snatching—it's so close to Surgeon's Square and all the schools—but thus far the men who work there have proven to be infuriatingly righteous and completely immovable to our way of seeing things. They call us heretics. And to be honest, there are plenty of men out there with the same way of thinking as them; we have to be careful whom we approach for favours. In fact, a member of our crew was arrested just last month—a digger who doubled as our driver. Asked the wrong chap for a cover story and got sentenced to four months hard labour. That's why we're working Greyfriars now—we're sorely short-handed for the digs and haven't got proper transport arranged to move specimens from Cuthbert's kirkyard, our preferred snatching grounds."

I took a moment to mull this over. "But didn't you say snatching was punishable solely by fine?"

"Solely by fine for men of a certain standing in the medical community. But for most—the diggers, the drivers, the lookouts—you rack up enough infractions, they'll sentence you to far worse than that. Luckily, the surgeons are decent men of considerable income who look out for their own; Malstrom's still paying the poor driver's wife for her hardship while her husband's locked away."

For a moment, I was mute, unable to think of an appropriate response. For all intents and purposes, Aneurin and his ilk were heretics; desecrating holy ground and paying off men of the cloth for the privilege. While I understood the necessity well enough, it was still a bitter truth to swallow.

Finally, I spoke again. "So why did you trust me? Tonight, when the sexton locked you in. You could have simply lain low overnight and left in the morning. Was it just to save the body?"

He appeared pensive for a moment, as if choosing his next words carefully. "May I be frank? I've been watching you in Malstrom's classes, James. The work you do . . . it's . . . well, it's quite brilliant, to be honest. Some of the best I've witnessed in my years working there. And seeing that, I had a feeling that, if push came to shove, I could trust you to come to my aid. See things my way. And I'm glad to say tonight has proven my initial suspicions correct."

Our eyes met, and I returned his smile. My chest filled with a bright, warm relief; he hadn't chosen me simply because I seemed desperate for money and dull enough to be fooled. He chose me because he *trusted* me. It was almost enough to make me forgive him completely.

Just then, the cart pulled to a halt, and I startled to realise we were in front of Number 14 Surgeon's Square. Aneurin hopped to his feet and briskly disembarked, and I helped him unload the trunk without a word exchanged between us. He glanced about the street to confirm the coast was clear before producing a key from his overcoat and unlocking the door to the school, gesturing for me to help move the trunk inside.

We deposited it in the main dissection hall, which was dark and vacant and chillingly still. Aneurin silently led me back to Malstrom's office and gestured for me to take a seat; the space felt considerably cozier than the stark sterility of the hall, and for that I was grateful.

"Wait here. I need to give Malstrom a full report; he'll undoubtedly be concerned if he hasn't heard from anyone else in the crew yet. If they were smart, they'll have disbanded after their escape; he'll be most relieved to hear we've emerged unscathed—and with a specimen, nonetheless! I assure you, James, he'll be most grateful for your service tonight."

"Might I not accompany you?" It was a bold proposition, but a part of me was eager to make my name known to Malstrom in person. If I could impress him with my willingness to assist his crew, perhaps he might show me favour in the classroom as well.

"I'm afraid not," Aneurin replied. "It's a calculated matter of discretion, you see: the surgeons never associate directly with the diggers. It provides them plausible deniability in the event of an inquiry. They rely on their assistants—such as myself—to act as their middle-men."

"Oh, of course—I understand." I was quick to withdraw my request, as the last thing I wanted was to be perceived as overstepping.

"I'll be back momentarily with your compensation." With that, he turned and opened a narrow wooden door situated in the corner behind Malstrom's desk. Internally, I was startled; I'd been in this office multiple times and had never even noticed the door before. And yet, of course, it made perfect sense; Malstrom must reside in chambers above his office.

I sat patiently for what felt like an uncomfortably long while. Occasionally, I thought I could make out the sound of conversation, but I couldn't be certain. Outside the window, the dim dawn gave way to a chilled, monochrome morning.

I shifted uncomfortably in my seat and unfastened the top button of my overcoat. Despite the fact that the fire was small, the size of the room made it feel unreasonably hot. I removed my gloves and waited some more.

Eventually, my patience wore thin. Though I didn't have any lectures that day, I'd had a rather eventful night and was keen to return to my chambers and be alone with my thoughts (or, depending on my mood, downstairs at the pub with the lads, drinking them away). I was a gentleman of a certain calibre, and being made to wait endlessly for my promised compensation was beginning to feel like a personal slight.

At last, I could stand it no longer. I rose to my feet, set my shoulders, and proceeded to pry open the door through which Aneurin had disappeared and ventured inside.

The scene that greeted me made my blood run cold.

What I'd assumed to be the entryway to a staircase was not, in fact, a portal to any such thing. Instead, the door gave way to a large, open chamber with a high vaulted ceiling not unlike the one in the dissection hall next door. But quite unlike the dissection hall, this room was windowless, dark, reeking with an unholy stench, and filled with grotesque horrors the likes of which my mind had never conjured, even in my darkest nightmares.

Splayed out on rough-hewn wooden tables a world away from the pristine marble slabs next door were a number of partially dissected corpses. On the table nearest the door was the body of a young woman with flowing brown hair who was missing both eyes, her throat laid wide open and pinned to a dissection board. Her head was missing its lower jaw, nose, upper lip, right ear, and a few select teeth, giving her mangled face a garish grin.

On the table next to hers lay the body of a man with his head cut off and entrails out, glistening ropes of gore nestled tightly in a nearby jar. His arms and legs had been amputated, the stumps left raw and exposed in the flickering lamplight. I stepped closer and recoiled in horror to see that his intestines were not alone; there appeared to be the entrails of no fewer than four other corpses in the jar along with them. Beside the jar was another of similar shape and size, but this one appeared to contain the man's severed head, nestling placidly with two others beneath it.

Beside these primitive dissection tables was stationed a makeshift desk, upon which rested a dozen jars, each containing a bobbing brain suspended in what I could only assume was embalming fluid. There were scraps of parchment strewn haphazardly across the surface of the desk; most seemed to feature anatomical illustrations, but one, to my compounded alarm, appeared to be an intricate series of jagged lines rendered in what could only be blood.

On the rickety shelves behind the desk sat another dizzying array of clear jars filled with dozens of macabre specimens, including one containing at least forty eye-balls suspended in an eerie green liquid. Positioned on the floor below the shelves stood a large vat in which was floating (by my initial approximation) three arms, several legs, and what appeared to be a disembodied spine. My stomach lurched, and I whirled away, only to find myself facing the fireplace over which hung pans of bones boiling in blood-coloured water, and a large iron cauldron containing more entrails, a heart, a liver, two kidneys, and a pair of lungs. The smell rising from the monstrous scene was beyond description, and I could stand it no longer. I lurched, heaved, and vomited upon the hearth.

"What the hell are you doing in here?"

I whirled around, my eyes still watering and faint with nausea, to see Aneurin descending from a wind-ing wooden staircase leading to a loft at the back of the room. Gone was the playful familiarity I'd grown accus-tomed to seeing etched into his features, now replaced with what I could only describe as cold fury.

I staggered, endeavouring to steady myself by grabbing the edge of a nearby table, but recoiling instantly upon the sensation of my hand landing in something wet and sticky.

"I—I was looking for you." The words felt hot and weak in my throat, thinned with bile and terror.

Aneurin's eyes narrowed. "I told you to wait outside. You weren't supposed to see this."

Suddenly, in the blink of an eye and a twisting clench of my heart, my fear and terror were replaced by unbridled, seething rage, the likes of which I had never before experienced.

"And what is this, Aneurin? What unholy abomination has been wrought here? Is this your doing? Malstrom's? For God's sake, this is the work of a sadist and a madman!"

Aneurin's expression remained cold, calculating. "James, you must understand, you're overreacting—"

I cackled, hysteria bubbling up inside me like a poisoned well. "Oh, I understand. I understand that I was right about you all along! This is an aberration, the work of a blasphemous, irreverent butcher! You, Aneurin MacKinnon, are kin to the Devil himself. This unholy lair can only be his workshop."

Aneurin blinked at me twice, his expression unreadable. "And that is your final conclusion based on all the evidence at hand? That I'm the deviant son of a butcher sent to raise Hell in Edinburgh as Lucifer's apprentice?"

I set my jaw and steeled my gaze. "I don't care who you are. But I'll never set foot in this place again. And may God have mercy on your soul."

And with that, I turned and ran from that hall of horrors, out into the streets and back to the naïve ignorance I once embraced, praying to God that the demon would not follow.

6.

An Arrangement

It was pure serendipity that my catastrophic fallout with
Aneurin happened to coincide with the break in term
for Christmas. I had to miss only one class at Malstrom's
school to avoid any awkward encounters, which was
simple enough to justify—I proclaimed a sudden bout
of illness and had Charlie send my regrets, which he
agreed to do, with an unmistakable air of suspicion.
Familiar as we were, he was undoubtedly keenly aware
of the fact it was quite unlike me to miss a lecture for
any reason, especially one of Malstrom's; in a class as
small as ours, my presence was sure to be missed and
duly commented upon. Fortunately, Charlie returned
that evening brimming with excitement and delivered
a dazzling description of the ocular dissection that had
been the coursework of the day, and I listened to his
vivid recounting of all he'd learned from the safety of my
bed, still feigning chill and fatigue. He later brought tea
and soup to my chamber, and I felt slightly remorseful

for my deceit, but I hadn't the words to explain what was truly wrong with me.

For my discovery of the dark underbelly at Malstrom's school had turned more than my stomach; I was forced to admit that it was impossible to imagine reconciling my Christian morals with the depravity I had uncovered there. What I'd witnessed in Aneurin's laboratory was utterly at odds with the sanctified scientific demonstrations that I participated in weekly under Malstrom's stern tutelage; Malstrom always insisted that every encounter with our cadaver be carried out "with the greatest decency and profound respect." But Aneurin's laboratory had been foul, chaotic, and sinister, brimming with sadistic cruelty and utter disregard for the unfortunate subjects interred there. I could not ever imagine looking upon Aneurin's face again without remembering the horrors unleashed by his hands.

And yet, that was precisely the crux of my dilemma: the laboratory was clearly not Aneurin's alone; it must be supervised by Malstrom himself. And if Malstrom condoned that carnage behind closed doors, how could I, in good conscience, operate within the confines of his pristine dissection hall, a clever façade for the house of horrors masked mere metres away? It was abundantly clear to me that, by allowing opportunity to corrupt my decency, I'd become a proponent of a practice most wicked. I should not—could not—permit such sins to be committed in the name of my education.

What's more, there was the lingering matter of Aneurin himself, which was a thorn stuck far deeper in my side that I cared to admit. While I was still reeling from the scale of his betrayal, what offended my disposition most was how clever and convincing his mask had been, and how utterly under his spell I had fallen. For while in the short duration of our companionship he had proven himself less than forthcoming in his intentions, bewilderingly mercurial in his affections, and more than a little opportunistic where my loyalty was concerned, he had never once struck me as malicious or insane. I could not seem to shake my memory of the man who had fearlessly scaled the wall outside my chamber, who had charmed me through the maze of Closes and shown me a glimpse into his world, who had been my partner in the most ridiculous (and admittedly first) crime I'd ever committed. The feeling of total and utter exhilaration I felt in his company— how was it possible that it was all a feint? Was I truly so gullible, so naïve, so desperate to feel a sense of belonging in this city that I'd allowed myself to be blinded by a degenerate scoundrel driven by sheer madness? Was he truly the snake in my Garden of Eden? Or was it possible that there was something more, something I had not yet seen, not yet known, not yet understood? Yet I could not doubt the horrors my senses had perceived in that laboratory, and I could not pretend otherwise.

These were the thoughts that cast a dreary shadow upon my mind throughout the long, dark, dismal winter days of my yuletide. I'd no plans (or funds) to travel South to see family, so I satisfied myself by remaining sequestered in my room for most of the day, studying and reading and attempting to distract myself from the dismal quagmire in which I'd found myself stranded. Fortunately, Charlie had remained in the city as well, as he was scheduled to give his

first-ever presentation at the Royal Medical Society
the Friday after Epiphany and had thus declared he
was too drowned in work to consider leaving Edinburgh. As such, though we spent our days in studious
isolation, we made a ritual of dining together each evening at the pub downstairs, often joined by Hamish,
who, as a local, had concluded he had nowhere better
to be (and was generally two pints past pissed by the
time we even joined him for dinner).

Such were our respective dispositions as the three
of us took our evening meal together on the fifth day
of Christmastide, the bitter wind whipping outside the
pub's glazed windowpanes audible even from the confines of our snug corner booth. Charlie was indulging
himself in a meandering monologue about the latest
research on the use of fumigators to ward off miasma.
Hamish was swilling the last of the third pint he'd consumed since we'd joined him, eyes glassy and unfocused. And I was lost in my thoughts, torn between my
desire to further my education and my moral obligation
to divest myself of involvement with Malstrom and his
ilk. All in all, it was a dismal dinner indeed, and I found
myself tracing lazy patterns with my fork through my
gravy instead of actually consuming a bite of what was
on my plate.

I should have known better than to let my current
state of malaise manifest itself so; mere moments later,
I caught Hamish eyeing my plate appraisingly, clearly
detecting that something was amiss. I gave him a defiant glower and attempted to turn my focus to Charlie,
but I knew once Hamish detected a whiff of drama, he
was loath to let it go.

"What's wrong with you?" His words were a bit slurred, his brogue nearly unintelligible under the influence of the ale.

Charlie paused mid-sentence and followed Hamish's gaze to my own. I politely met it as evenly as I could muster. "I beg your pardon?"

Hamish reclined further in the booth, propping his boots up on the seat and narrowing his eyes. "You're being odd. You've been being odd, but now you're even odder. Something's got you tangled up in yourself." He gestured vaguely in the direction of my torso, as if my intestines were somehow to blame for my ennui.

I cocked an incredulous eyebrow in his direction. "Nothing new. Just busy with my studies, busy with—"

"Bollocks," Hamish grumbled, draining the last of his pint. "We know you're a bookworm, but that's not it. You're distracted, distant. Charlie's doing a talk on fumigators, and I know for a fact you've got very strong opinions about them, but you haven't said a word since he started going on about it. You're a smug know-it-all, yet you're avoiding a debate. Why? What's wrong with you?" He was shaking his finger at me in a rather disrespectful manner, and I found myself rising to his taunts.

"Maybe I'm just being civil, seeing as it's Christmas-tide, and it's either you lot or my cadaver at Malstrom's for company."

Charlie snorted into his ale at that, then slapped his pint glass down on the table with an air of finality. "Ease off him, Hamish. It's the dead of winter, we're trapped indoors and haven't seen the sun for days, and we've been cut off from access to all our favourite toys at Malstrom's and have nothing else to play with except textbooks. We're allowed to be a bit tetchy."

I shot Charlie a grateful look, but Hamish just leaned forward with a hungry glint in his eye. "Ah, supplies running low at Malstrom's? I'd heard rumours as such. Seems only Knox has the fortitude to secure proper provisions for his pupils these days."

I was blindsided by the insinuation. None of my class-mates had ever mentioned our specimens in terms of supply and demand, and in light of my new knowledge on the matter, I was simultaneously bewildered and aghast at Hamish's brazenness—he must be far drunker than I thought.

"No, not at all, it's just the nature of the scheduled sessions—" Charlie began.

"Horsefeathers," Hamish quipped. "It's obvious to every student worth a wit that Knox will soon be the only game in town," he continued pompously. "Every other anatomist is living on borrowed time."

"And how would you know that?" I retorted, feel-ing a strange twisting in my stomach as I contemplated what he meant, now knowing what I knew about Aneurin and his ilk.

"Because Knox has all the best suppliers, of course."

"Suppliers?" I echoed. I was still reeling from the fact that this was the closest we'd ever actually come to discussing the underground trade amongst my friends, who were either wholly ignorant of it (as I had so recently been) or else entirely indifferent to it.

"Aye. Knox has been reeling in the freshest quar-ries around, thanks to Burke and Hare." He shot us a pointed look and took a long pull from his glass.

"Who?" I pressed, trying to understand.

"Burke and Hare," Hamish slurred, and Charlie and I exchanged a confused look. Hamish had clearly sailed right past drunk and well into rambling incoherence, and it certainly seemed his intention to impress us with these names, despite the fact we'd never heard them before.

"Sorry, mate, no clue what you're on about," Charlie insisted.

Hamish shrugged. "You will soon enough." He slumped back into his seat with a smug expression painted upon his bleary face.

"What are you talking about?" Charlie was clearly as agitated as I was, and a retort was just forming on the tip of my tongue when a shadow fell across our table in the imposing form of Angus himself, who rarely emerged from behind the bar unless under extreme duress.

"You. Willoughby." His tone was gruff and accusatory.

I blinked up at him. "Sir?"

"Your rent's past due."

I cleared my throat, taken aback by the fact he was raising an issue so personal as finances in the presence of my peers. "Surely there's been a mistake. My brother confirmed it would be delivered to this address on the fifteenth of every month. Could there have been a delay due to the holidays?"

Angus simply glared. "No delays. Everyone else paid up on time. As of this morning, you're in breach of agreement and subject to eviction."

A pulse of panic gripped my chest. Eviction? Surely he wouldn't turn me out into the dismal winter completely alone—

"Come now, Angus, it must be a simple misunderstanding!" To my great relief, Charlie once again came to my aid. "Look, I'll pay for James's rent this week myself, to give him time to get things sorted out. No need to evict anyone tonight, is there?"

Angus narrowed his eyes. "Fine. I don't care who's paying, so long as my coffer's not light."

Charlie gave an agreeable nod, extending far more graciousness towards Angus than I personally felt he deserved for such a violation of civility as discussing private business callously in public.

I could feel my cheeks burning with shame, my heart still pounding in distress; after all, I'd had no word from my eldest brother since I'd arrived here in Edinburgh with his (reluctant) blessing and affirmation that my allowance would remain in place. Where could the funds be, if not here? I realised in an increasing panic that I'd not even confirmed in my own accounts that my personal expense allowance had arrived this month; was it possible that it, too, was absent? I'd been so preoccupied with my studies and then all the bad business with Aneurin that monitoring my finances had completely slipped my mind—though being raised as a gentleman, concern about the state of my finances was not a habit that had been much ingrained in me.

"Angus, there hasn't been any mail for me, has there?"

"Just the letter last week. Slipped it under your door like usual."

My stomach clenched, and an icy-cold panic settled in my spine. "I didn't see any letter."

Angus shrugged. "That's hardly my problem. I delivered it." With that, he turned and ambled back to the bar, leaving me floundering in confusion and still mortified by my predicament.

"If you'll just . . . excuse me, lads. I've got to go check on the letter—surely it contains some explanation . . ."

"Of course, no worries."

"And, Charlie, I'll pay you back as soon as I have this worked out, I promise, I can't thank you enough—"

"Please, James, it's fine. Stop fretting, you're making me nervous."

With a tight-lipped smile, I rose and bolted to my chamber. A first glance confirmed my initial suspicion; there was no letter upon the floor. After all, I'd surely have seen it sometime in the past week; it seemed impossible I'd be blind to an envelope in the middle of my sparsely furnished room. Unless—

Cursing, I kicked up the edge of the threadbare rug, which had shifted from the centre of my chamber during the incident with The Beast and was now positioned more squarely in front of the door. Sure enough, beneath it was a creamy white envelope, boasting my address in my sister's unmistakable pristine script.

I blinked in disbelief. Why would Edith be writing? She was normally so aloof, so wrapped up in estate life in York, so devoted to her husband and children and household that she rarely made time for casual correspondence. I knew she'd intended to remain in Bath for a fair spell after my father's passing and my subsequent departure for Edinburgh, but it seemed impossible that the details of our estate would not have been sorted by now, allowing her to return to York. Puzzled, I tore open the envelope and scanned the pages within.

My dearest James,

It is with great reluctance that I write to you to inform you of an unforeseen circumstance regarding your future in Edinburgh. I pleaded with Richard to notify you earlier, but he has greatly abdicated his responsibilities as executor of Father's estate in the wake of our recent revelations. Therefore, it is I who am burdened with the task of conveying to you this most unfortunate of news.

The financial situation of the estate has proven to be even more precarious than we initially perceived. Father's debts are considerable, and the sums on hand were poorly invested in risky propositions, yielding meagre interest with which to cover expenses. We've been forced to drastically reduce the staff, forego entertainment, and make do without many of the comforts to which we are all accustomed.

Unfortunately, it is simply not enough. Richard has secured a loan, thanks to his connections at the bank, but we must conduct ourselves with due frugality until such a time that the loan may be repaid. As a result, we do not have the spare income with which to maintain your allowance and your current course of study.

I realise, little brother, that this must come as quite a shock to you, as we've all been most eager to shield you from unnecessary worry during this formative time in your education. However, it is no longer feasible to continue your training, as we haven't the money to cover your tuition, much less your lodging and expenses. It is therefore necessary that you return home at once.

But do not be disheartened! Though a career as a physician may no longer be within your grasp, Richard has laboured relentlessly to secure an alternative to ensure your future success. And, mercifully, his efforts have been rewarded: he has obtained an offer of apprenticeship for you at the East India Company! I am sure you will agree, a merchant's *life is one of comfort and prestige, and you will be able to maintain a life-style befitting of your upbringing.*

It is with this most fortunate of news that we eagerly await your return home before the end of Christmastide. It will take a few days to secure the final arrangements, and then you will be off to London to begin your new career!

With all my love and devotions,

E

I stared down at the papers in my hand, the wide world around me suddenly reduced to the size of a pale white rectangle, my greatest hopes and aspirations for my future dashed away with a few strokes of a quill. My life in Edinburgh—finished. My future as a physician—gone. My inspiration, my passion, my dreams—all apparently gambled away by my rogue of a father, who had the audacity to recuse himself of consequence in the coward-ice of death. My hands shook, and I felt suddenly faint. Was it truly possible to lose everything—everything—in the span of a mere minute?

I chuckled wryly to myself. While it had only taken a minute for my life to be reduced to ash, the process had surely been anything but sudden for my father. How many years had he spent in gambling halls and card rooms, exchanging the future of his family for the plea-sure of his present? How could he so sternly dictate the terms of my life to me from behind his great mahog-any desk, knowing full well that my efforts were to be for nothing? Perhaps he'd hoped to carry on the façade long enough that I could complete my studies and begin my career before his deceit was revealed, but what did he think would become of my mother? Of Richard, whose position in the landed gentry was meant to provide for his very existence? And of my middle brother Matthew who, while trained and practicing as a barrister, would undoubtedly not escape unscathed from the battering of his reputation once word of his family's disgrace became public?

Edith was the lucky one, I thought bitterly to myself. No wonder she could handle the situation with such infuriating pragmatism: she'd married exceptionally well (even by our family's standards), her dowry had been paid in full and was not subject to an income, and she'd promptly produced an heir and three more children besides. What did it matter to her if our family name was brought to ruin and I was forced to become a dull, petty merchant? She already had everything she'd ever wanted in life! The injustice was enough to light a spark of resentment in my belly that I could tell would not be easily extinguished.

I lowered myself into my desk chair, still stunned by this unanticipated turn of events. I cast a glance around my chamber as I envisioned packing my belongings back into The Beast and leaving this place forever. A deep melancholy settled over me; as dim and sparse as my chamber was, it had been home to some of the happiest hours of my life, spent reading and learning, questioning and knowing. The few short weeks I had been in this place had changed my view of mankind profoundly, from the friendships I had made to the anatomical miracles I had witnessed.

I could not envision a future for myself that did not involve the medical practice. To be exiled to London, trapped like a rat in a cage with the bankers and politicians and cits, so ordinary, so banal, seemed a fate worse than death. While I was certain that a career with the East India Company—normally reserved for those of the untitled but well-to-do middle-class—would serve me well financially, it held no wonder for me. I imagined exchanging my anatomy textbooks for dull financial tomes, spirited debates with my peers over pints of ale for capitalistic dealings in smokey cloisters over sifters of over-priced brandy, the visceral thrill that came from transcendent appreciation of the human form for the banal practice of balancing a ledger . . . the thought was nothing short of hateful. I could not—would not—renounce my ambitions so readily.

But what options did I have? I was barely making ends meet with my allowance in place, and no realistic means to procure further funds. Unless . . .

Unless.

My eyes flicked upwards to the beam that traversed my chamber's ceiling. Unbidden, the recollection of a corpse swinging gaily from its height manifested in my mind, and despite myself, a smile tugged at the corners of my lips.

But no. The act I had committed that night with Aneurin was dastardly, contemptible, illegal, and immoral. The mental contortions I'd performed to justify it in the moment no longer held traction when I weighed them against the horrifying reality of what I now knew occurred in Aneurin's laboratory. It had been a momentary lapse in judgement, a temporary blindness rendered by Aneurin's chicanery, an innocent mistake brought on by my infuriatingly persistent naïveté.

And yet.

And yet.

Aneurin's voice echoed in my mind. "Two guineas and a crown is the going price for the corpse of a grown man." Regardless of my feelings on the matter, he still owed me half. To be sure, that was more than enough to cover my monthly rent at the H&A. But what of tuition?

"Six shillings per foot and nine-pence per inch thereafter for a child."

It wouldn't . . . It wouldn't take that much effort to earn my tuition if those were the going rates. By my rough mental calculations, I'd need to participate in a mere two dozen or so snatches to cover the cost of my fees at both the University and Malstrom's. When I'd been serving as lookout for Aneurin and his crew, they'd employed me multiple times a week; I could make my expenses easily if I were to partner with them. And surely, if the trade was growing as competitive as Hamish implied, they could use an extra pair of hands to help them stay in the game. I could descend into their underworld for two months, maybe three, make my meagre fortune, and then recuse myself from the sordid practice as soon as I'd earned enough to cover my costs through the conclusion of the term. And surely by the end of summer my family's finances would be in order, and I could return to school in the autumn with a clean ledger and renewed commitment to my studies!

I bit my lip as my mind chewed over the idea. To earn a cut of each snatch, I'd surely need to be far more involved than simply maintaining my position as lookout. But Aneurin had mentioned they were short-handed and in need of a digger, and though my upbringing had spared me the brutality of most manual labour, I was young and healthy and of sound body— surely I could be an asset to the crew. Yet had I the stomach for such work? I'd held my own at Malstrom's thus far, but surely that was mere child's play compared to the foul business of exhuming the specimens themselves. Though if I'd sliced through the flesh of a man without so much as a flinch of hesitation, how much worse could it be to lift him, whole and unsullied, from beneath the earth?

I blinked and startled; a part of me could not believe I was even considering involving myself in such depravity! But what was the alternative? To abandon my passions, return South, and resign myself to a life of mundane servitude, devoid of meaning and wonderment? After all I had seen, all I had experienced in Edinburgh in my short time as a pupil of its Enlightenment, I could not envision a future without science. Without reason. Without passion.

Before I could even wrap my mind around my resolution, my feet had carried me halfway to Malstrom's. The rain was still whipping down in frigid sheets, and my overcoat offered me little in the way of protection. I'd neglected to don my hat or gloves in my haste, and I pulled my collar high around my neck as I wound my way through the familiar Closes until I arrived at Surgeon's Square. Upon arriving at the stoop, I realised I'd not even checked my watch to note the time; there was a distinct possibility I would find the hall vacant, Aneurin off the premises at dinner or in his lodgings . . . or perhaps engaged in something far more nefarious.

But there was nothing for it; I'd come that far, it made no sense to turn back. Steeling my nerves, I raised my frigid fingers to form a fist, and knocked.

There was an interminable pause, then the faint sound of footsteps, the rattling of a lock, and then the door swung open to reveal Aneurin himself. He looked dashingly disheveled in his apron with his shirt opened at the throat, once again with his sleeves rolled up his forearms and nary a cravat in sight. The bitter breeze whipped past me, tousling his wild hair, and I could see gooseflesh ripple over his skin upon contact with the glacial rain. His eyes narrowed, but he stepped aside and gestured for me to enter, clearly more to avoid prolonging his encounter with the inclement weather than out of any semblance of goodwill. Gratefully, I pushed past him and made my way to stand in the entrance hall, still shivering and soaked from the unpleasant walk.

"Mr. Willoughby. To what do I owe the pleasure?" His tone was terse, colder than cordial, and I felt stripped bare by his frigid gaze.

Steadying myself, I managed to reply. "I'd like to . . . I'd like to revisit the terms of my employment here."

He pursed his lips. "I was under the impression your employment had been terminated, as you seem to have taken the initiative to recuse yourself from the lectures."

"I . . . I had meant to. Recuse myself, that is. But I've . . . I've had a change of heart."

Aneurin's face remained cold, his moonstone eyes unreadable in the dim light of the hall. "You no longer think me a heretic in league with the Devil? I'm quite glad to hear it, as I can assure you I was deeply troubled by the prospect of a poor performance review by an outgoing pupil. Malstrom will be most reassured that you've no intention of blaspheming my name amongst your University brethren. However, I'm afraid we're no longer in need of your services, so while this olive branch is as delightful as it is unexpected, I'm afraid your attendance at this school will no longer be possible. Unless you've found a way to pay full tuition, that is."

The hardness of his demeanour was an icy scalpel to my chest. While I could in no way condone the atrocities performed in his lab, the fond memory of his laughter, his conspiratorial winks and witty jabs—all stirred within me a longing for companionship that I could not seem to shake. He had made me feel important, worthy, valuable, desired, yet now he looked at me as though I were no more than a pus-laced glaze at the bottom of a bedpan. Yet I refused to let his disdain detract me from my cause.

"You owe me." I kept my voice firm, determined.

He raised an eyebrow. "I beg your pardon?"

"You owe me. Half the price of the specimen I helped you procure. I was promised fifty percent, and I'm here to collect."

His eyes raked over my form once more, and I shivered into my soaking boots. He paused, considering. And then:

"Come to the office. And take off your overcoat; you'll catch cold." With that, he turned on his heel and led me down the corridor through the dissection hall and into the office, where, to my great relief, a fire was roaring merrily in the fireplace. I divested myself of my overcoat as instructed, draping it over the chair closest to the fire in the chance it might warm and dry slightly before I was turned out once more into the lingering storm.

Aneurin had fetched a key from the ring around his belt and used it to unlock the bottom drawer of the desk, withdrawing the same wooden till box he'd used to collect our fees during the first day of demonstrations at the school. He popped it open, counted out the coins, then slapped them on the desk with wholly more force than necessary.

"A guinea and a crown."

I swallowed. "That's more than half."

"For your trouble. And your silence." The last word was a crude, bitten command, harsh and impersonal. I flinched with the impact.

"Aneurin, listen, I—"

"Our business here has concluded, Mr. Willoughby, and our debts are squared. I've nothing more to say to you."

I met his eye and held it. "I want in."

"In?"

"On your . . . enterprise. I'd like to . . . assist you."

He froze, seeming to consider this turn of events, then gathered himself and settled casually into the chair behind the desk, closing the till and locking it back in its drawer, his movements measured and precise. "As I said, Mr. Willoughby, we no longer require your services as lookout."

"Not as a lookout. I want to be a digger." Aneurin's head snapped up, and I fumbled to continue my proposition, thrown off by finally obtaining his full attention. "I've heard there's . . . strong competition in town over the limited supplies available, and I want to help." It was a shot in the dark, but Hamish's words from earlier that evening were fresh in my mind; if there was indeed a chance I had some degree of leverage in this negotiation, I was determined to use it. "I know I'm not large, but I'm strong and willing and I . . . I find myself unexpectedly in dire financial straits. So I believe we could be of great service to one another and come to a mutually beneficial arrangement."

Aneurin was very still, the firelight flickering over his delicate features causing his cheekbones to look nearly painfully protruded, the hollows beneath his eyes rendering his expression distant and unreadable. The silence stretched between us, thick and palpable, but I held my ground and my tongue, forcing him to be the first to break.

At last, he spoke, his brogue soft and serene in the solitude of the room. "You called me a butcher. Evil. A sadist and a madman." He cocked his head. "Does this mean you've renounced your previous conclusion?"

I hadn't the words to fully express my current desperation; while I could not forgive all that I had seen in his laboratory, I could at least feign ignorance of it if that would allow me to pursue my chosen vocation. "Yes. Yes, I have. And for what it's worth, I'm sorry I said those things. I was . . . taken by surprise, is all. I don't think I . . . fully understood what your profession as a dissectionist and assemblist entailed."

Another pause. "And now you do?"

I could feel my heartbeat in my throat. "No. No, I don't, but I'm willing to look the other way, keep my mouth shut, and do the work, if you'll just give me a chance—"

Abruptly, he rose to his feet and rounded the desk, extending his hand in my direction. "Come with me." There was no question in his demand.

I hesitated. A mere fortnight ago, I'd been convinced he was an insane savage; was I really about to allow myself to be led away by him?

Well, I reasoned, better murdered and pinned to a dissection board than trapped for the remainder of my days as a dullard merchant in the offices of the EIC. Biting back a cynical laugh, I took his hand, startled by its warmth in my own. He turned and pulled open the door to his laboratory and led me inside.

The scene that greeted me was as grotesque as I'd remembered, though the corpse of the limbless man had been replaced by that of an elderly woman in a similar state of dismemberment. The jawless spectre closest to the door was still there, but now the cords of her throat were pried wide apart by an intricate series of clamps. I shuddered at the sight of them and steadied myself against the smell.

I tried to avert my eyes, but at that moment, Aneurin maneuvered himself to stand behind me, hands placed firmly upon my shoulders, forcing me to face the carnage laid out before me.

"On this specimen, Malstrom is conducting a detailed dissection of the throat by first treating the vocal cords with potassium hydroxide, rendering them more receptive to post-mortem stimulation. He will be giving a lecture on his findings and how they relate to our understanding of the human capacity for speech at the renowned medical school in Strasbourg in February." I peered closer. "The teeth we harvested from the extracted jaw will be repurposed and made into dentures for veterans of the Napoleonic Wars who suffered facial deformity from their wounds. Malstrom has been most sympathetic to their cause."

I had no more than begun to process this than Aneurin led me to the next table, upon which the body of the elderly woman was displayed, her intestines removed and fitted into the same large glass jar as the unfortunate souls who had come before her. Once again, the firm press of Aneurin's hands upon my shoulders prevented me from shying away.

"Here we are testing the influence of acidity upon the intestines by submerging them in solutions of varying components. Malstrom believes that the results of this experiment may be enormously instrumental in the treatment of gout."

He steered me onwards, to the desk whose contents had so horrified me that I'd been compelled to regurgitate. "The preservation of these heads and brains is essential to the work of our fellow physician across the Square who studies Phrenology, the correlation of shape and size of a skull to the personality traits of the man who possesses it. Though Malstrom is skeptical of this particular branch of science, he's willing to trade heads for other specimens that more closely pertain to his field of study.

"And here—you see this parchment?" Aneurin moved to stand beside me, gesturing animatedly towards the scroll upon the desk, which contained undeniable swaths of human blood. "Here we are conducting an experiment on the coagulative properties of blood when combined with various chemical compounds. Malstrom believes that we may find a way to reduce bleeding during surgical procedures, vastly limiting loss of life for those who must endure this risky undertaking. If we can find just the right compound—with coagulative properties and few side effects—we could change the course of surgical history forever.

"And here!" Aneurin's face was lit with enthusiasm as he slung his arm around my shoulder and pulled me up to the shelves behind the desk, eye-to-eye with the jar of eyeballs. "We are endeavouring to develop a surgery for the removal of cataracts, eliminating blindness in the elderly populace. Can you imagine, James, the possibilities of a world in which blindness no longer renders the elderly vestigial and obsolete?"

Before I could even formulate a response, he whisked me over to the fireplace, where the large cauldron of disembodied appendages was still bubbling away, just as it had been upon my last visit. But Aneurin only grinned wider, breathless with excitement. "And here, James, is where I do my work as an assemblist. I remove the organs and prepare them for study, I harvest the fat to sell to the candlemakers, then I boil down the bones, preserve them with a chemical wash, and assemble them back into their original form. Then they're delivered to Universities around the world. This one"—he pointed towards the cauldron's contents—"is destined for Malstrom's native Quebec, where it will be the first of its kind in the province. Can you imagine the impact it will have on the burgeoning field of medical study there?" I couldn't help but grin as I imagined the wonder on the faces of my peers, separated by thousands of miles but bound by our passionate quest for knowledge. It was a beautiful, poignant thought, and just like that, the fireplace transformed from a frame of horrors to a portal of possibility.

Aneurin finally turned to face me squarely, his expression solemn and his tone direct. "James, you cannot join this world out of necessity or because of your financial desperation. True, there are far too many scoundrels and wastrels in this game who do what it takes for profit and think of little else, but that isn't Malstrom. And that isn't me. We are members of the league of men who call ourselves not by the mantle of snatchers, but Resurrectionists. Our motivation is not the value of the bodies we steal, but in the second life we give them; each acts as a post-mortem Prometheus, bringing fire to mankind.

"If you are to become one of us, a true Resurrectionist, you must believe in the work we are doing, in our purpose and our plan. And until I'm sure you see it, I cannot let you be a part of it. You must understand that, just as actions have consequences, just as laws have repercussions, progress has a cost. And to join me in this, it must be one you are ready to pay."

That moment, in my mind, was akin to a microscope sliding into focus, the blur of confusing horrors that once surrounded me crystalizing to instead reveal a noble cause, pure and pristine. In the breath of a few mere sentences, Aneurin had transformed his world from monstrosity to marvel, and I felt the veil lift from my eyes, leaving me lucid and nearly blinded by its poignant truth.

I didn't blink, meeting his gaze unwaveringly. I knew in my very bones what my answer would be.

"I'm ready."

And I was.

7.

An Adventure

Returning to normal life at University seemed unthink-able after having struck such an arrangement regard-ing my newfound occupation, but Aneurin regretfully explained that there was simply no use for cadavers until the students returned to school. As such, I was forced to pass an interminable series of restless days that blurred into sleepless nights, attempting to come to terms with my newfound prospects and place in society.

My only respite was a brief visit to the Pig & Swin-dle at Aneurin's behest so that he might offer a vague summary of how a snatch was conducted. We were to meet the crew at the Greyfriars front gate, which Aneurin had devised a clever way to prop open; we'd be required to strip the corpse bare before stealing it to avoid a felony charge. We would use my chambers as the corpse's point of egress, and the milk cart to deliver us back to Malstrom's in the morning with our quarry.

He made the lot of it sound effortless, but I knew him well enough by then to deduce that the whole business was probably a fair bit more gruesome than what he'd described. I'd then find myself staring sleeplessly up at the ceiling as the hours ticked by, wondering if perhaps I'd gone mad myself and should be spirited back to the family stead immediately. But Edith's letter had left little room for interpretation; there was to be no more money coming my way for the foreseeable future, so it would be entirely up to me to ensure my own survival.

Such were the thoughts milling about my idle mind the evening before Epiphany. I'd dined with Charlie and Hamish as usual (doing my very best to seem engaged as Charlie rehearsed the finalised rendition of his RMS lecture for us) before retreating early to my chamber, claiming there were still a few chapters of text I needed to read before classes resumed; if either of them suspected that the true reason was simply that I couldn't afford to stay behind drinking and expend my meagre income on ale, they were at least too polite (or in Hamish's case, too drunk) to mention it.

I was gazing at my anatomy textbook with unfocused eyes when there came a sharp rap at my chamber door, nearly startling me out of my skin. My surprise quickly turned to curiosity, as I hadn't been expecting any visitors and Charlie and Hamish were still certainly downstairs enjoying their libations. I rose to open the door with a slight sense of trepidation, a part of me still worried that I'd garnered the ire of Angus once more for some perceived infraction.

To my considerable relief, I found myself face-to-face instead with Aneurin, dressed (for once) in a proper jacket, waistcoat, and cravat, hat upon his head, but somehow still looking no less wildly eccentric than he did dressed down in nothing but a loose-necked muslin shirt in his lab.

"Evening, James! Get dressed. We're going out."

I did my best to disguise my delight with a politely skeptical expression. "Is it your custom to call upon your acquaintances entirely unannounced?"

He remained undeterred. "At least I knocked this time." With a shrug, he pushed past me into my chamber, plucking my overcoat from its rack and tossing it in my direction. "Hurry up or we'll be late!"

Rolling my eyes, I slung the overcoat onto my bed and went to my wardrobe to procure a proper waistcoat, tugging up my suspenders in the process (silently grateful that I'd yet to change into my nightclothes, dashing any illusions of being an industrious young student engaged in rigorous, studious diligence). "If you insist upon showing up at my chamber door and making demands upon my social schedule, you can at least extend me the courtesy of allowing me a moment to pull myself together properly."

Aneurin sighed heavily and flopped into my desk chair looking well put-upon; I summarily ignored him and focused on fastening my waistcoat and selecting an appropriate cravat. Luckily, he was quickly distracted by the textbook displayed upon my desk, hunching over to peer at it more closely.

"Is this what they're teaching you with at the University?"

"Yes, that's the standard." I approached him to peer over his shoulder as my fingers worked the knot at my throat.

He snorted. "This thing is ancient."

I scowled. "It's not; it's only five years old."

He turned to shoot me an incredulous look over his shoulder. "Do you know how many advancements we've made in the last five years? Honestly, why anyone bothers with a University education at all is beyond me; everyone knows the Anatomy Schools are where the real work is done. This is frivolous nonsense."

I reached over him to slam the book shut, feeling mildly defensive. "Well, it's my frivolous nonsense, so you needn't worry yourself over it."

He grinned up at me. "Fine. As long as you continue to come to Malstrom's so a few years from now I don't catch you administering some antiquated, debunked remedy to your patients due to the abysmally out-dated anatomical knowledge acquired at your precious University."

I gave his shoulder a light-hearted swat. "That's the plan, isn't it?"

He responded with a devilish grin. "For now, if you hold up your end of the bargain."

I grinned back. "I'm certainly endeavouring to."

There was a strange beat, an undefinable pause, our eyes locked and lips upturned in a mutual companionable smile. A small part of me wanted to hold onto that moment as long as I could, but all too soon, the bright heat of awkward embarrassment flared across my cheeks, and I felt compelled to break the silence.

"So." I finished straightening my cravat and turned to retrieve my overcoat from the bed and pluck my hat off the rack. "Where are we off to this evening?"

Aneurin rose as well, brushing the creases out of his trousers and straightening the brim of his hat. "A dig."

I choked on my own breath, utterly gobsmacked by his casual demeanor. "Are you serious? You had me dress to go on a dig?"

"Of course! You'll need to make a good impression."

"Forgive me if I've misunderstood the assignment, but aren't we simply exhuming a body from the dirt? I could show up in a burlap sack and the corpse wouldn't bat an eye."

"I think that would rather depend on whether or not you paired it with trousers."

I glared at him. "Be that as it may, from my admittedly limited experience, we seem a bit overdressed for the occasion."

"Nonsense. Tonight, you're meeting the rest of the crew. I've told them a bit about you, of course, but I think it would behoove you not to show up looking like a run-of-the-mill vagabond I swept out of a gutter somewhere. I've informed them your University connections may prove invaluable to us at some point in the future."

I was quickly learning to translate Aneurin's silver tongue. "You mean, if we get caught, I'll make a delightful scapegoat."

Aneurin seemed momentarily startled by my prompt assessment, but his face quickly broke into an impressed grin. "Touché, Mr. Willoughby. Touché." With that, he turned and, with a swirl of his overcoat, strode out my chamber door, not even bothering to look back to be sure I would follow.

The short trek from my chambers to the gates of the kirkyard should have been tense indeed, but Aneurin wholly devoted himself to distracting me by inquiring as to my activities since our last meeting. I found myself slipping easily into our casual banter as I regaled him with the latest updates on Charlie's fumigator research, which he seemed to find amusing indeed.

"He's asserting that you can smoke away miasmas?" Aneurin's tone was tinged with laughter.

I threw up my hands helplessly. "I know! He's going to be torn to shreds by the Society, but he seems to believe that making any sort of splash is better than no splash at all."

"Well, for that matter, he ought to go in there and suggest smoking laudanum as a cure for hysteria." He chuckled at his own wit, and I elbowed him gamely in the ribs.

"Oh, please. Charlie may be audacious, but he's not a fool."

Aneurin cleared his throat and composed himself, a peculiar pause in his cadence. "So, Charlie is . . . a dear friend to you?"

I smiled in fond recollection. "He was my first friend here in the city; he took pity on me and helped me get The Beast upstairs when I arrived, alone and bewildered, on the doorstep of the H&A. He introduced me to the other lads from University as well—most of them are at Malstrom's now, too. Except for Hamish; he works for Knox, just down the way."

Aneurin's eyes narrowed. "Knox, you said?"

"Yes. You're familiar with his school, I'm sure?"

"Indeed I am." His tone had grown suddenly terse.

"I take it you are not a great fan of your competitor."

"It is not just Knox with whom I take issue, but his crew as well. They are an unscrupulous bunch, wholly without honour, and they have no qualms infringing upon the territory of the other snatchers working in this city. Knox is famous for his greed; he cares not whether there's enough specimens to go around, only that he corners the market and leaves the other schools wanting so that he may take more pupils for himself."

"Can't say I'm surprised," I replied, considering that my interactions with Hamish were often less than cordial. "Hamish is a loathsome little twat, it stands to reason he keeps similar company."

Aneurin snorted loudly, laughter ricocheting off the near stone walls as he clasped his breast in mock scandalisation. "Loathsome little twat? Good Lord, James, I didn't expect those words off the tongue of someone so high in the instep as yourself."

"Please, I grew up with two older brothers. The phrases they taught me would make a sailor blush." While this claim was slightly exaggerated (I'd never heard my brothers actually use any of the more colourful phrases they'd taught me), I was eager to prove that my horse wasn't too high to trade an occasional barb myself.

"Excellent news; you'll fit right in with our crew. I think you'll find our vocabulary dazzlingly colourful; perhaps we can all teach one another a thing or two . . ."

And with that, we arrived at the gates of Greyfriars, looming ominously against the darkness. I was able to make out a circle of shadowy figures huddled before them, offset in the pool of light cast by a nearby street lamp. Aneurin approached with such a boldness in his step that I didn't have time to hesitate.

"Gentlemen! It's my honour to introduce to you our newest fellow, James. As I mentioned, James here is from the University and has agreed to help us in our scholastic pursuits." Aneurin was all but bouncing on his heels in enthusiasm, a sentiment which, I quickly noted, his cohorts did not seem to share.

As my eyes adjusted to the dark, I could make out a grizzled old man leaning against a walking stick, eying me up and down suspiciously. "Him? He looks like a bloody dandy." His pronounced brogue dripped in condescension.

"For God's sake, Diggs, that's the point. Besides, James is the one who helped me procure the specimen we nearly lost at Greyfriars the night the sexton gave chase; I assure you, he's solid and strong and most sympathetic to our cause."

I felt myself stand a bit taller at hearing myself described as solid and strong. Regardless of my upbringing, I'd never been inclined to shy away from hard work.

"Have you dug before?" The stocky, broad-chested young man to his left piped up. Even from where I was standing, I could see the sinews of his tattooed forearms protruding from where his cuffs were rolled up past his elbows; he looked like he did little else but dig.

Startlingly, I realised I vaguely recognised having seen
him on occasion scuttling in and out of Malstrom's
office during our lectures.

"I—I haven't, no, but—"

"No matter," the man replied gruffly. "You'll at least
be more help than string-bean Willis over here." He
gestured towards a young boy standing beside him who
couldn't have been more than twelve, glaring up with
daggers in his eyes.

"Hardly my fault you're down a man," the boy protested. "At least I know how to keep my mouth shut—"

"Oy oy oy!" Aneurin waved his arms signaling a
halt to the volley. Much to my amusement, his accent
seemed to have grown even thicker in the presence of
his peers. "That's hardly the point. Gents, play nice. Stay
here while I take care of the gate." From his pocket he
procured an odd-looking tool that resembled a key ring
containing a confounding array of long, slender pins,
and strode off into the shadows, leaving the rest of us
lingering in an awkward silence.

Fortunately, the boy Willis broke it, apparently
unable to contain his curiosity about my background.

"Nye says you helped him move a body out of Greyfriars through the window of your lodgings. Is that
true?"

"Nye?" I was momentarily bewildered.

"Yes, Nye. Aneurin? Tall, dark-haired chap you
arrived here with?" He gestured vaguely in the direction of the gates.

"Oh!" It belatedly dawned on me that this must be
a nickname of his that I'd not yet been privy to; the
thought was amusing and a bit endearing. Nye. It suited

him. "Yes—we devised a pulley system to bring it up through my chamber window and then smuggled it out in a trunk right through the side door the next morning. I live directly above the Hope & Anchor, you see."

The stocky man exchanged an approving glance with his fellow diggers, and I could feel my confidence beginning to return. I occupied a position of considerable advantage, it would seem, and Aneurin—Nye—was clearly justified in bringing me into this circle.

No sooner had the thought crossed my mind than the man himself reappeared, pocketing his key ring with a merry jingle.

"So! James. The formal introductions. This over here is Diggs," Nye waved his hand in the direction of the hunched old man, the lines on his face so deep they appeared almost as gashes in the low lamplight. "He's a lifelong gravedigger employed at Greyfriars, and he's been on our payroll for years. And no need to mention his name; he's well aware of the irony." I held back a snigger.

"This here's Thomas; you may have seen him around Malstrom's. He works down at the quays most days, but helps us out on digs as well as with special deliveries when needs must. Malstrom relies on him to keep our product moving about the city." The broad-shouldered man nodded curtly in my direction, and I returned the favour.

"And of course, Willis. He's usually our lookout, but he's been helping us dig since we came up short-handed with our driver out of commission. That said, I'm hoping you'll be able to take his place with the spade and he with your lantern going forward."

Willis rolled his eyes petulantly. "Not sure you'll be any better off with this weakling."

Nye appeared undaunted at the boy's insubordination. "You'd best watch your tongue, Willis. If you'd seen James wield a scalpel as I have, you'd show him a bit more respect." He turned and offered me a still-audible aside: "Don't mind him. He's just irked to be losing out on a digger's income. Pays much better than a lookout, you see." Willis crossed his arms and gave a lazy shrug, clearly capitulating to Nye's assessment.

"Well then." Nye clapped his hands and rubbed them together enthusiastically. "Shall we?"

Without another word, I followed Nye's lead as four of us slipped into the shadowy cover of the gate. To my surprise, Willis scampered off in the opposite direction.

"Where's he off to?" I asked Nye; in all the details he had provided on how we were to execute the snatch, I had admittedly never inquired about the lookout's role.

"To your chamber," Nye replied casually as he twisted the latch open, the gates creaking menacingly in the silence.

"To my chamber?" I retorted, taken entirely aback. "How . . . how does he know where my chamber is? How is he going to get in? Does he know how the—"

The knowing smirk on Nye's face froze the words on my tongue as he pushed open the kirkyard gates and ushered us all inside.

Nye wordlessly signaled the way, and we fell in step behind him across the frosty lawn. Twice I nearly tripped over a headstone but was graciously spared the humiliation by Thomas, who appeared to have a knack for spotting such things and, in both instances, rapidly rerouted me with a curt shove of my shoulder. We circled around to the south side of the kirk and came to a stop when we reached an unremarkable patch of earth, beside which rested a small barrow covered in what appeared to be an inconspicuous white sheet. Diggs pulled the sheet away with an industrious yank, revealing beneath it the tools required for extraction of the specimen.

Suddenly, the whole situation became very real, and I could feel my hands begin to tremble at my sides. But before I could contemplate it a moment further, Aneurin reached forward and gripped a spade, which he thrust unceremoniously to my chest. The expression on his face rendered me defenseless even in my moment of deepest doubt; my fingers clasped the handle as if of their own accord. For a moment, I stood paralyzed, spade in hand, blinking down at the blanket of soft soil at my feet. Breathing deeply, I steadied my nerves.

Aneurin just smiled and nodded his head.

Before I could doubt myself, I drove my spade into the ground with all the fortitude I could muster, levied a heaping mound of dirt, and threw it back over my shoulder.

"Oy! What the hell are you doing?" Thomas's irritated hiss startled me after such a prolonged spell of silence, and I started upright in response to his tone.

"Nye, get your boy straight before he makes a muck of it; we don't have time for this shite," Diggs muttered softly as he spread the sheet carefully over the lower half of the grave, as if tucking in the interned corpse for a bedtime story.

I was about to protest the deep indignity at being called anyone's boy when Nye's firm grip on my shoulder pulled me away from the scene. The retort still bitter on my tongue, I loosed my vitriol in his direction instead, struggling to keep my frustration to a whisper.

"What the hell is their problem? You hired me to help; tell them to let me do so in peace."

Nye looked appropriately abashed. "A thousand apologies for their crudeness, James. I'm afraid it's my fault entirely. I realise now that, while I was quite specific about our order of operations, I rather neglected to elaborate on what, precisely, some of those operations entail."

I rounded on him defiantly. "I understood the plan perfectly well, thank you very much. Step one: rendezvous at the kirkyard. Step two: follow your lead. Step three: snatch the body. Do tell me: have I missed something, neglected some crucial detail in your infallible master plan?"

Nye shot me a look that was somewhere in the middle ground between remorseful and withering. "It's just . . . I fear I rather skimmed over the proper procedure for the snatching bit."

I pursed my lips skeptically. "We're digging up a dead body. It's hardly a great science."

Nye broke into another of his infuriating smirks. "As a matter of fact, it's a science of sorts indeed, and a precise one, at that. For a moment, let us observe." Wrapping one arm around my shoulder, he turned me to survey the scene, where Thomas and Diggs were making quick work of the layer of topsoil; in the minute or two that had passed, they were already nearly six inches deep.

Nye leaned in close to murmur his commentary in my ear. "You see how Diggs has placed the body sack on the lower half of the grave?"

I nodded, dutifully repressing my inclination towards a spiteful retort in exchange for a welling tide of curiosity.

"They're depositing the displaced soil carefully on top of the sack to avoid disturbing the grass around the burial site; if the sexton or a family member sees errant dirt strewn about the grave, they are liable to suspect a snatching."

I blinked; the thought had scarcely occurred to me as a threat before. After a moment of contemplation, another question arose in my mind. "But . . . why are they only digging up half the grave? Shouldn't they place the soil off to the side so they may extract the coffin in its entirety?"

Nye gave a brisk shake of his head. "A common misconception, that. You must remember that it is not our goal to extract the coffin at all; we are only after the corpse." I cocked my head, now curious as to how one could extract a body without first exhuming the coffin in which it was buried.

Nye continued, gesturing towards the scene playing out before us to illustrate his points as he made them. "We dig up only the top half of the coffin, you see, and use the displaced soil to weigh down the bottom half from above. Then when we reach our destination, we use a crowbar to snap the coffin lid at around the shoulder-point; the counterweight of the extra soil facilitates this process immeasurably. We use a rope to secure the specimen beneath the armpits and yank it out with a few quick tugs, the coffin never even leaving the earth. The corpse is stripped, the clothing returned to its origin, the lid closed and secured, the dirt replaced. Then we pop the corpse in the sack and, voilà!"

I was staring at him in a potent combination of admiration and horror. "I can't tell if that's genius or insane."

"Can't it be both? I've been at this for a while now, James, and I've brought our snatches to near perfection. It's . . . Well, I must say, it's rather a point of pride for me."

I rolled my eyes. "You're a mad man."

"A mad man who's got you on his payroll. Now, let's get back to work."

With that, we returned to the site. I picked up my spade once more and dug in, nary a word passing between myself and the rest of the crew as the minutes ticked by. Careful to deposit each spadeful of earth upon the designated shroud, I devoted all my attention to the task at hand. For a few blissful moments, it was easy to lose myself in the hypnotic rhythm of the dig, and I could all but forget the true purpose of our exertions.

The illusion of simplicity was shattered the moment my spade struck something solid beneath it. It was only in that moment that I noted the blade I was wielding was made of wood instead of the standard metal, and apparently for good reason—its collision with the lid of the coffin was muffled by the soft wood of the blade. My heart lurched in my chest as the heads of my companions pivoted towards me in unison, faces alight in anticipation.

I withdrew my spade ever so slightly and plunged it forward once more, the thunk of wood on wood unmistakable this time. Diggs, Thomas, and Nye exchanged knowing nods, and Thomas hauled himself bodily from the hole to procure a crowbar from the barrow, which he handed down to Nye.

Wordlessly, Nye maneuvered me out of the way and sank the crowbar beneath the light dusting of soil still coating the top end of the coffin. Once the crowbar was secured beneath the lip of the lid, all it took was a quick jerk of his arms and a resounding crack echoed across the frosty grounds as the coffin lid split square in two.

"Step back," Nye hissed. "Let the gasses escape."

As quickly as I could, I leapt back as a putrid scent infiltrated the pit; I was tempted to reach for my handkerchief but suppressed the urge, instead following the lead of the others and burying my face in the crook of my arm.

At long last, my eyes ceased watering. Without hesitation, Nye reached down and pried the loosed lid open before muttering further instructions to me.

"Reach inside. Tell me if it's the head or the feet."

I stared at him, mortified at the prospect of sticking my hands into a coffin, sight unseen. "How . . . how do I know if it's the head or the feet?"

"For Christ's sake," Thomas muttered from above us as he brushed the dirt gruffly from his knees. "What kind of physician are you that you can't tell a man's head from his bloody feet?"

Biting back an impolite retort, I simply crouched and thrust my hands inside the gaping opening, refusing to allow myself time to think. My fingers met something soft, supple. Hair. Human hair.

I snatched my hands back from the abyss. "Head. We're at the head end." Impressively, the tremble in my voice was scarcely audible.

"Excellent." Nye's tone was professional, unperturbed. "Now find the neck. Do you feel anything fastened around it?"

I stared up at him, mildly offended that he appeared to be asking me to insert my hands back into the coffin once more. I'd rather envisioned the process to be far less personal than it was revealing itself to be.

"Like . . . cloth?"

Nye shook his head. "No, like metal. Some families have taken to using coffin collars as a deterrent to snatchers; they fasten a metal ring around the throat of the corpse and secure it to the coffin, preventing us from extracting the body cleanly."

Swallowing hard, I plunged my hands back inside and allowed my fingers to map a path from the corpse's scalp, down the familiar shape of a protruded forehead and angled jawbone, then further below to his throat. There, sure enough, I detected a cool, smooth ring of metal.

My eyes darted up to meet Nye's. "He has a collar."

Nye swore silently under his breath, then straightened his back to issue an order to Thomas. "Get the saw and get down here. We'll have to decapitate."

It took every ounce of fortitude I possessed not to swoon. "You . . . you want me to decapitate him?"

Nye shook his head silently and extended his hand, which I gratefully took and allowed him to pull me upright. "Come on. Thomas will take it from here."

Bracing himself on either side of the pit, he hauled himself up and out of the grave, then aided me in following him. Thomas descended in our place before using the saw to quickly separate the split part of the coffin lid from the remainder, casting it aside. I deliberately averted my eyes as the corpse's gaunt face finally came into view, internally praying none of the others would notice my squeamishness.

Beside me, Nye was either oblivious to my discomfort or doubly devoted to relieving me of it. Lowering his head to mutter quietly in my ear, he proceeded to describe the events unfolding below us. "Thomas will sever the head from the body to allow us to extract it despite the collar. The severance is costly; it means we can't sell the corpse as 'untarnished' or 'whole,' which fetches the best price on the market. The decapitation means we'll have to sell it piecemeal instead."

Below us, the disconcerting sound of the saw teeth hitting what I could only assume was bone resonated from the open grave. I willed myself to ignore it. "So how does . . . how does a piecemeal sale work, exactly?"

Nye continued to hold my gaze, clearly diverting me from the unfolding scene. "We can parcel out the hair, the teeth, the organs, and the humours and sell them to physicians who specialise in each field. Malstrom will keep the eyes, a sample of blood, and perhaps the colon for use in his current experiments. Hammond across the way will take the limbs and heart. Knox will want the lungs. And Holmes will take the head."

Across the pit, Diggs let out a derisive snort. He had planted his spade in the dirt and was leaning against it at a jaunty, cavalier angle, nursing a flask that had materialised in his grisled hands. "Oh, Holmes'll take the head alright," he sniggered. Then he poured a few drops from his flask onto the open grave, shaking his head in derision. "Poor bastard."

I turned back to Nye inquisitively. "What's wrong with this Holmes character?"

Nye grinned deviously. "He's the expert in Phrenology I told you about before; he believes one can determine a man's personality traits based on the shape and size of his skull."

"And . . . you're skeptics of this branch of science?"

Nye exchanged a knowing glance with Diggs, who cackled quietly under his breath at my apparent naïveté. Composing himself, Nye finally mustered the breath to answer.

"Our quarrel is not so much with the science as it is with the scientist himself. You see, a few years back, Holmes got himself arrested for breaking into a vault and stealing the heads of three corpses. He pled not guilty to the court on the grounds that the undertaking was purely for the 'advancement and development of medical understanding.' The court was convinced, so he was fined a mere twenty pounds and released to continue his research."

By this time, Diggs's sniggers had digressed into quite near full-blown hysteria, tears trickling from the corners of his eyes as he took another swig from his flask and attempted to suppress his laughter. Based on our previous interactions, I found this behaviour to be most out of character and proceeded in my inquest with due caution.

"And then what?" There was clearly far more to this story than I was being led to believe.

Nye cleared his throat and bit back a smile, clearly struggling to remain objective in his recounting of the facts. "The court showed him mercy on the grounds that 'merely his love of scientific investigation' had motivated the act."

"But you don't believe that?"

"Not once it was revealed that one of the purloined heads belonged to his own mother."

I could not so much as attempt to disguise the expression of disgust on my face at this revelation. Meanwhile, Diggs appeared so delighted at my reaction that he was forced to lean heavily on the handle of his own spade in order to remain upright despite the heaves of wheezing laughter racking his tottering frame, and even Nye was chuckling to himself as I processed the tale he had just unearthed.

"Of all the ghastly, abhorrent, perverted tales . . . his own mother—"

Nye gave a nonchalant shrug. "Perhaps he wanted to involve the head of the family."

And it was that—that simple, honest, irreverent gesture—that sent me teetering off the edge as well. Waves of laughter overtook me, and I was forced to crouch, hands clasped over my mouth, to prevent the evidence of my delighted scandalisation from reverberating across the dim kirkyard. Beside me, Nye clapped his hand across my back as he, too, fell victim to the tide of hysterics—apparently much to the chagrin of Thomas, who, even from the bottom of the pit, I could tell was glaring fiercely at the lot of us. Willing myself to maintain control, I took a few steadying gulps of air and managed to right myself.

"Rope." At Thomas's barked command, Aneurin was his rigid, professional self once more, procuring a coil from the barrow and tossing it into the pit. I could see Thomas's form stooped low over the open coffin as he maneuvered the rope within, and I was silently grateful that I'd been excused from my position below ground in his stead.

"Heads up." With no more than this briefest of warnings, Nye and Diggs hopped back from the edge of the pit, and I quickly followed. A mere second later, a human head flew up over the rim and landed in the grass with a sickening thud before rolling a few feet and coming to rest at the base of the next tombstone over.

"For Christ's sake, Thomas, how many times must I tell you to treat the specimens with care?"

"For all the care Holmes is about to give that cap, I'd say rolling a few feet in the kirkyard is the least of its worries. Let him enjoy his last few moments of innocence, eh?" Thomas's wry response was muffled by his depth, but we had no trouble mistaking his intentions.

Nye simply muttered under his breath and stooped to scoop up the head and deposit it gently into the barrow. Fortunately, the eyes were closed, but the grotesque gape of the dead man's mouth was unavoidable, and I could see Diggs peering at me closely, awaiting my reaction. I willed myself to remain unmoved.

"Got 'im, Nye?" Thomas's voice remained low and curt, and Nye returned to the edge of the grave, whereupon Thomas tossed the rope back up into his waiting arms before emerging from the pit in a fluid, graceful motion completely at odds with his stocky workman's frame. He resurveyed the scene above ground, his gaze coming to rest upon me. "Ready to pull?" He eyed me steadily, and I nodded in grim determination, taking my place behind Nye, who passed back the tail end of the rope. I wrapped it firmly in my hands as Nye turned to convey further instructions.

"It's important we jerk rather than drag; do you understand? We have to move in tandem here."

I nodded earnestly.

"On my count of three, we pull. Then step back, reposition, and wait for my count again. Understood?"

Another nod.

"Good. One. Two. Three."

On the count of three, I gave a mighty yank and was surprised when the rope instantly yielded a foot or two. This was easier than I had thought, with two men taking on the weight.

Nye seemed pleased as well. He took two large steps back, and I followed suit, then bent low and tightened my fingers, awaiting his signal.

"One. Two. Three . . . One. Two. Three. Again. One. Two. Three . . ."

My fingers trembled and my calf cramped, but I remained mute and undeterred.

"And one! Two! Three!" With this final count, the counterweight gave way, and Nye and I both tumbled to the ground in a most ungraceful manner. But I hardly had time to contemplate my wounded pride for there, mere feet before us, was the decapitated corpse, still shrouded in his Sunday best.

For a moment, I just blinked, dumbfounded, but an elbow to the ribs courtesy of Nye snapped me from my stupor, and I rose quickly to my feet, scurrying forward to join Diggs and Thomas, who had descended on the specimen like hounds upon a fox.

Their nimble fingers made quick work of the man's flimsy clothes. He'd clearly been poor; the suit was shabby and the material thin, the buttonholes too large for the cheap wooden nubs meant to substitute for metallic finery. Before I had time to process the situation, I found myself aiding in divesting him of his coat and shirt, wresting off his suspenders and cravat with nary a second thought. His skin was ice-cold and disconcertingly clammy as his bare form revealed itself before us, but I did not so much as shudder; my time with my corpse at Malstrom's had, at the very least, steeled me to the presence of death. And this process was nothing more than an extension of that, I reasoned, ridding a body of the unnecessary vestments of life in preparation for further purpose in death.

Nye made himself useful in the removal of the man's boots, undergarments, and trousers, then took charge of collecting all the discarded clothing and tossing it haphazardly back into the pit. For some reason, I found this action more shocking than the stripping of the corpse, though I wasn't sure what I'd been expecting; for him to fold it lovingly and place it back in the coffin like an offering? Such actions were borne of sentiment, an impulse which, I was quickly discovering, had no business in the world of snatching.

The corpse stripped nude, the others returned to their spades and began to shovel the heap of dirt back into the grave, still not a word exchanged amongst them. Averting my eyes from the indignity of the headless man now lying fully exposed on the grass, I redirected my attention to the task at hand and joined them.

Just as Nye had described, once the grave was refilled and the sack shaken out, it was impossible to discern that the ground had been disturbed at all. It was shocking to me how clean and precise the process was, and how the members of Nye's crew moved like dancers in choreographed motion, synchronised and silent and disconcertingly fast. All in all, the extraction had taken, by my internal estimations, less than a half hour. It was, as Nye had promised, a science unto itself.

I made myself useful holding the open end of the sack so that Nye and Thomas could maneuver the corpse's shoulders inside. I did my best to ignore the gory stump where his head had once been, but the physician in me was secretly slightly delighted to catch a furtive glimpse of the severed spinal cord up close; we'd yet to embark upon any skeletal dissection at Malstrom's, so this sneak peek was a treat indeed. Nye gave me a knowing nod as we pulled the shroud down past the corpse's feet and secured it into a knot, then positioned ourselves at each end to hoist it up and tote it over to Diggs's barrow, where we deposited it as gently as we could muster.

Our trek back across the silent kirkyard was more tenuous than our first; maneuvering the barrow between the headstones was an ordeal within itself, and the added weight of the corpse on top of all the tools slowed our process considerably. Nonetheless, at long last, the welcome sight of my chamber window came into view from around the hulking shadow of the kirk, and I felt that I could almost breathe freely once more. I quickly admonished myself with the recollection that we weren't out of the woods yet. There was still much more to our plan if we were to pull off the snatch flawlessly, and much of it came down to me.

Our party came to a halt beside the shrubbery directly beneath my chamber. I stooped to collect a pebble, then threw it up to connect with the window above. There was a pause, a collective intake of breath—

And the window swung open, Willis peering down at us in the dark before offering a quick wave of affirmation. Nye returned it, and moments later, the coil of rope descended once more.

Nye gestured for me to go first. I was a bit nervous, hardly being a pinnacle of athletic prowess, but Nye had assured me that ascending was as simple as descending, if I only remembered how to work the physics in my favour. I merely needed to remember to lean back and brace with my legs, instead of pulling with my arms. Simple.

Initially, all was as easy as Nye had described. Midway up the wall, however, my boot hit a loose stone in the façade, and I found myself suddenly, dizzyingly swinging to and fro against the rough wall, the fibres of the rope dragging precariously against the uneven surface. For a moment, I panicked, certain the rope would be torn to shreds and would surely split, and I'd fall to my ultimate demise in the shrubbery below. A backwards glance over my shoulder, however, revealed I was perhaps no more than six feet off the ground. I therefore found the resolve to steady myself, recapture my form, and continue my ascent relatively unfazed.

Crawling through the window of my chamber had all the surreal qualities of returning to a former life; I could scarcely believe that I was the same person now as the boy who had whiled away his hours lost in books and thought, innocently lighting a lantern for the depravity occurring below. Depravity of which I was now, undeniably, a part.

I had no time to mourn my loss of innocence, for right on my heels appeared Nye, swinging into the room like an avenging angel, full of newfound swagger and beaming from ear to ear. Leaving no time to exchange a word between us, he immediately turned and peered back out the window to monitor Thomas and Diggs's progress below. Moments later, two quick jerks of the rope still tied to the rafter above my bed signaled that it was time to bring our plan to completion.

Grabbing the loose end dangling from the knot above, Nye untied the bind to create a pulley, much like we'd used that first night he'd appeared outside my window. Silently assuming our positions once more, rope gripped tightly in our fists, I waited for his signal.

"One. Two. Three." We heaved. "One. Two. Three." Again. "One. Two. Three . . ."

In tandem, we laboured until at long last, the familiar bulk of the white corpse sack appeared in my window. This time, we were not caught off guard; as the bag swung into the room, we gracefully dodged it. Keeping the rope secure, we worked together to lower the sack gently to the floor, creating nary a disturbance in the process; my neighbours would be none the wiser about our deeds.

Satisfied, we stepped back to grin down at our haul. I looked past Nye's pleased expression to where Willis was stationed, lounging in my desk chair as if he owned the place. "Am I done here?" He sounded so bored I almost laughed aloud.

Nye turned to him with a benevolent shrug. "Your part is complete. Come by Malstrom's tomorrow, at eleven. He'll pay us out then."

"Thanks." And without so much as a by your leave, Willis hopped up onto the window ledge, grabbed the rope, and swung out into the darkness below.

Nye pulled up the rope and closed the window, latching it tightly, then turned to face me once more. I was about to heave a sigh of relief when my eyeline was unfortunately redirected to the lump of a cadaver sitting in the middle of my chamber floor.

"Well," said Nye, his voice splitting the silence like a spade. "I hope The Beast is hungry."

To our credit, we were considerably more efficient packing the body away the second time around. The first time had been unbearably disgusting and awkward, all odd angles and stiff joints, but this time we were aided by previous experience (and perhaps the fortuitous lack of an attached head). All in all, we made quick work of packing it away, barely working up a sweat in the process.

I slapped the lid of The Beast shut, and we fastened the clasps in unison before both sinking to the floor and lapsing into a stunned, exhausted, elated silence.

It was then that I realised I had absolutely no idea what to say. Should I comment upon our adventure? Ask for Nye's feedback and advice? Or should I change the subject entirely, pretend we were simply sprawled out upon my chamber floor for some completely unrelated reason, perhaps as if he'd stopped by for tea and a chat and it just happened to be after midnight and for some reason we were both covered in damp soil and sweat and drunk off the thrill of victory?

I settled for something in between. Pulling myself wearily to my feet, I gestured towards the basin placed upon my vanity. For all it lacked in amenities, the staff at the H&A at least had the decency to provide a fresh pitcher each day, and I found myself greatly in want of its services.

"Would you care to wash up a bit? You're welcome to use my basin. I believe I have a spare flannel on hand."

Nye grinned and clambered to his feet. "God, yes. I must admit, no matter how hard I work to refine my process, there is simply no way around getting one's hands dirty in this line of work."

I tossed a grin at him over my shoulder as I rummaged through my wardrobe, procuring two muslin flannels and handing him one as I poured some water into the basin. "I imagine that in your line of work, your hands get dirty with things far worse than a bit of loose soil."

He laughed—a warm, honest sound—as he divested himself of his overcoat and tossed it over the back of my desk chair. Then he casually rolled up his shirtsleeves, dipped his flannel into the water, and commenced carefully sponging off his hands. "Far be it from me to argue that, though I prefer to keep my hands clean in the presence of company. One must maintain appearances, or the next thing you know you're accused of being a sadist and a madman."

Abashed, I silently shrugged off my own overcoat and hung it on the rack, removed my cufflinks and placed them on the desk, then rolled up my sleeves and joined him at the basin, dipping my own flannel in and diligently scrubbing at the stubborn dirt caked between my fingers.

I chose my next words carefully. "I am truly sorry for that, you know."

He swirled his flannel in the water and rung it out, the grime from his hands leaving a cloudy haze behind. He raised it carefully to his brow and then ran it down his neck, wiping away the perspiration from our exertions, his cheeks still flushed from the evening's excitement. My gaze felt riveted to the damp trail the wet muslin left upon his porcelain skin.

When he at last spoke again, his words were soft, unassuming. "I know. And I . . . I'm sorry I deceived you. Not just about the nature of the laboratory, not just about Malstrom's connection to the kirkyard, not just about my role in it . . . about it all. I was . . ." He seemed lost in thought, lowering the flannel to the water again, unnaturally focused upon the act as if he could not stand to look me in the face as he divulged this sudden confession. "You must understand; throughout my life, I have learned to be cautious about whom I trust. I have been betrayed many times over, and always to a sorry end. And while I realise my defenses must make my actions appear unforgivably ruthless upon first blush, I assure you, James, it was never my intention to cause you harm through my deceit."

"I know." My hands were frozen in the act of washing, my heart hammering a distracting staccato against my ribs. "Why else would I be here?"

At last, Nye's eyes met mine, and we were once again caught in a crystalised moment of paralysing uncertainty. I wanted, I wanted, but what, what? And I could see he wanted, he wanted, too—

"I should go." He dropped the flannel with a wet plop upon the vanity, the moment snapped and shattered with his decision.

"Oh! Um, yes, of course, you'll . . . be back in the morning for the trunk?" I knew, of course, that we wouldn't be moving the trunk to Malstrom's until we were able to catch the milk cart again at dawn. But I'd thought perhaps—

Perhaps what? Perhaps Nye would stay here in my chamber all night, keeping me company instead of leaving me alone with a trunkful of corpse and a headful of gnawing anxieties? The idea was absurd, preposterous; he was a grown man, with his own lodgings, his own occupation, his own master to serve and his own crew to oversee, perhaps his own sweetheart to visit, like the beautiful Mary Paterson. Though he'd denied a romantic entanglement with her, a man would have to be made of stone to deny the affections roused by her beauty, and Nye hardly seemed impervious to the indulgences of mortals. Why on earth would he waste his night with the dreary likes of me—

"Unless . . . would you care for a drink?" He was paused in the act of grabbing his overcoat, bent awkwardly, head twisted to gauge my reaction to his proposition.

"Yes." The word was out of my mouth before I could so much as contemplate an alternative response.

He righted himself and turned to face me once more, an expression akin to relief on his face; he seemed honestly delighted I'd acquiesced. "Excellent! I do apologise for not offering sooner. You should know drinking and snatching often go hand in hand; it's honestly inexcusable of me to have even considered taking your leave without so much as a nip of something to rekindle your fortitude after so dismal an undertaking." The words escaped him in a frenetic jumble, the sentiment endearingly earnest, and he seemed flustered for the first time I could ever recall.

Eager to put him back at ease, I offered a reassuring smile, but suddenly realised a slight wrinkle in the plan. "I . . . I haven't got anything to drink."

Nye just winked. "Never fear. Stay here." Before I could get a word in edgewise, he'd flung open the door to my chamber and strode off down the dim hallway towards the staircase to the pub.

I wanted to shout after him that it was after hours; the pub was closed, and Angus did not take late-night requests, but it was far too late. By the time I'd made my way across the room and poked my head out the door, he'd disappeared entirely. Flummoxed, I lowered myself onto my bed, toed off my boots (I was well aware of the fact that Nye and I were far past the parameters of proper dress at this point), changed out of my soiled socks, and proceeded to wait.

No more than two minutes later, Nye reappeared, a half-full bottle of whiskey in his hand. Waggling his eyebrows, he merrily waltzed in and shut the door behind him with his foot, depositing his catch upon my desk with a flourish.

I stared up at him in astonishment. "Did you just steal that?"

He shrugged and flung himself into my desk chair, popped out the cork, took a fortifying pull, and extended the bottle in my direction. "Problem?"

I opted to leave morality out of it, as it seemed Nye operated on his own rather unique set of principles. Instead, I focused upon the logistics. "Angus locks the liquor cupboard more securely than his damn safe. How did you break in?"

"Angus is a moron who stores the key to the liquor cupboard on top of the liquor cupboard. I learned that last season, when Willis was employed here as a dish boy."

I accepted the bottle and took a swig. It was good whiskey, smokey and sweet, a far cut better than anything I'd ever ordered for myself. I quickly took another pull before handing it back to Nye. "I take it the dish-boy job was a cover?"

Nye raised the bottle in my direction. "Astute observation indeed, James. I believe you're getting the hang of this criminal business."

"And I assume that has something to do with you being banned from the premises for life?"

"Another excellent deduction! It's true, we had a rather clever operation set up here at the H&A last season, but it all went completely to shite when one night the sexton took an unscheduled walk and Willis had to abandon his post at the dish bin to warn our sorry skins. Took Angus about two seconds to put it all together after that, so"—he took a mournful sip from the bottle—"suffice to say, he's not so friendly with our lot anymore."

I shook my head and grinned. "You're all mad, you know."

"Well, I'd say you have to be, to make a living poking about corpses, but at least it pays well. Now, Mr. Willoughby, what's your excuse? What do you think your newfound vocation says about you?" His tone was chiding as he tipped back in his chair, propping his feet up on my desk. For some reason, the gesture felt relaxed rather than disrespectful.

I took his cue and leaned back against the headboard of my bed, stretching my legs out in front of me, allowing myself to sink further into the warm comfort of the whiskey.

"I think it means I was meant for this life."

"In that case, it's fair fortune you met me."

"Yes. Fair fortune indeed." He leaned forward and passed the bottle back to me.

So we sat and talked and drank and laughed as outside my window, the night faded into a crisp and rosy new dawn.

8.

An Awakening

In my brief sojourn at Oxford, I attended a philosophy lecture in which the professor posited the question How does one discern wakefulness from dreaming? How may we be certain that what we perceive as our reality is not, in fact, the fevered nocturnal manifestations of a distant, unknowable consciousness? The peers in my class made arguments aplenty in their lilting Latin platitudes: that dreams lack Reason, which is the Truth of all matters. That dreams defy Logic, which is the Root of all things. That in dreaming, we recuse our enlightened mindfulness to beastly baser instincts and, in doing so, negate the essence of our humanity. I listened to the arguments unconvinced, for it often seemed to me that I was more human for dreaming than any beast I'd encountered yet.

And thus was the paradox of my divergent parallel lives as they unfolded before me in the nascent new year. For in each separate life I lived, I became convinced that the other must surely be a fiction, an elaborate fantasy conjured by my preoccupied mind, only to find, a matter of hours later, that I was quite convinced of the opposite. As I passed my days in the presence of my peers, attending lectures and anatomy lessons, dining with chums at the pub, studying and reading and devoting myself to rigorous scholarly pursuits, I could not conceive of my other life in the Underworld—or the origins of the persistent dirt beneath my fingernails.

But at night, I felt so truly alive that the genteel pastimes of my days seemed but a pale distraction from the invigorating exploits of my nocturnal being. Under the intoxicating influence of adrenaline, each moment I spent with Aneurin and his crew further cemented my place in the shrouded shadows that clung to the corners of the city I had come to call home. With each snatch, my personal technique grew better, quicker, more refined. I mastered the elegant choreography of the practice with a surgeon's precision and a convert's devotion, and developed the stomach to endure even the grisliest of digs. I could feel my body changing in response to my newfound labours, my lean limbs defining with novel musculature I'd never before possessed, and it was with a sense of pride that I found myself well and truly pulling my weight within my unlikely circle of colleagues.

My dedication did not go unnoticed. Though Diggs could hardly be said to have warmed to me, both Thomas and Willis moved quickly from cordial to friendly as I proved my worth time and again. Our crew met regularly at the Pig even on nights we weren't snatching under the noble guise of "refining our process," but business matters were rarely the main topic on hand; we'd more often simply drink and joke and catch up on the gossip about town. Sometimes Mary Paterson would join us, and, despite my lack of experience in conversing with ladies, I was gradually learning (with varying degrees of success) not to stumble into a tongue-tied travesty each time she cast her eyes at me. She seemed to find my bashfulness in her presence particularly endearing (if not a bit entertaining) and had a penchant for making me blush—which delighted Nye to no end.

And Nye. Every moment with him felt like a dream decoded, a riddle unravelled in a foreign tongue. Whether drinking by my side at the Pig, eyeing me appraisingly across the hall at Malstrom's, or splayed out casually in my desk chair recovering from the rigors of a dig, he was my North Star whenever the darkness of doubt threatened to envelop me. When I could not tell dreams from wakefulness, he remained my touchstone and my Truth; a glimmer in his eye and a quirk of his lips were all that it took to make me feel manifest, whole, and worthy.

We made a habit of our post-dig drink. Some nights, he'd nick a bottle from the pub downstairs, some nights he'd procure a flask from the folds of his overcoat, and some nights I'd use my earnings to buy us a bottle of something proper to split. But it quickly became obvious that it wasn't wholly about the drink; often we'd drain no more than a glass apiece over the course of an evening, scarcely pausing to wet our lips as we talked ourselves hoarse over all manner of topics. We'd collaborate, we'd quarrel, we'd provoke and retaliate and retort, but above all we'd laugh. Truth be told, there was an effortlessness to our rapport that eluded definition, for the circumstances that brought us together were grim and grotesque indeed. By all accounts, our alliance should have been a sorry one. Yet I found it instead full of joy and deep affection—albeit tinged with a dark, macabre humour that doubtlessly would have offended anyone but ourselves. With him, I could share my thoughts on anything—from discontinuous capillaries to Divine Creation—and know that I was in the presence of a kindred spirit.

It was, I believe, firmly because of this cherished friendship that I was able to maintain the duality of my existence for as long as I did. Though none at Malstrom's were aware of my connection with Nye, his lingering presence at the periphery of the dissection hall was grounding to me, a constant reminder that my night-life was not merely a twisted anomaly but instead a natural extension of my academic exploits. With each fresh corpse we procured for the school, my knowledge and that of my peers was expanded tenfold under Malstrom's tutelage and demonstrations, and the correlation between my private proclivities and public progress felt most visceral to me. As deplorable as my newfound vocation may have seemed to an objective outsider, to me it felt duly justified in a tangible way: my hands brought forth and gave new life to that which had been seized by Death—a power so heady it was intoxicating to wield.

This is not to say that my existence was wholly without conflict. For one, there was the niggling matter of my family, who were (perhaps predictably) concerned as to my whereabouts when I failed to report back to the familial stead in response to Edith's summons. I first received several correspondences from Edith demanding the details of my travel plans, followed by a more pointed inquisition from my mother, and then, eventually, a harsh rebuke from Richard himself, penned under the guise of deep brotherly concern but clearly merely a façade for sheer annoyance. I initially considered responding but found myself wholly at a loss for what to say; even if I claimed to have secured an apprenticeship in town, no such position would pay well enough to cover a full University tuition on top of room and board, so I'd be forced to either hide my continued pursuit of a medical degree or somehow convince them that I'd found complimentary lodgings courtesy of my employer—neither of which would hold true upon further inquisition. I resolved instead to avoid the topic entirely and promptly burn every letter that appeared upon my stoop—an admittedly cowardly resolution which apparently amused Nye to no end.

"You're not even going to open it?" He pressed one night, post-snatch, from his standard spot in my desk chair as I tossed yet another ludicrously embossed white envelope into the embers smoldering in my fireplace.

"They all say the same thing," I responded dolefully. "Come home at once. You are in dereliction of your duties. Stop ussing with the dregs of the earth and rejoin proper society this instant."

Nye raised his eyebrow. "You made that last bit up."

"I paraphrased."

"Embellished."

"Interpreted."

"Touché."

On a more positive note, my financial situation proceeded to resolve itself with surprising haste and continued to improve exponentially the longer I remained
engaged in my newfound position. Whereas at first I
had been secretly concerned that my share of the compensation might be insufficient to cover room, board,
and tuition, I soon found myself flush with cash, paid
in full upon delivery to Malstrom's the morning after
each snatch. Our new setup in Greyfriars eliminated
much of the risk that had previously prevented the
crew from operating freely, and as a result, we soon
found ourselves employed upwards of three times a
week, every snatch fetching a prize sum for the fresh-
ness with which we were able to procure it. Though
Nye remained the middleman between Malstrom and
the rest of us, I could tell from the generous bonuses we
began to receive that Malstrom was impressed with our
performance. With each passing week, my confidence
and commitment grew ever deeper, and I soon could
not picture my life at the University without the elegant
counterbalance of my conquests in the kirkyard.

As time went by, I became increasingly immune to
the gruesome nature of my profession, which not only
aided me in the dissection hall but turned the details of
each conquest into a pleasant, anonymous blur. While
it was true there were some digs that were more mem-
orable than others (the excavation of a pair of twin girls
buried head to foot in the same coffin, my first unpleasant encounter with a corpse too far past fresh, and the
unforgettable prize of a man who measured nearly
seven feet in height, yielding an unexpected windfall so
generous that I could have renounced my new career

that very night and been set financially until next term, and yet . . .)

The downside to the effortless predictability of our brilliant process was that it lulled each and every one of us into a state of oblivious complacency so total that when, one unremarkable Wednesday night, Diggs happened to glance across the kirkyard and see Willis's lantern burning bright in my chamber window, it startled him so profoundly he nearly tipped back into the grave.

"Lookout! Lookout!" His voice was gruff and gravelly from underuse, as we always undertook our labours in silence whenever possible.

Like a pair of startled moles, Nye and I popped our heads out of the hole we were lodged in, having just cracked open the coffin lid. Blinking into the darkness, we stared in disbelief at the flame flickering resolutely above the scene, unmistakable in its implication. Thomas, who'd been occupying himself knotting the ropes and clearing out the barrow for our quarry, swore quietly under his breath and leaned down to converse with Nye.

"What'll it be, boss? Stay, or run?"

Nye hesitated.

My heart was hammering in my chest at a most unnatural rate, my limbs all but vibrating with the instinct to flee. "Are you serious, Nye? We have to go! Now! If the sexton keeps his usual route, we have five minutes, maybe less—"

"Unless . . ." mused Nye.

I gawped at him. "Unless what?" He couldn't honestly be considering trying to pull off the snatch with the sexton on the loose! We were a mere twenty feet from the western path; there was no way we could be missed.

He exchanged a look with Thomas, who gave a resolute nod in apparent concurrence and then dashed off into the darkness. My head whipped over to Diggs, who simply cordially tipped his hat and tottered off in the opposite direction, leaving only myself and Nye in the wretched pit with a broken coffin and our livelihoods on the line.

"Are you out of your mind?" I hissed. "We have to go!"

Nye shook his head. "No. We're too close. I'm not giving up on this one."

I clenched my teeth and attempted to steady my swelling temper. "The sexton will—"

"Be distracted by Thomas. We've done this before, James, just relax and keep working. Eyes on the prize." With that, he knelt and pried open the coffin, then extended his hand in anticipation of rope.

At a complete loss for words (and, frankly, too terrified of raising my voice to argue), I grabbed the coil from where Thomas had left it graveside and helped Nye secure it under the corpse's arms. Fortunately, it was a small one—a boy, no more than twelve, still well-preserved. Easy bait. I could see that Nye's reckless obstinance might just pay off.

We moved through our paces swiftly and methodically, securing the body in the barrow and tossing the funeral vestments back into the earth before tipping the mound of soil back into place. I reached out to bag the body, but Nye shook his head and simply threw the sack over it to obscure it. "There's no time," he murmured, and I nodded in assent.

I gripped the handles of the barrow and resolutely turned to maneuver it towards my chamber, but Nye quickly steered me in the opposite direction, towards the outward-facing gates of the kirkyard. We walked quickly but cautiously, our movements meticulous and mindful. As soon as we reached the main path, Nye leaned in closely to whisper in my ear.

"We'll walk the barrow out the main gate and make for Malstrom's. The chances of encountering the sexton are too great to hoist it to your chamber. We'll have to be quick on the streets; if we're caught, there's little denying what we're up to. Do you understand?"

I nodded mutely, my palms sweating in nervous anticipation.

"If we become separated"—he ignored my horrified expression at the thought—"it's essential that you carry on to Malstrom's yourself. Use the back entrance; as always, it's unlocked. Put the body in the tea-chest in Malstrom's office; don't leave it in the lab. Then make for the Pig; we'll rendezvous there. Yes?"

"Yes." The word felt tight and stilted in my throat, the threat of imminent capture becoming real to me for the first time. While I had, of course, contemplated the risks of this vocation, it had never occurred to me what I would actually do if faced with such a scenario, and suddenly relying on my family name and smart dress seemed rather a farce indeed.

We reached the familiar bend in the path that led along the south side of the kirk, presenting a straight shot to the main gate, and I could feel my pace quickening. We were so close to escape, so close to freedom—

From behind us, a shout echoed across the frosty grounds. Was it Thomas? It was impossible to tell. Nye's eyes grew wide, and he shot a wild glance back over his shoulder. His gait, which had quickened to match my own, measurably slowed.

"James—"

"No. I'm not leaving without you! You can't go back for him."

Nye shook his head determinedly. "James, I'm sorry, I have to. I run this crew, I can't leave one of my men behind."

My breath was coming in frantic, panicked heaves as I ground to a halt as well, resolved in convincing him otherwise. "What good'll it do us if you're both arrested? Thomas will be fine, Malstrom will take care of him—"

"I'm sorry; I can't leave him. If my men can't trust me, they won't follow me. If there's even a chance I can help Thomas escape, I have to try."

His expression was one of steadfast resolve, and I knew in my heart that there would be no convincing him otherwise. After all, I realised, would I not want him to show the same loyalty to me, were our fortunes ever reversed?

"Alright. Go."

He clapped my shoulder affectionately. "Godspeed, James. Make haste for the gate. It will appear secured, but the pin's wedged in the lock; take care not to disturb it." I nodded earnestly, doing my best to breathe around the lump of panic wedged in my throat. "Then straight to Malstrom's. Quickly. Don't stop for anyone. I'll see you at the Pig." And with that, he turned on his heel and disappeared down the shadowy path and into the yawning darkness.

I turned back to my own trajectory, the handles of the barrow slippery from the sweat of my palms. While

I knew my escape from the kirkyard lay unimpeded before me, there was no way to guarantee my safe passage all the way to Malstrom's. The quickest route involved the steep stairs of the Closes, rendering it unusable under the burden of a full barrow; I quickly concluded I'd have to use the main streets, which offered little cover and no plausible excuses for my presence there were I to be spotted. My only salvation was to be my speed, aided only by the heavy fog rolling in from the sea, shrouding the city in a misty cloak of obscurity. If I could perhaps avoid the street lamps, keep my footing on the rain-slick cobblestones, keep my head down and my resolve high, then perhaps, perhaps . . .

I veered unsteadily out of the main gates onto Candlemaker Row with all the countenance of a man possessed. The barrow, though not heavy, was not built for precision or hasty maneuvering, and I found myself struggling to maintain my velocity as I peddled it down onto the familiar straightway of Chambers Street with as nimble a hand as I could muster. The ungreased axles seemed to groan obscenely in the oppressive silence that enveloped the Old Town at that late hour, and the rattling of the wheels against the cobblestones sounded unholy to my keen ears. The streets were all but abandoned, and never before had I yearned so acutely for some obscure company, whether it be a gang of hooligans or a gaggle of sailors, simply to drown out the sound of my own deafening undertaking, but alas, I had no such luck. I was utterly alone, an obvious target to any impartial observer as I hastened my way towards my destination, pleading my case with any deity who might happen to observe my predicament to grant me mercy, despite my less-than-pious objectives. But the singular thought that blazed bright in my mind and fortified my resolve was that I could not disappoint the crew. I had come this far in service to them; now was no time for turning back.

By the time I reached the crossing at South Bridge, I had foolishly convinced myself that I was in the clear. I'd navigated myself most fortuitously thus far, and the remaining trek up the length of Infirmary Street seemed hardly a threat in the least, as most buildings on either side consisted of vacant University lecture halls. Pausing momentarily, I'd just allowed myself the luxury of wiping my sweat-slick palms on the fleece of my trousers when a voice erupted behind me from out of nowhere.

"Oy, you! Stop right there!"

I froze in place, tempered in sweat, heart racing and breath reeling, eyes narrowing to assess the figure emerging from the swirling mist surrounding us. To my utter dismay, a young, portly constable emerged from the fog, the silhouette of his hat and baton striking a mortal fear into my clenching heart. It was my worst nightmare manifested, and a part of me scarcely believed he could be real, for the sheer dumb luck of it all. I was still attempting to conjure an appropriate (if dismissive) response when he strode purposefully to a parade rest a mere two feet in front of me, towering over me with a dour grimace completely at odds with the rosy-cheeked youthfulness of his face. I blinked up at him, attempting to square his formidable stature with the boyish appearance of his visage.

"What's in the barrow?" His brogue was as thick as Hamish's, and once again I thanked my lucky stars

I'd had enough experience with the locals that I could parse out the rolling syllables.

I had no formal alibi and had rehearsed nothing with my cohorts of what my story was to be if I ever found myself thus compromised. Floundering, I could feel a cold layer of perspiration formulating on my brow which had nothing to do with the inclement weather.

"Simply . . . a delivery. An urgent delivery, sir, of utmost importance."

The constable took another step forward, close enough that his daunting presence all but made me shirk my position at the helm of the barrow. He more than made up for his lack of years in his knack for intimidation, and I found myself mealy-mouthed beneath his stern gaze.

"And what could possibly be of such importance at this late hour?" he sneered, eyes narrowed and lips pulled tight into a disdainful grimace.

I swallowed hard, the back of my tongue making an awkward dry click against the palate of my mouth, and I maneuvered to square my shoulders against the impending imposition; after all, there was little recourse for escape on such a narrow thoroughfare, so it seemed standing my ground would be the only recourse worth pursuing.

"It's . . . Well, you see, it's precious cargo, sir, of a most time-sensitive nature, so I really must be on my way."

I moved to the left as if to round him, but the constable's eyes flared with newly kindled intrigue no doubt spurned by my evasiveness. I could nearly feel the desire to unleash exemplary justice emanating from him in palpable waves. A wicked grin manifested itself upon his face, predatory and pronounced. "Why, is that so? I think perhaps I ought to inspect it myself." He reached forcefully past my shoulder towards the sheet.

I tipped the barrow just in time to pivot it out of his grasp, angling myself deliberately between the intruder and my quarry. "I don't know what you're implying, sir. But I really must be off, the delivery is of the utmost urgency—"

The constable darted round the barrow straight into my path, cutting off my only clear point of egress, barely able to disguise the look of sheer delight upon his face. "Ah, ah, now not so fast there, sonny. Seems I ought to check up on your story now, seeing as we've had some troubles round these parts with the illegal nature of a few so-called special deliveries."

My gaze flicked appraisingly to my left. I was within dodging distance of Robertson's Close; were I to abandon the barrow and make sufficient haste, there was a chance I could outrun the prowling constable despite his current advantage in both stature and station. As discreetly as I could, I relinquished my grip on the handles and readied my legs for flight.

Leering, the constable gripped the front corner of the barrow firmly with one hand and used the other to whisk the sheet away with a flare so dramatic it was as if he were mentally performing a one-man show to a rapt audience of no one but himself.

And there, laid bare between us, was the nude corpse, so ghostly white in the lamplight it seemed nearly to glow. The sight of it, curled in a foetal position in the muddy bed of the barrow, was so horrifically incriminating that I could not parse out a word in my own defense. For a moment, I felt like a disembodied soul hovering above the scene, the dire predicament of my situation incomprehensible in its magnitude. I was to be arrested, tried, and publicly fined—and that's if I were lucky! Though Nye had always been adamant that the lawmen were lenient towards students of genteel households, the dour disdain with which this constable had confronted me left little reassurance that they would be as kind as Nye had so confidently described.

There was simply no other choice; I'd have to make a run for it. If I could make it down the Close and onto the Cowgate, there were a fair number of taverns and public houses where I could perhaps take refuge if I had enough of a head start—or if not that, at least circle back by way of High School Yards and lose myself amidst the familiar architecture of the University. Resolved, I took a step back, swiveled on my heel, and darted for the Close—

Only to run bodily into a shadowy stranger who had been pelting in the opposite direction at full speed. The collision nearly knocked me off my feet, and I reeled, stunned, as the constable shouted in alarm at the sudden ruckus. I was doubly dumbfounded when a parting of the mist and a beam from the street lamp revealed the figure to be none other than Aneurin himself. For a split second, he just gawped at me, then a quick glance over my shoulder revealed the precariousness of the situation, and his expression instantly transformed from one of relief to one of hastened panic.

"James! There you are! Oh thank God, you've found assistance. Constable! Are you here to aid us with our transport?" Nye brushed past me to approach the stupefied constable, whose expression displayed the same element of disbelief that I feared was mirrored upon my own.

"What is the meaning of this?" The constable righted himself, dropping the sheet and reaching menacingly for his club.

"Constable Murray, I'm sure my friend James here has enlightened you to our most pressing errand, for the life of this precious boy is at stake!" With that, he gesticulated grandly towards the barrow where the corpse remained, unsurprisingly, quite dead and pale as a gutted fish in the wan light.

The constable scowled. "You mistake me for an imbecile, MacKinnon? The boy's clearly already dead as a doornail, and you lads are in for a world of trouble."

Nye shook his head fervently. "You misunderstand, sir! For this boy here, you know him! It's wee Willis, from the quays!"

The constable (Murray, apparently), cocked his head. "I can't be expected to keep track of every wretched urchin scuttling about Old Town."

Nye earnestly maneuvered closer to Murray, his stature suddenly transforming from frenzied to fetching in the mere blink of an eye. His gait was instantly infused with a charismatic, casual swagger that I was learning to recognise all too well, and sure enough, when he spoke once more, his silver tongue wove a tapestry of lies so elaborate I could scarce keep my jaw off the cobblestones.

"Don't be ridiculous, Murray. Wee Willis works at the quays—along with his cousin James, here. Good, honest, noble work, befitting of these two God-fearing gentlemen. But I'm afraid that, tonight, there was a terrible accident, and Willis took a wrong-footed step off a barge and found himself submerged in the frigid current of the Water of Leith. He was underwater nigh on four minutes before James and the lads found him and pulled him out—a dreadful business, a most miserable fate, don't you agree?"

Murray glowered. "Aye. But we also agree on the main point: Willis is dead. And that means you are in possession of corporeal contraband, so I'll now take the liberty of escorting you both—"

"Ah ah, not so fast! You see, my friend James here— being the clever, quick thinker that he is—correctly recalled that, besides being a most cherished companion, I am also quite well connected in the field of medical science. Upon retrieving Willis from the icy depths, he immediately sent for me, knowing that perhaps I alone would have the connections to revive him!"

At this, Murray openly scoffed. "You're full of shite, MacKinnon. You may be a surgeon, but you're not God. The boy's dead. And stripped bare, I might add—"

"Of course he's stripped bare, his clothes were near frozen to his flesh! I instructed they be removed at once, and the boy covered in whatever linen we had on hand for immediate transport to Malstrom's laboratory."

"And then what, Lazarus? You raise the dead?" An expression of utter disdain had reappeared upon the constable's face, and my heart felt ready to hammer its way through my ribs. I had no idea where Nye was going with any of this, but I couldn't imagine an outcome that didn't involve the two of us being carted off to gaol.

In that moment of doubt, Nye lowered his voice conspiratorially. "Murray, as long as I've known you, I've taken you to be a good man. But now I must ask, upon the life of your mother: are you a trustworthy man?"

Murray blinked. "What's that got to do with any of it?"

Nye licked his lips and leaned in closer. "What I'm about to tell you is a secret so great, the risk of its exposure could compromise the very future of mankind."

Murray appeared stunned at this revelation. "What . . . what sort of secret?"

"It's to do with Malstrom's research at the medical school, you see. We all know that Malstrom is well-regarded as a genius in his field"—Nye glanced at me for confirmation and I nodded resolutely; though I wasn't sure the nature of the part I was playing, I knew enough to go along with it—"truly one of the great medical minds of his generation. And in his laboratory, he's currently researching . . ." he trailed off and glanced around, as if checking the road for nefarious eavesdroppers. Seemingly satisfied, he continued in a whisper: "the Galvanic Battery."

"And what . . . what's that?" The constable had lowered his voice to a whisper when he replied, and I nearly choked on my own saliva; was it possible he was actually buying this? Lord in Heaven, Nye was even better than I'd given him credit for.

"A Galvanic Battery, my dear sir, is an electrochemical cell in which a current is generated from spontaneous redox reactions. The brilliant Italian scientist Galvani pioneered its usage in the reanimation of frogs, but his work was later eclipsed when his nephew demonstrated the use of the battery upon a human corpse in New-gate—perhaps you heard word of it?"

Murray shook his head, still rapt with intrigue.

"It was a marvel beyond compare, I'm told by my colleagues in the know. Unfortunately the reanimated corpse in Newgate did not survive for long, but Malstrom believes he is on the precipice of a great breakthrough on this front! If his methodology is correct, the Galvanic Battery may very well be the key to Life Everlasting! Can you imagine, Murray? The proverbial fountain of youth, sprung forth from our very own city! Ay, what a feat!" Nye's eyes were bright with manufactured wonder, and he sounded flushed and breathless at the (imagined) prospect.

"Has he . . . has he succeeded before?" Murray's eyes were wide as saucers.

Nye raised his finger to his lips and shook his head coyly. "Ach, I'm afraid that I'm not privileged to dis-close. For how would you feel, knowing that the dead now walk these very streets amongst us?"

Murray's face went chalk-white, his breathing quite irregular as he considered the prospect, and cast a glance over at the corpse in the barrow. Nye took the opportunity to wink impishly at me, and I had to use all my willpower not to roll my eyes at his audacity; we'd barely managed to collect ourselves back into the guise of dignity when Murray turned back to face us.

"So . . . you believe you can revive Willis?"

Nye nodded solemnly. "I know I can, sir. But time is of the essence. Please—dear James here cannot bear to lose his cousin, his family has suffered so much loss already—what with the pox and the war and the rest of it . . ." (I took the liberty of rounding the heel of my boot squarely upon his toe; for he was laying it on awfully thick, even by his standards). "Please, Murray. We must help. We must. It's the least we Christians can do."

Murray barely paused to consider this, and when he replied, it was with all the somber, dire solemnity of a soldier called up to duty. "Alright, MacKinnon. Take the boy. And may God have mercy upon his soul—may it be departed no more." And with a pious tip of his hat, he stood aside.

With a gracious bow, Nye grasped the handles of the barrow and turned to me, his eyes gentle and reassuring. "Come, James. We won't let Willis perish; I swear it!" And with a final flagrant flourish, we made haste at full speed down the street, never once daring to glance back.

* * *

An hour later, we found ourselves gathered in the safe embrace of the Pig, Nye recounting our narrow escape with all the drama of a minstrel as he summoned more whiskeys. Willis was all but weeping with laughter, Thomas had buried his face in his hands in sheer disbelief, and even Diggs had allowed an audible chuckle or two to escape during the account, shaking his head as he downed the last of his third glass.

"You're mad as hatters, the lot of you," he wheezed, but the bemused expression upon his haggard face betrayed his softer sentiments.

Willis, still tittering helplessly (the whiskeys having clearly caught up with him more quickly than the rest of us), attempted to wipe his eyes dry between gasps. "I can't believe you told him I was dead. I should probably resent that, you know."

"Nonsense. The corpse was far better-looking than you; you ought to take it as a compliment. A little decomposition was still better than your ugly mug." Nye ducked just in time as Willis chucked his cap at him, laughing uproariously at the slight.

I grinned. The adrenaline from our escape was still coursing through my veins, and I felt a sense of giddy elation that put me completely at ease, despite the raucous setting.

"And you, Thomas?" I inquired. "You've yet to convey us your tale."

Thomas took a swig of his drink and shrugged. "Not much to tell. I led the sexton on a rousing chase, but nearly found myself cornered before I could make it to the MacKenzie."

"The MacKenzie?"

Thomas grinned. "Aye, the MacKenzie mausoleum. A while back, our girl Mary, clever as she is, picked and swapped the padlock on the mausoleum door, providing us a stealthy hiding spot within the kirkyard grounds, were we ever to be in need of one."

"Did I hear my Christian name upon the tongues of this motley crew?" Mary's husky voice emerged from the crowd behind us as she sauntered up to our table, half-drained pint glass in hand, cheeks rosy from the libations, her lips curved in apparent amusement at having overheard Thomas's mention.

"Mary, love! We didn't expect you here this fine evening!" Nye rose to his feet to take her hand, give her a twirl, and bring them both back down to the chair with her perched coquettishly in his lap. She pressed a jovial kiss to his cheek, and again I was startled to feel a flare of something red-hot in my belly at the sight, which I quickly tamped down.

"Aye, business was slow at the Hart tonight, so I decided to pop in for some refreshments. Now, on what account were you lads dragging my reputation through the mud?"

Nye gave her waist a playful pinch, and she giggled (I could feel my brow knit into a glare and took a sip of whiskey to distract myself from their most improper display). "You know fair well we'd all die before slandering you. Thomas was merely singing your praises to James, on account of your brilliant maneuvering at the MacKenzie. Your hideout saved us again tonight; we owe you our skins many times over."

"Well, that's a debt I'll gladly collect one of these days," she replied with a wicked wink in my direction.

Eager to redeem my composure, I ventured: "My peers at University have mistaken you all for ghosts, you know."

Thomas seemed delighted by the prospect. "Really?"

"Indeed. Rumours are rife within the student body of sightings of shadowy figures about that mausoleum; you've made quite the contribution to the local lore, apparently."

Thomas and Diggs laughed heartily at this, and Nye took the opportunity to shoot another pointed glance over at Willis. "You see? You're not the only one to get off on playing dead."

Willis cackled. "Then, to Death!"

"To Death! And all the joys thereafter!"

We drank.

By the time we departed the Pig an hour later, we were all one peg below steady. Thomas and Diggs took their leave to travel north to their lodgings, while Nye, Willis, and I turned onto South Bridge, pulling up our collars against a newly falling rain. The air was so chill that I was, for once, grateful for the amount of whiskey in my belly, as it was the only measure to fortify me against the inclement weather. We walked briskly and in silence, too exhausted from our revelries to muster more conversation. We'd just crossed over Cowgate when our footfalls were met by the echo of an unfamiliar pair, rapidly approaching us from behind.

"You there! Halt!"

We three whirled in place to face our aggressor and found ourselves in the presence of—to my eternal dismay—none other than Constable Murray, stalking through the rain like an angry tomcat on the prowl. I froze in mortification; there was no way he could fail to recognise us, and we'd be caught bold-faced in our lie! My hands began to tremble at my sides, now more certain than ever that my inevitable ruin at last was neigh.

"Constable Murray! A fine coincidence, crossing your path once again this fair night." Nye tipped his hat in a flourish of civility, but I merely stiffened in my shoes; I doubted good manners would provide us the necessary grace to escape unscathed from this unlikely encounter.

Murray squinted through the rain at the three of us, and it was all but possible to see the wheels turning inside his head. Upon registering the presence of young

Willis, his eyes flew open comedically wide, and he leapt backwards in dismay.

"Wee Willis? Is that . . . is that you?" His tone was wonderstruck.

"Aye, that it is, Murray. Back from the dead and out for a pint. The afterlife has the most dismal libations, I'm afraid to report."

For one brief, breathless moment, I thought Murray might actually be dumb enough to buy it. But a half breath later, his eyes narrowed, his face flushed an odd shade of puce, and his hand flew to his baton with a fevered grip.

"You!" He shouted, brandishing the baton dangerously close to Nye's nose. "You lying, dirty scoundrel! What have you got to say for yourself?"

There was a deafening pause.

"It worked?"

I had no time to process the consequences of Nye's cheekiness, for by the time Murray was charging forth swinging his baton wildly in our direction, Nye had gripped my hand firmly and pulled me into an all-out sprint down the bridge, veering abruptly to the left towards a hidden flight of steps I'd never before even noticed. I vaguely registered the sound of Willis making his own hasty retreat in the opposite direction, but it was obvious that Nye was the true target of Murray's ire; the sound of his boots echoed menacingly behind us as he engaged in dogged pursuit. We took the steps two at a time, still keenly aware of Murray's footfalls close on our heels, and descended further into the rising darkness. It then occurred to me where Nye was leading us: to the Vaults.

No sooner had our feet hit solid ground than Nye was yanking me down a narrow passageway illuminated by a single flickering lantern. It was scarcely wide enough for us to fit through shoulder to shoulder, and our footfalls seemed to my discretion obscenely loud as they echoed off the damp stone walls. We pelted full-speed ahead despite the limited visibility, and I once again found myself placing all my trust in Nye's guidance as we wound deeper below ground.

All at once, the passageway widened, and we tumbled through a low stone archway into a cavernous expanse, brimming with torchlight and acrid with smoke, and the raucous, raunchy vision of the true Underworld swam into focus before my very eyes.

I scarcely had time to process the scene as Nye led me, still running full-tilt, through the crowded, teeming masses of the Vaults' sordid inhabitants. Flickering glimpses of unsavoury scenes flashed before my eyes: of taverns, dice games, cards and guns, rail-thin wretches begging in tattered rags, and bawdy women dressed so provocatively that I had never before seen so much exposed flesh (well, on a living woman, at least). The stench was so thick it was palpable, as if misery itself had congealed into a reeking miasma, and I found myself thinking wildly of Charlie's fumigators and rather wishing I had one on hand. But there was no time to ponder such frivolities; with an elated shout, Nye glanced back over his shoulder to meet my eye.

"I think we've nearly lost him! Come on!"

Another harsh yank upon my hand, and we veered suddenly to the right, around a hairpin turn, whereupon we found ourselves at the base of a steep staircase.

Ascending in a flurry of frantic footfalls, we emerged from our subterranean escapade suddenly, startlingly into the thoroughfare of Chambers Street. Utterly disorientated, I froze in place, but Nye showed no such trepidation; he merely dragged me along down the road, still running at top speed, and didn't slow until we arrived, panting and trembling, at the side door of the H&A. We hastened up the stairs to my chamber, whereupon he spun and slammed the door shut behind us before leaning against it, breathless and grinning like a maniac, his hair wild and expression wholly untamed.

I made an honest effort to return his enthusiasm, but found myself much too consumed, leaning bodily against my wardrobe as I willed my heart to slow and my lungs to fill, the sudden madness of the chase still swirling my thoughts into a dizzying flurry incapable of manifesting into coherent speech.

I'd barely regained my balance when the silence was broken by a bout of hysterical laughter. I glanced over at Nye and found him a vision as he threw his head back in reckless glee, howling in mirth at our daring escape. I yearned to glower at him, berate him, accuse him of endangering my illustrious future once more, but in the moment our eyes met, any illusions of stern stoicism evaporated in the warmth of his delight. I began to laugh as well.

We laughed and laughed, gasping and staggering as we came together in a hearty embrace, the shared thrill of our adventure more intoxicating than the whiskey by far. He pulled me tightly to his chest and slapped me jovially upon the back.

"Well done, James. I always knew you were made of thicker stuff."

I returned his affections willingly, the proximity of his body to my own suddenly making me feel more unsteady than I had even moments before. As he pulled away, I was overtaken by the urge to hold him, which unfortunately manifested in me awkwardly clasping his hands in my own.

He stilled, staring down at where we were joined, the laughter dying in his throat. Then his gaze flicked up to meet mine, his sea-grey eyes dark and inquiring. I could not be certain what his question was, but I knew with all my being that my answer was yes.

And with that, he stepped forward and pressed his lips to mine.

The strangest thing was, it was not at all strange. Surely, that moment should have felt momentous and burdened with meaning and profound purpose, but instead it felt startlingly casual, effortless, and sure. Our lips slotted together naturally, as though they'd met a thousand times before, our movements intermingling in a soft, steady exchange.

Nye's lips were warm and his hands firm as he cupped my face to gently tilt it upward towards his. His tongue met mine without hesitation or fanfare, his every breath an echo of my own, as though we'd been moving in tandem from the moment we met and this newfound intimacy was simply a most natural extension, born of some divine inevitability.

Suddenly, Nye startled and pulled swiftly away, leaving me panting and dumbstruck before him, flushed and flustered and desperately unmoored. His expression was one of utter mortification.

"James, I'm so sorry, Christ, so sorry—I shouldn't have . . . I didn't mean to—"

Before I could doubt myself, I reached out and twisted my hands firmly into the lapels of his waistcoat, preventing any further retreat. When I spoke, my voice was low and commanding, leaving no room for interpretation.

"Don't stop. For the love of God, don't you dare stop."

And with that he was upon me once more, a tangled clash of tongues and teeth, his fingers threading through my hair as I pulled him helplessly closer to me. The world around us seemed to spin and dissolve.

I closed my eyes, and let go.

9.

A Complication

If I had previously thought that the delicate balance of
moral complexities my lifestyle in Edinburgh required
me to maintain were fraught, this fresh intimacy with
Nye added yet another layer of secrecy upon my already
burdened conscience. Though by day I played my role
of "dutiful academic" with diligence and devotion, it felt
more and more that the gentlemanly pursuits that filled
my time at the University were merely an inconvenient
distraction, distant and trivial, compared to the rush of
elation I experienced after nightfall. Lectures, no matter
how informative, paled in comparison to the dissections
at Malstrom's. And dissections at Malstrom's were no
match for the thrill of the dig. And the thrill of the dig
was all too soon forgotten once Nye and I were sequestered alone in my chamber thereafter.

As such, I was ill-prepared for the sudden drought in
correspondence which settled upon us during the first
fortnight of March. The nascent days of the month were

marked with snowfall (rendering clean snatches impossible), so I'd reluctantly resigned myself to a reprieve in nocturnal activity until the weather cleared. But a mere six days later, the dreary weather lifted and ushered in a series of crisp, moonlit nights: ideal snatching weather. Yet still, no summons came.

I did my best to hide my agitation each time I combed through my dissection tray with the fevered focus of a madman, searching in vain for any sign of that familiar summons: Tonight. More than once, I caught Charlie giving me quizzical stares from across the slab as I flustered and fretted, irritable and distracted as Malstrom's droning faded into the background of my preoccupied mind. My eyes were persistently drawn to where Nye was stationed at the back of the hall, elegantly composed and utterly oblivious as he busied himself with the maintenance of the lab. Though he would occasionally deign to offer me a vague, tight-lipped smile on the rare occasion he met my eye, for the most part, he remained remote and infuriatingly aloof. Even if there were no digs, I fretted, surely he missed my companionship as much as I missed his... unless his affections had already waned? I began to wonder if perhaps I was losing my mind, and he'd never taken anything but a passing interest in me in the first place—professionally or otherwise. The thought was abhorrent on a number of levels I felt ill-prepared to dissect.

By the end of the second week of silence, my nerves were frayed past any point of plausible denial. What was worse, I could not bring myself to conjure a believable excuse for my current malaise, which the lads at University unfortunately mistook as a slight. I felt deeply guilty about this, for they had been nothing but supportive of all my University endeavours; Phillip and Charlie had even gone so far as to nominate me as a speaker at the following month's RMS meeting in the hope of raising my spirits. Yet I'd turned down the offer in a fit of pique, and they'd been understandably resigned towards my disposition ever since.

It had been with heavy feet that I accompanied the two of them towards Surgeon's Square in the brittle winter sunlight for our class. The thought of enduring another interminable afternoon at Malstrom's gazing moon-eyed at my former companion while being summarily ignored was unpleasant in the utmost, and there was a persistent gnawing sensation in my abdomen that I resoundingly wished would go away.

"What is going on with you these days," Charlie muttered as I clumsily dropped my scalpel for the fifth time in as many minutes, nearly botching the delicate tonsillectomy that was our current assignment. Mercifully, Malstrom's back was turned, sparing him witness to my continued humiliation. "Used to think you were some sort of wizard, the way you wielded that thing. Now I'm not that confident standing next to you, to say nothing of the poor fellow lying on your slab. Promise me you'll warn me if you feel the sudden need to flail in my direction?"

His jab was good-natured, but his words still carried a bite. I wasn't used to floundering like a novice in the dissection lab; prior to my current mental state, my skills had continued to exceed even Malstrom's expectations. I was growing acutely aware that my reputation would be in serious peril if my performance over the last two weeks was any indication of my future as a surgeon, and the thought of losing my spot at the top of the class added to the growing anxiety mounting within me.

I took a deep breath, rolled my wrists, and reached back down to pry my specimen's mouth open. "It's nothing, honestly." I flinched as the tip of the scalpel grazed the uvula quite by accident, and I let out a rather uncharacteristic curse under my breath.

"James, mate." Charlie took a step away from his own specimen to move closer to me, allowing us to continue our conversation in low tones. "Whatever it is, you've got to get ahold of yourself. At some point, Malstrom's going to notice his golden boy's lost his luster, and then you'll have a steep mountain to climb to get back in his good graces. Believe me, I know." Charlie had had the misfortune of getting on Malstrom's bad side following an innocent mistake pertaining to an ocular incision a full month prior and was still the subject of many a withering glare from the master.

I nodded resolutely and willed my hands to steady, but at that very moment I had the uncanny sensation I was being watched. My eyes flicked up across the room to find Nye staring at Charlie and me, his searing gaze so brazen that I physically startled and stumbled back from my slab. The sudden motion jarred Charlie as well, who gave me a pointed look before backing away to resume his position beside his own cadaver.

That was the final straw. Straightening my spine, I summoned my courage and resolved to act. "You know, I think I need . . . I think I've done something to this scalpel. The handle's loose."

"Yes, I'd assume throwing it to the floor might do that to an instrument," Charlie quipped and ventured a good-natured wink at me over his shoulder as I rolled my eyes and turned to make my way deliberately across the hall.

Nye was standing behind the long counter at the back of the room, polishing several dozen pairs of surgical shears of varying lengths. His sleeves were rolled up casually to reveal his forearms, and his hair seemed even more disheveled than usual. I did my best to ignore on both counts.

Much to my chagrin, he was puttering about with a look of innocent disinterest upon his face, as though his pointed glare in my direction mere moments ago had simply been a figment of my imagination. But I refused to be fooled.

"Pardon me, Mr. MacKinnon."

His eyes darted up to meet mine, and he plastered his most placating smile upon his face. "Why, Mr. Willoughby! How may I help you?"

I raised my scalpel with a flourish. "I need a new scalpel. The handle on this one is loose."

"Is that so?" He extended his hand to receive the instrument, and I pointedly ignored the way my heart fluttered at the sight of his graceful fingers curling around the handle. I refused to demur in his presence under such circumstances.

He licked his lips pointedly and examined the tool, his expression a careful portrait of dignified professionalism. "Ah yes, right you are. Astutely observed, Mr. Willoughby, my sincerest apologies. Allow me to fetch you a replacement."

He turned to the cupboards to retrieve a large bin, which he deposited upon the counter between us with what appeared to me to be unnecessary force. Prying open the lid to reveal the heap of scalpels within, he proceeded to pick through them as if searching for the perfect fit amongst the seemingly identical items.

Was he buying time? Did he expect me to say something to him? No sooner had the panicked thought crossed my mind than I recalled that I was indeed over here to say something to him, though I couldn't for the life of me remember what, except that it was perhaps a rather rude accusation wholly inappropriate for our current setting.

"We need to talk." I whispered, bowing my head towards his as though I, too, were intent upon locating the holy grail of scalpels.

"Quite so." His fingers flicked nimbly through the dazzling array of blades, his eyes still lowered and his tone neutral.

"Quite so?" I hissed. "No word from you for nigh on two weeks, and all you can say is, quite so?" Perhaps I was being dramatic, but my temper was rapidly getting the better of me.

"There's been a . . . situation, of sorts. An unforeseen turn of events."

It took all of my willpower not to openly scoff at so flimsy an excuse. "I can think of several unforeseen turns of events in recent weeks, but I must confess I'm at a loss for which of them might necessitate your ignoring me entirely."

At last, his eyes met mine, if only for the briefest of instants. "It was for your safety."

Through a sneer, my retort was uncharacteristically harsh. "My safety? I know you to be a liar and a rogue, but this I've got to hear."

He appeared wholly unimpacted by my outburst. "Not here. Malstrom's office after class. Yes?"

Biting back an exasperated sigh, I acquiesced. "Yes."

"Excellent." With that he suddenly straightened, plucking a scalpel from the bin seemingly at random and proffered it to me. "Your sabre, sir."

I remained unamused and kept my response dry as I plucked it from his hand. "Thank you." I turned to return to my station.

"Oh, and Mr. Willoughby? Just a tip: it works best when you resist hurling it to the floor repeatedly."

Throwing caution to the wind, I tossed a rather crude gesture his way before stalking back to my place, glancing about for anyone who may have noticed his sly smile in my direction or the blooming blush upon my face.

Surprisingly, this short exchange did wonders to cure my nerves, despite the lack of conclusive answers derived from it. It would appear that simply the promise of attention from Nye was enough to steady my hands and sober my mind, and I was able to complete my tonsillectomy without further incident (and still finish before Charlie, much to his apparent chagrin). Malstrom dismissed the class shortly thereafter, and I made my excuses to Charlie as best I could while deflecting his continued inquiries into what business I could possibly need to conduct with Malstrom's assistant after hours; I was eventually forced to perjure myself in the interest of stifling his curiosities.

"If you must know," I uttered conspiratorially, "I'm being considered for an apprenticeship here." The lie was sour on my tongue, but regretfully unavoidable considering the circumstances.

Charlie's eyes grew wide at the prospect. "Are you serious? With Malstrom?"

"Shhh!" I hushed him vigorously and glanced around at the few straggling students still milling about the room completing the day's tasks. "It's not for certain yet."

"So that's why you've been acting so peculiar!" Charlie exhaled. "No wonder. Don't want to botch your big chance, eh? I'd be nervous too, mate. Still, that's fantastic—congratulations!" He seemed honestly glad for me, which only compounded my guilt over the falsehood.

I managed a meek smile. "Thanks. But if you don't mind, I really must . . ." I gestured vaguely towards Malstrom's office, where I knew Nye was undoubtedly waiting.

"Of course! Will you be at dinner tonight?"

I considered the prospect. There was a decent chance I'd be back at my lodgings before sundown, but I was secretly rather hoping to be otherwise detained with Nye after our lengthy separation. "Erm . . . not sure, sorry. I'll join if I can."

"Too grand for the likes of us already, eh?" Charlie grinned playfully as he donned his cap and shook his head in feigned exasperation. "Honestly, though, best of luck to you. You'll have to tell us everything as soon as you know for sure!"

"You know I will."

The odd twisting sensation in my stomach hadn't quite dissipated by the time I entered Malstrom's office, shutting the door behind me more out of habit than intent. I turned to find Nye busying himself over a stack of letters on the desk, which to my untrained eye he seemed to be shuffling entirely at random, but I elected not to press the point.

"Hello."

He stilled and met my eye. "Hello."

There was an infinite lull, in which my mind unhelpfully conjured the phantom sensation of his lips upon my own during our last encounter a fortnight past, and my cravat seemed suddenly unnaturally tight about my throat. Unthinkingly, I reached up to loosen it.

"How have you been?"

His voice, so familiar and foreign all at once, ignited an empty, lurching feeling deep inside me. How have I been? Miserable, mortified, sleepless and bereft, lovesick as a guileless maiden and angry as a scorned bride.

I shifted awkwardly in place. "Well enough. And you?"

He offered me a slow, wan smile, as if he could see clear through my skin and detect my inner turmoil. Gesturing towards the open chair, he extended an invitation. "Join me?"

A part of me wanted to remain haughty, indignant, and remote, to see if I could make him squirm and suffer under the oppression of uncertainty as I had done for the past two weeks. But I had not the heart for it, and I assumed the position with barely a beat of reluctance.

"Drink?"

"No, thank you."

Another pause. Nye fidgeted with the stack of letters, making undetectable adjustments to further square the corners. At last, he spoke.

"I do not wish to keep secrets from you, James, and I see now that, in the act of attempting to protect you, I have caused more distress than good. Please know it was not my intention to alarm you, though in retrospect my actions did little to prevent this."

"Your actions? What actions? You ignored me, disregarded and discarded me; it is your lack of actions to which I take offense." For the first time in my life, I felt the compelling need to assert myself fully and without compromise; for too long I had been at the mercy of the discretion of others and was in no mood to follow that pattern a moment longer.

"And for that the blame is solely my own, and I can offer little in the way of excuse that feels sufficient for the extent of my oversight. But I found our crew in a sudden, unexpected predicament, and I fear it's one that we are yet to be clear of. I wanted to come to you with answers, not mere warnings, yet I'm sorry to report that, as of now, I have none." I was startled to see him looking so browbeaten and weary; it was most uncharacteristic to his disposition and was undoubtedly cause for alarm.

"Warnings of what?"

"There is trouble brewing in the Underworld, James, and we Resurrectionists have found ourselves in the gory heart of it. You know that ours is one of many crews that operate within the boundaries of this city and its outskirts, do you not?"

"I do." Though I knew no other snatchers personally, it was clear that we were not the only game in town, considering the number of Anatomy Schools propped up about the Square, each promising fresh specimens to eager students.

"Lately, we have been the victims of a sudden incursion by a gang brought up from London, under the direction of a fellow named Crouch. We were initially unclear who had hired his mercenaries to intrude upon the soil of our city, but their actions were swift and fierce. Several crews found themselves cut out of their staked grounds, others were blackmailed or robbed of their quarries under the threat of violence. As for us, we are a small and private enterprise by comparison, so it was to our advantage to simply lie low and keep our methods to ourselves until the upheaval died down."

My pulse was racing in my temples at the thought. "But it hasn't?"

Nye rubbed his eyes, which I noted seemed more tired and hollow than usual. It was clear the stress of the situation had taken a great toll upon him, and it took considerable restraint to keep myself from offering immediate comfort. "Not in the way I had hoped. Many of the crews have capitulated to the gang's demands and are falling under their influence of power."

I furrowed my brow. "Why not just band together and refuse?"

Nye steepled his fingers under his chin. "Because when I say gang, James, I mean it; these are not merely a ragged group of snatchers gone bad. They are trained, organised, and efficient. They wield influence over local authorities, they have unlimited funds, and they have no mercy to offer those who resist them. Quite recently, a medical school in London attempted to cut ties with them for gouging the prices, and they responded by hacking every corpse in the school to bits, rendering them useless and bankrupting the institution."

I blinked in horror at the prospect. "That's abominable."

Nye shook his head in despair. "The fate of those bodies is better than that of some of our colleagues. Word is they've faced capture and torture, many emerging with broken fingers, burned brands, and sealed lips as souvenirs of their encounter."

"My God." I shuddered at the image of such a fate awaiting Nye or one of his men.

But he didn't stop there. "What's more, there are rumours afoot just this week that poor dear Daft Jamie, a member of the Cuthbert crew, found himself in over his head with Crouch's men and has since conveniently disappeared."

My mind suddenly conjured up a memory of a familiar face from Nicolson Street, just outside the Square: of a jolly, portly young beggar with a malformed foot, often singing and telling jokes for the amusement of the students who might spare him a few coins.

"Daft Jamie was a digger?" I could scarcely hide my incredulity.

"No, a lookout, but he's been on the job since he was scarcely old enough to talk." Nye pursed his lips, his brow furrowing over this latest revelation. "He's as embedded in the trade as any of us; if Crouch took aim at him, he's been emboldened indeed. I do not scare easily, James—one must have a steady confidence to compete in this nefarious game—but I must confess, these recent events have left me shaken indeed. This line of work was risky before, of course; there was always the possibility of gaol, or hard labour, or perhaps the occasional tussle with a rival gang. But this? This smacks of murder, and I cannot ignore the sensation that we are all caught in a net that is slowly closing in."

I resisted the urge to reach out and clasp his hand; the gesture felt too patronising in such a moment of vulnerability.

"So . . . what do you intend to do?"

He pursed his lips. "I intend to find a hole in the net and make sure we slip through it unscathed."

I furrowed my brow. "How?"

"So far? By keeping our heads down and our eyes and ears wide open. Fortunately, it seems most of Crouch's minions have retreated back South, though they've left a few spies in place to keep watch over things and make sure the new recruits stay in line. And thanks to my connections with reliable sources, I've been able to . . . trace that line, as it were."

"Trace it? Where?"

Nye looked me straight in the eye. "Straight to one Dr. Robert Knox."

I was stunned. Suddenly, echoes of Hamish's veiled warnings from that night at the pub several lifetimes ago reverberated through my mind; was this the threat to which he'd so casually alluded? "To Knox? But why would he want a crew of interlopers disrupting the trade?"

"As I told you before, he's an unscrupulous, greedy man who cares less of his own profits and more that others have none," Nye replied with a sneer. "This new alliance with Crouch is a deal with the devil, to be sure, but that's of no concern for a man with so wicked a soul. He's long been in a feud with the University proper, so a desire to monopolise their cadavers would hardly come as a surprise, but to cut out his fellow Anatomists as well? To wage war upon their diggers, even their lowly lookouts, and not just over their livelihoods but their very lives as well? The man is a snake. He's aimed to drag us all asunder no matter what the cost, but if he thinks our crew will go quietly, he's in for quite a shock."

I couldn't dismiss the look of firm determination on his face. "So . . . how will you outwit him?"

He exhaled, long and low, leaning back wearily in his chair. "For now? I've determined it's safe enough to carry on as we were while I look for confirmation of Knox's next move. We can resume digging this week, as the main battleground has been the kirkyard at Saint Cuthbert's; Greyfriars has been mercifully spared on account of its small size. Considering that we do not use a common method of egress, I believe we'll be hard to detect for those unsure where to look."

I offered a reassuring smile at this. "So that's . . . good, isn't it?"

To my relief, Nye returned my smile, though his eyes still seemed tainted with concern. "Yes. Good, for now. But I worry about what this means for the future of men like us. Knox is playing with fire here, and he seems to care not if he burns the world down with him. I can't stand by idly and watch this city's most promising schools be reduced to ash over one man's pride."

"And so that is what has preoccupied you so? I wish you'd simply have trusted me, Nye. You should know by now it would take more than this to scare me off."

He leaned forward suddenly, his expression transforming to one of earnest sincerity, hands clasped dutifully before him. "James, I need to . . . I must make something clear."

A swell of trepidation rose up inside me, which I did my best to temper. "Go on."

"In our conversation earlier, you accused me of being a liar and a rogue—"

"I merely meant—"

But he held up his finger in protest, and the words died on my lips. "Let me finish, please. I will be the first to admit to you that, in a professional capacity, yes, I am both of those things and, quite honestly, worse, but they are traits required of my vocation. I do not find them admirable qualities, but I also do not find them disdainful enough to dissuade me from what I believe to be my calling, which is to aid in the advancement of medical science for the benefit of all mankind."

I nodded solemnly in agreement; he and I were kindred spirits in this respect.

"But in matters of a personal capacity, I must urgently impress upon you that I endeavour to conduct myself as a man of honour. I have no desire to inflict pain upon your sentiments or shame upon your pride. My intentions towards you are born of deepest affection, and they were never—and will never—be otherwise. Do you understand?"

My cheeks felt red-hot with so personal a revelation, and I could only offer a small nod in response, such was my surprise at his sudden declaration. Gone was Nye's perpetual air of mischief and whimsy, suddenly replaced by a visceral vulnerability that struck me to my core.

"In that case, should you wish to continue our . . . companionship, I must know that you are not uncertain of my motives in regards to you and your personal well-being. I, of course, would not admonish you for questioning my methods as your colleague, for in that regard I am quite without scruples and often in need of a check; but if we are to be companions, James, we must trust one another in at least that much."

I willed myself to speak through the tide of emotion ebbing within me at this unexpected proclamation. "Yes. Yes, Nye. I can trust you. I will."

The relief that radiated from his face was all but palpable. "And I, you."

I grinned. "Good."

He grinned back. "Good."

I cleared my throat. "So. Will that be all, Mr. MacKinnon?"

He paused for a moment, appearing deep in thought. At last, he spoke again. "Yesterday I extracted the most enlarged spleen I've ever seen. Would you care to see it, Mr. Willoughby?"

I was instantly invested. "Please."

"Right this way."

Despite our frequent associations on digs and at the Pig, Nye and I had spent little time together in Malstrom's laboratory since my disastrous introduction to the place. Aside from brief forays inside to deposit The Beast the morning after a snatch, I'd not lain eyes on it with any degree of scrutiny in weeks.

It remained largely unchanged, though the cast of characters deposited upon the dissection slabs had been predictably refreshed (though their degree of macabre mutilation, I quickly noted, had not). Nye ushered me excitedly across the room to the specimen shelves and plucked a large jar from one before depositing it upon the desk in front of me with a flourish.

I gazed in amazement. "That's a spleen?" It hardly seemed feasible; the organ was at least three times the standard size.

"Indeed!" Nye was unable to disguise his enthusiasm. "Malstrom believes the swelling was a result of infection, but here's the curious bit: the only other organ to be impacted was the heart."

I shot him a skeptical look. "But . . . there's no connection between the two. They're part of entirely different systems."

"Precisely! It's a total mystery. Malstrom is thrilled."

"Is the heart enlarged to the same degree?"

"Not quite, sadly, though the affliction is noticeable."

"May I see it?"

There was an astute pause, and I was startled to see a flush of colour bloom upon Nye's cheeks. "It's. Well, it's . . . in my chambers."

I blinked. "And your chambers are . . ." Strangely, it had never occurred to me to ask where Nye lived. For some reason, I could not imagine him doing things as mundane as eating or sleeping on his own; he appeared to me a character in perpetual motion, and the thought of him in a domestic habitat was foreign to me.

"Just upstairs." His eyes shifted downwards in a gesture that ought to have seemed demure, but instead appeared to me downright calculating.

I bit back a smile at his coy display. "Is that a formal invitation?"

"If you'd . . . like it to be."

"Indeed, I would."

Nye cleared his throat. "Then if you'll just . . . follow me . . ." His sudden bout of bashfulness was endlessly endearing, and I felt emboldened in my newfound assertiveness.

I followed him up the spiral stair at the back of the laboratory into a loft overlooking the hall which appeared to serve a second office for Malstrom, this one dedicated to the more sensitive materials that would be frowned upon in his proper, outward-facing study. There were illustrations of the grisliest nature scattered haphazardly about, more stacks of jars containing odd and noteworthy specimens, and a dazzling array of surgical instruments the likes of which I'd never before seen and whose usage made me feel quite light-headed to contemplate.

"This way." Nye's voice interrupted my distraction, and I turned to watch as he pulled a rope adjoined to a hatch in the ceiling, revealing within it a retractable ladder which he extended to its full height. "Apologies, I realise it's a bit . . . undignified, but—"

"I'd expect nothing less," I quipped as I brushed past him and ascended as gracefully as I could (which wasn't saying much); I felt undeniably awkward in such a position, but my self-consciousness was swiftly forgotten as I properly took in my surroundings for the first time.

The hatchway had opened up into a lofty, airy attic space in which soaring wooden beams vaulted up to a high ceiling above. Though the few windows were small, the sheer height of the room made it feel near-cavernous in size, and the space felt warm and dry despite the singular diminutive fireplace. The furnishings were sparse: a bed, a rickety dining table surrounded by three mismatched chairs, an ancient-looking wardrobe and vanity of similar styles, and a crude bench upon which were perched a kettle, a pot, and a few utensils. A large desk was positioned nearest the western window, outfitted with a predictable array of ink, quills, and sealing wax.

But what drew my gaze above all was the ornamentation. For upon every accessible inch of the towering walls were displayed a wild and wonderful array of oddities the likes of which I had never before seen. There were skeletons of various exotic creatures affixed to oaken backboards and strung in wild mobiles dangling from the rafters, shelves laden with domed jars displaying a marvelous array of taxidermied wildlife, framed display cases of insects and foreign botanicals. Alongside these were stacks upon stacks of books, dusty and dated but clearly well-used. And upon every inch of space not occupied by a shelf was displayed a brilliant array of the most gorgeous anatomical drawings I had ever seen; they were so exquisite my breath caught in my throat as I hastily approached one, utterly mesmerized, my eyes eager to drink in the beauty before me.

It was an illustration of a skull: standard enough, by normal accounts. But labeling each element was an elegant, ornate calligraphy I more often associated with medieval manuscripts than anatomical manuals. The lettering, gilded and aureate, was positioned so as to echo the curvature of the bones, and was festooned with woven knots of vibrant ink. The overall effect rendered the scene into a stunning work of art, and I was dumbfounded by its beauty, struck mute in wonderment.

I made my way slowly around the perimeter of the room, gaping unrepentantly at each illustration in turn. There were manuals of the eye, the brain, the circulatory and skeletal systems, each one more disarmingly exquisite than the last. I was wholly transfixed, and it was not until I'd nearly traversed the circumference of the room and came to stand before the desk that I discerned what lay upon it: a work in progress of the heart, half-rendered but still staggering in its impact.

I stared awestruck before gathering my bearings enough to whirl about and face Nye, who was hovering shyly by the fireplace, a look of earnest trepidation upon his face.

"These illustrations . . . they're yours?"

"Yes." He slowly approached and came to stand behind me as I turned back towards the work upon his desk, dimly registering the jar sitting upon it containing a peculiarly enlarged heart, which was apparently serving as the model for his latest work.

"They're . . . Nye, these are incredible."

He let out a huff of apparent satisfaction and peered over my shoulder. "Thank you. They're not much, just a hobby."

I reached out to trace the edges of the parchment before me, so delicate beneath my fingers I scarcely dared breathe. "You could illustrate manuals, you know."

"Mmm." His affirmation sounded wistful, distant. "Maybe someday."

My eyes wandered to the lettering, of so distinct a style that it nearly threatened to upstage the organ it described. "Where did you learn to do this?"

He leaned over my shoulder, and I could feel his breath warm against my neck. "The isle I am from—Iona? It is the seat of Christian artistry of this type. The very birthplace of the Book of Kells, perhaps our only claim to fame."

I ventured a glance sideways to look at him, his face distractingly close to my own. "And you studied this there?"

"For a spell, yes. I was destined to be a butcher, but I once considered relinquishing my duty as a firstborn son to join the Church."

I paused to contemplate this. "What happened?"

"For some bizarre reason, it didn't stick. Can't imagine why."

I snorted at his cavalier dismissal, and he took the opportunity to wrap his arms fully around my waist, pulling me back against the flat planes of his chest as he pressed a soft kiss to the nape of my neck. It was as if he had ignited my very blood, and the rush of heat that descended upon me made my knees feel weak.

"I can't believe you never showed me this before."

"Wasn't—sure—you'd like—my other—decorations." He punctuated each pause in the sentence with a press of his lips against the exposed column of my neck, and his fingers rose to begin unfastening my cravat.

"You mean all the bones and bugs and dead bits?" I asked, struggling to keep my breath steady despite his ministrations. A nip of his teeth against my earlobe sent my hands flying forward to grip the edge of his desk, and my eyes fluttered shut.

"Mmm. I realise it's a bit unconventional, but—"

"From you? I'd expect nothing less." This resolution spoken, I whirled to face him and drew his lips to mine at last.

* * *

"I've made a decision." My voice was muzzy, words slurred with satiated fatigue.

"And what's that?"

"I like your chambers."

"Oh you do, do you?"

"Indeed. You have the loveliest blankets." I was nestled under several layers of warm, soft tartan wool, feeling cozier and more content than I had in recent memory. "I can't believe we've wasted so many nights at the H&A when you had all this to offer!"

"By all this, I must assume you mean bat skeletons and beetle carcasses."

I tilted my head to gaze up at him as best I could from our reclined position. "Obviously. What else would I be referring to?"

Nye laughed at that and continued carding his fingers through my hair, where I distantly noted he was tracing the approximate location of the fissures of my cranial plates.

"Are you analysing the anatomy of my skull?" I was so content, I could barely bring myself to be indignant.

"Don't be ridiculous. I'm taking measurements to see if the skin of your forehead could be tanned and bound into a pocketbook."

I swatted half-heartedly at his shoulder. "You're a mad man, you know that."

"You're the one in bed with me."

I sighed, the cavernous space above us feeling distant and blurry. I felt boneless and utterly at peace. "Tell me something about yourself," I murmured. "Something I don't know."

"You think I'm that mysterious?" He quirked an eyebrow.

"I think you're that surprising."

"And yet you wish to be surprised upon command, which I'd say quite negates the point."

The edges of my lips turned up despite Nye's obstinacy, and I endeavoured to clarify my request. "Tell me something of your childhood."

"Like what?"

"Like . . ." I searched my vaults of memory for a suitable example. "I am the youngest of four siblings. Two brothers, and a sister."

"Hmm." Nye's response was neutral.

I pressed on. "I was first designated for military life and, upon failing at that, for the clergy and, upon failing at that, for medical school, and have since been redirected to a life of business with the East India Company. I am in dereliction of my apprenticeship there as we speak."

Nye snorted in apparent surprise. "So that's why your family keeps summoning you?"

"Indeed. As much as I'd like to believe they greatly miss my dazzling charisma and invaluable company, I fear they're more concerned with ensuring my future as a gentleman of means, upholding the family name."

"Hmm."

"Your turn."

Nye pondered for a moment. "English wasn't my first language."

"Really?" Once again, I found myself floored. I'd heard accounts of foreign speakers in the furthest western isles, but had never dreamed I'd meet one.

"On the island, we all spoke English in town on account of the pilgrims and outlanders, but in my house, I learned the Gaelic tongue first."

"Do you recall any of it?"

"Some."

"Say something."

"Tha gaol agam ort, mò chridhe."

"Pretty. What's the meaning?"

"Your forehead would make a lovely pocketbook."

I groaned and punched him squarely in the arm, and he snickered at his own jest.

"Alright, you arse. Teach me to say something," I implored impishly.

He grinned. "Try this: Mac Fhionghuin."

My mouth twisted and slipped treacherously over the guttural consonants, and Nye laughed jovially at my failed attempt.

"Very funny. What does this one mean?"

He paused for a moment. "It's my name."

I startled. "Your name's not MacKinnon?" Once again, Nye had managed to catch me completely unawares with another of his seemingly endless casual revelations.

"Well, in English it is. But to me, it's Mac Fhionghuin."

I tried once more to repeat it, the rolling singsong of foreign syllables that sounded so effortless in Nye's low brogue somehow stilted and halting in my own.

"You're being too shy with the consonants," he scolded, amusement painted upon his soft features.

"You've got to let them move." He paused to consider this. "I know: say it again, but this time do it like my tongue is in your mouth."

"Nye!" I was simultaneously scandalised and charmed by his brazen vulgarity, which left me entirely vulnerable to his next attack, rolling me bodily onto my back to brace himself over me. I laughed and fought back half-heartedly, but he remained unmoved.

"I think I ought to give you a brief refresher, purely for pronunciation purposes . . ."

Once more, the world stretched and contorted, soft and hazy, a sweet surrender more profound than oblivion.

10.
An Intermission

"Hot pie?"

"What?" I could scarcely hear Nye over the din in the main barroom at the Pig. It was unusually crowded that night, overflowing with a rowdy band of sailors on shore leave who appeared to have wandered in more out of happenstance than any calculated desire to have a drink in the blissful anonymity which the habitual purveyors of the Pig so resolutely prided themselves in preserving. We'd only managed to secure a table when one particularly inebriated seaman passed out beneath it (and I did my best to disguise my disgust as Nye casually rolled the man over and propped him up beside the fireplace, wholly at the mercy of his cohorts), and I was beginning to regret ever agreeing to tag along to this meeting in the first place.

"I said, hot pie?" Nye gesticulated animatedly in the direction of the large, portly woman currently stationed beside our table, looming over us with a gaze I feared was intended to be hospitable but, due to her lack of teeth, was more menacing than anything else. Propped beneath her generous bosom was a shallow wooden box affixed to a strap which fastened about her neck, and I finally registered that she was selling the item in question.

"Erm, no thank you," I shouted back.

Nye shrugged good-naturedly. "Your loss." He gave the portly woman his most winning smile. "Two for me, please."

With another gummy grin, she procured two steaming pies from the box with her bare hands and plopped them down straight on the table in front of Nye. It took all my willpower not to shudder at the thought of what gruesome grime the bottoms of the pies were now in unholy communion with.

Nye, entirely unaffected, procured a coin and thanked her profusely, and she disappeared into the crowd.

"Not hungry?" He plucked up a pie and took a generous bite, and I was forced to admit that the wafting scent of a hearty gravy was actually quite tempting indeed. My stomach grumbled in consensus, incensed that I was once again diving into the whiskey without a proper dinner first.

"No, I'm . . . I'm fine." I pointedly looked away from the crispy flake of pastry stuck to Nye's lower lip.

"Bollocks. Try a bite, won't you?" He extended the pie in my direction.

"What kind is it?"

"Steak and kidney." He sounded oddly sarcastic.

"Why do you say it like that?"

"Well, the butcher's from the Vaults, so . . ."

"So, as likely, rat and tail."

Nye rolled his eyes in agreement. "Whatever it is, it's delicious—May's pies are the best in Old Town. Come on; try a bite." He dangled the pie tantalisingly before me, and my willpower could no longer withstand the temptation. I leaned forward and took a measured nibble.

He observed my reaction with barely disguised glee.

"My God, that's delicious." It truly was—the pastry was decadently buttery yet hearty, enveloping the most savoury, tender meat I'd ever tasted. It was salty but flavourful and perfectly balanced, and I leaned back in for a second mouthful before Nye could withdraw the offer.

"See? I told you rat was tasty."

My mouth was still too full to retort when out of the crowd emerged a windswept, harried-looking Mary Paterson. Her auburn locks were wicked with rain and her nose red-tipped from the cold, but she still looked more gorgeous than ever, and the eyes of the surrounding sailors trained after her as she approached our table.

"Ah, there's our girl!" Nye sprung to his feet, pie still in hand, and somehow managed to sweep Mary into his arms and give her a twirl without spilling so much as a drop of gravy. She laughed uproariously at this greeting, her expression instantly transforming from one of distinct harassment to one of extraordinary fondness. I observed the eyes of the surrounding sailors narrowing in jealousy at the display, but felt no such malevolence myself; ever since Nye had adamantly reassured me that his affections towards Mary were not of a romantic nature, I found their friendship most endearing. Mary was a true gem: witty, cunning, more than a bit cheeky, a vibrant, joyful soul who left my former resentment of her perplexing to my present self (though it rarely hurt that Nye often took extra care to reassure me of the true nature of his affections following our meetings with her).

"How are you this evening, love? Fancy a pie?" He held up the half-eaten fare with a flourish.

"I fear thirst far outweighs my hunger for now. I've had the most dreadful day."

Nye pulled out the spare chair and ushered her chivalrously into it. "Then be seated, m'lady, and I'll procure you a dram! James? Anything for you?"

"I'd settle for the last half of that pie."

Nye groaned but handed it over. "I've created a monster."

I grinned and indulged in another delicious bite as he winked and elbowed his way through the crowd towards the bar.

"James, how've you been, lovie? Besides half-starved, from the looks of it." Mary seemed pointedly amused at the rate at which I was scoffing my dinner.

"Sorry," I muttered through a mouthful of pastry as I attempted to chew the last bite as quickly as possible. "Have you tried these pies? Nye bought them from a woman named May, though I'm inclined to believe she may have been an angel in disguise, if this pie is any indication."

Mary threw back her head and howled with laughter. "Christ, I know May, darling, and trust me, she's no angel—though I'll admit she's got a real gift for pies. Her husband runs a butcher shop smuggling in contraband horsemeat from Ireland."

I choked a bit and took a hearty swill of whiskey. "I'm sorry, horse, you said?"

Mary looked pensive for a moment. "I mean, the meat was either horse or peasant child, though right now I can't seem to recall which—"

"Oh, spare me." I groaned as she cackled at her own jest, divesting herself of her cloak and rubbing the warmth back into her hands. "Long day, you said?"

"Ach, and a discouraging one, I'm afraid. I hate being the bearer of bad news for you boys, but these days, with the trade being what it is, I fear I never hear anything but."

I leaned forward to clasp her hands in mine encouragingly, startled to find them ice-cold from the weather—Mary exuded such warmth at all times, I occasionally forgot that she was real flesh and blood, susceptible to the inclement elements of Edinburgh the same as anyone else. "Well, if it's any consolation, hearing bad news from you always makes it sound better."

She smiled at that. "Thanks, James. That's sweet of you to say."

"Oy! Willoughby! Are you attempting to make an adventuress of m'lady?" Nye slapped down the two drams of whiskey upon the table in faux indignation.

Mary leaned back in her chair with a practiced swagger, crossing her arms and cocking her head. "I'm hardly the type to be tempted by the likes of either of you blades—what sort of girl do you take me for? You should know by now my taste in men is far worse than what you lot have on offer."

Nye barked out a laugh at that, but he did discretely comb his fingers through the hair at the nape of my neck as he settled into his seat beside me before promptly withdrawing his hand to pick up the spare pie. The gesture was subtle enough that a casual onlooker would be none the wiser, but I did notice a sly smile tug at the edges of Mary's lips as she gave the two of us a fond appraisal, and I could feel a flush spread in my cheeks, an uncanny combination of embarrassment and pride at the thought of her discerning gaze.

"So, my dearest,' Nye continued. 'What news?"

Mary sighed and drained a full glass in a single swill before pulling the second towards her; Nye didn't bat an eye at her rapaciousness, and I had learned well enough that Mary could outdrink us both (any preconceived notions I'd had about the fragile sensibilities of women who imbibed had been thoroughly disproved the first time I'd watched in astonishment as she downed six brimming glasses before taking her leave, her gait as steady as a vicar's upon her departure).

"More of the same on my end, I fear. All the local crews have been cut out of Cuthbert's save for those reporting to Knox, and New Calton reports more of the same."

Nye shook his head in clear distress. "Any word on Daft Jamie's whereabouts?"

"I'm afraid not. I shudder to think of what's become of the poor lad. His mother hasn't slept since he's been gone, offering the few shillings she has as a reward for any news—but every man bearing Crouch's brand has kept his lips sealed." To my surprise and earnest distress, her eyes welled up with tears. "Jamie was such an honest soul; the boy wouldn't hurt a fly! Why, he saved my skin five times over with alibis when I was recognised at funerals—and to no gain of his own. He believed in honour amongst thieves; he'd never cause trouble intentionally! What quarrel could Crouch have with him?" Nye plucked out a kerchief to offer her, which she promptly refused, settling instead for wiping her face with the hem of her sleeve.

Sighing, Nye pocketed the square of linen and soldiered on. "I suspect it wasn't Crouch's quarrel at all: it was Knox's."

Mary shook her head, sniffling indignantly. "But why would a surgeon want a petty lookout dead? It makes no sense!"

"The best I can tell? Jamie found out something he shouldn't. Whatever Knox's end game is, it's about more than just cowing rival crews into complacency. I doubt Jamie was looking for trouble; it just happened to find him."

Mary shook her head woefully. "It's bad business all around, lads, and I fear it's only a matter of time before Knox's men centre their target on you."

Nye popped the last bite of pie into his mouth and licked his fingers (I could not will my eyes to avoid this display, resulting in my momentary distraction; fortunately, Nye ceased his ministrations before my hypnosis was complete, reeling me back to business). "But they haven't thus far. We're a small operation, Mary; surely they don't need every corpse in Edinburgh upon their infernal slabs."

Mary took another hearty pull from her glass. "What worries me, Nye, is that that hardly seems to be the point; Knox has made this about power, not prosperity. He's still slighted by the snub from the University last year, and rumour has it his lectures have become increasingly critical of both the University and his fellow independent anatomists alike. It's only a matter of time before he sets his sights on your school."

Nye paused to ponder this. "So what, then, would you have us do?"

Mary clasped her fingers tightly around her glass. "Hell if I know, love. Malstrom's living on borrowed time as it sits."

"And you've no more leads on Knox's next move?"

"I'm close enough to the danger as is. To a crowd of mourners, I can blend in as a pretty, innocent afterthought. But to a gang of professional thieves? I've got red hair and a fair face, sweetheart. I'm rather hard to forget." Sorrow receding to mute resignation, she settled back in her chair, and I was regrettably forced to agree with her conclusion; as vital as she was as a spy for our crew, her notable beauty made her ill-suited to blend in.

The wheels were turning inside my own head. Though I ordinarily deferred to Nye in all professional matters, I suddenly had a proposal of my own.

"What if . . . what if I could get us in on the action with Knox?"

Mary raised her eyebrows. Nye shot me a suspicious glance. "How so?"

I rushed to formulate my plan. "I'm well acquainted with Hamish, who is employed as one of Knox's assistants." (I pointedly avoided using the word friend to describe my relationship with him, as ours was still strained, at best). "He's mentioned two of Knox's snatchers—Burke and Hare? Apparently they're churning out the best quarries Hamish has ever seen, and Knox is paying a pretty penny for the prize."

Nye's looked incredulous. "Burke and Hare, you say? Never heard of them. Mary?"

"Afraid not," she replied with a bewildered shrug.

Nye paused, and I could see the gears turning inside his head. "Odd, isn't it? We know every crew in this city—their turf, their men, their means—yet these two appear out of nowhere with unlimited quarries pristine enough to catch the eye of the one man vying for monopoly of the trade?"

"Perhaps they're from Crouch's crew?" Mary posited skeptically.

"Unlikely. Crouch's men were merely a gang of mercenaries for hire, all threats and muscle; they hadn't the finesse of snatchers themselves. There's no way a pair of Outlanders could slip invisibly into the folds of our trade without their competitors taking note."

Mary tipped her head. "Then I agree; it's odd indeed. But what can be done about it?"

Nye drummed his fingers upon the tabletop, chewing his lip in thought. "Burke and Hare. We need to know more."

A plot was rapidly taking shape inside my mind, so mad and risky I'd never have mentioned it if I were not so desperate to help my dear friends out of their present conundrum. Before I could censor myself, I ventured forward. "What if . . . if I were to approach Hamish, beg for a favour, ask that he bring me in on the racket; perhaps he'd be willing to introduce me to Burke and

Hare's crew of diggers? From there, I could assess their plots, motives, and future stakes—and give you fair warning if you found yourself targeted by them."

Nye steepled his fingers, brow furrowed in thought. "But to what end, James? If you get caught up with the likes of Knox's men, there's no sure way of extricating yourself."

"I'll simply give Hamish the same tale of woe I gave you: that I need enough money to finish the term and pay off my debts, I'm willing to take the blame in the case of a failed operation, and my family ties are surely sufficient to mortgage my risk in the game. Make it clear my lot is a temporary state, though admittedly a desperate one."

Mary downed the last of her whiskey and raised the empty glass in my direction. "That's a fine fair idea, love. You'd make more headway with these unscrupulous gents than I ever could. You've got the face of a cherub and the name of a noble—a rather irresistible combination, wouldn't you say, Nye?"

Nye shot her a wry look before turning back to me. "You really think Hamish would cut you in with Knox's prime suppliers?"

I shrugged. "No idea. But it's worth a try, isn't it? Far better than languishing here, griping over our misfortune and leaving our fate to the wind, as we've done the past three sennight."

Mary eyed me shrewdly. "Well put, James." She turned her attention to Nye. "He's right, love. We've got to try a different approach; I can't simply waltz around the outskirts of a criminal enterprise on a weekly basis and expect to remain unnoticed. I've got a suspicion that a few of Knox's men already have sights on me. James would be a far less conspicuous target."

Nye nodded slowly, locking eyes with mine; I remained utterly resolute in my determination to offer myself as our saving grace and offered a solemn nod in return. "Well then. Another drink to toast our new fortune?"

"Aye," Mary replied. "To our fortune, indeed." I tried not to notice the fear in her eyes.

*   *   *

To his credit, one of Hamish's most admirable qualities was his steadfast reliability. Perhaps not in matters of professionalism; of that element of his life, I was quite ignorant indeed. But any moment he wasn't in service of Dr. Robert Knox, one could count on Hamish to be posted up in his booth at the H&A, holding court over the throngs of admiring students from the University who came by to hear his stories or gawp at the specimens he lifted from the lab with his perpetually sticky fingers. In exchange for this entertainment, he accepted drinks of any sort, and as a result, I rarely saw him short of five pints in, regardless of the day of the week.

While his pompous attitude and voyeuristic indulgences had long rubbed me the wrong way, I was eternally grateful for both as I joined my peers for dinner the following night, during which we predictably found ourselves pulled into Hamish's theatrical orbit as he recounted a particularly macabre dissection he'd witnessed earlier.

"The laceration had punctured the stomach, you see," he whispered conspiratorially over a row of empty pint glasses. "And the poor lad had been none the wiser! By the time he realised his predicament, he was vomiting blood by the bucket-load. Ghastly scene, honestly. Shame Knox couldn't do anything for him, but the extraction of the gut was sublime."

"Christ, mate, that's dark." Phillip pounded the last of his drink and wiped his mouth with his sleeve; it was clear my companions had all been imbibing for some time, but for once, I was grateful they had Hamish amongst their ranks.

"Anyone up for some cards in my chambers?" Charlie offered.

"Don't be such a stiff! Stay and have another, lads." Hamish implored (I was observant enough to know he truly meant, 'Buy me another,' but this time I held my tongue).

"Nah, I ought to call it," Phillip sighed in resignation. "We've got an oral exam in botany tomorrow; can't risk a bottle-ache."

He and Charlie rose and turned to look at me expectantly. And for good reason: I was often the most outspokenly studious amongst us (though, as of late, most of my excuses pertaining to "studying" or "the library" were code for something else entirely, though my peers were fortunately none the wiser).

"Erm, I'm actually . . . You know, I think I'll stay for one more. What'll it be, Hamish? Ale?"

Hamish looked as startled as Phillip and Charlie were, whether as a result of my shirking academic responsibility or my willingness to remain in his company alone. Regardless, he merely nodded and settled lazily back in the booth, propping his boots rudely on the spare seat.

"Right then." I turned to Phillip and Charlie. "See you in the morning?"

"Sure . . ." Charlie gave me another odd look as he and Phillip took their leave. I knew my behaviour was undeniably uncharacteristic, but I'd have plenty of time to conjure up an excuse before class tomorrow, I reasoned.

Returning with two foaming pints, I shoved Hamish's foot off the bench with my own and settled in, sliding my offering across the sticky wood surface of the table. Hamish, eyes glassy, peered at me accusatorially.

"What do you want, Willoughby?"

I was admittedly startled; I'd rather hoped for a more informal transition into my request, but it appeared Hamish had no illusions about my motives.

"I was wondering . . . If maybe . . . It's, well, it's a sensitive topic, you see." I attempted to conjure an aura of embarrassed humility, befitting a nobleman fallen from favour.

Hamish's eyes narrowed. "Go on, then."

"I find myself rather urgently in need of employment."

Hamish rolled his eyes and took a gulp of his ale. "Sorry, mate, I've told you before: Knox is full up at the school."

I took a steadying breath. "I don't mean at the school. I mean in the kirkyards."

Hamish stilled, pint still halfway to his lips. He blinked. I took internal pleasure at having caught him off guard.

"And what does a toff like you know of the goings-on in the kirkyards?"

I leveled my gaze. "Enough to know there's fast money to be made. And I need money. It's . . . quite urgent."

He pursed his lips. "Get it from your family, like any normal blue-blood."

"It's not that simple. It's just . . . I've accrued some debts. Debts which . . . about which I cannot tell my family."

A sly, self-satisfied smile crept over Hamish's smug face. "Ooh, naughty naughty, Willoughby. What is it? Dice? Dens? Women?" He seemed utterly delighted at my humiliation, and it took all my willpower not to counter him.

"Some ill-advised gambling upon a boxing match, if you must know."

He didn't bother to disguise his disappointment that I was not secretly a womanizing drug fiend. "Oh. How much do you need?"

I tabulated a wild calculation. "Twenty pounds." It was a solid number, I reasoned; high enough that it wasn't something I could easily swing from a gentleman scholar's allowance, yet not so high I'd be indentured to Knox and his crew forever.

Hamish let out a low whistle. "Hell of a boxing match, Willoughby."

I shrugged. "Like I said, it was ill-advised. So, can you help? I've tried more respectable avenues of income, but it's mid-term, and none of the laboratories are hiring."

Hamish traced his finger lazily around the rim of his half-full pint, peering intently at the froth settling slowly down the sides. "We don't need diggers; our rolls are full-up, thanks to Knox's powers of persuasion. But we do need transporters."

I paused. "Transporters?"

"Young men, University students if possible, well-dressed and well-groomed, to move the product to the Square without attracting the attention of the law or ire of the University."

I swallowed. "What would it entail?"

"It's easy work, if you're willing to do it. I'll introduce you to our supplier, and they'll determine your schedule from there."

"Burke and Hare?" I asked, perhaps a bit more earnestly that I ought.

Hamish shot me a suspicious look. "How do you know about Burke and Hare?"

I shrugged, playing it off as casually as I could muster. "You mentioned them one night while we were drinking, that they were on Knox's payroll, et cetera. I just . . . put two and two together, as it were."

Hamish still appeared guarded, but, to my relief, he didn't rescind his offer. "Cleverer than you seem, aren't you? I admit I underestimated you, Willoughby; I had you pegged for the type to believe their school specimens appeared out of thin air as some sort of benevolent act of God."

I laughed at this, determined to play up any budding comradery. "I admit I was naïve at first, but trust me, Hamish; I've no illusions about this business. I'm eager for a cut, and I need it fast."

To my relief, Hamish grinned. It appeared that greed was the common tongue he spoke. "Well spotted, toff-boy. There's a fair killing to be made in this trade, for those with the stomachs for it." He took another swig of drink, and I resolutely tamped down the uneasy tightening in my chest. "To answer your query, yes, your supplier will be Burke and Hare, of Tanner's Close. They're the best in the business and Knox's prized pets, so you'll get a fair deal from them. When they have product to move, they'll contact you, and you'll see it safely to Knox's lab. Your status is your cover; Dr. Knox has made an arrangement with law enforcement not to question gentlemen of high station in the vicinity of his practice." I shuddered at the recollection of the methods Nye mentioned Crouch's gang had used to persuade the magistrates to agree to such a measure.

I banished all trepidation from my response. "Very well. And the pay? By the delivery?"

Hamish nodded his head. "Aye. The more product you run, the more you make."

"And no contract? I must be clear here, Hamish. I've no desire to become involved in this sordid business permanently; I merely need to settle my debt and return my focus to my academics."

His smile was dangerously close to a sneer. "'Course, toff-boy. Wouldn't expect anything less from the likes of you."

I gave him a sarcastic grin. "Excellent. So when do I start?"

"Tomorrow night. The White Hart Inn. I'll make your acquaintance there."

"Very well, then." I rose to my feet, pushing my still-full pint towards Hamish, who snapped it up without hesitation. "Until tomorrow, Hamish."

"Until tomorrow, toff-boy."

* * *

The White Hart Inn proved to be much the same as every other High Street pub in Old Town. A mere five-minute walk from the H&A (if I cut through the kirkyard), it boasted a nearly identical dark oak bar, low-beamed ceiling, and wide assortment of clientele, ranging from weary travellers to thirsty University students to the common, haggard labourers looking to spend a day's wages in a reputable haunt. The scene was coarse but familiar, and I found myself immediately at ease, relieved that, for once, I wasn't floundering entirely out of my depths in my latest escapade.

I had just commenced a subtle scan of the room in search of Hamish when a gruff clap upon my back startled me quite severely.

"What ho, toff-boy. Where the hell's your drink? They'll think you're a bloody snitch."

"Hello, Hamish," I replied wearily, already irritated with his petulant swagger. "I was merely displaying some manners by awaiting my companion, or am I mistaken that you'd accept a pint yourself?"

"Aye, that's the spirit. Order us a drink, and I'll see if the suppliers are here."

I obediently procured the ale and then made my way across the tavern to where I'd observed Hamish in animated conversation with two men seated at a table with their backs to me. I deposited the pints upon the surface, pulled up a spare chair, and settled into a seat across from my newest colleagues.

It took the span of a mere moment for me to realise that I was not in the presence of gentlemen. The men facing me were at least ten years my senior and the very definition of rough, with unkempt hair, darned clothing, and cracked-lipped grins that displayed rows of dismayingly discoloured teeth. The one on the left had a mawkish, hollow look to him, with a slender, angular nose, a prominent brow, and a dead-eyed stare that caused an odd pit to clench in the region of my stomach. The fellow to his right was marginally more favourable to behold, but the rounded boyishness of his face was near thoroughly offset by his stocky, imposing frame. His weathered hands, currently wrapped around the neck of his pint, were so large the glass appeared dwarfed by them. It was clear from the outset that these were not the types of men one trifled with, and for the first time that evening, I began to have some doubts about my plot.

Hamish grinned at me—an insincere, calculated sliver of a thing—and I struggled to respond in kind. Something about the mere stature of these two strangers had put me on edge, and I felt as if I were floundering at the edge of a great abyss, a wildness thrashing darkly beneath the placid calm of still waters. I took a deep breath and steadied myself; certainly my imagination was running away with me.

Hamish swilled his pint with a flourish in my direction. "Gents, allow me to introduce my esteemed colleague from the University proper, James." The two men tipped their hats and leered at me most unpleasantly as Hamish looked on, unimpacted. "James, may I present our illustrious suppliers: Messieurs Burke and Hare."

* * *

"What are they like?"

Nye's inquiry was punctuated by the swings of his spade hitting the soft soil of the grave in which we were currently submerged up to our shoulders. We could hear Diggs and Thomas working diligently in tandem on the plot beside ours; a husband and wife had passed of consumption within hours of one another, and our constitutions were much improved by the prospect of a double payday after such a long drought.

"They're . . . Irish," I offered, unsure of where else to start.

Nye shot me a look so full of exasperation I could sense it even in the darkness. "Let me get this straight: you volunteered to be our inside man on the most high-stakes operation we've yet ventured, and your formidable intelligence-gathering has led you to the groundbreaking revelation that your suppliers are Irish?"

I snorted at his sarcasm, then paused briefly to empty a particularly rocky spadeful of dirt carefully over my shoulder. At last, I continued.

"Shut up, I'm setting the scene. Have you no appreciation for the classic art of storytelling?"

"I'm more a cut to the quick of it sort of fellow, myself."

"Why, got somewhere to be?"

"Well, no, as a matter of fact, I believe I'm the definition of a captive audience."

That sent us both into a round of undignified tittering, leaning back against the damp soil walls surrounding us until we could catch our breath.

I'd not had the chance to speak with Nye since my meeting with Hamish and his associates at the White

Hart. There'd been several lengthy University lectures I was required to attend that week, and my time in Malstrom's laboratory had been dominated by the master himself, leaving me no chance for sly asides. As such, I'd been endlessly relieved to find the familiar phrase Tonight scratched onto a tightly wound square of parchment tucked beneath my scalpel earlier that day. And as much as I wanted to blame my excitement upon my earnest desire to convey my findings at the White Hart to Nye, the truth was that I was also veritably itching for a dig; Now that the practice had become routine to me, my muscles ached for the labour, and my lungs yearned for the unparalleled refreshment of crisp kirkyard air. All in all, it had become a fair way to pass a night, and the unwelcome interruption to our operation caused by Knox's infringement had irked me in more ways than one.

Having finally recomposed myself, I returned my attention to digging. "They run a boarding-house in Tanner's Close. That's where we're to collect our quarries."

Nye paused and glanced up from his spade. "We?"

I grinned: this was the revelation I'd been most excited to share with him. "Indeed. As I haven't a cart of my own, they insisted I'd need a companion to help bear the load, and I said I had just the chap."

Nye's reaction was less enthusiastic than I'd hoped. He glowered as he flung more dirt up over his shoulder, expertly landing it atop the growing pile. "And how am I supposed to show up at Knox's lab unrecognised? His assistants know me, James. We all know one another around here."

I eyed him skeptically. "They know you dig?"

"Not officially, no, but they know I serve Malstrom. They'll undoubtedly be suspicious if I suddenly start transporting bodies for Knox."

I bit my lip and pondered this unforeseen conundrum. "Well, maybe Charlie—"

"Never mind, I'll work it out," Nye hastily retorted. "Perhaps I'll wear a disguise or something."

It took considerable effort not to snigger at the prospect, but I was quickly learning that Nye was rather sensitive where my companionship with Charlie was concerned; whether he considered him a true competitor for my affections I couldn't be sure, but I was at least conscious enough to have picked up on his reticence.

"It'll be a relief to have you along," I continued. "I have to say, the suppliers are . . . odd."

"Odd, how?"

I tried unsuccessfully to quantify it: that strange, crawling sensation that crept up my spine as I sat across from the men discussing our future prospects. "I can't quite describe it, really. They're not like our crew, they're . . . rougher, more uncouth."

Nye arched an eyebrow at me. "Are you certain you're not just judging them because they're poor?"

"No, honestly, it's not that," I sputtered indignantly. Though I was growing more aware of my aristocratic tendency to pass judgement on those of lower stations, that didn't explain the discomfort I'd felt in Burke and Hare's company. "They're just . . . intense, I suppose. They seemed new to this trade and were very obsessed with the particulars of payment."

Nye sighed and wiped his brow. "I warned you, James. If these men were part of Crouch's ploy to put

Knox in power, they're not your average low-level crooks. Despite their rough looks, they're businessmen; that much you must remember."

His lecture was punctuated suddenly by a loud curse from the plot next door.

Nye turned and pulled himself up onto his forearms to peer over at the neighbouring grave. "Diggs? Thomas? You boys alright over there?"

Digg's voice floated out of the pit, his tone thick with dejection. "Bloody coffin's cracked. He's got corpse rot; utterly useless. We'll cover him back up."

Nye swore loudly and slid back into our hole. "Here's hoping we have better luck with ours; we all could use a cause for celebration."

Fortunately, luck was in our favour, and we soon procured a female specimen in excellent condition. The extraction was swift and clean, the body procured whole and unmarred. The promise of a decent payout was enough to raise everyone's spirits, and we all maneuvered with practiced professionalism as we executed yet another elegant, expert snatch. I could feel my own disposition improving considerably as I devoted my energies to the easy fellowship of our crew, my niggling concern over Burke and Hare a now-distant folly.

What's more, after expertly hoisting the subject up to my chambers and interring her in the belly of The Beast, Nye and I took advantage of our solitude and indulged in a little celebration of our own—no whiskey required.

11.

An Interruption

I awoke to the soft glow of a cool, grey Edinburgh dawn. Acclimating slowly to my surroundings, I took in the familiar shapes that comprised my chamber—most notably the one beside me, in Nye's slumbering form. A smile tugged at the corners of my lips unsummoned, but I regretfully rolled away to fetch my pocket watch off the nightstand to check the time. It was early yet, and I still felt dazed and bleary-eyed as I watched the delicate second hand perform its journey around the face. A memory of sitting upon my father's knee observing this very timepiece emerged unbidden from the recesses of my mind, accompanied by an unwelcome pang of grief followed swiftly by anger, the once-fond memory now tainted with the knowledge of his manipulation and betrayal. The emotion was bitter to endure.

Fortuitously, my angst was interrupted by the soothing sound of Nye's slumbering breath. Though I could not yet bring myself to tear my gaze from the cursed heirloom cradled in my palm and all the heavy history it held, I consoled myself instead by measuring Nye's inhalations and exhalations to the rhythmic tick of its cadence, and soon found myself lulled back into a soporific stupor. In, tick-tick-tick, out, tick-tick-tick, in, tick-tick-tick, out, tick-tick-tick . . . My eyelids grew heavy once more, and the face of my watch blurred as the vexing memories of the past were overwritten by the tender rhythm of my newfound life. My dear one slept peacefully beside me, and I dreamt.

The unexpected slide of frigid toes against my bare calf elicited an undignified squawk from me, and I thrashed about clumsily beneath the blankets, struggling to roll back over and confront their source. Nye sniggered cheekily at my flailing and doubled his efforts, pressing the whole of his freezing-cold foot against mine. I finally managed to extricate myself from the confining tangle of bedclothes with a triumphant yelp and maneuvered nose to nose with him, the edges of his ash-grey eyes crinkling with mischief.

"Get your bloody ice-block toes off of me, you. You'll give me frostbite."

He pretended to look incensed. "And you care not if I'm frostbitten myself, as you deny me the courtesy of your warmth?"

I rolled my eyes but pressed my forehead against his, allowing our breath to intermingle. "You just have poor circulation."

"Then come here and help me improve the flow of my humours, will you? I'm liable to freeze to death in this hovel you call a home." He reached out to pull my body closer, wrapping his solid arms around me in a tender embrace. Feigning exasperation, I groaned but conceded, pressing a kiss to his suprasternal notch before letting my head loll back against his shoulder and slinging my arm heavily around his waist, melting against him in fond familiarity.

"Hardly my fault we're here," I murmured against the warmth of his skin. "If you weren't so eager last night, we could be back in your chambers, sleeping amongst all the disemboweled guts and dangling bones like proper gentlemen."

Nye laughed heartily at this, and I shifted to peer up at him. His hair was splayed in wild tangles across the pillow, and the angles of his features looked even more ethereal than usual in the dim morning light. He was beautiful—always—but especially now, in this quiet moment of singular solitude, and my heart seemed to swell in my chest with unanticipated emotion.

"What time is it?" His fingertips traced lazy circles between my shoulder blades, eliciting a shiver of goose-flesh across my back. I leaned into his touch and let my eyes flutter shut.

"Early yet. We've time before class."

"Mmm. Lucky, that, as I've just had a most brilliant idea about a different way to improve my circulation." Without further ado he rolled me swiftly to my back, grinning down cheekily as he rose to settle himself above me with now-practiced ease. His body felt warm and solid upon my own, a gift and reassurance all in one, and I marveled at how perfectly we fit together like this: two pieces of a puzzle sliding into place, magnets drawn effortlessly into alignment. It was an indulgently sentimental thought, I realized, but I could scarcely bring myself to feel ashamed of it—for if Nye's embrace was any indication, he felt entirely the same.

The nature of our shared affections was still so new to me, the sensations I experienced in his arms so unlike anything I had dared to imagine in my previous life. I wondered if I would ever grow used to it: to the earth-shaking intermingling of intensity and desire, to the strange, mercurial shivers that flared like webs of lightning up my spine with each oscillation of Nye's form against mine, to the ecstasy that washed over me at the mere sight of him falling apart in a shattering swell of passion and pleasure. Even a thousand lifetimes upon this earth would not be enough to render it all predictable.

He kissed me gently as he rolled his hips in mesmerising undulations, and I could feel him chuckle smugly against my mouth as he perceived my obvious eagerness. Not one to be idly subjected to such judgment, I guided my fingers in a calculated path along the familiar ridges of his ribs before skimming across his vertebrae, then down past his sacrum before coming to rest lower still, clutching for purchase, spurning him on and eliciting a surprised gasp from his lips. He blinked down, gaze wide and hungry, and I returned it with a coy smile. He dropped his forehead to meet mine, a low moan rumbling in his chest, and I arched my back in silent consensus, seeking only more, more...

"James... James..." Nye's voice was soft and desperate. My world was unravelling at a perilous pace, when loud footfalls in the hallway jolted us abruptly from our mutual bliss.

We instantly froze in place. Though there were occasionally comings and goings at early hours amongst the lodgers, it was rare for there to be much movement before dawn—especially with the city still very much in the dark, gloomy grip of winter—so a stir at that hour was unusual indeed. What was more, one set of footfalls undeniably belonged to Angus; the telltale rattle of his unfastened boot buckles was the equivalent of a cat bell on the stroppy proprietor, and most of the tenants at the H&A had learned quickly to avoid them if at all possible.

To my increasing agitation, the footfalls came to a halt directly outside my chamber door, followed by a succession of three sharp knocks.

"Willoughby! Open up! Visitor!" Angus sounded beyond irritated.

I sat bolt upright, sending Nye tumbling off of me and clutching the blankets desperately to my chest, the ardent spell of our encounter instantaneously broken.

"I'm—I'm not expecting anyone, Angus! I'm not fit for company!"

There was a pause, then a sharp, unintelligible exchange of voices—one female—followed by three more bangs.

"Last warning, Willoughby."

"Please, Angus, I'm not—"

But before I could utter another plea, there was the distinctive rattle of a key in the lock, and to my compounding horror, the door flew wide open, allowing for the wildly rude imposition of—

"Edith?"

It felt just as it had when I was a young boy and had fallen through the thin ice covering the pond on our family estate. The air rushed from my lungs all at once, leaving me paralyzed, trapped in suffocating, unyielding pressure. I ceased to see or hear, all that surrounded me giving way to instant darkness. Everything was frozen in that single, infinite moment as Edith's eyes grew wide, taking in the scene before her.

To her credit, Edith abruptly regained her composure and sprung hastily into action. She whirled towards Angus and slammed the door squarely in his face, sparing him the view of my interior chamber as though he were the interfering party. For a breath, she just stood there, staring at the door, clearly collecting her thoughts. At long last, she straightened her spine, drew back her shoulders, adjusted her hat, and spoke, her tone brittle and stern.

"You have one minute to make yourselves decent before I turn back around."

I scrambled out of bed so quickly I nearly tripped, Nye right behind me. From there, it was a frantic fumbling through the crumpled piles of clothing we'd abandoned in our wake the night before, the licentious memory of each item's removal flaring bright in my mind as I hastily rushed to rectify my state of undress, acutely aware of Nye's equally humiliating struggle.

We were still hopping about in a most undignified fashion, attempting to yank our boots on without unfastening them, when Edith turned, her eyes cold and expression blank, with no remnants of the sisterly fondness I recalled from our childhood. Her gaze landed squarely upon Nye, and he halted in place as if stunned. I realised I had never seen Nye look afraid before, yet here, in the presence of my most diminutive kin, he looked nothing short of terrified.

"You. Out. Now." Her command left no room for argument.

Nye didn't even spare me a glance as he snatched up his overcoat and hat and scurried out the door, slamming it shut behind him with an air of finality that shook me to my core.

I realized then that I was trembling. I had never before felt so uncompromisingly exposed, and it was as if every nerve ending in my body was vibrating with the duress of my continued violation.

"What are you doing here?" I couldn't bear to look at her, but I could at least speak, so I kept my gaze on the floor despite the defiance in my tone.

"What am I doing here? I think the better question is, brother dear, what you are doing here, seeing as you were due in London two months ago and none of us have heard from you since. We rather thought you dead." I swallowed, still unable to look up, my cheeks flaring hot.

Despite my silence, Edith soldiered on. "If you'd bothered reading the multitude of correspondences I sent you, you'd know that Lord Harrison and I have been disposed in Glasgow the past fortnight, and will be staying on until next month. When your absence dragged on without any word, Richard implored me to make the voyage to Edinburgh to be sure you were unharmed, though I see now we are altogether too late for that."

I flinched at her insinuation, mortification quickly morphing into indignation. "I've not been harmed, Edith. I am safe, healthy, and providing wholly for myself, independent of our family's struggles. I've continued my classes at the University—which, I might remind you, is the most prestigious medical institution in the western world—with great success, and I intend to complete my degree as planned. I can fend for myself, I'm a grown man—"

"A grown man?" Two bright spots of pink had emerged high on her cheekbones, and I knew from experience I was about to receive one of Edith's infamous dressing-downs. "A grown man? You're nothing of the sort, James, and your situation here is evidence enough of that. You're a petulant, ungrateful, lost little boy, living in squalor above an inn, entertaining—" She lowered her voice and glanced about, as though we may somehow be in unanticipated company— "gentlemen callers overnight! Have you any idea what fresh ruin you'd cause our family if your current vocation were to be made public?"

I startled, taken entirely aback by her misunderstanding. "My vocation? For Heaven's sake, Edith, I'm not a whore, any more than I am a 'lost little boy.' The man who was here, that..." The words caught around a lump in my throat, but I forced it down. "That's Aneurin. He's my... my colleague. My companion. He is... he is dear to me." Quantification eluded me along with my eloquence, but it felt essential that I impress upon her that Aneurin was wholly without blame.

Her eyes were dark and dangerous when at last I dared to meet them. "So his company is merely a pleasurable dalliance for you? He does not support you financially?"

"God, no, Edith, nothing of the sort," I rushed to reassure her. "My association with him is wholly voluntary; I enjoy his company a great deal, and we—"

To my utter shock, she appeared even more infuriated by this assertion, the bright flush of anger spreading past her cheeks and tinging the tip of her nose. When she spoke again, her words were full of vitriol. "And it has never once occurred to you what the consequences would be if anyone were to discover the unnatural quality of your relationship? You simply promenade openly about town with this man with no consideration for your own reputation, let alone that of your family? I've heard this city is filled with degenerates, but that doesn't mean you're entitled to act like one."

I could feel the anger rising in me equal to her own, her fiery accusations setting my temper alight. "I believe I'm entitled to nothing except perhaps a bit of privacy. Besides, this is hardly worthy of a scandal in the scheme of things; what should society care if a third son does not engage in proper methods of courtship?"

Her expression revealed a disdainful scoff. "Society tolerates deviance in families whose clout demands it be so. But ours certainly hasn't that sort of clout anymore, surely you know that! Must I remind you of all that is at stake here? Richard's petition to be reinstated to the House of Lords, Matthew's new partnership with a merchant in the East India fleet—we fell so far, James, and it's only now we're finally at the precipice of clawing our way back. Can you truly prioritise your unorthodox proclivities over the well-being of your very family?

I always knew you to be a bit conceited, but I never thought you selfish until this very moment. I can only pray you'll endeavour to prove me greatly mistaken."

"How dare you call me selfish—casting judgement against me when you had everything you ever wanted simply handed to you for the taking as soon as your dowry was paid in full! What would you know of selflessness?"

"We were all born into privilege," Edith interjected before I could inquire further. "And it is our solemn responsibility to maintain it. On that matter, I believe Richard will be unyielding in the utmost; for this you should be prepared. And I must warn you, brother mine: the stresses of his position as head of the household have not made him a forgiving man of late."

Something lurched inside my chest at the thought of my proclivities being exposed to my brother. "You . . . you won't tell Richard what you found here, will you?" Though I desperately wanted not to value his opinion whatsoever, the thought of my humiliation upon this revelation made my cheeks flame in anticipatory mortification.

Edith let out a derisive snort. "For now? Of course not. I'll not elaborate upon what I've found here, save that you're not dead; no one else need be unduly burdened by your disgrace. God knows we don't need you chasing Maman into an early grave as well."

Her words struck me like a blow to the face. Despite my mother's inane insistence that I was somehow to blame for my father's death, my siblings had never once shown an inclination to indulge this outlandish assertion until now.

"Get out." My petulance was a thin mask for my fury, and I wanted nothing more than to escape this unbearable confrontation and retreat back to the safety of my established independence—and most importantly, were I being honest, to Nye's steadying embrace. The threat of his absence from my future life felt unendurable, and there grew a staggering ache within me at the very thought.

Edith didn't budge. "Listen here, brother mine: you will meet me for dinner at Tipton House tonight, and we shall finish this conversation then."

I stood my ground as well. "There's nothing left to say, Edith. Leave me be."

She refused to flinch. "There is far more to be said than I've had the opportunity to convey here, due to the deeply inappropriate circumstances." She cast a scathing glare behind me at what I hotly remembered was my incriminatingly rumpled bed. "We shall convene at the Tipton and conclude our dialogue in a civilised setting and with the dignity our family and station commands. I will not negotiate with you on this."

I stared mutinously back at her. "And if I decline your invitation?"

She sighed. "If you do not attend, I'm afraid I shall have no choice but to inform Richard of my findings here, as much as it would pain me to witness his disgust. I believe we can both agree that it is in your best interest to avoid such a fate." With that, she turned to make her exit, but, in the process, clipped her toe upon the edge of The Beast, which, to my horror, I realised that Nye and I had carelessly left directly beside the door. It had not occurred to us in our haste to place it somewhere less prominent, and my heart leapt into my throat as Edith glared down at it, clearly suppressing an exclamation not befitting of her station.

She cast one final disdainful glance back at me over her shoulder. "For Heaven's sake, James. Have you not even bothered to unpack?" With that, she flung open the door and marched out, slamming it behind her.

For a moment, I stood petrified, attempting to process everything that had transpired—to cool my churning blood and steady my racing mind. Then my eyes flicked back to The Beast, where it lay innocently upon the floor, its latched jaws locked in a knowing smile.

My knees went weak and my head light, and I collapsed into my chair to bury my face in my hands, at last succumbing to the enormity of what had just transpired.

Some time had passed before I was able to regain control of myself; I came to my senses gradually, like a sailor thrown suddenly overboard but then buoyed ashore by a rolling succession of waves. When I eventually revived some semblance of sanity, I took stock of my situation and found it less than ideal: I was hunched in a ball like a pettish child recovering from a tantrum, which was greatly at odds with the maturity and dignity required of my newly declared self-determination, which must remain intact were I to have any chance of altering Edith's mind over dinner.

There could be no question of avoiding her: I could not risk her divulging my secret to Richard, and I still clung to hope that her opinion may be swayed if I were able to convey to her the reality of my lot in Edinburgh in a far more . . . *civilised* setting. Hoisting myself up to stand,

I brushed the creases from my trousers, then promptly checked my pocket watch for the time and cursed outright; it was imperative that I converse with Nye before our scheduled lecture at Malstrom's to convey my remorse for Edith's egregiously improper intrusion.

I granted myself entry through the unlocked back door of Malstrom's school (not even bothering to ring the bell), briskly traversed the laboratory (barely batting an eye at the fresh array of horrors on display there), and ascended towards Nye's chambers, anxious to notify him of my impending ultimatum and to beg his assistance in helping me prepare my plea for emancipation.

I was unsurprised to find the ladder to the attic already extended, so I took the rungs with practiced ease and emerged with as much dignity as one could be expected to muster when making an entrance through a trapdoor in the floor.

To my astonishment, I found Nye not engaged in his morning routine, as I'd anticipated, but instead still in his dinner clothes and rummaging about frantically through his wardrobe. Propped open beside him was a half-full valise.

I was dumbfounded. "Nye? What are you doing?"

He let out a shout of such alarm that I startled and nearly fell straight back through the trapdoor, managing but by the grace of my reflexes to catch the narrow bannister. Nye whirled to face me, and it was only when I saw his eyes, blown wide and wild with terror, that it occurred to me that something was truly wrong.

"What are you doing here?" He was staring at me as though I were a ghost, some ghastly manifestation conjured up solely to torment him.

I hesitated. "I . . . came to see you."

He blinked, an infinite pause stretching between us. At last he broke the silence, but his tone did little to reassure me. "Why?"

It was at this juncture that the first inklings of irritation settled upon me; he was treating me as if I were some foreign interloper intruding upon his space. "Because I thought perhaps we had a few matters of a personal nature to discuss?"

Nye cleared his throat and bent to stuff the waistcoat he'd procured from the wardrobe into the valise at his feet. "Fair point. I suppose I should beg your pardon before I take my leave."

It was my turn to be caught speechless. "Your leave? To go where? Malstrom's session starts in an hour."

"I'll be long gone before he gets in."

Something inside me twisted and jerked. "Gone? Gone, where?"

He remained half-buried in his wardrobe, flinging out two pairs of trousers in the general direction of his luggage. "Away from the noose. They won't catch me waiting around here like a spare gander."

"Nye, what are you talking about? Nobody is coming for you with a noose!"

He whirled to face me once more, hands frantically clutching an unfamiliar cloak between them, knuckles white and shaking in apparent terror.

"Your sister did not report me?"

I took a step towards him, holding up my hands like I was attempting to gentle a spooked foal. "I'm certain she didn't."

This gave him pause. At last, his eyes narrowed, and he seemed to truly see me for the first time since our interaction began. "She could not have misinterpreted the scene she happened upon."

I shook my head. "She did not."

Nye swallowed. "And she doesn't plan to tell the authorities?"

His terror felt visceral in a way I could not define. I felt I had no choice but to reassure him, to talk him down from whatever fit of displaced panic had currently set in. And for all Edith's threats, I knew she would rather die herself than risk our family's reputation by bandying about accusations in public. "Under no circumstances."

This seemed to confuse him even more, and it was with a degree of agitation that he finally responded. "Does it not bother her to know I have taken liberties with you? Has she no concern for your honour?"

I was secretly endeared by Nye's chivalry, however misguided. I set my shoulders and issued my retort. "I've made it clear that any liberties you have taken were given freely of my own accord. God, Nye . . . Come here."

But Nye stood still, his face still disarmingly vacant. In four quick strides, I was across the room, pulling him to me, clutching him to my chest. He wrapped his arms around my body willingly before slumping against me, head dropping heavily to my shoulder. In that moment, all I could do was hold him as he shook. He seemed so unbearably young, and I realized with a pang that our ages were perhaps much more similar than I'd previously thought—that it might just be his wisdom, aged beyond his years, that made him seem so stoically sage at the onset.

"It's alright." I brought my fingers up to card them through his unruly mane of curls. "We're alright."

While this was true in the moment, the precariousness of my situation was becoming clearer by the second. While Edith was of no real threat on account of her desperation to leave our family name untarnished, I could not guarantee the same of Richard. He had always been hot-tempered an impulsive, and I shuddered to imagine what his reaction would be if Edith were to divulge my secret.

Well then, I concluded. *I must simply convince Edith to keep it, at all costs.*

Nye seemed to calm but did not loosen his embrace, and I allowed myself to lean into the gesture, my desire to protect him overwhelming in its intensity.

I knew, of course, that the way Nye and I were was . . . not accepted. I knew it in that hazy, vague way one knows it is unacceptable to utter a curse, or blaspheme the name of the Lord, or covet thy neighbor's wife.

And I knew, I suppose, that this particular sin of which Nye and I were guilty was more serious than any grave we have disturbed in the kirkyard. I'd heard how couplings like ours were described—devious, blasphemous, lustful, even unnatural, as Edith had so cruelly asserted. And if the police were to discover us our punishment would be far worse than a few days' hard labour. The noose would likely be the verdict.

And yet.

How could anything be unnatural when our coupling felt as easy as breathing air? How could the life I'd found with Nye be anything other than a benediction, full of grace? How could Nye ever be less than everything?

For he was everything. And for all my inexperience and shy trepidation, for all my bashful fumblings and insecure ramblings, he was all I could want in moments of intimacy: tender, patient, and endlessly joyful. For all the daily mischief he pulled me into, the thrill of it could never compare to the gleam in his eye when we were burrowed beneath the blankets, sequestered in our own private Eden as he guided me along winding pathways in a maze of unprecedented pleasure.

It could never be unnatural.

It was as easy as breathing.

"Breathe." I murmured the word softly but sternly.

Nye sighed deeply into the crook of my neck.

"Breathe. Again."

His chest expanded beneath my hands. His latissimus dorsi flexed in time. He breathed.

At long last, he lifted his head from my shoulder. His eyes were wet when mine met them, the tears setting grey all to silver alight, and I brought up my thumb to wipe them away.

"There's something I have to tell you." His words were soft. Even.

My heart seemed to twist in my chest. "Alright."

"Sit down?" He gestured towards one of the chairs perched at his small dining table.

I glowered at the implied formality and instead made my way resolutely to the bed, flinging myself down upon it with a defiant finality. "Much obliged."

Nye rolled his eyes at my obstinance, and I found myself hard-pressed not to grin back as he joined me upon the bed, kicking up his feet beside me.

He launched forth without preface or prelude. "When I told you that I came to Edinburgh for opportunity, that wasn't the whole truth."

I quirked an eyebrow at him. "Go on."

"The truth is . . . I was exiled. From Iona."

"Oh." I paused to process this.

Suddenly, Nye barked out a laugh. "Christ. That's a lie."

"What?"

"Here I am trying to confess to you, and I'm still beating around the bush like some cowardly halfwit. The truth is that I was sentenced to die on Iona, so I escaped and ended up here."

I was stunned. "You . . . were sentenced to die? For what?" I was reeling at this revelation, my brain frantically attempting to keep up.

Nye cleared his throat and shifted his gaze away. "So, the island . . . remember I told you it was home to a holy site?"

I nodded.

"I was caught by the Abbott in a . . . delicate situation with a young pilgrim who was living there."

The thought of Nye in a delicate situation with anyone besides myself stirred something treacherous within me, but I duly suppressed it in lieu of the far more pressing matter at hand. "So what happened? They sentenced both of you to die?"

Nye gave a baleful snort. "Both of us? No. Me? Yes. You see, the pilgrim in question was from a noble and wealthy family in Spain who wielded quite a lot of influence—both at the monastery and abroad. So instead of confessing, he claimed I was a demon that seduced him—he was 'utterly powerless against my wicked wiles.' So they sentenced me—the son of a poor butcher—to death, and the fair young nobleman was granted safe passage back home to Spain."

I could tell my mouth was unflatteringly agape at the injustice of it all. "How did you escape?"

"The gaolkeeper's wife took pity on me and let me make a run for it—I was scarcely more than a child, for God's sake; her mercy was the one glimmer of humanity in that forsaken place. I stowed away on a fishing boat and made it to the mainland. I intended to carry on to the Continent, but at my sojourn here in Edinburgh, I had the supreme fortune to cross paths with Miss Mary Paterson. She was sleeping rough, same as me, but she knew this city inside and out, and taught me what I needed to know. We learned to trust each other, to depend on one another. She became as a sister to me."

A deep melancholy washed over me, imagining the unbearable circumstances of their combined poverty and desperation. Though I could not fathom the suffering they'd endured upon the streets, I'd seen enough of the miserable urchins begging upon corners to know that their life could not have been kind. It was clear me, at last, that the intimacy of their friendship was born not of romantic desire, but of a pain only the two of them could understand. "How old were you then?"

He sighed, the weight of the memory heavy upon him. "We were but fourteen. I'd arrived with no plan and no prospects, but Mary quickly turned all that around as soon as she had me as her accomplice. She already knew of the city's affection for the butchering arts, and it was through her observations and subsequent connections that we came to be as we are today; I owe it all to her."

I gave him a rueful smile, a grasping effort at reassurance. "Nye, I'm so sorry. I'm glad you and Mary found one another, of course, but I'm sorry any of that happened to you."

He shrugged. "It's not your fault. Besides, I should be grateful; all that I endured on Iona, that's what brought me here to this city. It's what brought me to this school. To Malstrom."

"It's what brought you to me." The words were bold and rich on my tongue, but I meant them.

Nye's eyes leapt up to meet mine, and his smile echoed my own. He kissed me briefly, but for once did not endeavour to carry on. Instead, he pulled me into his arms and lowered me until we were lying side by side, limbs wrapped up in one another like the knit of his tartan wool. Silence descended.

And it was in that moment that I knew there was no going back. Everything that had come before this city was gone: my family, my house, my future, my name. The cracks I'd previously barely perceived widened into a yawning chasm between myself and all I had known before, an unbreachable distance spilling across vast swaths of inescapable memory. Edinburgh was my life now. This was the only home I would ever need to know.

Nye pulled me closer. We breathed.

But even as we dissolved into a quiet, poignant truce, a fresh spark of fear ignited within me.

What would happen at my impending dinner with Edith? What would become of me and Nye if our discourse dissolved into further animosity, and Edith took it upon herself to divulge my secret to Richard?

The consequences were too dire to comprehend. Admittedly until that point I'd assumed the worst thing that could befall me as a result of my many transgressions in defiance of Richard's orders would be that he may call me a disgrace, berate me, perhaps publicly disown me, but none of that had seemed of great importance until now.

As I lay in the tangle of Nye's knowing arms, I could not help but contemplate the fate of the Spanish pilgrim: he'd been spirited away, perhaps to a life of sheepish penance, but he'd been allowed to *live*.

Whereas Nye . . .

I shuddered, but then steeled my resolve. I'd have to use every ounce of wit and wiles I possessed to turn Edith's mind, but I *would* protect Nye, no matter the cost

12.

A Chastening

I entered the hall at Tipton House a full half hour before dinner was to be served, and was immediately escorted by a porter to a dazzlingly appointed parlour to await Edith's arrival. I was relieved to have the spare time to collect myself, as I'd spent the past four hours in Nye's company, rehearsing my role for this very encounter.

I was determined to be calm, even-tempered, and practical, arguing my case like a lecturer at the RMS. In no uncertain terms, I was to simply present the facts: that my education and vocation in Edinburgh were of no cost to Richard, that I did not take unnecessary risks where my reputation was concerned, and that my only wish was to be left in peace. If she agreed, I would guarantee that I was no threat to the family honour in my current state—far less so than if she were to force me to return to London to intermingle with the peerage. For all intents and purposes, I would conclude, it was in the best interest of us all that I simply be written off as a harmless, if frivolous, black sheep.

Nye hadn't been entirely convinced by my arguments, and was treating the appointment as if I were headed to the gallows myself. "But James, there are laws about what she saw. There's no way she'll disown you if she believes your morality is at stake. Surely, she wouldn't turn her back and leave you to rot in sin." I'd never heard him sound so bitter.

"You don't know Edith like I do," I'd dismissed him curtly. "My immortal soul is of no concern to her. Her only goal in life is to maintain her position in society and eliminate anything that threatens it. I'm less of a liability sequestered up here than at the family stead or in London among her society friends. I need only remind her of that." I prayed that I sounded more convinced than I felt.

I reviewed these points for what felt to be the millionth time as I positioned myself into a chair by the fire and graciously accepted a glass of wine, settling in to wait. An indeterminate length of time later, it became quite evident that Edith, in her predictably conniving manner, was content to arrive well past the allotted hour, no doubt as a ploy to sow deep seeds of worry in my mind when left to my own devices. Even as I accepted another offered glass of wine, even as I purposefully paced the circumference of the room admiring its lavish decorations, even as I stood lost in melancholy thought, staring out at the rain-spattered street below, I willed myself to not spiral into treacherous self-doubt. To emerge from this encounter victorious, the burden of convincing Edith to abandon me to my chosen fate would fall entirely upon me and me alone; for once, I could not depend on Nye's casual swagger and endless reserve of confidence to buoy me through.

The minutes dragged on. Despite my better judgement, my fingers closed around my pocket watch, and I flicked it open to check the time. Edith was more than twenty minutes late. I snapped it shut and proceeded to turn the item over in my palm, thumb tracing the lines of the family crest that was, to my estimation, the sole cause for my current conundrum.

My mind wandered back through the recesses of memory to one event that took place beneath the likeness of this very crest, which had christened the entrance hall of our summer estate. I had been no more than seven and stood quaking with unsuppressed sobs over my brothers' mutual cruelty as their laughter echoed off the marble floor.

"Wee Miss Molly, tricks and folly, paint her lips and call her dolly!" Richard cackled, shoving me into Matthew's waiting hands. Matthew uttered a shout of delight as he wrenched my arms behind my back, painfully pinning my wrists together despite my best attempts at escape. I wriggled and wailed as Richard advanced once more, pulling one of Edith's dressing gowns over my head, which he and Matthew then proceeded to wrestle me into.

"Stop, stop, please," I gasped, trembling from head to toe in mortification.

"What's the matter, *Miss Molly*?" Matthew hissed as he plopped my mother's bonnet onto my head and yanked the ribbons into a knot at my throat. "You like Edith's toy dollies so much, why don't you dress like one?"

"Please, no, stop! Edith, make them stop!" Desperately, I turned to my sister, still holding one of her precious dolls in her arms, watching ambivalently over the whole scene from the staircase.

She simply blinked back at me, expressionless. "I told you not to play with my things, James." And with that, she'd turned and walked away, leaving my brothers to their fun.

At that very moment of recollection, as if on cue, the door to the parlour swung open once more, announcing Edith's arrival and catapulting me back into the present. I shoved the watch back into my pocket and rose to my feet to greet her, my memory of her girlish distain blending seamlessly into the present look of deep ambivalence imprinted upon her face.

She had donned her finest travelling cloak coupled with an almost humourously anachronistic shawl of tartan for the occasion, and I suppressed a laugh at what was clearly her attempt at a genteel display of local flair. She looked for all the world like the high-class Southerners visiting High Street, as out of place in the North as in Timbuktu. She stood before me, haughty as ever, and I braced myself for the impending tirade.

Strangely, it did not come. She simply stared, mute and paralysed, as behind her the porter hovered awkwardly.

She cleared her throat. "Mr. Willoughby. I believe this is generally the point in conversation in which you wish me a good evening and inquire as to the comfort of my journey here. Or perhaps too much time spent alone has dulled your manners beyond repair."

My mind reeled with curiosity. Was she truly not going to spend the evening berating me, forgoing her prior threats in favour of a far more gracious approach? I took the bait with an air of caution.

"But of course, Lady Harrison, please forgive my impropriety, as my mind had momentarily wandered elsewhere." I fell into a low bow, and she returned it with a practiced curtsy. "Good evening to you. I trust your journey here was without incident?"

"Aside from the dreadful weather, I'm pleased to say it was." She gave a curt nod to the porter, who divested her of her shawl and cloak and escorted her to the table, where we were seated without delay.

Edith adjusted the ruffles at the throat of her gown and smoothed a manicured ringlet of her hair. "So, Mr. Willoughby. Is it always so relentlessly rainy in this city? I fear Lord Harrison and I haven't seen a ray of sunshine in weeks. It appears a most dismal affliction, does it not impact your disposition so?"

I could scarcely believe my ears. Were we truly about to sit down and play-act a society dinner, knowing full well the daggers that we had hurled at one another mere hours before? I remained incredulous, but what point was there in forcing the topic? Perhaps Edith had changed her mind in the interim and was now simply going to resume ignoring my existence altogether. I scarcely dared hope for such a turn in fortune.

"Indeed, Lady Harrison, the weather here in the North leaves much to be desired, but one becomes accustomed to it. I find myself no more seeking sunshine than I would a flying unicorn."

At this, Edith laughed. Though it was far from the sincere chortles I'd once earned from her in our child-hood, it was still a pleasant, if measured, thing, and for a moment I could almost pretend that all between us could be turned right once more.

It wasn't until we'd had our first bite of pheasant (the food a transcendent pleasure I was forced to admit I'd missed) that the true interrogation began. To her credit, she'd trod lightly upon the topic of my education and vocation up to that point (and I'd remained appropri-ately vague about both my classes and my work for Malstrom). But it was clear that she was eager to assess my current prospects further, and I wished for nothing more than to impress upon her the worthiness of my endeavours.

"The University sounds excellent, to be sure," she replied warily, dabbing her lips. "But you must also tell me more of your employer! You say he's one of the fin-est surgeons in the city?"

. "Indeed," I said, crafting my reply with care. "Doc-tor Malstrom is renowned worldwide, in fact, as a physician, surgeon, anatomist, and professor. He even operates his own private institution, the one at which I am currently employed."

Edith raised her eyebrows. "Is that so? A private institution—is that more prestigious than what's on offer at the University?"

"Oh, absolutely," I replied shrewdly, easily interpret-ing Edith's true intent. "The University in Edinburgh, while excellent in its own rite, does not teach in the Parisian method, you see. Only the private schools do, which is why only the best students from the University are accepted there—myself among them. I was at top of my class, and as soon as I attended a demonstration at Doctor Malstrom's institution, I was singled out for an offer as an assistant. It is through this generous opportunity that I am able to support myself without our dear brother's assistance." It was an embellishment, of course, but I knew for my own benefit I must emphasise the importance of my attendance at Malstrom's— not to mention the financial security afforded to me by my (less scrupulous) activities on the school's behalf.

She paused to consider this. "It seems a worthy vocation." I let out a breath I scarcely knew I'd been holding. "However, I've come with news that I believe you'll agree will make your continued pursuit of such an undoubtedly exhausting profession entirely unnecessary."

Of course. Of course she would not let go so easily of her bull-headed insistence that I become a merchant. I internally chided myself for thinking that a battle against a foe as formidable as my sister would be won with so little persuasion.

I proceeded as diplomatically as I could. "Edith, while I appreciate the offer with the East India Company, I assure you that this vocation is equally profitable and well-respected amongst the intellectually enlightened circles here in Edinburgh. Why, I'm able to afford my tuition at not one but two institutions, my lodging at a reputable inn," (I ignored the flinch that crossed her face as she undoubtedly recalled our encounter there this morning, and barreled on with fervor,) "and a fine lifestyle amidst the esteemed echelons of the New Enlightenment! By the time I've finished my degree—"

"I'm not speaking of the East India Company, James. In fact, the offer that I bring forth will make such fortunes seem folly."

This admission rendered me speechless. Edith looked insufferably smug at having apparently caught me so off guard.

"Apologies, sister, but I've no idea of what you speak."

"Of course not, how could you, for I've only just received the news before I departed for Edinburgh." Her voice was an infuriating sing-song trill, patronising and placating and causing my blood to go hot in my veins. "You see, it's nothing to do with your vocation, James. It's to do with your marriage."

The world did an odd sort of tilt to one side. I blinked, dumbstruck. "My . . . My what? I'm not betrothed!"

"Of course you're not, dear, but that's just the thing. Lord Harrison and I received the most flattering correspondence from his dear cousin, Lady Witherspoon—I believe you are acquainted with her daughter, Violet?"

My brain grasped at straws. I knew of Lord and Lady Witherspoon, of course—they were legends in Society circles, stewards of the largest estate in Derbyshire, a sumptuous residence in London, and a series of apartments in the Royal Crescent so grand that my mother had spoken of little else for a full week after attending a dinner there. Edith had been so thrilled when the Witherspoons confirmed their attendance at her own wedding that she'd squealed like a child and then flown instantly into a fit of extreme agitation, insisting that the floral arrangements must be upgraded immediately so as not to bring dishonour upon our family name.

Yet what did any of that have to do with me? I was aware the Witherspoons had a multitude of children, but it was a fair few seconds before my mind finally unearthed a fond memory of an ivory-skinned girl with an upturned nose, raven hair, and deep brown eyes, laughing over her teacup on the terrace at the breakfast following my distant cousin Lydia's nuptials with some haughty Lord the previous summer.

"I believe we exchanged a few words at Cousin Lydia's wedding?" I posited politely. Our encounter had been brief indeed; we'd reached for the same lavender cake and bumped fingers quite by accident. I'd offered a gracious apology, and she'd responded with an unusually witty quip that had taken me by surprise. I'd been charmed, to be sure, and had taken the liberty to engage her in a light-hearted volley of pleasant banter. Even so, the exchange had lasted no longer than a few minutes at most; I'd known better than to risk being deemed improper in the company of a girl of her status.

Edith gave me a knowing smile. "You needn't be modest, James, for it appears you made quite the impression on her. She'll be coming out this summer in London and specifically inquired as to whether you'd be in attendance this Season."

I was utterly confounded. "I've no reason to attend. I've not finished my degree, I have no allowance or inheritance, and what's more, I still have one elder brother who is yet to be betrothed!" In my youth, marriage had always seemed to me an inevitable but distant reality, a vague, nebulous responsibility for which I would—at some magical, as-yet-undefined juncture in the future—feel wholly prepared to undertake. It was not until this very moment that I'd dared acknowledge that the duties of marriage were distinctly at odds with my continued companionship with Nye.

"None of that matters now, James. Violet's set her sights on you, and what's more, Lord and Lady Witherspoon approve."

"But . . . why?" I wasn't being modest: I was an absurdly unlikely subject for such a match—no money, no influence, no notable pedigree in the grand scheme of things; even prior to my father's death and our family's subsequent struggles, I'd have declared the thought audacious.

Edith shrugged casually and took a measured bite of pheasant before responding. "The Witherspoons are fortunate to be in a position such that they encourage their daughters to marry for love, so long as it's amongst the peerage. And it would seem your fair face and fine manner have at last served their purpose; Violet has set her sights firmly upon you as her impending suitor."

I meekly struggled to articulate my thoughts. "Though our encounter was pleasant enough, surely it was insufficient for a lady of her station to draw such a dramatic conclusion."

Edith tittered dismissively. "Well, of course she's prone to silly conjectures; she's a girl of romantic notions and endless means. But the point is, dear brother, she wants to affirm your acquaintanceship during the Season this summer! Lady Witherspoon is, of course, aware that your studies have not yet concluded, therefore throwing your attendance into doubt—hence she reached out to Lord Harrison and myself personally so that we may guarantee their daughter not be disappointed."

A cold, heavy weight settled in my stomach as the reality of my predicament slowly slid into focus. "But if I've not completed my studies by the time I'm betrothed—"

"You'll complete your degree at Oxford over the duration of your engagement, of course, there's no harm in that. You'll be a proper physician by the time vows are exchanged."

I faltered. "But how will I establish a surgical practice—"

A laugh so shrill I was shocked it didn't shatter the goblets erupted from Edith, who fanned herself in mock amusement. "Practice? Surely you understand that when you come into a dowry of that size, you needn't trouble yourself with engaging in something so mundane as a surgical practice. The Witherspoons would never allow it!"

"But then how shall I pass my time?" I countered obstinately. "Is Violet as yet unaware that I am ill-suited at the art of fox-hunts, shooting, gambling, and other such boorish occupations?"

"Quite to the contrary," Edith maintained. "It would seem she's most intrigued by your more scholarly pursuits. She quite fancies herself an intellectual, apparently, and desires to continue circulating in high-minded circles. An Oxford physician for a husband, to her, seems quite the thing. Lord Harrison himself is the very one who affirmed the benefits of the match; he wants to ensure his niece's whimsical mind is appropriately occupied until such a time when she may otherwise engage in her wifely duties. Once children are in the picture, of course, she will doubtlessly resign to her softer nature."

At the mention of children, I could feel my face flush, my mind drawing an unhelpful parallel between myself and a prize stud at auction.

"To what, then, shall I devote my time if I am to be housebound like a lapdog?"

Clearly agitated, Edith polished off the last bite of her pheasant before placing her silverware squarely down upon the plate with a decisive clack. "Surely, brother, for a dowry of twenty thousand, you can devise something."

A hot, molten panic swirled in my chest. Edith's words felt like a net cast over me, dragging me back to the unwelcome reality of my family's turmoil and our precarious station in society—all trappings of the hateful world that existed outside my life in Edinburgh. I felt sick at the thought. To imagine a future without all that brought me joy: my schooling, my friends, my very place in the progress of the Enlightenment, and that was all to say nothing of Nye.

Nye, Nye . . . His very being flooded my consciousness. A life without him was worth nothing—not even twenty thousand pounds.

I steeled myself. "I'm not going home, Edith. Or to London—or Oxford, for that matter. My life is here now. I will earn my degree and practice medicine. I will keep my head down and my persona proper. I will not disgrace our family, nor will I cost any of you a penny for your troubles. I'm hard-pressed to see your quarrel with that."

Her expression cooled in an instant, lips drawn into a thin line, eyes gone cold and full of judgement. "Don't be ridiculous, James. This is your duty."

"I don't see it as my duty."

An odd, blotchy blush was spreading across Edith's face, and her tone revealed just how close she was to losing her temper entirely. "It will be, and sooner rather than later. In fact, Richard is relying upon it: a dowry like that in the family will do wonders in reestablishing the standing of the estate. Not to mention the entwining of our fortunes with a family as esteemed as the Witherspoons; why, Richard was all but beside himself at the prospect! It's the happiest I've seen him in months."

I set my jaw and my intentions. "Well, then, Richard may find himself sorely disappointed."

Edith tilted her head, her expression still dangerous; it was apparent I was treading on increasingly thin ice. "Have you no sense of obligation towards your kin? Your own mother? Your father's memory? Your family name?"

"The kin who taunted and bullied me? The mother who blamed me for our father's death? The sire who betrayed and bankrupted us? The name of which I am the third in line to carry, and which has been nothing but a weight upon me since I left the family stead?" Like water breaching a dam, a lifetime of suppressed slights was pouring forth from me, and I could no sooner stop it than halt the flow of the Water of Leith. I knew how I must have appeared in this moment: a stubborn, obstinate boy engaging in a miserably childish squabble with my wretched sibling, but the truth was, I no longer had the capacity to care.

Edith, for what it was worth, was all too eager to dismount her high horse. Her response was issued as a disdainful sneer: "Oh, don't act as though your childhood was naught but suffering; every young boy faces the torment of his brothers and the scolding of his Maman. You're hardly an exception."

More memories of my childhood resurfaced unbidden, mementos of what felt like a different lifetime: the ill-intentioned jeers, the brutish slights, the relentless shame of being so obviously and deliberately excluded from the unspoken tenets of brotherhood seemingly effortlessly afforded to the other male members of my family. It all rose up inside me as a chaotic cacophony that, in boyhood, would have paralyzed me with mortification, but here and now instigated nothing but indignant rage.

I would hold my tongue no more. "Easy for you to say," I retorted. "You were up in your cloisters with your poetry and embroidery and music and books, tasked only with curating your beauty and manners. Meanwhile, I was dragged about and subjected to all manner of cruelty, both verbal and otherwise, be it from Father, our brothers, even distant kin who found my gentle disposition most amusing. I was never part of this family, Edith; you were all just too polite to say it. And now, I'm afraid, it's simply too late."

And with that, I stood so forcefully I nearly overturned the chair, ignoring the gawping horror on Edith's face. I turned to the exit and ran as fast as I could, not even bothering to pause and request my overcoat from the butler.

I burst out the doors of Tipton House and into the embrace of Edinburgh's chill, my boots pelting against the cobblestones as I careened down High Street, running as fast as my lungs would allow. My blood thundered in my ears, my breath a sodden mist around me, and I lost myself in it entirely until my body could sustain me no more.

I emerged from my exertion as if from a trance, only to find myself (rather bewilderingly) perched upon the stairs outside Malstrom's. It was as if my legs had intended to carry me to the sanctuary of my chambers, only to abandon their mission in favour of the solitude of my asylum. I leaned back against the stone bannister, feeling its piercing cold sear through my waistcoat, and cast my gaze to the night sky. Ever so gradually, my pulse resumed its normal rhythm. The aura of red about my vision seemed to melt away, my respiration slowed, and my muscles relaxed against their strain. All too quickly, my view of the stars was blurred with tears.

What had I done?

Merely what I needed to do, Reason informed me. My family was desperately trying to pull me back into their mire when I'd only just found the fortitude to claw my way out on my own. I didn't need them anymore, I reminded myself. I had my vocation—profitable and sure. My path was set. I was a Resurrectionist now, risen from the dead as surely as those whose forms graced my slab. This would be my new beginning.

"James? What are you doing here?"

I was jolted from my thoughts by the familiar voice of my dear companion. I should have perhaps been startled that he'd been so quick to find me, and yet surprise eluded me; he knew me all too well.

I bowed my head to wipe the tears from my face as subtly as I could before turning to greet him. He emerged from the doorframe of the school like a beauteous vision, dark hair swirling in the wind, his pale angelic face the purest image of compassion. Extended in his right hand was his overcoat; it was only then that I noticed I was so cold I was shaking.

"Thanks." A smile tugged at the corners of my lips as he threw the coat around my shivering form and lowered himself to sit beside me, close enough I could feel his heat against my shoulder.

We sat in silence for a spell. I knew he was waiting for me to speak first, allowing me space to formulate my thoughts. At long last, I found the fortitude to articulate them.

In as simple terms as I could muster, I told him the sum of my conversation with Edith: her forced ignorance of my companionship with Nye, her insistence upon my return to London for the Season, and most importantly of all, her utterly misguided attempt to provoke me into a proper society match with Violet. His brow knitted together with concern when I told him of my abrupt departure from the negotiation, and I knew instantly where his mind had turned.

I hastened to assuage his fears. "You don't... we needn't be concerned about her reporting... what she saw between us."

"You needn't worry about our secret, Nye. I have a plan." Never mind that my brilliant *plan* was a mere thirty seconds old; I hoped I sounded more certain than I felt. "I'll return to London as Edith demands, but I'll be thoroughly horrid to Violet: cold and standoffish and entirely unpleasant. By the time July arrives, she won't be able to stand the sight of me!"

An odd smile formed on Nye's face. "*You*? Cold and standoffish?"

I gave a resolute nod. "Indeed. Violet will lose interest entirely, I'll have fulfilled Edith's ultimatum; there will be no proposal, and I'll be free to return to Edinburgh by the start of the digging season."

Nye raised his eyebrows, his expression of amusement on his face. "Forgive me, James, but I have a hard time imagining you putting off Violet with haughty stoicism. Why, don't you know that when it comes to the fairer sex, the more standoffish you are, the more intrigued they become? You're going about this all wrong!"

"Oh, what do *you* know of the fairer sex?" I shot back, and he pulled a rude face before responding.

"Enough to know you may well find yourself backed into a corner despite your best efforts."

I sighed. I couldn't burden him with Edith's threat of divulging our secret to Richard; his experience in Iona would undoubtedly send him into a blind panic at the thought, and he was burdened enough already by the unrest facing his crew.

"Please, just trust me, Nye. I'll take care of it." Internally, I resolved to write Edith the following day. I would not beg her forgiveness, but I would at least offer her a vague assurance of my presence for the Season. That ought to be, by my calculations, enough to buy her silence for the time being.

Nye shifted uneasily, putting space between our shoulders. I shivered as the wind whipped a chill through the gap. "I do trust you, of course. But, James"—his tone had grown guarded—"twenty thousand pounds is—"

"Pointless." I interrupted him before he could perjure himself any further. "It's just as I told you before, Nye: I'm not like Edith, or Richard, or any of the rest of my family. Their only goal is to secure a place in society and sail obliviously through a life devoid of any consequence or meaning. And that's precisely what I came to Edinburgh to escape; I yearned for purpose, and it was here that I found it. For the first time in my life, here— at the University, at Malstrom's—I feel that I matter."

Nye's silver gaze bore into mine, and he clasped my chilly hands within his own. "You certainly do to me."

It was an admission so profound that it took all my willpower to not lean in and kiss him then and there. I could tell he felt the same, but instead settled for a firm squeeze of my hands and a soft, sweet smile.

"Come to bed." He stood and tugged me towards the tempting glow of the hall.

I hesitated for a mere moment; a part of me wanted to continue to sulk in the cold and lick my wounds, but all it took was one look at Nye's earnest face and I knew I couldn't resist. Rising to my frigid feet, I let him lead me home.

13.
An Upending

I had little time to reflect further upon all I stood to lose as a result of that singular spectacular falling out with Edith, for, as if on cue, the demands of my current livelihood seemed at once to conspire against me. A particularly ghastly strain of cholera tore through the West Port, so I was soon gainfully employed at Greyfriars with Nye and the crew on a near-nightly basis. What's more, my classes at the University seemed to double in workload entirely without warning ("They're sorting out the boys from the men in preparation for exams," Charlie grumbled over a particularly taxing essay as we hunched side by side in the library, he struggling to conform his thesis and me attempting to ward off sleep after a three-body haul from the kirkyard the night before). And though I'd thus far received no summons from Messieurs Burke and Hare, Hamish had taken every opportunity to remind me (in some ways more subtle than others) that I was in his pocket now, an indebted member of Knox's ever-growing sphere of influence. My nervousness over my impending role in that operation exacerbated my anxiety greatly, and the lack of a clear assignment left me feeling like I was a man living on borrowed time.

As such, it came as more a relief than anything else when Hamish sought me out in my chamber early one morning to notify me that my services would be required at the boarding-house on Tanner's Close that day.

"And you've secured a second man to help you with the carry?"

"Yes, Hamish." I resisted the urge to roll my eyes at his relentless meddling. Did he truly not think I was capable of a task so simple as carting a body from one end of Old Town to the other?

"Good. Knox's assistant will be expecting you before two o'clock. Don't be late."

"Do I seem to you a gentleman prone to tardiness?" I knew I should hold my tongue, but Hamish's lauding of his position over me was fraying my patience to shreds.

Hamish shot me a lopsided smile. "Dunno, toff-boy, didn't take you for a gambler either, and yet, here you are! A nobleman on my payroll. I wasn't certain the gentry occupied themselves with things so mundane as timeliness, so I thought I'd best give note." He appeared nothing short of gleeful at my subordination to his whims.

I yearned to verbally eviscerate him for his arrogance, but managed to hold myself back. Instead, I feigned a sniveling smile. "Consider it noted, Hamish. I shall be on time. Now, by your leave, I'm ironically late for class."

Nye, I was amused to note, had changed his tune considerably regarding his involvement in the Knox scheme. When I intercepted him in Malstrom's office following my morning lecture, he seemed veritably delighted at the prospect of our first delivery.

"Today? Finally? Oh, excellent, I've been preparing for this!"

"Preparing? For what, exactly? We're just carrying a tea-chest a half mile up the wynd." My peevishness regarding the task had more to do with Hamish's attitude earlier than the assignment itself, but Nye seemed wholly undeterred.

"Why, my disguise, of course! Wait here."

With that, he bounded out of the room, leaving me alone amongst Malstrom's dusty tomes. I occupied myself perusing the bookshelves, tracing my fingers carefully along the well-worn spines, familiarising myself with all the titles—each reflecting a new beacon in medical advancement. I wondered absently if Nye could ask Malstrom to let me borrow a few. My scholastic reveries were shattered moments later, when Nye burst back into the room so abruptly I yelped in alarm. I whirled around to find him standing in a posture of abject triumph, clearly awaiting my verdict.

"So? What do you think?"

I bit back a laugh. His clothing was different, to be sure: he was wearing a new waistcoat in the more modern style favoured by the University elite, along with a matching cravat which, for once in his life, was properly tied and perched primly at his throat. He'd also donned a new hat, the design of which I recognised well from one of the University shops, making the guise of student all the more believable. But the most notable change was what was emerging from beneath the cap in question.

It was a tousle of white-blonde hair, lightly curled, longer than his natural cut but similarly disheveled, the anachronistic colour so at odds with his native tone that it washed his whole visage into a ghostly pale palette, the overall effect disconcerting in the utmost.

He spun around smugly, apparently mistaking my silence for stunned approval. "Good, isn't it?"

He did look different, to be sure, but not in the subtle, anonymous sense he was clearly aspiring to capture.

I measured my response. "It's . . . wait, where did you get that wig?"

He demurred for less than a second, but I still registered the guilty shift in his gaze. "Borrowed it from a friend."

I narrowed my eyes. "Because it certainly looks like the hair of a specimen I recall us exhuming last week."

Nye shrugged. "Well, he wasn't using it anymore."

"Oh my God, Nye, that is absolutely vile."

He feigned innocence as he twisted one of the locks in question around his fingers. "What? It would be a shame to let a perfectly good wig go to waste. Besides, it alters my appearance completely, would you not agree?"

I shook my head in exasperation at his heresy but allowed myself to consider his point. After all, perhaps I was not the most objective audience, for would anyone else have so diligently memorized the precise slant of his cheekbones? The gentle slope of his nose? The sharp angle of his jawline, the perfect plush curve of his lower lip? To me, these features would be recognizable anywhere, even in pitch darkness or infirm blindness. I had memorized them all in pristine precision with not just my eyes, but my fingers, my mouth, my tongue, my breath. I would recognise his face always, in any manifestation, in this life or any other.

He must have caught me staring and known I was beaten, because his mouth quirked into a smug smile. "You agree with me. It's a marvelous wig, and a perfect disguise."

I shrugged. "It's alright. You look like an albino dandy, to be honest, but I suppose we've got to work with what we have."

"Oy, rude!" He gave my shoulder a playful shove and my aura of disdain shattered completely, giving way to an undignified bout of giggling that overtook us both.

The walk to Tanner's Close was brief but grim. Despite my residency at the University, I'd spent little time out and about on that side of the West Port, and for good reason: the poverty and squalor in the tenements there was infamous, and my brief foray into the Vaults with Nye had given me little reason to seek out such conditions. Nye had told me stories of the suffering endured by those who lived there: the disease, the violence, the persistent spectre of death that claimed dozens of victims each night, their bodies flung carelessly into mass graves on the outskirts of the city with no fanfare or remorse. It seemed an existence more brutal than any I could fathom, a casual disregard for the sanctity of human life that was foreign to me in the utmost.

I did my best not to stare at the miserable urchins and piles of human excrement lining the Closes as we wound our way down King's Stables Lane. The decrepit tenements loomed so high on either side of us, they seemed liable to blot out the sky altogether, and I felt agonisingly aware of how out of place we must seem amidst the fetid grime surrounding us. I nearly reached out to clutch at Nye's arm in a vague plea for reassurance, but he moved two steps ahead of me, head raised, gaze acute, gait steady with purpose. I duly followed his lead.

To my surprise, when we reached the assigned address, Nye stepped aside and removed his hat while gesturing for me to proceed. I hesitated; my stomach felt suddenly heavy and hollow, the daunting scale of the risk we were taking by involving ourselves in yet another unsavoury vein of the Underworld swiftly sliding into focus. I was so far beyond my depths in this, in all of this. Around our table at the Pig, it had seemed rather a merry game, but here in the ash-grey light and fetid stench of the Close, I was a man adrift.

Nye somehow understood my reticence implicitly. He reached out and gave my shoulder a firm squeeze. "It's alright, James. It's as you said: 'We're just carrying a tea-chest half a mile up the wynd.' No more, no less."

I took a deep breath and offered him a half-hearted smile, doing my best not to be further disturbed by the unnerving effect of his disguise. Besides, this was my world now: Nye, the school, the crew, and all that went along with it.

I raised my hand to the door and knocked. Moments later, it swung open, revealing the now-familiar leer of Mr. Hare. Though his lips were set in the semblance of a grin, the black pools of his eyes reflected no such mirth, and it was with a degree of relief that I could sense Nye recoil slightly beside me: it was clear I was not the only one disturbed by his demeanour.

"Ach. It's the boys from the school!" He called out gruffly over his shoulder before disappearing back inside, not even bothering to offer a proper welcome. We followed him in, squinting as our eyes adjusted to the dark. There was an odd smell about the place; of cold and damp, mouldy hay and rotted wood. I breathed through my mouth and willed myself not to think of Charlie and his fumigators and the dangers of miasmas.

The scene indoors was as bleak and cheerless as the exterior had been, and I found myself increasingly sobered by the inhospitable surroundings. When I'd been informed that the Messieurs operated a boarding-house, I'd mentally conjured images of an establish-ment much like the H&A, though perhaps with a shared lodging space containing multiple beds (a hum-ble arrangement amongst the lower classes I'd merely heard described but never witnessed). The reality was infinitely more depressing: the front room consisted of nothing more than a decaying clapboard floor and a soot-caked fireplace, in front of which squatted a homely woman stirring something unidentifiable in a pot hanging above the low flames. She didn't so much as lift her eyes or offer a single word of acknowledgement, and the shadows cast eerie hollows into the angles of her face. I shivered: despite the fire, it felt somehow colder inside than it had out on the street.

There was a ramshackle collection of tables and chairs strewn about seemingly at random, and an unmade straw bed was shoved haphazardly into the corner. I grimaced in horror: is that where these men slept, in the same common room where they entertained their lodgers? The shameless familiarity was obscene to my sensibilities, as base and raw as an unexpected exposure to nudity, and I quickly averted my gaze from the bed back to Mr. Hare, who disappeared wordlessly through a low-arched doorway to his right. Nye and I exchanged a quick glance, but there was nothing we could do but follow.

The lodging room was a similar picture of grim destitution: twelve "beds" (that seemed to me merely rugged troughs filled with hay) were arranged in two rows of six. The only indication that their contents were intended for human respite and not for animal consumption was the presence of a threadbare woolen blanket folded at the foot of each; clearly pillows were out of the question in accommodations so primitive. There were no washing basins, and no chamber pot to be seen. The place reeked with the stench of stale sweat and alcohol, and the complete absence of windows only compounded the dismal effect. It was, in sum, precisely the type of place I would expect two such men as Burke and Hare to operate.

Burke was in the process of fastening the familiar form of a tea-chest with a coarse length of rope to serve as handles for transport. He acknowledged our arrival with a curt nod of his head before immediately diverting his attention back to the task at hand; clearly neither he nor his partner were much for pleasantries. Nye and I pulled to a halt and stood in awkward silence as we watched Hare kneel to assist him; I knew not where to cast my eyes, as observing the men's labour before me felt rudely impatient, but to spare a glance at Nye seemed a danger in itself. I instead settled for an undefined point in the mid-distance, as though deep in thought, devoid of judgement or opinion upon this sordid situation—or any other.

At last, the Messieurs rose to their feet, the trunk well-trussed and ready. I was instantly reminded of just how large Burke was; he towered over Hare (who was admittedly slight) and still seemed nearly a head above Nye, who was notably taller than average. Despite myself, I shied from his imposing form, but did my best to disguise it as a casual shiver brought on by the dank cold.

"You remember your contact's name?" Hare's tone was artificially neutral, the Irish lilt in his accent doing nothing to erase the undertone of malice.

"Fergusson," I replied without hesitation.

"Aye. And the compensation?"

"Accept no less than a credit of eight pounds, to be collected by yourself, in person, within the hour," I recited.

Apparently satisfied by my response, he issued a brusque nod of approval. "Well enough, then. Off with you."

He took a step back to allow Nye and me access to the chest. Burke, I noted, remained unmoved and persistently mute, a towering presence above us as we assumed our positions on either side of the quarry, wrapped the rope loops about our wrists, and hoisted it up. It would have been a fair struggle for one man, but between the two of us, the load was not much, and I was pleased we'd remained nimble enough to maneuver quickly in case of any trouble.

For a moment, I considered whether I should issue a proper word of parting or perhaps tip my hat, but decided better of it; it was clear that when it came to doing business with Burke and Hare, the less said, the better. So it was wholly without fanfare that Nye and I retreated from the rotten trappings of the boarding-house with our cargo in tow, wound our way down the Close, and emerged onto the Grassmarket thoroughfare with nary a backwards look.

We walked for a time in wordless lockstep, navigating our way through the crowds and chattel clogging the street. Normally, I'd've balked at moving such a delicate haul in broad daylight, but I soon discovered that the throngs of pedestrians provided excellent cover for our purposes, however nefarious. We could disappear here, I realised, hidden in plain sight.

"So," Nye ventured, his voice raised above the chatter, "curious fellows, Burke and Hare."

"Told you so."

"And you've still no idea how they're connected to Knox?"

I was admittedly surprised that he'd so brazenly broached such a delicate topic in public, but I reasoned our chaotic surroundings left little opportunity for eavesdroppers. "Like I said, Hamish didn't give details when he introduced us."

Nye pursed his lips, brow furrowing in thought. "It's so odd, though, isn't it? That I've run in these circles for years, and yet I've never seen the two of them about. Mary confirmed they're not part of the current crews that operate out of the cemeteries at Cuthbert's, Calton, or Canongate. I've never crossed them at Greyfriars, yet their location in the city makes it unlikely they're sourcing their specimens from surrounding parishes—if their product is so fresh as to be worth eight pounds."

"And you still don't believe they're on Crouch's payroll?"

"As I said before, the men Crouch left in place to consolidate power for Knox would be henchmen, not low-level suppliers eking out a meagre living in a boarding-house."

"So the question remains: where are they getting their supply?"

"Precisely. According to Mary, Crouch's gang put most of the crews out of work; the few still employed are frequenting their old hunting grounds, but are forced to report to Knox, cutting the other anatomists out of the trade entirely. But Burke and Hare—"

"Don't fit that pattern."

"Just so. They report to Knox, of course, but from what source?" He paused to consider this further before continuing. "Did they tell you of their day trade?"

"They just said they worked at the canals. General labourers."

"Mmm." Nye's brow was knitted in apparent consternation, pearls of sweat forming at the hairline of his preposterous wig. I wiped my face with my own sleeve; despite the chilly weather, we were maintaining a brisk pace, and the weight of the chest felt increasingly cumbersome with each step.

It was with a degree of relief that we emerged off the Cowgate onto Nicolson Street and into the familiar surroundings of Surgeon's Square. We made haste to Number 10 (Knox's famous abode, seeming a world away from Malstrom's, despite being just footsteps down the lane) and sidled about to the back-alley entrance without drawing unwarranted attention, much to my relief; though our dress and manner would provide us a degree of protection from the law, it was best not to dawdle about the Square with a trunk in tow and risk disturbing the fragile peace with the authorities who sometimes patrolled there.

Three brisk knocks and the door flew open, revealing a tall, lean man with a disarmingly large moustache perched upon his thin face. He wore small silver spectacles, a spotless white canvas apron, and an expression of reserved disinterest.

"Mister Fergusson, I presume?" I spoke with an air of authority I did not at all possess.

His eyes narrowed as they fell upon the tea-chest suspended between us. "Who's calling?"

"Delivery from Messieurs Burke and Hare, sir. We were told you were expecting us."

His thin, pale lips turned downwards into a resigned moue. "Very well, then. This way."

He ushered us inside and down a long, dim corridor. I was struck by how different this venue seemed from my own school; it contained none of the light or airiness of Malstrom's operating hall, and it seemed to have all the dour malice I'd once superstitiously expected of a place such as this one. If anything, the lanterns lining the hall seemed almost intentionally low, as if the eerie ambiance were created more out of theatricality than necessity. I recalled the throngs of gawkers who, it was said, paid admission to Knox's demonstrations in his renowned operating theatre; was this design for their benefit? To spook them, and set the mood? How positively gauche. I wrinkled my nose in disgust at the thought.

We took a sharp left and entered a small office, then briskly carried on through a door at the back into what was clearly the entrance to Knox's private laboratory. Fergusson gestured vaguely towards an empty slab, completely ignoring the two other assistants already hard at work over their own specimens.

"Just there is fine. Open it up, and I'll give you your price."

Nye and I nodded resolutely and hauled the chest up to the surface before proceeding to untether it from its leather strappings. We stepped back to allow Fergusson to observe as we lifted the lid in unison.

And there, in solemn, stoic beauty, lay the pristine corpse of Mary Paterson.

It was as though the floor had dropped out from beneath me and I was still hovering there, midair, jarringly aware of my dire predicament but unable to do so much as flap my arms to keep from falling. The world grew suddenly weightless, dim, sticky-slow, surreal in shape and dull in sound, reality hazy and amorphous as it eluded my grasp.

She looked for all the world as though she were merely sleeping; her flame-red hair shone just as brightly in death as it had in the flickering firelight at the Pig, her pale skin as unspoiled as her youth would advise. Were it not for the unnatural curl of her limbs to accommodate the tight enclosure in which she was so unscrupulously restrained, I would have mistaken her repose for one of serene slumber.

"My God." To my shock, Fergusson was the first to speak. "I know this girl."

My head pivoted on my neck as mechanically as a bird on a cuckoo clock; I felt separate from my body, unable to form a coherent thought. My gaze came to rest on Nye, who was staring down at the tea-chest, his expression hauntingly blank. It was as if he could not believe what was transpiring before him.

"You know her?" Nye's voice sounded glassy, strange and hollow.

"Aye, she's a regular at The Drop—Jones! Miller! C'mere!"

The two nearby assistants ceased their work and crowded in around the chest, peering down at Mary's exposed body with impunity.

"Well, I'll be damned," one exclaimed, sounding more entertained than anything else.

The other let out a long, low whistle. "My, my, would've been a pity to waste that flesh on the worms—"

"Don't look at her!" It was as if something inside of Nye had snapped, and before I could react, he was lunging forward, slamming the chest shut and whirling about to face off against the rest of us, as if raring for a fight. The other assistants seemed as startled as myself at this sudden outburst, but it was Fergusson who gathered himself enough to intervene.

"There there, my good fellow! You needn't worry, we are all professional physicians here, the young lady's modesty—"

"The young lady's modesty is none of your goddamn business," Nye hissed dangerously, his expression feral and wild. "I won't let you lay a hand on her!"

"It's a bit late for chivalry, I'm afraid," Fergusson continued, seeming to mistake Nye's impertinence for a newcomer's malaise at the whole ordeal. "This poor young lady is quite irreversibly deceased, and her corpse is officially the legal property of Dr. Knox, as per the arrangement with his esteemed colleagues."

"Like hell she's his property," Nye snarled. "This isn't some anonymous old wench who turned belly-up in the Vaults! You know her! I know her! This is Mary! She's my"—his voice faltered, if only for a moment— "she's my friend."

"Sorry, sonny," the other assistant chimed in. "But Mary here had plenty of 'friends.' Dunno what she told you up against the alley wall, but—"

Before I could react, Nye lunged forward and punched him square in the face. A spray of blood erupted from his nose, splashing theatrically across Fergusson's spotless apron, and all three men were suddenly so violently entangled I had no idea how to even begin to extricate Nye. Knox's third assistant stood beside me in a similar state of paralysis; it would seem neither of us had the slightest idea what to do. Diving into the fray seemed ill-advised, but a split second later, the combatants rammed squarely up against the dissection slab, threatening to overturn the tea-chest entirely, and it became obvious the scrum could not continue unchecked. We reached this conclusion in apparent unison and simultaneously dove head first into the fray.

As fights go, this one was not particularly brutal. Growing up with two older brothers, I'd learned early on to sustain the abuses of poorly thrown fists, elbows, and knees, and frankly, my fellow physicians were not half the brawlers my brothers were. That said, the unique circumstance of being veritably surrounded by half-dissected corpses did indeed raise the stakes, and I found myself pulling my punches more out of caution for the deceased than concern for the living. I've no idea how long we'd carried on for, save that it was long enough for me to deal and receive a fair few blows, but not so long as to allow either side to establish an upper hand. I'd just begun to consider whether we might be in a bit over our heads when a voice rang out, low and sharp, loud enough to startle us into instant submission.

"ENOUGH!"

The three assistants jerked immediately to attention like foot soldiers in the presence of a general. For an instant, Nye and I continued to flail half-heartedly in their direction, but we quickly realised that the interloper commanded an immediate truce and composed ourselves as readily as possible, considering the circumstances, and turned in the direction of the sound.

Silhouetted in the doorway was the imposing figure of a man, stooped in frame yet still broad in appearance, draped in the folds of an elaborate overcoat and leaning heavily against a cane. For an eternal second, he said nothing: he simply stood, taking in the scene before him. I detected a distinct tremble in Fergusson and realised that, while the man's silence meant nothing to me, it was speaking volumes to his minions.

At long last, he emerged from the shadows in a series of slow, deliberate strides, his pace making the reveal of his facial features all the more dramatic; for the man's face was truly that of a monster—and I am not one to speak in hyperbole. It was pockmarked and lined with deep crevices in the flesh, giving the impression of having been clumsily hewn from rough stone. His left eye was missing, its absence poorly disguised by the presence of a ragged eye patch. His lips were pulled into a grisled, sneering scowl, and what little hair he had stood out from his head in sparse, unkempt tufts.

So this was the esteemed Dr. Knox! His name was common enough on the lips of every University student that I'd always felt him a formal acquaintance by association, but it was true that I'd never actually seen the man. He rarely ventured outside of his school, and word was he lived in the New Town—the wealthy part of the city. Before this moment, I'd assumed the tall tales of his appearance to be greatly exaggerated, but was now forced to admit they were, if anything, more forgiving than the reality of it.

He ventured forward until he was a mere foot in front of Fergusson, who by that point was quite literally quaking in his boots.

"Fergusson, what is the meaning of this?"

"Apologies, sir. A minor dispute with the porters."

"The porters, eh?" Knox's singular eye slid over myself and Nye in turn; I silently prayed that Nye's disguise was more convincing than I found it to be. Nye remained stoically mute beneath Knox's scrutiny, while I took the opportunity to readjust my hat in an effort to regain a semblance of propriety. To my horror, Knox's gaze slipped straight past me to linger suspiciously on Nye, as if wondering if he recognised him.

"A thousand apologies, sir," I ventured, desperate to distract him from Nye's visage. (God, was I really speaking out of turn to Dr. Knox? Had I lost my mind?) "But we're under strict orders from the suppliers to guarantee a fixed price for our quarry. When we could not reach an agreement, my associate here and I ventured to reclaim it."

Knox took a step back and seemed to assess me for the first time. I straightened my back and met his gaze unwaveringly, assuming an expression of snobbish disdain; after all, was I not a student from a well-bred family, no different from the ones filling his pockets at the endless demonstrations he provided in his famed theatre? He could not possibly know my true status and thus would owe me the benefit of the doubt.

"Reclaim it, eh? That's a bit unconventional, lad. You should know we've a set arrangement with all our suppliers; what my assistants have offered you is what's been decided."

"But, sir, I think you'll agree, this particular specimen is of such unique quality, it ought to fetch a finer price than what's on offer."

Knox paused. "Cancer?"

I was caught off guard. "Sorry?"

"Does the subject have cancer? Elephantiasis? A conjoined twin? A deformed limb? A foetus?"

"No?"

"Then what can you possibly be offering me that would warrant more than the standard sum?"

I was grasping at straws. It was clear Nye was in no condition to defend himself against interrogation, and I knew I must therefore hold Knox's attention at all costs. "Why don't you . . . see for yourself, sir?" With that, I stood aside and gestured extravagantly towards the chest, a magician performing the prestige. Knox took a measured step forward and drew open the top of the chest, then uttered an exclamation of what I could only describe as delight; it would seem my instincts about the man had been correct.

"My goodness, she's exquisite! And in such a pristine state, not a smudge of dirt or waft of rot! A true prize, my boy—you've an excellent eye." I couldn't stand to watch him leering at poor Mary, but I quickly remembered myself: the situation at hand was well past dire, and I would count us lucky if I could get Nye and myself out of it with merely a couple of split lips to show for our troubles. Still, if Knox saw me as an enthusiastic student, he would expect me to play the unscrupulous lickspittle, and I dared not disappoint.

"Why, thank you sir." I offered a cordial bow.

"Did your suppliers tell you her cause of death?"

"I'm afraid not, sir."

"Curious, how marvelously curious! Fergusson, we will assess the specimen in the theatre immediately."

Fergusson startled and stuttered, clearly caught off guard. "But, sir, I'm afraid the theatre hasn't been properly cleaned from this morning's lecture."

Knox's face transformed in an instant from one of merry mirth to one of downright disdain. "Then fetch the bloody slop-boy and have it cleaned, for God's sake!" With a brisk bow, Fergusson scurried out the door, and Knox turned his attention back to me. "Now, my good fellow, fetch that chest and follow me." Without waiting for a response, he whirled on his heel and disappeared once more into the shadows.

I tried to catch Nye's eye as we grasped the opposing handles of the chest and gingerly lifted Mary and her casket from the slab, but his gaze was distant and unfocused. He was surely dazed with grief and shock; I myself could barely comprehend this turn of events, and I'd known Mary for far shorter a time than Nye. The scale of his loss was incalculable.

Yet we somehow soldiered on, following Knox's hobbled gait through the winding hallways of half-lit lamps. He never once turned to see if we were in pursuit—he merely assumed his bidding would be done. I swiftly concluded that Knox was an arrogant, hubristic man, far from the entertainingly rebellious folk hero of University lore. He seemed every bit as immoral and selfish as Nye had described, and I dared not wonder what awaited us at the end of this journey; I could merely persist in placing one foot in front of the other.

We at last emerged from the maze of narrow hallways and into an operating theatre so large it took my breath away. I'd been in the grand theatres at the University, of course—the type that sat a fair four hundred men, making it nearly impossible to observe the lecturer without a pair of opera glasses. But this theatre was different: intimate rows of narrow wooden seats rose up on all sides of the chamber, stacked so steeply that they disappeared into the cavernous darkness above the upper tiers. The stage was brilliantly illuminated beneath a soaring, domed-glass window, haloed in a series of glowing lamps that gave the whole scene a serene, heavenly aura. The only indication that this theatre was intended for dissection—as opposed to, say, the royal ballet—was the presence of a singular stoic pedestal and slab positioned prominently in the middle of it.

Currently crouched beneath the pedestal was a small man frantically scrubbing away at what (to my horror) appeared to be an alarming amount of fat, tendon, and blood strewn about the floor. I was beyond appalled: Malstrom never made a mess of his subjects, for he insisted it was an insult to their posthumous dignity. But what stood before me looked to be the aftermath of savage butchery, not scientific dissection. It was abundantly clear that Knox was no proper scientist: he was clearly a madman, if this was the nature of his demonstrations! No wonder his audiences spoke with such awe of his methods; this was theatre, plain and simple. Entertainment.

"You! Boy! Have you not finished yet?" Knox's voice echoed menacingly through the chamber, and the man jerked upright. I nearly stopped dead in my tracks: it was Hamish.

"A thousand apologies, sir, we didn't know you'd be needing the theatre—"

"Enough!" Knox snarled and, without warning, dealt a brutal backhand across Hamish's flushing face. "Get the slab cleared for now; leave the rest for later."

To his credit, Hamish barely flinched. "Yes, sir."

It was in that moment that his eyes flicked past Knox to rest on me. They grew wide for a moment, knowing that his lie had been at last exposed: he was no assistant to the great Dr. Knox, he was merely a slop-boy at his theatre, charged with clearing out the grisly bits of gore (and, evidently, pinching what he could for the amusement of his admirers back at the pub). He was even lowlier than I! And to think, from the way he talked at the H&A, all confidence and swagger—I never would have guessed his secret. But here in this moment, it was all revealed between us. Momentary relief surged through me: from now on, I would be indebted to Hamish no more.

Hamish swiftly turned away and proceeded to give the dissection slab a perfunctory wipe-down, but it was still a far cry from anything resembling clean when Knox summoned Miller and Jones to lay Mary out for assessment. Nye and I stood side by side and could only watch in mutual helpless despair as her corpse was positioned, all modesty disregarded. I desperately wished to take Nye's hand, to squeeze it, to offer some reassurance that this was all simply a terrible nightmare, but I knew in my soul that there would be no waking from this. Whatever nefarious plot we were caught up in, it had cost Mary her life; this was the price and penance for our vocation, and it would seem our debt was now due.

Knox at last scaled the dais and stood peering lasciviously down at the figure displayed before him. Mary looked for all the world like a sacrifice laid out in supine surrender, her familiar red hair a halo of flames crowning her beatific face. When juxtaposed so severely against Knox's monstrous visage, the scene, in sum, was so utterly grotesque that I yearned to turn away. Yet I could not afford to betray my repulsion, for just then Nye swayed slightly as if suddenly unsteady upon his feet. I instinctively maneuvered to prop my shoulder against his own; it was clear that I would need to be strong enough for the both of us.

Knox proceeded to run his hands up and down the length of Mary's body, examining her state, muttering to himself. "Superb, simply superb. Most excellent, indeed." After a seeming eternity, he at last withdrew his lecherous grip and straightened his back. "Well, my dear boy"—Knox's gaze fell once more to me—"she is a marvel. And you're quite right; please tell the Messieurs I'll give them a full nine pounds for such a catch, available for collection this afternoon. And to you, for your prodigious observation—a full ten shillings to you and your companion, for your diligence and discretion."

He turned his attention back to his team. "Fergusson, fetch a whiskey barrel from the stores. Jones, Miller, prepare the body for preservation; we'll sell tickets at double-price for this one; she'll be a marvelous show indeed. And you, boy"—he spoke sharply to Hamish, and it was abundantly clear he had no idea what his proper name was—"pay out the porters, then get back to work on these floors. This hall is a disgrace." And with this final barked command, he took his leave, offering no word of parting.

In an instant his team sprang into action, his three assistants bursting into a flurry of activity while Hamish merely gave me a jerk of his head to indicate that I was to follow him. We made our way to the back door in silence. It was clear we were each preparing our gambit; Hamish surely knew I wasn't about to let his secret go unmentioned, and I was not inclined to let Mary go without avenging her circumstance. And as for Nye—he remained disconcertingly quiet, still apace beside me but perceptibly distant. Without ado, Hamish ushered us outside.

The moment we set foot in the narrow alley, however, Nye whirled about and forcibly grabbed Hamish by the collar, pulling him straight out the door behind us. He spun him and slammed him bodily against the rough-hewn stone of the building, eliciting a desperate yelp from a similarly startled Hamish. I was once again forced to attempt to regain control of the situation.

"For God's sake, Nye, stop it, you're acting insane." I yanked him back by the collar, and he gave a frustrated snarl as Hamish escaped his grasp, dodging Nye's thrashing and making a break for the door. "Hamish, don't you dare set foot through that door, or I'll tell everyone at the H&A about this little farce you're putting on. I doubt they'll be so willing to spare you a pint when they find out you are more proficient with a mop than a scalpel."

Hamish's hand froze upon the door handle. He didn't turn around, but he at last spoke. "You're bluffing."

I lowered my voice dangerously. "You know I'm a gambling man, Hamish. Do you really want to take that bet?"

With a resigned sigh, his hand dropped to his side, and he turned back around to face us, shoulders drooping in apparent defeat. "Fine. What do you want?"

"We want answers," Nye growled, eyes still dark and dangerous, fists curled for a fight.

"Who the bloody hell are you?" Hamish paused and squinted, then jerked back in sudden realisation. "My God, you're Malstrom's man!" He whipped around in my direction. "What is going on here? Why've you brought him into this?"

Nye cut in before I could offer any semblance of explanation. "Because that girl lying on the slab in there was our friend. A member of our crew. And now she's dead, and I know for a fact her body never went below ground. So you're going to tell us everything you know about Messieurs Burke and Hare."

Hamish stared defiantly back at Nye. "I don't know any more than you do."

"You're full of shite," Nye spat, and I internally flinched at his indecency. "How long have they been suppliers for Knox?"

"Five or six months, thereabouts."

"How regular?"

Hamish paused to consider this. "Once a fortnight or so, more or less."

"And what's their source?"

Hamish shrugged. "Never asked."

Nye took two commanding steps forward to loom over Hamish, the intensity in his expression flaring bright, even in the dim light of the alley. "Now listen here, you little weasel: whatever Knox is up to in the kirkyards of this city, that's business. But what happened here today? That's personal. So I'm asking you plainly: where did Knox find these men? And where do they get their quarries?"

Hamish set his jaw. "I don't really see how that's my problem."

"Because," retorted Nye with a menacing grin, "you're going to help us catch the bastards."

14.

A Revelation

Hamish glared skeptically out from beneath his wide-brimmed hat at the sparse crowd gathered at the Pig, taking in the ambiance. For all his measured swagger when he was holding court at the H&A, it appeared that being put out of his element was enough to reduce him to a series of nervous twitches and tics. He'd barely even touched the pint I'd placed before him, a clear indication he was feeling quite unlike himself.

Truthfully, I wasn't faring much better. The two days that had passed since our encounter with Knox had been fraught and filled with tension, primarily because Nye had insisted upon breaking the news about Mary to his crew on his own. Though I initially took offense, I knew deep down that I was still an interloper amongst their tight-knit family—a foreigner, an outlander, and while they'd come to tolerate (and even, dare I say, accept) me, I would always be cut from a different cloth than they.

I'd paid a visit to Nye's chambers the following night to check on his welfare, and he'd been so sullen and short-tempered I'd left in a snit of my own. Though I could not yet comprehend that we would never again share a laugh with her over a dram and that her seat at our familiar table was to be permanently vacant, my grief paled in comparison to Nye's. I yearned to console him, but I had to acknowledge that Mary's loss had cut him far deeper than I could comprehend, and I knew him well enough to allow space for his sorrow.

I was therefore startled to discover a note left upon my tray at the onset of Malstrom's lecture the very next morning:

Tonight

The Pig—10 o'clock sharp

Bring Hamish

I hadn't the faintest idea what Nye had in store for his newly marked adversary, so it was with bewildered resignation that I was forced to confront Hamish in his customary booth at the H&A, fully prepared to extort him into joining me. Much to my surprise, he agreed without a fuss; it would seem that my knowledge of his dearest secret afforded me considerably more power than I'd previously dared hope.

"So how long have you been messing about with Malstrom's man?" Hamish spoke apropos of nothing, gaze still firmly locked on the unfamiliar crowd surrounding us.

"I beg your pardon?" The question caught me so entirely off guard I nearly dropped my pint, humiliation and indignation swelling hotly at the back of my tongue. My God, were we so obvious that someone as obtuse as Hamish could discern the true nature of my companionship with Nye? We'd have to be more careful—

"I mean, how long have you been digging with his crew? And don't be coy, Willoughby; I know damned well you're a digger and not just a porter. The second I saw you with MacKinnon, it all fell into place."

I attempted to shirk my persistent paranoia and instead eyed him appraisingly. "What gave it away? My hands?" They were now undeniably the hands of a digger, boasting the trademark calluses of a man who made his way in the world with a spade.

Hamish pursed his lips. "Your fingernails—far more dirt under them than there should be for a man of your station. You diggers are a filthy lot, aren't ye?"

"Says the slop-boy."

"Says the—"

"Gentlemen! Kind of you to join me." Three drams of whiskey dropped to the table with a clatter as Nye folded himself elegantly into the chair beside me, not even bothering to divest himself of his overcoat. "Drink up."

Hamish glared at him. "The hell, MacKinnon. I'll not touch a drop until you tell me why you've brought me here."

Nye just grinned and threw back his drink with abandon, smacking his lips and slapping the glass to the table with a flourish. "And I won't speak a word until you've enjoyed my hospitality. So it seems we find ourselves at an impasse, McGregor." I was consistently startled at how much thicker Nye's accent became when he was amongst his own countrymen, and between him and

Hamish, I was becoming increasingly uncertain that I'd even be able to follow the conversation without a translator.

"So your plan is, what, to get me drunk enough I'll willingly go along with whatever hare-brained scheme you've cooked up?"

Nye shrugged. "No, I'm certain you'll go along willingly regardless, unless you'd like the details of your position at Knox's to be made public amongst the many admirers James tells me you've made amongst the gullible University boys. Oh, and I'm sure the good doctor's assistants would be thrilled to know you've been passing yourself off as one of their own—"

"Yes, alright, we've established you've got me cornered here, but could we perhaps pass over the niceties"—he gestured towards his glass—"and get on to business?"

"Oh, I assure you these aren't niceties." Nye's gaze was cold, his tone suddenly laced with vitriol. "I fear rather they're essential for the business we're about to conduct tonight."

My head whipped towards him. "Tonight?" What on earth was Nye going to have us do? He couldn't seriously think the three of us could take down Burke and Hare on our own; though we were all sturdy enough, Burke and Hare were hardened criminals of the tenement lot. I wouldn't bet against them in a fight.

Nye remained unfazed. "Indeed, tonight. Drink up, James. We'll need to steady our stomachs."

I caught his eye and attempted to hold it, willing him to somehow communicate to me exactly what wild vengeance was in store, but he simply blinked and turned away. Once again, I would have to trust him blindly.

Without allowing myself a moment more to think, I plucked up my glass and threw down the contents. I noticed that the whiskey no longer made me sputter. Reluctantly, Hamish followed suit.

"Excellent!" Nye clapped his hands together in a disconcerting display of manufactured mirth. "Now let's be on our way; we haven't a moment to waste." With that, he rose and, from beside his chair, picked up a handsomely embossed leather bag I'd never seen before—I'd been so distracted by his entrance with the whiskey I'd failed to even note he was carrying it. Its contents made a most disconcerting metallic clatter, and I could feel inklings of hesitation welling traitorously in my chest.

Hamish and I followed Nye in silence as he led us (quite to my surprise) not towards Tanner's Close at all, but instead along the familiar path to Surgeon's Square. The hour was late and the streets eerily deserted, void of the bustle of students and faculty that rendered life into the place. We passed Malstrom's school and carried on straight to Number 10, my anxiety swelling with each passing second. What could Nye be planning at Knox's establishment that required a strong stomach enforced by drink? We maneuvered our way through the shadows to the back door, at which point Nye performed a startling about-face, nearly causing a collision with myself and Hamish (who'd been following lock-step behind him).

"Open the door." His tone was low and commanding, eyes black and stern, his expression unreadable beneath his pale skin alight with the reflection of the moon. I had never before feared Nye, despite his sordid occupation and dubious morals, but here in this moment, his feral intensity sent chills down my spine.

Hamish glowered but dare not protest; he produced a ring of keys from the chain on his waistcoat, fitted one into the door, and pressed it open with a long, low groan of the hinges which echoed deafeningly down the alley. We slipped inside wordlessly, only to be simultaneously startled by the slamming of the door behind us.

The now-familiar hallway was predictably dim, the only lit lantern the one positioned beside the door. Nye gestured towards it with a curt nod.

"Take us to Knox's stores."

Hamish cocked his head dangerously. "You can't be serious."

"Does it appear that I'm joking? To the stores, slop-boy. Now." With that, Nye pulled the lantern from its peg and thrust it into Hamish's hand. Grudgingly, his fingers closed around the handle, and he turned to guide us into the impending darkness.

We wound through the narrow hallways until we reached a stone spiral staircase descending into a cellar. My breath felt hot and tight in my lungs; I knew not what Nye's designs were, but I knew that nothing good could be found in the stores of an anatomy school.

We descended briskly, unable to let Hamish get too far ahead, lest the light of his lantern disappear around the coiled stairwell, and at last emerged into a dank, low-ceilinged room lined with whiskey casks stacked in a sturdy iron rack. In the center of the room was a long wooden table bearing stains of an unmentionable source, and the smell of rancid alcohol permeated the stale air.

Wordlessly, Nye snatched the lantern from Hamish's grasp and used its wick to light three more, illuminating the room in a sinister glow. Placing the last of these upon the table, he uttered the first words since we had entered this forsaken place.

"Which ones were Burke and Hare's?"

Hamish shifted nervously. "Most of 'em are gone. Already used."

Nye narrowed his eyes. "But not all."

With a resigned sigh, Hamish appeared to capitulate and turned to face the wall of barrels, pointing to select ones in turn. "Ostler. Simpson. Haldane. Wilson. And, of course, Paterson over there." He gestured vaguely towards a cask still top-up in the corner, and I shuddered with dread.

Nye appeared unimpacted. "Good man. McGregor, go fetch the intake records. James, help me get these down."

Hamish disappeared back up the staircase, lantern in hand, and I was still so speechless with shock and dismay that I uttered not a word as Nye and I worked in tandem to pull the designated casks from their shelves. They were awkward and unwieldy, and I strained to shoulder the load as we maneuvered them into a scattered row before the table. As soon as we rolled the last one into place, Nye knelt over the suspicious leather bag on the floor, popped open the clasp, and procured a crowbar.

"Nye, what are you—"

Before I could finish my sentence, Nye had cracked open the top of the nearest barrel and pried open the lid, and I was hit squarely in the face with the most nauseating stench I'd ever encountered in my natural life. Retching, I retreated backwards as my eyes overflowed and my stomach threatened to upend its contents.

"You alright?" Nye sounded, if anything, slightly amused by my reaction.

"Christ almighty, Nye, give a man some warning! And would you care to enlighten me as to what the hell we're doing here?" I'd intended to be benevolent and indulge whatever plot he'd cooked up in an ill-fated effort to avenge his grief, but the current circumstances were trying my patience.

"We are testing a hypothesis." With that, he rolled up his sleeve and plunged his hand into whatever substance was raising the infernal stink permeating the room. He shook his arm a bit and sank deeper, as if fishing for something, and then his eyes lit up as he produced (to my infinite horror), a gape-mouthed head attached to what was evidently a submerged cadaver.

The look on my face must have been worth a thousand words, because Nye didn't wait for me to inquire before proceeding to explain, apparently entirely unimpacted by the grotesque contents of his right hand. "Knox is famous for preserving his most prized specimens in whiskey for months at a time, waiting for the most opportune moment to perform high-demand demonstrations—for which he doubles his admission fee, of course."

I blanched. "So these barrels all contain—"

"Preserved corpses, yes. Now stop flapping about and help me get this one up on the table."

"Not until you tell me why you need it on the table! For Heaven's sake, this is ludicrous! And what's any of it got to do with Mary's death?"

He dropped the head unceremoniously back beneath the brim of the barrel with a troubling splash and turned to look me straight in the eye, his gaze blazing with intensity. "You know as well as I do that Mary didn't die, she was murdered. And I intend to prove she wasn't the only one. So, are you going to help me or not?"

As if he even had to ask; as always when it came to Nye, I was already in over my head. Before I could doubt myself, I strode forward and hastily rolled up my sleeves before plunging my hands into the barrel, gripping the corpse beneath the arms and giving it a firm yank. Nye rushed in to catch the knees as it slithered perilously towards the floor, then aided me in hauling it up to spread it supine upon the weathered table.

We were just wrestling the third specimen (Haldane, M., according to the chalk scribble gracing the lid of the barrel) out of its container when Hamish reappeared with a thick leather bound tome in hand. He deposited it with a flourish upon the end of the table not currently dripping with corpse-whiskey, apparently disconcertingly unimpacted by the smell or the proceedings unfolding in front of him.

"Here you are, sir."

Nye glanced up from our labours with a satisfied nod. "Excellent, I'll be right there. We just need to—Good Lord, is this Daft Jamie?" We'd just cracked open the fourth barrel, and upon closer inspection, I could confirm we were regrettably familiar with its occupant.

Hamish gave a sly shrug. "And if it is?"

Squinting at the corpse in the barrel, I could now detect a distinct resemblance.

Nye appeared incensed. "His crew's been scouring the West Port looking for him for weeks, to say nothing of the heartbreak his mother endured following his disappearance! You mean to tell me that none of Knox's men recognised him? Even with his club foot?"

Hamish was unmoved. "Knox took care of the problem with a falciform knife immediately upon delivery."

"He—oh, for the love . . ." With that, Nye bent and hauled the body fully out of the barrel and cast it dripping onto the table beside the others.

I blinked in disbelief. The cadaver's feet were gone, the elegantly hewn edge of the resulting stumps an unmistakable trademark of the falciform.

"He destroyed the evidence." Nye's voice was low. "He knew."

"Knew what?" Hamish sounded unimpressed.

"Knew that Burke and Hare are no average snatchers. Daft Jamie may not have been of sound mind, but he was young, healthy, and strong as an ox; there's no way Knox would mistake him for the victim of a natural death."

"Never said his death was natural." Hamish reached down and gave the bound book on the table top a little shove in our direction. "I do believe there was drink involved."

Nye snatched up the volume and flipped through the pages, running his finger down the lined ledger until it came to rest upon the name Wilson, J.

"*Intake date: 14 February. Suppliers: W.B. & W.H. Cause of death: Alcohol-Induced Asphyxiation.* And—just as I suspected—no source."

I glanced over Nye's shoulder and furrowed my brow. "There's no column for *Source*," I observed.

"Not officially, no," Nye replied. "But look here: see these symbols at the end of each row?" He pointed to a series of delicately drawn marks etched in the margins of the ledger. "Each of these corresponds to the insignia of a kirkyard in the city: Cuthbert's, Calton, Canongate. He kept records of where the bodies were snatched from, which crew was responsible."

The enormity of what he was insinuating washed over me. "And Jamie's . . ."

Nye grinned up at me, face alight in revelation. "Had no origin. And look here . . ." He flicked through more pages, scanning the margins for the telltale omission. "The same goes for Haldane, Simpson, Ostler . . . all Burke and Hare's quarries! And Christ on the cross, there's more . . ." He commenced counting under his breath each time he crossed a line with an absent source.

Each was the same:

Suppliers: W.B. & W.H. Cause of death: Asphyxiation.

I could feel my blood run cold.

"Fifteen." Nye's voice was barely a murmur.

"What?" I could scarcely believe my ears.

"They've produced fifteen cadavers since November last. The first apparently died of dropsy, according to the official records, but after that . . ."

"Asphyxiation," I whispered. It was murder, as certain as could be.

Nye slapped the book shut so abruptly that Hamish let out an undignified yelp, and I nearly jumped backwards straight into the open barrel of whiskey.

"Now!" Nye declared, casting the book aside. "For the final proof."

He knelt before his open bag and rummaged through it, eventually producing an array of syringes, a series of delicate vials, and a corked bottle of an unidentifiable substance. He deposited the lot upon the table and rose, spreading his hands benevolently before him, a conductor captivating his chorus before the opening downbeat.

"Observe!" He plucked up a syringe and decapped it, then approached the body of 'Olster, J.'. With nary a temporisation, he took the needle and stuck it directly into the trachea, then proceeded to slowly withdraw the plunger, gathering the lingering fluid from the lungs. Once he was satisfied with the volume, he withdrew and deposited the secretion meticulously into a clear glass vial. Then he briskly popped the top from the mysterious bottle, tipped a few drops into the vial, inserted a stopper, and gave the whole thing a hearty shake. To my surprise, the mixture within transformed from its original grey-brown hue into a striking blue one.

"What the devil?" Hamish approached out of the shadows, suddenly seeming as fascinated as I was.

"What is that?" I demanded, stepping closer to observe the metamorphosis.

"This, gentlemen, is a solution used to indicate the presence of either cresol compounds alone—in which case, the solvent turns blue, or if there is an additional presence of bile acids—in which case it will turn a rather impressive shade of chartreuse."

I was floored. "Where did you get the solvent?"

"I invented it," he replied nonchalantly. "A few years ago, when Malstrom suspected a declared outbreak of consumption was, in fact, the result of a bad batch of spirits brewed in the Vaults. We needed to be able to verify the presence of bile in the lungs: a sure sign of asphyxiation due to poisoning. Consumption would leave no such trace."

My mind was racing a mile a minute, and when I spoke, it was in a tone of hushed awe. "So in this case, if all the specimens were truly the victims of alcohol-induced asphyxiation, there'd be bile present in the airway. And"—I turned to peer more closely at the swirling blue contents of the vial—"in this case, it's clearly not."

"Nope." Nye plopped the vial down on the table, picked up another syringe, and continued on with a second extraction courtesy of Simpson, A. "And I'm guessing there will be no bile in the rest of these, either, but science demands we be thorough with our evidence. Lend a hand?" He gestured towards the pile of syringes. With a grin, I took my place beside him.

Moments later, we had our results: none of the cadavers had asphyxiated upon their own expulsions, rendering the declared cause of death an obvious fallacy. It was a brilliant maneuver, swift and damning, and I beamed over at Nye in anticipation of his shared exaltation.

To my bewilderment, he looked more troubled than elated. I capped my last vial and placed it on the table beside the others, all a perfect hue of cerulean. "What is it?"

His lips drew into a thin line, and his eyes narrowed as he leaned over the body of Daft Jamie, running two fingers firmly along the centre of the corpse's throat. "It doesn't make any sense."

I moved in closer until our shoulders were brushing and placed my fingers beside his own where they were still tracing the length of the trachea, trying to feel what he felt.

"Do you feel that?" His fingers bumped against mine, guiding my search.

I shook my head. "I don't feel anything."

His hand suddenly closed over mine, stilling me mid-thought, drawing my gaze to his. "Exactly."

I just stared back at him, utterly lost.

"There's no damage to the trachea. If these people had been strangled, there would be trauma, possibly bruising, signs of a struggle . . . but there's nothing. Yet no bile in the lungs, so they clearly couldn't have asphyxiated upon their own vomit, which coincidentally rules out poisoning as well. So how do Burke and Hare do it?"

He released my hand and began to pace the small space. For the first time in several minutes, I registered the presence of Hamish, who was watching the proceedings with an air of mild curiosity. My fingers suddenly burned red-hot where moments mere moments ago they'd been entangled with Nye's own.

"Burke is large, strong, capable. He could easily crush the throat of an old woman in her sleep, or perhaps entice her to over-imbibe and take advantage of her incapacitation. Daft Jamie, though—he was a fortress, a gentle giant. And I know for a fact the boy didn't drink to excess. There's no way Burke could have overpowered him on his own; the alcohol they served him must have been mixed with something much stronger, yet not poison or there'd be signs of emesis." He paused his monologue just long enough to hover at the head end of the line of corpses, leaning in so close to their bloated faces that I couldn't fathom how he didn't retch from the stink. Then without further ado, he reached forward and one by one pried their mouths open.

"Ah. Aha." He snatched up the nearest lantern and held it aloft to illuminate his subjects.

"What is it?" I approached once more, still carefully breathing through my mouth to avoid the odour.

"Look here." Nye picked up a spare syringe and used the needle end to point into the mouth of the nearest victim. "The back molars are cracked. Could be common wear-and-tear were it a one-off, but see: it's the same in all the others, even Daft Jamie, and he was young and in fair health."

My mind quickly drew a conclusion. "You think their jaws were forced shut."

Nye shot me an approving smile. "Indeed I do. And see here?" He traced his fingers along a web of inflamed blood vessels surrounding the nostrils of the nearest victim. "I'll bet this is bruising. Ordinarily we'd assume it was common inflammation or acne rosacea caused by the recent inhospitable weather, but in this case, I think not. It all makes sense: tainted alcohol to incapacitate, and brute force to extinguish."

I peered closer, still harbouring my own doubts. "Perhaps. But you must agree, the bruising could very well be incidental—"

"In an isolated incident, yes. But for it to present in all four bodies? It would be a most unlikely coincidence. Combine that with the damage to the molars and the absence of bile? I believe we have ourselves a modus operandi: they lure the victim with unlimited drinks of dubious origins, then suffocate them by sealing their mouth and nose simultaneously. I'd venture there's trauma to the ribs indicating they place a weight of some sort upon the chest, but, unfortunately, confirming that would require far more invasiveness than we're currently afforded. We don't want to be fined for the destruction of Knox's property."

I paused to consider this. "Do you think four specimens is enough to make the case?"

Nye straightened, a pall of grief falling across his angular face. "Five." He gestured towards the barrel in the corner: Paterson, M.

I shook my head. "Nye, no, we don't have to, I'm sure the police will—"

"Bungle it royally. I'm not leaving Mary's justice to chance." He set his jaw in grim determination. "Come along, James. Help me with her."

It was a sorrowful unveiling indeed. We uncoiled Mary from her provisional coffin, Nye tenderly cradling her lolling head as I wrapped my arms around her lifeless limbs. We placed her gingerly beside the others, her beauty all the more acute in opposition to their bloated state. I watched in stoic silence as Nye drew his sample from her lungs before handing it to me to process, then he gently pried open her lips to examine her teeth as I procured the solvent results. When all was finished, he closed her mouth with benevolent tenderness, and

I placed the fifth and final vial of blue fluid upon the table beside the others.

Then Nye simply stared down at her for a seeming eternity, his eyes distant and expression vacant. It was as if he were forcing himself to look at her as a type of penance, and eventually I could not stand to watch him torture himself any further.

"She would be proud of you, Nye." I wrapped my arm around him and gave his shoulder a squeeze. "You'll get her justice now. I know it."

He placed his hand solemnly over mine and gave me a wan smile in return. "God willing, James. God willing."

Our eyes met, and I yearned to kiss him, but abruptly remembered Hamish's presence and pulled curtly away. My reaction seemed to shake Nye from his stupor, and a moment later, he was himself again, turning to bark out more orders.

"Alright, McGregor. Put these back where we found 'em." He gestured towards the bodies, then turned to pick up his bag and began to fill it with his equipment and our collection of evidence.

"And just where do you think you're going?" Hamish retorted haughtily.

"We're taking this"—he held his bag aloft—"and this"—he snatched up the records book—"to the proper authorities."

Hamish glared. "Like hell you are. You're not putting me out of a job!"

Nye rolled his eyes. "Oh, don't be dramatic. Knox will come out of this unscathed; you know as well as I do how the law works in this town! He has money and means and prestige; the police won't touch him. He needs only to feign ignorance and let the paupers take the fall. Same as always." And with those bitter words on his tongue and a jerk of his head in my direction, we hastily took our leave.

I was still coming to terms with all that had just transpired as we wound our way through the Closes at a brisk clip, Nye's strides purposeful and his expression determined. I at last felt compelled to speak, if only to assuage my own lingering doubts.

"I still don't understand it, though. Why would they have gone after Mary?"

"As part of Knox and Crouch's plan to undercut all the other crews; Mary herself said she was sure their gang had noticed her observing their activities, and it's no secret in the trade that she was associated with our lot. They picked her off to shut her mouth. Same with Daft Jamie; he worked with the lads at Cuthbert's for years and must have resisted Knox's efforts to expunge their crew from the territory."

I puzzled over this for a moment. "But the other victims we saw, they were all old women—poor, connectionless old women, foreign to the city, if they were residing in a boarding-house and associating with the likes of Burke and Hare. How could a bunch of old crones be involved in the trade?"

"They weren't," Nye replied simply. "It's my belief that Burke and Hare are opportunists turned executioners." I eyed him quizzically, and he proceeded to elaborate. "For the most part, they'd kill the elderly and infirm merely for profit, a crime which Knox was willing to overlook in exchange for such excellent specimens. But once Crouch and his ilk became involved,

Knox used Burke and Hare to murder for political gain, not just financial; hence the calculated elimination of Jamie and Mary. It's a rather brilliant model if you think about it: disguising their targeted kills within a series of utterly random ones."

I shuddered. "It's wicked and perverse."

Nye shot me an appraising glance. "It's a step removed from the graves we upend."

I set my jaw, and spoke no more.

*   *   *

"And so, Constable, you'll note that our findings prove beyond any doubt that all of this is—"

"Utter shite." Murray leaned back languidly in his chair, a look of complete indifference upon his face.

I was stunned. Nye had presented the evidence in a most compelling fashion, simplifying the scientific elements in layman's terms for the benefit of our audience—which consisted of the now-familiar constable and his secretary (a heavyset, moon-faced lad who appeared even younger than myself). The secretary had observed Nye's theatrics with starry-eyed awe, but was now fixing his expression into one of neutral disdain to match that of his superior officer, to my considerable chagrin. How was it possible that they could ignore the undeniable proof of foul play that Nye had so eloquently placed before them?

Murray answered my question before I could even posit it. "You know the rules, MacKinnon: no body, no crime. These men you speak of—Burke and Hare?

Unless they're currently in possession of the deceased, you've got no leg to stand on."

"But on the orders of Dr. Knox—"

Murray let out a patronising chuckle. "You can't possibly expect me to bring a case against one of the city's most renowned surgeons based on some shoddy record-keeping and a magic trick involving blue dye. You think I was born yesterday? A jury would never convict, and I'd lose my job."

"But the Crouch gang—"

"Has put your lot out of business. You think I don't know what's happening in your line of work, son? You're here framing your adversaries on some trumped-up evidence because you've found yourself cut out of a job—and now suddenly, conveniently, you've decided to make the law your ally? Please. You've spent years waving your exploits under my nose, all but daring me to prosecute you, and now you think I'll be on your side?"

Nye stiffened. "I thought you were on the side of justice."

Murray smirked. "Indeed, I am. And which side do you fancy you're on, hmm? Desecrating the graves of upstanding Christians, pissing on the sacredness of human life itself, carving up men for entertainment like a bunch of mad butchers—you lot are bound for Hell, MacKinnon. So forgive me if I don't risk my neck for you."

Nye persisted. "If not for me, then what about for the victims? You knew Mary, you knew Daft Jamie—"

"The Mary I locked up in the tank on countless occasions for unvirtuous conduct? The Jamie whose relentless singing drew more complaints on my beat than any other panhandling swindler on High Street? You must be joking."

Nye looked as though he'd been slapped, and my fists clenched in sympathetic indignation: to hear an officer of the law say that these people meant nothing because of their station was an affirmation of Nye's deepest suspicions. Without warning, he stood up so abruptly that his chair nearly tipped over with the force of it. "Come on, James. We're going." He leaned over and hastily began to shovel the evidence back into his bag.

"But . . ." I couldn't believe he was just going to give up, but I could think of no other recourse in our current position.

"I said, we're going." Nye had never spoken to me so sharply before, and my body reacted in total compliance before my brain had the chance to take offense. The next thing I knew, we were bursting through the doors and back out onto the street. Nye turned towards Malstrom's and set off at a pace so brisk I nearly had to trot to keep up with him.

"What are we going to do now?" I knew better than to assume that this was surrender.

"Simple: we're going to catch them in the act."

15.

An Entrapment

The dour mood at our table was amplified tenfold by the merry reveries involving what appeared to be every other patron of the Pig save for our crew. There was some sort of dice tournament in session, and the place was packed with rowdy gamblers, their mingled shouts of elation and dismay making it infinitely more difficult for us to focus on the pressing matter at hand.

"So you want to bait these madmen into committing a murder?" Diggs shouted so loudly that in any other circumstance I'd expect our imminent arrest, but in this situation drew nary a sideways glance.

Nye rolled his eyes. "Don't be ridiculous, of course not. I'm merely proposing we use Willis as a lookout to alert us if they lure anyone back to the boarding-house with the promise of drink."

Thomas looked skeptical. "But that's common practice for proprietors of a boarding-house. How will we know if they intend to murder?"

"Because as far as I can tell, they're not running a boarding-house at all; it's simply a front for their nefarious occupation. According to my research, they've killed mothers, wives, strangers, and innocents—not to mention Burke's own sister-in-law."

Willis spit his mouth of whiskey onto the table in astonishment. "His own sister-in-law? Are you sure?"

"I cross-referenced her name with lodging records and her travel ticket from Falkirk; the evidence doesn't lie."

"Well, can't be said I hadn't considered it with my own sister-in-law at times . . ." Diggs muttered into his pint. Thomas sniggered; Nye ignored him.

"The point is, lads, the objective is simple: we need to catch them with a fresh body."

I remained unconvinced. "Why does Willis need to be involved at all? After all, as the Messieurs' official porters, aren't we the first ones to know when they procure a new quarry?"

Nye shot me a withering look. "I said a fresh body, James. Still warm. If we alert the authorities to merely the common presence of a body in a trunk, Burke and Hare will simply claim it's from a kirkyard and be fined for the misdemeanour—which completely misses the point."

I paused to consider this, still unconvinced. "But who will report it? If the authorities wouldn't take your word for it, why would they take any of ours? It seems they've dismissed our lot outright."

"We'll need a man on the inside, someone posing as a potential lodger to file an official report."

"I could do it," Thomas offered. "I've got a respectable day job at the quays; I may be a labourer, but my name is untarnished when it comes to the law."

Nye shook his head. "Burke and Hare would recognise your tattoos immediately."

"His tattoos?" I was flummoxed.

"The five dots on his flexor pollicis," Nye quipped. "Common for men who work on the Water of Leith, but the symbol is reserved for locals; they'd never mistake you for an outlander."

"How do you know all this?" I was still sometimes taken aback by the breadth and span of Nye's seemingly infinite knowledge of the city's inner workings.

Nye just grinned and carried on. "So the point is, none of us can serve as the whistleblower: either the authorities know us and will discount our testimony, or Burke and Hare will recognise us as locals with connections in the community."

"So what's the answer?" I was growing irritated with the present conundrum, and it was all too obvious that Nye was simply holding back in order to reveal his solution with as much drama as possible.

Nye turned to me. "You are."

I eyed him skeptically. "Me? Burke and Hare know me best of all; they've had drinks with me, entrusted me with their quarry—"

"Not you specifically. Your connections."

"My—" The realisation of what he was implying instantly dawned on me. "No. No, Nye, absolutely not. It's bad enough I've gotten myself into this insane mess; there's no way I'm dragging more of my friends down with me."

"Come on, you know Charlie and Phillip are always angling to get on Malstrom's good side!"

"I didn't even think you knew Phillip's name," I grumbled mutinously.

Nye carried on as if I'd not even spoken. "If they help us with this, I can guarantee that Malstrom will extend their studies to include access to his private laboratory next year. Think of the opportunity."

I was appalled at his boldness. "You're an absolute menace, you know that, right? How is it you seem to know every man's pressure point and just how hard to press it in order to get what you want? You're a conniving, manipulative git—"

"Which is why you admire and adore me," Nye firmly concluded. "Come on, James—there's hardly any risk at all!"

"You're asking me to use my friends as bait to catch two murderers."

"You're being a fatalist. Think of it this way: they need only convince Burke and Hare to take them in for a drink, stay long enough to have established a sign of their presence within the boarding-house, then mosey on down to the station and report a murder. Then the authorities will search the property and inevitably find the body, wherever Burke and Hare have stowed it."

I took a fortifying swill of my drink as I considered this. "It's still a risk. Those men are dangerous."

"They're dangerous to people of a particular station, as you well know. But so long as Charlie and Phillip know what they're up against, they won't be taken in and tempted to imbibe like drunkards. They need only keep their wits about them long enough to be able to prove they were present inside the house, giving them grounds to issue a report. Burke and Hare will be none the wiser."

Diggs nodded thoughtfully. "It's a good plan."

I shot him a dirty look. "You only like it because it doesn't involve your life on the line." I was still resentful at being asked to further exploit my University connections and potentially put my friends in the path of two unhinged murderers.

To my surprise, Thomas was the next to speak up in Nye's defense. "It's a good plan because it's a sane plan, James. We can't take vengeance on Burke and Hare ourselves if they've got Crouch's gang backing them, and the law will continue to turn a blind eye so long as their victims are undesirables and missed only by the likes of us. Burke and Hare will keep killing unless we stop them—and who knows, any one of us could be next."

And that to me struck home. They had already taken Mary from us; what would happen if (when?) they set their sights on yet another member of our crew? To lose Diggs, Thomas, or Willis? Though we could sometimes be at odds as a result of our varied backgrounds, I had come to cherish these men as friends and comrades.

And I could not even bear to think of what would happen were they to move against Nye. The mere thought of losing him, of being here, without him, filled me with a deep and bitter dread that I couldn't even begin to quantify.

No. That could not—must not—be allowed to happen.

"Alright. Let me talk to Charlie."

* * *

"Are you bloody serious right now?"

"Look, Charlie, I know, it all seems quite mad, but I assure you Mr. MacKinnon and I will have the situation under control. And he's offered to guarantee both you and Phillip a proper position at Malstrom's this autumn—"

"Not about the proposal, you idiot—about the part where you've been serving as a digger for Malstrom this whole time!" Charlie looked sincerely flabbergasted, and I rushed to quantify my involvement.

"I just . . . look, I didn't want to ask you for more money, and I was too ashamed to make my situation known amongst our friends. I was desperate—"

"You sly bastard." Phillip's expression, to my surprise, was one of utter delight. "So that's how you came into Malstrom's inner circle?"

It took considerable effort to mask my displeasure at the insinuation. "I'd like to think that my surgical skills had more to do with it—"

Charlie groaned and rolled his eyes. "Come on; we all know you're a wizard with a scalpel, no need to rub it in. But honestly, mate, this sounds like some dodgy business you're caught up in. Are you sure you don't just want a loan?"

I shook my head vehemently and recalled the lessons I'd learned from Nye about identifying each man's pressure point when entering a negotiation. "No, it's not about the money, it's not about that at all. It's about . . . well, it's about Malstrom, and the school! If Knox and his cronies have their way, he'll put every private anatomy school in town out of business, save for his own, and hoard all the specimens for himself. Without access to a proper anatomy school, you'll be no better off studying here in Edinburgh than you would be at bloody Oxford studying Latin and Medical Theory." I could see both Charlie and

Phillip balk at the prospect of so grim a fate and knew I had them beat.

"So," said Charlie as he folded his hands primly in front of himself. "What exactly do you need us to do?"

* * *

The White Hart Inn was nearly vacant, which was surprising considering that it was nearly dusk on an unseasonably warm Saturday—perfect cavorting weather. I was posted up in a corner booth with Nye, Charlie, and Phillip, who had made each other's acquaintance outside the anatomy hall for the first time mere moments prior but were apparently already thick as thieves, judging by the gusto with which they were carrying on their conversation.

"So Malstrom's theory of coagulation posits that copper may be the key to presurgical preparation?" Charlie appeared utterly entranced by Nye's effortless wisdom and seemed to me so eager to pick his brain that the fact that he was about to come into contact with two proven killers seemed to have abandoned his mind entirely.

"It's down to that or iron, though, with both, there's a very thin line between helpfulness and harm when administering doses." Nye took a measured sip of his drink, somehow managing to look characteristically sage despite the fact he'd donned his "disguise" for the occasion, and the disarray of his blond wig set against his dark, perceptive eyes conjured up notable similarities to a disgruntled barn owl.

"Of course, of course," Phillip mused. He was understandably rapt, considering that his latest lecture at the RMS had to do with the ineffectiveness of presurgical bloodletting. "And how have you administered the compounds?"

"We've tried both orally and intravenously, though it would seem—"

"Oy." It was impossible to mask irritation from my tone. "Could we please focus on the matter at hand here?"

Nye shot me an exasperated look. "Calm down, James. There's nothing more for us to do until the Messieurs arrive."

"And you're sure they'll be here?"

"If Hamish values his life, then the tip is good, and Willis confirmed the old woman seen in Burke's company this morning appears to have vanished into thin air. All we need to do"—he gestured casually at the array of pint glasses scattered before us—"is occupy ourselves long enough to appear reasonably drunk by the time he and his companion arrive."

We were being cautious, of course—Nye had slipped the barkeep a few coins to spare us a stack of empty glasses, so we certainly had the appearance of having partaken in far more than we had in actuality. Even so, the casual air with which my companions were approaching the entire endeavour was grating on my already-frayed nerves.

"Fine." I glowered as I took a spiteful sip of my drink. "I just don't find it wise to be so cavalier about the whole situation."

Charlie gave me a lopsided grin. "It's fine, James. It's a simple plan; hardly surgery, eh, fellows?" The rest of my cohorts chuckled at his jest, and I resigned myself to mutinously stewing in silence.

A mere moment later, however, the door to the pub swung open and the mood at our table viscerally shifted. I didn't need to turn around to know without a doubt that our targets had arrived.

Nye was sitting across from me and caught my eye, giving me a firm nod. "Patience. Be casual; don't look up. Trust me; they can't miss us."

Sure enough, the next thing I knew, I felt a jarring clap upon my back, and a booming Irish brogue echoed from above me. "Well, if it isn't our merry porters! James and—sorry, lad, I never caught your name?"

"John," Nye responded effortlessly, offering a hand for Burke to clasp in his own monstrous one. He gave it a hearty shake, and I shuddered at the sight; even from where I was sitting, I could smell the stench of whiskey on Burke's breath. Hamish had confirmed the two men often drank to excess, and I could tell by Hare's unsteady motions as he maneuvered towards us with two drams from the bar that those claims were not exaggerated.

"Oy, if it's not the boys from Knox's lot!" Hare's sudden bout of loquaciousness was so unlike the man I'd known from my previous encounters that I was caught rather off guard. "You've no doubt received our summons for tomorrow morning?"

"Mister Hare," I rose to shake his hand. "And Mister Burke," I offered my hand and a strained smile. "What a pleasant surprise. Yes, my colleague and I were planning on taking up your quarry first thing tomorrow, as requested. But in the meantime, we thought we'd nip out for a drink."

"Ay, a fair night for it, innit?" Hare leaned in close, as if sharing a treasured secret, and I was struck by how unnaturally sharp and jagged his teeth looked.

"A fair night, indeed," I concurred, taking a measured step backwards. "And what a coincidence that we've crossed your path! These two lads"—I waved towards Charlie and Phillip, who tipped their hats in turn—"are strangers from out of town and in need of lodging for the night. I was just telling them we knew of two fine gentlemen who own a renowned establishment just up the road—and speak of the devil, here you are!"

"In the flesh," Hare sneered. Burke let out a menacing chuckle. (Could it be that these actions were only sinister in my mind, knowing the horrors these two men had committed? Were I not in the know, would I find their manner to be friendly, gregarious, perhaps even charming? It was impossible to tell.)

"I'm Edmund Gray," Charlie interjected, using the ubiquitous alias we'd concocted. And this is my brother, Bernard." Phillip offered a curt nod in response. "We're just passing through on our way south, but our coach broke an axle and is moored in town overnight. Have you beds to spare?"

Hare offered him a calculating smile. "Indeed we have, sir. Nothing fancy, but a place to rest your head. You'll have the lodging house to yourselves."

Just then we were interrupted by the barkeep, apparently intent on providing us all another pint (entirely unrequested, and clearly keen to keep clearing us of our coins). He gave Burke and Hare a disapproving glare. "What happened to that old bag Docherty you were in with earlier? Didn't you say she was your cousin?" he posited to Burke.

Burke's demeanour changed in an instant to one of keen irritation. "She was a useless drunk; we had to kick her out," he snapped.

"Vile, irritating creature," Hare corroborated haughtily.

Across the table, Nye and I exchanged a pointed look: this woman was clearly the unfortunate soul Willis had seen the Messieurs ushering into their abode mere hours before, presumably destined to meet her untimely end; it would seem they'd brought her here drinking prior to luring her into their trap.

"Well, that's a stroke of luck for us, I suppose!" Charlie interjected merrily, and his optimism appeared to have the intended effect upon the Messieurs.

"Indeed, indeed." Hare threw back his whiskey in a single gulp before wiping his lips wetly on the back of his hand. "Don't suppose you fellows would be willing to obtain a bottle of something for us to bring back to the stead? I fear our stocks are perilously low these days."

I had to press my lips together to keep from grinning as I dutifully avoided Nye's gaze: this was going precisely to plan. I could scarcely believe our good fortune!

"It would be our pleasure," Phillip acquiesced, nodding pointedly to the barkeep, who hastily retreated to purchase the desired item.

"Excellent!" Burke downed his own dram and slapped it heartily upon the table. "Always more pleasant to drink surrounded by the comforts of one's home, is it not?"

It was mere minutes before the bottle of spirits had been procured and Burke and Hare were excitedly ushering the "Grays" from our booth towards the door with promises of the fine food and cordial atmosphere they could expect upon arrival at Tanner's Close. It filled me with dread to think what would have become of Phillip and Charlie were they unaware of the savage plot forming against them. Would they have been so easily drawn in had we not placed them so squarely in the path of destruction?

Burke was just fastening his overcoat when he turned back towards Nye and myself, still positioned in our seats. "Well, come on then, we haven't got all night."

Nye waved his hand dismissively. "Sorry, gents, we can't join the revelries tonight. But you all enjoy."

For a moment, Burke's grin faltered, and his fingers stilled upon the buttons of his ragged lapel. "Oh, but you and James must join us, we insist!" There was an undertone of malice in his voice that caused my palms to burst out in a cold sweat.

I cleared my throat. "I'm afraid we're otherwise engaged this evening. But we'll be around tomorrow morning at eight sharp for—"

"Nonsense." Burke's enormous hand clamped down on my shoulder and tightened like a vise. "We at least owe you a drink for referring two such esteemed guests to our humble abode." He spared a glance towards Phillip and Charlie, who were being briskly herded out the door by an overly enthusiastic Hare.

The sight gave me pause. Could I truly allow my friends to face these madmen alone, even if they were to remain sober as church mice and devoted to our mission? Could I really be so sure that Burke and Hare would allow them to take their leave without harm when the time came? Nye had been so certain that they would only attack once their victims were incapacitated, but what if, what if—

"Well, I suppose, if you insist," I capitulated as I rose to my feet, deliberately ignoring Nye's reaction. "I suppose a dram or two wouldn't set us far behind."

"Ach, now that's the spirit, sonny!" Burke's hand squeezed my shoulder impossibly tighter, and it took all my willpower not to flinch.

"So, John," I finally dared to meet Nye's eye, steeling my own expression into one of defiance. "Come along."

The walk to Tanner's Close was one of dichotomous extremes. A half dozen paces ahead of me, Burke and Hare were engaged in an animated exchange with Phillip and Charlie, the details of which I couldn't quite overhear. Phillip and Charlie performed their roles to perfection, putting on an act of mild inebriation so convincing that, more than once, I had to remind myself that they'd each consumed less than a pint during our short stay at the Hart.

Beside me, Nye was stalking along in a mutinous snit, clearly furious I'd deviated from the plan.

I finally dared to speak, keeping my voice below a murmur, lest we be overheard. "I couldn't let them go it alone."

"They'd have been fine," Nye hissed. "Willis would have had an eye on them the whole time."

"No offense, Nye, but what's bloody Willis going to do if Burke and Hare decide to have a go? Burke could crush him with a single backhand."

Nye set his jaw, clearly displeased at having his authority on the matter questioned. "Burke and Hare are killers of opportunity. They're not in it for the fight, James. And now we have to somehow account for our own presence at the crime scene, unless we find some way to—"

"For Christ's sake, Nye, these are my friends. I know to you this is all a great game and you delight in deploying your pawns on a whim"—he huffed indignantly but did not argue at this accusation—"but there are lives at stake. You understand that, don't you?"

Nye's jaw was set, his expression cold. "I may not wear my emotions on my sleeve, James, but Mary's death has been a weight upon me that I cannot shake. What we are doing here is as much for her as it is for the rest of us, and I need you to believe me—to trust me—that I do not take your friends' peril lightly. I will protect their lives as I would my own, or that of any member of this crew. You cherish them, James, and I cherish you. They are therefore as dear to me as family."

I was once again caught off guard by Nye's earnest vulnerability. His disposition was so mercurial that even after all this time, I could often forget that beneath the calculated exterior of a devoted scientist and shrewd businessman was a tender heart and wary soul—and an inherent goodness that glimmered through the cracks of his stoic façade. Throwing caution to the wind, I took his hand and gave it a squeeze. My affection was rewarded with a smile, but the levity did not reach his eyes.

The house on Tanner's Close was every bit as dismal as I remembered, and the festering knowledge that there was a fresh body stashed somewhere on the premises did little to assuage my discomfort as Burke and Hare made a theatrical demonstration of hospitality, pulling up chairs around the fire for us and pouring generous servings of the rum we'd procured from the pub. The two of them made disconcertingly quick work of theirs and encouraged the rest of us to do the same; I couldn't discern if they were imbibing with such enthusiasm simply to set a precedent for their guests, or if this was how they steadied their nerves against the sacrilege of purloining human life. Either way, Nye, Phillip, Charlie, and I exchanged measured glances as we in turn waited for the proprietors to turn their backs long enough for us to dump the contents of our drams into the sputtering fire.

After a brief spell in their company, however, it quickly became obvious how Burke and Hare ingratiated themselves to their guests. Upon polishing off the rum, they promptly produced a bottle of bootleg whiskey (over which Nye and I exchanged a pointed glance, remembering that it was undoubted laced with something much stronger), all while regaling the lot of us with colourful tales of previous lodgers and nefarious characters they'd encountered in their time as innkeepers. I couldn't help but notice that the two of them were masterful storytellers, and more than once, I found myself taken in and laughing at some proclaimed exploit. It was so at odds with their prior disposition towards me that the nefarious charade made my head spin. They seemed unbothered that the rest of us remained relatively reserved; so long as they were able to keep filling our cups, they seemed to care not whether we were pleasant company ourselves.

The world had grown dark outside the grimy window overlooking the alley when the dowdy woman I remembered from my previous visit to the place appeared with a basket of hot rolls for the lot of us. Her disposition, like that of our hosts, was night and day from our last encounter; on this night, she was jovial and hospitable, even requesting a song from Burke, who dueted with Hare and demanded we all sing along. Midway through the second chorus, I locked eyes with Nye, and he gave me a pointed look: so this was how they did it—create an atmosphere of companionable merrymaking, one of relaxation and intimacy, and then twist it into a cruel advantage. It was brilliant. Wicked, yes. But brilliant.

After one more song, I observed as Charlie deliberately set his glass down upon the buckled wooden floor and stood (swaying a bit unsteadily, in an excellent parody of inebriation). "Alright, gents—I think we're in need of another bottle, eh?"

"Nonsense," slurred Hare from where he was stoking the roaring fire. "We've got plenty of bootleg on hand."

Charlie shook his head. "Your constitution is greater than mine, I'm afraid. Let me go procure us something proper; I'll be back in a flash, you'll scarcely miss me."

I could see Hare shoot Burke a pointed look over his shoulder, but Burke appeared unphased. On cue, Phillip cast his glass aside and stood as well, placing his cap lopsidedly upon his head. "I'll come with you. Best not wander these streets alone."

Before our hosts could protest, the two of them staggered out the door, slamming it behind them. Silence echoed in their wake.

For a long, tense moment, there was nothing but the sound of Hare raking the poker through the coals. Burke stilled as well, his bloodshot eyes going dark and solemn.

Nye cleared his throat and readied himself to rise from his chair. "We'd best be on our way as well, what with the early delivery tomorrow—"

"I don't think so, do you?" Burke's voice was low and sounded strangely far away.

"No," Hare replied into the fire. "I don't think you're going anywhere."

Nye's eyes flicked back and forth between the two men. "I'm sorry?"

Hare kept his gaze fixed firmly upon the flames. "You think we're going to let two of Malstrom's men slip through our grasp? Not on Knox's watch, my boy. You're in far too deep for that."

My breath caught in my throat. Nye shifted in his chair. "I'm afraid I don't know what you mean. We work for Knox, as porters—"

"You think Knox is that stupid, boy?" Hare slowly turned to face us, his eyes two black embers glowing with malice. "He has eyes everywhere. On you, and your pathetic little crew. On that fool Malstrom and his joke of a school. And on your friend here"—he turned to leer at me—"who thinks he's clever enough to hoodwink us."

I opened my mouth to protest, but before I could utter a word, I was interrupted by the unmistakable sound of iron sliding into a latch.

Burke had locked the door. We were trapped.

16.

A Conclusion

The resulting silence was infinite. I could feel the heat of my blood rushing through my veins in time with my hammering heart, see the realisation of our peril reflected in Nye's eyes, smell the liquor and smoke and the rank stench of doom hovering around us in a suffocating cloud. This would be the end of us. By this time tomorrow, we'd be submerged in barrels of whiskey stashed away in Knox's stores, another box for Hamish to smugly tick in his daily inventory. I wondered wildly what our Cause of death would be listed as. Please, I thought helplessly, let it be strangulation, and let it be quick.

Across from me, Nye rearranged his features into a now-familiar mask of polite indifference, leaning back in his chair as if settling in for a lengthy philosophical debate instead of a fight for our very lives.

"So you've found us out." He shrugged. "What exactly do you intend to do about it?"

Hare rose from his place by the fire, still brandishing the poker in front of himself menacingly. "Nothing much, if you play along. We just need to ask you a couple of questions, and then we can all be on our merry way. No harm in a civilised little chat, eh?"

Nye peered up at him with an appraising smile. "No, none at all. Fire away."

I was still paralyzed with fear, watching the scene play out before me with a surreal sense of detachment.

"How do you do it? Crack Greyfriars?"

Nye steepled his fingers beneath his chin. "Same as anywhere else. Set a lookout, pay off the sexton, pull the quarries."

"Liar," Hare snapped, suddenly crouching until his nose was mere inches from Nye's. "We've tried for weeks to strongarm the sexton, and he'll find himself upon a slab before he complies. The gates remain locked and the fence unscalable. Yet your merry little team of bandits continues to strip the place clean. So I'll ask you again: how do you do it? And this time, be precise."

Out of nowhere, two broad hands clamped down upon my shoulders, and I realized with a surge of renewed horror that Burke had maneuvered from his post by the door to position himself strategically behind my chair, his monstrous paws coming to rest mere inches from my trachea.

Nye observed this all with a neutral expression. "The key, lads, lies less with one's connections and more in taking proper precautions to defend one's own." No sooner had the proclamation left his lips than there was a flash of silver seemingly manifested from within Nye's sleeve, and the next thing I knew Hare was staggering backwards, gripping his cheek as blood poured forth from between his grasping fingers. Nye was on his feet in an instant, whirling to face me and charge Burke head-on, scalpel clutched firmly before him.

Burke made to counter, mercifully relinquishing his grasp of my neck and lunging towards Nye like a man possessed. Nye expertly pivoted past his reach, sending a staggering Burke crashing into his previously occupied chair. Nye used the momentary distraction to turn his attention back to Hare, who, in his injured state, had dropped the fire poker upon the floor. Nye scooped it up in a single elegant motion and whirled back around to wave it threateningly towards our attackers.

"James, the door!" The sound of my own name knocked me from my stupor, and I sprang to my feet and bolted towards the exit.

But not fast enough. Burke managed to flail and right himself just enough to catch hold of my ankle, yanking me bodily to the ground with an animalistic shriek. The next thing I knew, the full weight of him was upon me, his fists striking out at me with blazing efficiency. I curled in against the onslaught, struggling to raise my hands to protect my head, crying out helplessly against the relentless brutality of violence and pain.

Across the room, I could hear sounds of a skirmish as Hare quickly regained his bearings and refocused his assault upon Nye. It was from the corner of my blood-ied gaze that I could catch mere snippets of the action: Nye brandishing the poker and scalpel in tandem, Hare rushing him like a feral beast, the deafening sound of breaking furniture and flesh upon flesh as they tumbled to the ground in fortified combat.

I cannot recall how long we endured, only that the edges of my vision began to dim and my lungs felt empty and spent. Would Burke truly beat me to death? It was a fate so savage, so intimately visceral that my mind could not wholly comprehend it. Strange for this to be the end of me, I thought, in a dilapidated tenement in the West Port at the hands of this hulking brute—a world away from the life I'd once known and renounced all the same. Strange, strange, how perfectly strange . . .

"OY! Magistrate! Open up!"

All at once, the scene froze once more, and the four of us lay paralysed in shock upon the gritty clapboard floor, heads pivoting in tandem towards the voice emanating from the other side of the door. A sharp series of knocks confirmed my greatest hope: the authorities had arrived! We'd be saved!

"OY! Open up at once!" More pounding.

There was a scuffle of movement to my right, where I could dimly perceive Hare rolling off of Nye's supine form. To my horror, he was holding Nye's scalpel in his hand, which he wordlessly passed off to Burke—who promptly grinned down at me and pressed it firmly to my throat, the metal ice-cold against my fragile skin.

"What's the problem, officer?" Hare shouted through the door. He made no move to unlatch it.

"Noise complaint. Open the door."

"No need, officer," Hare's tone was sweet and even. "Wife and I had a bit of a row is all. We're quite finished now."

"This is your third *row* this month, you brute. If you and the missus can't mind your manners, I'll be taking the both of you to the station."

"Ach, now, there's no need for that; this is an honest matter of a domestic disagreement," Hare simpered. "We'll keep it down, you have my solemn word."

A hesitation from the other side of the door. When the reply came, it was considerably less stern than before. "And enough with the singing, as well. Your neighbours have about done had it."

"Just shows there's no accounting for taste."

Was I mistaken in that I heard laughter from the magistrate? It began to dawn on me that this magistrate was clearly not one summoned by Phillip and Charlie for a report of murder, but was simply a patrolman paying lip service to nosy neighbours.

"Just keep it civil after dark."

"Ay, officer, with pleasure. Will there be anything else?"

"That'll be all. Good evening."

"Good evening, sir."

My eyes darted over to meet Nye's. He was still on the floor, but to my considerable relief, he'd managed to pull himself into a sitting position, and while he appeared a bit flushed and roughed-over, he looked far better than I myself was feeling. I couldn't speak for the blade against my throat, but surely Nye would help us—

It was as if Burke read my thoughts and moved instantly to counter them.

"Have you ever watched a man die?" Burke's voice was so low it was barely more than a whisper, loud enough for Nye to hear him, but far too quiet for the magistrate to detect.

Nye's gaze abandoned mine for Burke's, and I stared up defenseless as Burke's mouth turned into a leering grin. He pressed down harder with the scalpel, eliciting a shudder from my battered body.

"I don't just mean, have you seen a dead man—I know your profession, the things you lot do, the vile, stinking masses of flesh you trundle to and fro like nasty little butcher boys," Burke continued, tracing a lazy pattern with the blade across my thyroid cartilage and down towards my sternal head. "But I mean, have you watched a man as he dies? The way the light leaves his eyes, the way his body shivers and stills, the way his mouth gapes and gasps?"

He smiled victoriously over at Nye as he drove the tip of the scalpel gently through my epidermis—not deep, just enough to elicit a pained gasp from me, which I heard echoed in Nye's response. He seemed so helpless where he sat impotently looking on, bearing the marks of Hare's assault, so utterly undone by our imminent demise. I felt the foolish urge to reach for him, to ask for his hand, to beg for him to hold mine while I left this world so that I might remember one last good thing before the light was gone.

We stayed silent.

Outside the door, footsteps receded—along with what little hope I had left.

A chuckle emanated from somewhere behind me: Hare, in triumph, having thwarted the guard. I could feel a trickle of blood seeping down the side of my neck from the puncture of the scalpel. I wondered if there would soon be more.

Sighing, I looked once more to Nye. The least I could hope was that his face would be the final token I could carry with me from this world.

Everything that occurred next happened in one dizzying instant. Nye's hand flew to his head, tore off his wig, and dipped it deliberately into the open fireplace beside him, setting the whole frizzy nest ablaze. Then in a single, calculated maneuver, he elegantly lobbed the flaming ball of hair across the room, landing it directly upon the straw bed—which promptly set the whole of it alight.

Burke's weight evaporated off of me as he dashed to assist Hare in suppressing the blaze. The room was a tinderbox, from the straw bed to the brittle floor boards to the sagging wooden beams of the ceiling, and I knew as well as anyone that unless contained, the fire would consume the lot of it in a matter of minutes.

"Come on." Before I could process anything further, Nye was hauling me to my feet. We spared a single glance towards the front door but inevitably reached the same conclusion: to make a run for it would put us easily within an arm's grasp of Burke, and we couldn't trust the fire to keep him distracted long enough to ensure our escape. Pivoting, Nye pulled me deeper inside, through the low-arched doorway into the lodging room. Nye slammed the door shut, and I scrabbled for the lock—only to discover, to my compounded dismay, that there was none.

Nye remained undeterred. In the time it took me to register our newfound predicament, he'd already made his way over to the closest trough-bed and threw his weight bodily behind it, shoving it until it came to rest squarely in front of the door-frame.

Nye turned and looked me over, cupping my face gently in his hands. "Are you alright?" I stared dumbly

back at him. I could feel the echoes of Burke's beating vibrating through my aching bones and bruised
flesh, but I could at least finally determine that nothing seemed life-threatening. Blearily, I nodded. Nye
smiled at me, and I smiled back, but the reprieve was
short-lived.

"James, we have to keep moving: that barricade
won't hold them off forever; as soon as they get the fire
under control, they'll take on the door with a hatchet."

"Alright," I managed muzzily and turned towards the
interior of the room.

Only to promptly remember that the lodging room
had no windows.

Or doors, save the one we'd entered through.

We were trapped again.

Panic welled up in my chest as I glanced around frantically, looking for any point of egress but finding none.
I turned to Nye, who was doing the same, but looking
considerably less concerned about it.

"There's no way out!" I exclaimed in acute agitation;
how was it that Nye could look so infuriating calm in
such a dire moment?

"Nonsense." He pointed straight upwards, and upon
following his direction, my eyes fell upon a fire hatch
nestled in the roofing above the rafters. There was just
one problem.

"Nye, that has to be twenty feet up. How do you pro-
pose we reach it?"

Nye was already a step ahead of me, pacing the
perimeter of the room before zeroing in on one of the
trough-beds and bending to lift it. He cleared one end
a foot or two off the ground, then swore as he dropped

it. "They're too heavy; no way we could stack enough to reach the beams." Undeterred, he spun around and made his way to the corner, where there were four tea-chests propped innocuously in a haphazard stack. I'd not registered them the first time I'd been inside this room, but I now eyed them with a sense of foreboding. Nye popped the top one open.

"What are you looking for?"

"Rope. That's how they secured the tea-chest we picked up from them, so there must be a coil around here somewhere," he replied matter-of-factly. "In the meantime, you gather up the blankets. Worse comes to worst, we can attempt to knot them together . . ." I hastened to do his bidding and scampered to the closest trough, yanking up the blanket with little fanfare—

Only to be confronted by the bloated corpse of one (presumed) Mrs. Docherty.

I shouted and leapt backwards, so startled by my discovery that I forgot what an impact my reaction would have upon Nye, who appeared at my side instantaneously.

"Are you alright? You—oh." His expression turned somber as he took two steps forward and leaned over the body, eyes combing over every detail of the scene, nodding and muttering to himself as he took it all in.

He glanced up at me, eyes full of delight. "James, look! I was right! Blood about her nose and mouth, signs of trauma but none of vomit. She still smells of alcohol, but that's clearly not what did her in—you see the bruising here? It's obvious now, so perfectly obvious, we simply must—"

"Nye, hate to interrupt, but need I remind you—"

"Right, right! Her corpse will do us no good if we're on the slab beside her, eh?" And with a jovial wink he veritably skipped back to inspecting the tea-chests. It took all my willpower not to roll my eyes. Sometimes Nye's obsession with science could be a bit more than inappropriate, considering the circumstances.

My irritation was short-lived, however, as seconds later Nye uttered a shout of elation as he waved a long coil of rope aloft; I instantly rushed over to join him in inspecting our newfound lifeline.

"It's narrow, but strong," Nye mused, running his fingers along the rough fibres. "I doubt we could climb it, but if you wrap your hands, we can always—"

I caught his eye and gave him a grin. "Use the pulley system?"

In no time flat, we'd devised our rig; countless nights of practice in the safety of my chambers had prepared us well. Nye expertly triangulated his position, bracing against a steady support beam at the far side of the room as I hastily wrapped my palms in the tatters of a blanket, doing what I could to save myself further injury. Then I coiled my hands within the strand and nodded.

Nye pulled. It was difficult going, the rope of a much narrower width than the one to which we were accustomed, and I could feel it chafing savagely against my palms despite the meager coverage offered by the blanket wrappings. Yet I held fast, eyes focused upon the rafters above me, drawing nearer and nearer until at last I could grasp one and swing myself the rest of the way up.

Straddling the beam, I looked down at Nye, who whooped and pumped his fist triumphantly. At that very moment, there was a dangerous bang from the other side of the door, startling us both—our victory was short-lived. We hadn't much time; Burke and Hare had evidently contained the fire and immediately set about attempting to breach the door. Suddenly, I realised the flaw in our plan.

"Nye . . . how are you going to get up here, too?"

He shook his head. "You go on and get help. I'll hold them off."

I glared down at him in disbelief. "Are you insane? I'm not leaving you here! Who knows how long it will take me to find an officer and convince him to come back with me—you'll be dead before I return!"

Another bang against the door, and we both jumped as it rattled precariously on its hinges. Nye turned back to me imploringly. "Please, James, just go."

My heart hammered mutinously in my chest. "Not without you."

He threw up his hands in surrender. "Then how?"

I wracked my gaze frantically over the contents of the room. There must be a solution somewhere! Suddenly, I felt a smile blossom upon my lips.

Nye peered up at me like I'd gone spare. "What?"

I shot him a cocky grin. "Lucky for you, I did start paying attention in physics class." He stared back at me blankly. "What do you know about counterweights?"

My proposal seemed to dawn on him as if we were of one mind. "You mean—"

"Docherty. Come on, quickly!"

Poor Mrs. Docherty was not, lightly put, a small woman. She was nearly twice the width of Nye if but a half-head shorter than he, and the rope creaked and groaned with strain as Nye hauled her up into the rafters from his triangulated position by the door at the far side of the room, using the distance to strategically diminish the force required to lift her off the ground. I hovered above in worried anticipation, distantly clocking the increased frequency of bangs against the door and fretting about how much longer the barricade might hold. Mercifully, I was soon able to grasp the corpse and secure her slumped between two beams.

"I've got her! Come on, Nye, quickly!"

Nye didn't take reminding; he hustled from his position by the door to stand directly beneath the beam upon which I was perched over Docherty's wilted body. The blanket wrapping his hands was already shredded, I noted, but he seemed unbothered by that fact as he wound his fingers through the base of the rope and held tight.

"Are you ready?" My inquiry was punctuated by another menacing bang, and I could see the trough shift slightly in front of the door.

Nye grinned up at me. "Better be. One, two, three!"

And with that, I shoved old Mrs. Docherty bodily off the rafters, sending her careening to the floor below.

Just as intended, with a great jerk her descent propelled Nye upwards at a most alarming rate; I scarcely had time to process Docherty's departure before Nye was catapulted upwards into my company, grasping frantically for purchase. I reached down to catch his hand and haul him up onto the beam beside me, and for a moment we just sat there, grinning stupidly at one another.

I could have kissed him were it not for another bang emanating from the doorway, louder this time, and the trough creaked ominously as it slid further across the floor. We scrambled to our feet and braced ourselves against the rough under-thatchings of the roof as we maneuvered our way along the narrow beam and over to the trapdoor above. I reached up to fling it open, only to discover—

"It's locked." I could scarcely believe the sheer silliness of our predicament: for the door to the lodging room to have nary a lock in place, and yet the hatch to the roof was fastened with a sturdy padlock? The odds were unthinkable.

I turned back to Nye, who was glancing about frantically in search of a solution. Not a moment too soon, his eyes lit up.

"Hand me your pocket watch."

I did so without thinking, only to watch as he smashed the glass face upon the beam beside him, sending shards scattering down the precipitous drop below. I must have made some sound of indignation, for he looked at me with an inquisitive air.

"What?"

I cleared my throat. "Sorry, it was . . . that was an heirloom."

Nye looked caught-out. "Apologies. Desperate times, you know. I'll replace it."

For a moment, my father's stern face flashed before me—his disapproving eyes, his mouth pressed into a judgemental moue, tongue twisting treacherously over continued accusations of weakness and ungrateful insolence—

"On second thought? Forget about it."

Nye smirked and then turned his attention back to the watch. I observed in fascination as he plucked the two hands cleanly from the face, pocketed the shell, then turned back to the lock preventing our escape. He inserted the pointed ends of the two hands into the keyhole, one above the other, and fidgeted them about, tongue poking from the corner of his mouth as his brow furrowed in utmost concentration. I held my breath as, below us, another resounding bang followed by a triumphant shout heralded the progress of our pursuers. Not a moment too soon, the hands seemed to slip miraculously into place, and the lock fell open with a satisfying click.

There was no time for celebration. Nye tore away the lock and cast it aside, then flung the hatch open with a mighty heave. The fresh night air cascaded over us, and I gasped my first breath of freedom since our horrid ordeal had begun. Then Nye reached up and braced his hands upon the frame and hauled himself through the hatch and onto the roof before turning to extend his hand to me. Clasping it gratefully, I held fast as he pulled me to safety.

Though safety was, for all intents and purposes, a fairly relative term for our predicament. Despite having escaped the boarding-house, we were now perched precariously on a rooftop composed of slick, moldy hay, a full twenty feet above the ground. Nye turned to lead me towards the edge, and despite my best intentions of bravery, I hesitated.

That was all it took for him to slip. The next thing I knew, the two of us were tumbling down the slippery incline, shouting in simultaneous shock and fear as we hurled towards the edge. The split second before we fell, our eyes met.

Nye grasped my hand. And down we went.

I would like to say that, in that moment, my life flashed before my eyes, but to be quite disappointingly honest, the drop was far less perilous than it had looked from atop the peak of the roof. Distance notwithstanding, our dramatic exit was further tamed by the fact that we landed utterly unscathed in a large pile of discarded thatching hay abandoned in a heap at the alley's end.

For a moment, we both simply blinked up at the night sky, uncomprehending. The stars were wild and clear that night, and it dawned on me that for the first time in ages, the clouds had lifted.

Nye started to laugh.

So did I.

So that is where, moments later, Phillip and Charlie found us. They were accompanied by an impressive throng of officers from the guard—summarily proving Nye's point that the lawmen could be roused to action, if summoned by the right kind of citizen.

"Just here, officers! These are our friends—they saw the body!" Charlie cried out, committing to the act with such gusto that I was nearly convinced he'd actually seen Mrs. Docherty himself.

A gruff-looking constable with a grizzled beard peered down at the two of us with a combination of curiosity and suspicion. "Is that the truth, lads? Is there a body inside this lodging house?"

"Ay, there is," Nye replied, composing himself as well as he could considering his rather undignified circumstances.

"What state was the victim left in?" demanded a young officer from behind him.

Nye and I exchanged a knowing look. "Well, officer," I ventured. "She seemed rather the end of her rope."

17.

A Commencement

The day of William Burke's hanging was unseasonably grey and cold, an unforgiving departure from the breathless emergence of spring that had enchanted the city over the previous five weeks. The sudden break in season was met with affronted resentment by the throngs of bystanders gathered to witness the event, relentlessly complaining of it all—the rain, the cold, the thick fog that obscured the view of the action for those sequestered at the back of the crowd. It was a miserable affair, all things told.

To me, the scene seemed fitting. For once, we were past the initial flush of triumph; the past few fortnights had been marked with naught but dreary disappointment.

First and foremost was the matter of Nye's testimony at Burke's trial. Following the dramatic arrest of the Messieurs, Murray had called Nye back in to present his evidence to the leads of the prosecution.

I attended the demonstration for moral support and was once again struck breathless with admiration as Nye walked the stern-faced officials through the scientific evidence at hand, which was now corroborated by the presence of the body recovered from the house on Tanner's Close. Nye was both charismatic and direct in his account of his investigation into the crimes and patiently answered the barristers' endless lines of inquiry into his findings. By the end of the day, his testimony was approved and his date scheduled in court. Nye was beside himself with excitement at the opportunity to bring his particular branch of science before the jury.

Yet two nights before he was scheduled to testify, we were flabbergasted by a message from the Magistrate's office: the prosecution had instead opted for a plea bargain, offering Hare full immunity if he turned on Burke. Which, of course, he had—without hesitation or remorse.

Nye had stormed down to the station with me on his heels, demanding answers. Murray was characteristically unhelpful.

"What can I say? The barristers know full well it's easier to convince a jury based on firsthand testimony than to try and convince them that your hocus pocus is anything other than magic tricks."

"But I've presented you with scientific proof—"

"From the mouth of a snatcher!" Murray scoffed. "Don't you forget, boy, that to the God-fearing people of this town, you and your lot are depraved heathens, and your so-called schools are dens of sin and debauchery. To call the likes of you to the stand to convince them that your kind holds the keys to justice? Not in this lifetime, sonny. Not in this lifetime."

As if to add insult to injury, the prosecution had decided—just as Nye predicted—not to pursue Knox. He was too far outside the realm of Hare's testimony to prove he had full knowledge of where the Messieurs had sourced the specimens they'd provided and was made too untouchable by his lofty station in society to be the subject of any sustained investigation by the lawmen.

For what it was worth, the sordid details which emerged from Burke's trial had made Knox a pariah about town, and he had wordlessly taken his family and absconded South a mere few days after it began. It would seem no one knew exactly where he'd gone, but rumours were he was still somewhere about London; he'd not even had the decency to venture overseas.

So it was with a bittersweet melancholy that our crew assembled at Malstrom's and made our way together towards the square to witness the hanging. For as hard-fought and hard-won as this victory had been, the sour taste of injustice still lingered bitterly in our mouths.

The crush of spectators descending upon the square was far beyond anything I could have previously imagined; though hangings in Edinburgh were common enough, the salacious details of Burke and Hare's vile plot had electrified the city in the daily news reports on the trial, and it would seem that now every citizen in town, no matter their walk of life, wanted to witness the downfall of the devil in their midst. Not only that, but in a final coup de grâce, the University itself had guaranteed intake of Burke's corpse and had promised a public post-mortem dissection, tickets for which were now the hottest item on the market. Rumour had it they'd already sold a thousand, and attendees would be ushered through the operating theatre throughout the proceedings (inevitably leading to wild speculation regarding which bit of the dissection would be the most enjoyable to watch).

So massive was the crowd that morning that, by the time we reached the Cowgate, it had become nearly impossible to move. Thomas hoisted Willis up on his shoulders to see what he could observe, and he dourly reported that it appeared we could get no closer; the throngs of spectators were simply too thick to penetrate. For a spell, we simply milled about in place, but the circumstances grew less and less ideal. The mob only grew thicker, drunker, more rowdy, and their irreverent gossip regarding the case was like knives to the hearts of us directly impacted by it.

We'd endured no longer than a half hour before Nye finally spoke up. "Gents? I think we ought to get out of here. What say you?" There was a murmur of agreement, and with that, Nye shepherded us all against the tide of onlookers out of the fray and up Queen Street instead, circumventing the worst of the crush. We didn't stop walking until we arrived at Bell's Brae, a rugged stone wall upon an outcropping overlooking the tranquil Water of Leith. Without hesitation, Nye clambered atop of it and came to settle, and the rest of us followed suit. He wordlessly produced a bottle of whiskey from the folds of his overcoat and passed it somberly down the line.

We drank to Mary, and to Daft Jamie, and to the other nameless souls whose lives were brought short by the deeds of unscrupulous men. We drank to the bravery of Phillip and Charlie, and to the wisdom and generosity of Malstrom, even to Hamish's shameless immorality. Before too long, we were toasting to May's pies, to the blundering Greyfriars sexton, to Murray and his cursed band of good-for-nothing goons, to Angus and the Pig and bootleg whiskey, to Edinburgh and Scotland and Long Live the North, and as the kirk bells tolled one, somewhere in the distance a roar erupted from the crowd, and William Burke at last met his end.

We barely noticed.

The dreary weather did not relent. Diggs was the first to surrender, rising unsteadily from his perch with a tip of his hat, sauntering away down the road and into the thickening fog with nary a word of parting. Thomas and Willis were next, exclaiming that all the talk of May's pies meant they could think of nothing else, and the two of them ventured off in the direction of the Vaults.

For a long time, Nye and I sat in silence, staring at the river. He took one last pull from the bottle, then tipped the rest of the whiskey into the churning water below. I pressed my hand upon his own where it was resting on the wall. He did not turn to look at me, but at least he smiled, though his eyes remained full of tears.

At long last, when we could take the cold and rain no more, he led me through the emptying streets in the fading light, back to the warmth and safety of his chamber, and reminded me what it meant to be alive.

* * *

Summer descended upon us like a suffocating blanket
of unwanted comfort and light. The breeze grew warm
and the days grew long, what should have been a much-
needed respite at our northern latitude. Before I knew
it, digging season was over, and I assisted Nye in closing down the dissection hall for summer. Our classes
there adjourned for the season, and it was with great
humility that I accepted an offer of apprenticeship for
the upcoming scholastic year, which was to commence
in September. As promised, Phillip and Charlie were to
come on board as assistants.

It was all so simply perfect, it was too good to be true.
For with the absence of Knox's schemes inciting terror
amongst our crew, I at last had the unfortunate opportunity to confront a far more nebulous threat: that of
my continued absence from London. As the start of
the Season drew ominously nearer, it became glaringly
obvious that my willful avoidance of the predicament
could not persist. Per my last placating correspondence
with Edith a month prior, I had agreed to return to our
London stead at the conclusion of the term, and her
approving (if curt) reply indicated that she intended to
hold me to my word. As such, I would be forced to
either announce my imminent departure from Edinburgh or risk Edith divulging my secret to Richard—
endangering not only my future vocation, but perhaps
Nye's very life. For so long the summer had seemed
a distant ultimatum, and then all at once, in a blaze
of infernal sunshine and hateful heat, it was barreling
down upon me like a wave upon battered rocks.

I turned all the more eagerly to Nye to fill my hours
with joy in the hopes of displacing the pervasive dread

festering within me. Though my University classes still required my utmost attention (as exams were not to be held until the end of April), I found Nye only too eager to mix work and pleasure. Most days that the sun appeared, we'd meet up after my classes and walk to the Meadows. Nye would spread out a blanket, and we'd spend the afternoons lounging about, me with my nose stuck in a textbook, him with his sketch-pad and inks, or sometimes reading one of Malstrom's heavy tomes. In this blissful respite, we'd pass the time until the light grew dim, then retire to enjoy one another's company in a far less scholastic manner.

My favourite days were the ones in which we could secure a small patch of grass hidden amidst a grove of trees at the far end of the promenade. The foliage there concealed the site from prying eyes, and in this privacy, I could lay with my head in Nye's lap. He would caress my hair gently as he leafed through my textbook, quizzing me on all manner of facts and figures to prepare me for my upcoming exams—between savage quips about the antiquated information I for some reason insisted upon retaining for the purposes of my continued education. I'd swat at him good-naturedly, he'd press a kiss to my lips, and we'd carry on like that for hours, such that by the time we departed, I'd be dizzy with simultaneous pedagogic delight and consuming arousal.

Yet as the last vestiges of spring waned in a simmering haze of earthly delights, I was forced to at last confront the reality of my fate. The thought of returning to Society was hateful to me, but could I truly be as sure as I'd professed that my secret was safe with Edith? If I neglected my duties and slighted Edith's demands, I estimated there was a fair chance she'd dispatch Richard himself to kidnap me back into the coils of their control. Yet if I left Edinburgh of my own volition and bent to my family's will, I'd be caught in the quicksand of their social scheming before I even knew I'd lost my footing. And what of Nye's assertion that I was sure to make a mess of my plot to dissuade Violet's affections? What if I somehow found myself ensnared, mollified, or worst of all, *betrothed*?

As grim as my fate was sure to be if I fell subject to my duties, a lifetime of domestic misery paled in comparison to the noose that would await Nye if Richard were to report him to the authorities. I found myself thinking more and more often of the Spanish pilgrim, whisked away back to his life of privilege and leaving Nye to take the fall from the stocks for his sins. The injustice of it all was infuriating.

I was utterly convinced I was being quite secretive about my inner turmoil, until one afternoon, in our spot at the Meadows, mere days before my exams were scheduled to commence. Nye suddenly slapped the textbook down and tossed it to the side, a look of flagrant irritation upon his face. My eyes sprang open from where they'd been lulling half-lidded as I stumbled to recite the common treatments for indigestion, instantly wary of this change in routine.

"Alright, out with it."

I peered up at him from his lap. "Out with what?"

"Whatever's on your mind. You've been odd all week."

"Odd how?" I could feel my cheeks flushing in desperation to maintain my nonchalance.

"You know the common treatments for indigestion like the back of your hand, yet you've just listed laudanum amongst them."

"Honest mistake."

"Twice."

I paused, but soon resigned myself to my fate. Pulling myself into a sitting position, I turned to meet him eye to eye. He deserved the truth; that much I could give him. "I've been turning it over and over in my mind, Nye, and I must confess, I've been more worried than I've let on about Edith, and the tenuous terms of her silence. I fear I really will have to return to London."

Nye looked at me quizzically. "Of course you must return to London. Was that not always your plan?"

I was admittedly a bit chapped by his cavalier affirmation of my impending departure. Would he not *miss* me, as I dreaded missing him?

"Well . . . I mean, yes, obviously, but I thought I might somehow . . . wriggle out of it."

Nye shot me a withering look. "*Wriggle out of it*? Forgive me if I've misjudged, but your sister hardly seems the type to let you wriggle out of any net she's woven."

I groaned at the sheer *unfairness* of it. "*I know*, of course *I know*. I'm just . . . not keen to be apart from you."

A slow, hesitant smile emerged on Nye's face. "Nor I, you. Which is why I think perhaps I ought to accompany you. As your . . . *professional advisor*, as it were, as you navigate the uncharted waters of society courtship."

I was stunned. "You'd . . . come to London?"

"Well, you see, I've had a job offer there."

He cleared his throat and shifted his eyes, and I suddenly realised that I was perhaps not the only one between us who'd been keeping a secret. I could scarcely believe what he was saying. "Where?"

"The headquarters of the new national police. There's a young sergeant there who heard about my work on the Burke case from Murray's assistant, and he's asked me to do a residency there; to study and present some of my findings to the new members of the force. He believes—as do I—that science has a place in the enforcement of law, and we can use our medical knowledge to solve cases that were previously unsolvable."

I paused to consider this. "A residency? For how long?"

"I've been guaranteed a position for three months."

I could hardly believe my ears. "And . . . you'd really go? What about Malstrom?"

Nye shrugged. "He was completely understanding when I told him I was considering the placement. He knows that this is an opportunity to promote our profession in the realm of acceptable society; he encouraged me to pursue it to the fullest. I told him I'd not yet made up my mind, though I confess my only hesitation was that I first wanted to affirm your desire for my . . . continued company."

I took his hands eagerly in my own. "Yes, Nye. Yes. Come with me! We can make it through the summer together."

Something shifted in his expression at that, and he withdrew his hand from my grasp. He swallowed, suddenly unsettled and infuriatingly aloof. It seemed to me an eternity before at last he spoke, and when he did, his words were measured and maddeningly precise. "No. No, I can't. It was unforgivable of me to even suggest such a thing."

I shook my head, infuriated with this abrupt turnabout. "But why? Why not?"

He took a long, measured breath. "James, I have brought ruin upon myself time and time again. Be it my nature, my proclivities, my selfishness, my greed, I am not an honourable man. If I am spotted in London with you, what will be said? What excuses will you make for our acquaintanceship? For our familiarity? And how long do you think your circles in the city will turn a blind eye before you, too, are disgraced? Is there an end for us that is not at best a bucket of tar and a barrel of feathers—or, at worst, a hangman's rope?" To my astonishment, his eyes welled up with tears. "I have brought you low, James. I must now merely offer you an escape, a chance for redemption, for a respectable life separate from my sins. Go to London on your own, as you planned. Make amends with your family. I mustn't keep you from it."

The words felt like a punch to the gut. I could scarcely believe that Nye could be so callous as this; I'd thought our bond was holy, sacred, forged in gore and gristle, blood and bone, and yet here he sat straight-faced before me, dismissing it all as if it were simply an ill-advised transgression.

I refused to take such indignity lying down. "How can you tell me to move on, having seen what we've seen, and done what we've done?" I could feel a hot swell of mortification rising in my chest, and suddenly,

I could bear it no longer. "Do I mean nothing to you?" I spat. "Nothing more than the bodies we exhumed from the ground? Because I must confess, you have flayed me open, plucked me apart, laid me bare before you, and now you intend to walk away as if I were simply another cadaver on your slab?"

In that moment, I saw his willpower break. He surged forward and kissed me fiercely, passionately, as if there were no one in the world but the two of us.

I should have known better, as the act was so typical of Nye: feigning aloof disinterest as a guise for hopeless self-preservation, sacrificing his own happiness for my enduring protection. I had known him long enough by now that it was foolish for me to doubt the good in his heart. Though he knew not how to show it, his love and loyalty was unfailing.

I couldn't react quickly enough. I reached forward and cradled his face in my hands, willing him with all my soul to understand. "I crave no absolution but yours," I murmured between breathless kisses, stilling him so that I might look him in the eye. "You have not brought me low; you have raised me from the utmost depths of despair and longing. I did not follow you out of desperation, I followed you out of desire. Do you not see that? Do you not see that all we have done, I have consented to do? This is my will, Nye. My truth and my reason, it's all with you."

And then there were no more words, just the feverish caress of fingers and palms and the tender press of lips and tongues. I breathed him in, my heart sang with elation, for this, this, was all I would ever desire.

When at last he pulled away, he looked almost smugly satisfied as he combed his fingers sheepishly through his disheveled hair. "We must be discreet once we arrive in London," he ventured. "Edinburgh affords us freedoms that I fear your society circles in the South will not extend."

"Of course," I concurred (perhaps a bit too quickly). "We'll be prudent. Cautious. Sensible."

Nye snorted. "Us? Sensible? Cautious? Prudent? Sounds unlikely at best, intolerably bland at worst."

I let out a laugh. "At least we'll endure the blandness together. And be back to our capers in Edinburgh by the end of the Season."

At last, his expression softened, and I knew I had won him over. "Well, if that be your desire, James Willoughby, far be it from me to deny you."

I grinned at him. "That is my desire, Aneurin Mac Fhionghuin."

He grinned back. "Then sit for your exams as planned, and I will depart one week hence. We shall meet again in London, as colleagues and companions both."

We sealed our pact with a kiss.

* * *

It just so happened that the day of Nye's departure coincided with that of my very first University exam. I was relentlessly nervous despite having spent hours in preparation, and it was with butterflies in my stomach that I approached Malstrom's school to say my farewell to Nye before sitting for my test. I found him there scurrying about the entrance hall, surrounded by a staggering array of travelling trunks.

"My, you don't pack lightly, do you?" I quipped. "Did you exhume the whole kirkyard to bring with you as a souvenir?"

Nye turned to face me, eyes bright and cheeks flushed with excitement. "Hardly; it's all my equipment. You've no idea what it takes to transport a laboratory from one end of the country to the other! They offered to provide me with a brand-new lab, but how was I to guarantee that it would be to my standards? This seemed the only way."

I took in the scene, impressed. "No offense, Nye, I'm starting to think your new benefactors may be mad as hatters to give you free reign of the place."

He put on a face of faux scandalisation. "How dare you! I'm apparently 'one of the brightest young minds in the medical field,' if you're to believe the report I received courtesy of my patron."

"Well, wait until they hear about your hobbies," I replied with a wink, and Nye chucked in return.

"I can't stay long," I continued wistfully. "My exam starts in a half hour."

"I'd wish you luck, but God knows you don't need it. You've a brilliant mind and a brave heart, James. You'll blow them all away, I know it."

I shook my head at his lavish praise. "Thanks. But I should be off; don't want to be late—"

Nye raised a finger to interject. "Which reminds me! I have a little something for you."

I watched in curiosity as he rooted about in his pocket before withdrawing a small item which he held towards me, cradled in his palm.

It was my father's pocket watch. For a moment I froze, confused. "You had it repaired? I told you that you needn't bother—"

"Open it."

I plucked up the item and popped open the clasp, and my breath caught in my throat.

Where the face should be was now a gorgeous rendering of a Lover's Eye: an intricate portrait of Nye's crystalline iris, immaculately shaded in his remarkable kaleidoscope of grey, the lashes a dark web from beneath which his gaze peered back at me, piercing the soul of my desire and causing my heart to clench painfully within my chest.

But what stunned me most was the illustration that opposed it: nestled into the lid of the watch was an anatomical rendering of the ocular cavity, each part of the eye neatly labeled in Nye's unmistakable hand. It was as if Nye had captured his entire essence in a single locket: the beauty and the science, the sentiment and the mind. It was perfect.

I finally tore my gaze away from the trinket to take in his expression. He hovered before me expectantly, awaiting my verdict. I simply clasped him firmly by the cravat and pulled him towards me for a very fond farewell.

Whatever awaited us in London, I concluded, we would brave it together. I could scarcely wait for our next adventure to begin.

* * *

Seated in the lecture hall between a nervous-looking Phillip and a disputably cavalier Charlie, I set up my ink pot, parchments, and quill with trembling hands. Though I knew I was well-prepared, my mind kept conjuring up impossible scenarios: of a question the subject of which I'd somehow entirely forgotten to study, or perhaps that the pages of my textbook had stuck together during my preparation and I'd missed a whole chapter unknowingly . . . As unlikely as it all was, my future still depended upon my performance, and I knew better than to take the opportunity for granted.

A hush fell over the hall as the professor entered. With a curt bow to the class, he overturned the large hourglass positioned on the lectern at the front of the room, then pulled back the canvas that had been covering the topics etched upon the board.

First day examination:

lst. Describe the Cochlear apparatus.

2nd. What Arteries are given off by the Aorta in blood's passage through the Arm?

3rd. Which chemicals can be used to detect the presence of bile in the esophagus?

4th. Describe the chambers of the heart.

A sudden flash of memories—of a discarded ear upon the surface of a gritty pub table, of hot wax solidifying in a web of veins, of cerulean blue swirling in a transparent tube, and finally, of a diagram of a heart tacked haphazardly above a bed, conjuring precious recollections of Love, of Joy, of Life.

I dipped my quill in the ink and lowered my head to write.

Author's Note

I first learned the truth about Burke and Hare, Scotland's most notorious serial killers, in an episode of Aaron Mahnke's podcast Lore. As a true-crime junkie, I'd heard their names in passing, but it wasn't until Lore that I fully understood their peculiar place in history, as the world's most famous grave robbers . . . who never robbed a grave. That alone was enough to catch my attention, but my interest was only compounded as I learned more about the Resurrectionists and the society that gave rise to them. Listening to all the weird, wild, fantastical (and, frankly, ingenious) methods they devised to hone their craft, I was enthralled. Everything about these Resurrection men—their trade, their exploits, and the moral code by which they operated—was all so fantastically unhinged that I couldn't stop imagining what it must have been like to spend time in their company.

The story of The Resurrectionist came to me in increments. I was initially tempted to simply write a work of historical fiction centered around a body snatcher and his crew, but the story of Burke and Hare kept drawing me back. It was such a poignant microcosm of the colliding ideals of the era: the breathless excitement of the New Enlightenment and the scientific progress that it brought, completely at odds with the religious and ethical norms that dominated the legal framework and social mores of the time. There was simply no better parable to highlight the consequence of these unresolved tensions.

And thus I landed here, at this strange little intersection between historical fiction and true crime, where real-life figures make coy cameos against a wholly imagined backdrop. Burke and Hare are real, of course, but so are Dr. Knox, Mary Paterson, Daft Jamie, Fergusson, and even the Grays (the pseudonym taken on by James's friends when they go undercover to expose Burke and Hare's crimes). It was my goal to make the story compelling for readers who had never heard of the original murders, but also to include enough Easter eggs that those familiar with the legend could enjoy some dramatic irony as the real-life individuals commingle with imagined characters. Admittedly my favorite cameo is that of Dr. Holmes, who was arrested for stealing his own mother's head; when I read that anecdote in Suzie Lennox's Bodysnatchers (the ultimate resource on the topic), I had one of those priceless laugh-out-loud-from-sheer-horror moments that define a project like this.

I must also credit Kate Winkler-Dawson, the true-crime historian, with humanizing Burke and Hare's victims. In her podcast Tenfold More Wicked, she delves into the humanity of each of these individuals in a way that made them feel viscerally accessible to me, and it's a must-listen for anyone curious to know more about these events.

Cameos aside, I delighted in creating the cast of fictional characters that populates this book. James, the narrator, came to me nearly fully formed. He is the quintessential Dr. Watson character, through which a reader can be exposed to a strange and wondrous new world and learn through his experience as he seeks the answers we're looking for. Aneurin was—perhaps unsurprisingly—much more of an enigma. Everything about him, from his looks to his mannerisms to his backstory, revealed itself in fits and starts. For a long time, he was nameless, until I happened to catch an episode of a TV series in which an actor named Aneurin appeared, and my jaw literally dropped as I recognized, That's him!

I did not initially set out to write a love story, but as I started to delve into the nuances of James and Aneurin's relationship, it became very clear to me that they were attracted to each other as more than friends. After years of consuming frustratingly queer-coded content, it felt essential to remove any nuance or ambiguity from the text regarding their sexuality. It was important to me that these characters be canonically romantically involved.

I also felt it was crucial to make James's sexuality simply a part of his coming-of-age story—a piece of the puzzle, not the whole of it. While it's true that an element of James's character growth is embracing his sexual identity, it was equally important to me that he be recognized as a driven student, a loyal friend, an advocate for justice, and an indispensable accomplice to Aneurin's brilliant detective work. His romantic attachment to Aneurin is a consequence of all that, not the driving force behind it, and it's my hope that this is apparent in the way the whole of his life is portrayed.

Harper
North

Book Credits

Tk